The Sound of Breaking Ice

THE SOUND OF BREAKING ICE

LEE RICHIE

RIGHT TRACK PUBLISHING
AUSTRALIA

Lee Richie/Right Track Publishing
AUSTRALIA
www.leerichie.com

Cover art and design by Richard Austin Lee
Front cover photography by Daniel Lee

The Sound of Breaking Ice/Lee Richie.
1st edition published 2026
ISBN: 978-0-6482564-8-9 Paperback
ISBN: 978-0-6482564-9-6   E-Book

For Dad

For Dad, who fought in distant wars
Ended up on Dunkirk's shores
Relived the horror every night
Awoke in terror, screams of fright
Dad, who read me tales for bed
Adventures swirling in my head
Dad, who laughed at Benny Hill
Perhaps upstairs, he's laughing still
Dad, who dreamed of Kathmandu
Of mountains high in skies of blue
I never said, I hope he knew
Not just my dad, my hero too

Loved and never forgotten

Author's Note:

The Two Faces of Winter

When I lived and worked for ten years in the Great Lakes snowbelt, I learned that winter is a season of profound deception.

It presents itself as a portrait of serene beauty—a world muffled under a blanket of fresh snow, skies of brilliant blue, and a silence so profound it feels sacred. This is the postcard winter we all know, a picture of untouchable peace.

But beneath that pristine surface lies the other winter. The bleak one. The force that leaches the color from the world and, sometimes, from the soul. It is the raw, untameable power that howls at the windows, reminding you of your own fragility.

It was this obsession—how something so beautiful can feel so isolating, so menacing—that became the beating heart of *The Sound of Breaking Ice*. The setting is not merely a backdrop; the winter is a character in its own right, mirroring the tension that lives inside our protagonist, Ray Waring.

This story is northern noir: the chilling truth hidden within a frozen landscape. I hope you feel the cold as you read, and listen for the sound of the ice finally giving way.

Chapter 1

"Mr President, they're breaching the school."

Crisp dropped the memo on the Resolute Desk and strode to the anteroom, where a television blared. Newtridge, his chief of staff, trailed him, already snapping orders into his phone. The secretarial staff stood frozen, their faces washed in the blue glow of the screen.

"Turn it up," Crisp said.

A banner scrolled beneath shaky footage: **CNN LIVE: Siege at Lilyfield Elementary—Day 4**.

"Thank you, Jan." Studio Anchor David Turner shuffled his paper, his attention divided between the camera and his earpiece feed. *"Just to recap then; we are live on day four of the harrowing siege at Lilyfield*

Elementary School, where four armed men took dozens of children and two teachers' hostage. The situation has escalated dramatically in the last hour as FBI agents have begun their final assault. Let's go straight to our team on the ground. Sarah Bennett, our correspondent on the story. Sarah, what are you seeing?"

"David, it's absolute chaos here. Moments ago, FBI tactical teams initiated their assault after what sounded like an explosion from inside the school. Shots were fired, multiple shots, and we saw agents push forward before suddenly falling back. It appears there was heavy resistance from the suspects."

"Sorry to interrupt, Sarah, we have Mark Reynolds in the chopper. Mark, what's happening?"

"David, Elena, this is Mark in Chopper Five. We have a bird's-eye view as the scene unfolds, and the FBI perimeter is tightening. There's another push to breach the front foyer, but, bizarrely, they are falling back yet again. There seems to be a lot of confusion. Hold on! One agent, dressed in black tactical gear, did not retreat. He's continued alone into the building while the rest of the teams seemed to regroup outside."

"What the hell?" the president muttered.

"Sarah, this is Elena in the studio. We're also getting reports that this agent is inside amid significant gunfire. Can you confirm?"

"What is going on with these people?" Crisp said, irritation clear in his tone. "Why did they drop back?" No one answered.

"That's right, Elena. Just minutes ago... Wait! Someone is coming out of the building. Yes! Elena, David, this lone agent has emerged with a teacher and a large group of children, we believe at least fifteen. They are being rushed to waiting paramedics. But what's extraordinary is that after handing them over, this agent has turned right around and gone back in." The reporter ducked at the sound of an explosion and gunfire heard from inside the school. *"Elana, that gunfire had everyone ducking for cover. Now, incredibly, that agent is coming out this time carrying two small children. The crowd here is in shock. Law enforcement is swarming, but this one agent appears to be the only one who successfully breached the heart of the siege."*

The president's team stood mesmerized, watching events unfold. President Crisp had his left hand cupping his right elbow, and his right hand pushed against his mouth, his teeth biting into his fingers, his intent focused on the action. No one spoke.

"David, Elena, this is Mark in the chopper. There's still heavy activity near the rear of the school where the suspects initially tried to escape in a catering truck. We're seeing multiple armored vehicles moving in, but the situation remains volatile. Shots were fired just seconds ago; it's

unclear if the remaining suspects are still active or if this is law enforcement clearing the building."

"Mark, do we have any confirmation on the status of the terrorists? As we reported on Monday, intel suggested they are linked to the Muslim Brotherhood, but there have been shocking developments early today."

"David, Sarah here. That's right. Sources inside the investigation are now telling CNN that these men may not be who they first claimed to be. Remember, they broadcast a video with ISIS flags, but during the initial confrontation, a teacher pulled the mask off one attacker, revealing his face before being shot. Law enforcement is now investigating whether these were actually far-right extremists attempting to frame Islamic groups. This could be a horrific false-flag operation."

Low murmurs rumbled around the anteroom. The group had grown to overflowing as staff came to see the action.

"That is a staggering development. And as we await official confirmation, our focus remains on the hostages. Sarah, any word on casualties?"

"Elena, we know at least one teacher was killed during the initial confrontation. One school security guard was also fatally shot when the suspects tried to flee. I'm being told that the first batch of children and the teacher brought out by this FBI agent appear to be traumatized but otherwise unharmed; many are being treated on-site. The two subsequent children

brought out in his arms are said to be in critical condition. They are being airlifted to the hospital. We still don't know if all hostages have been recovered."

"Jesus Christ!" Crisp said, his fist clenched.

"I'm told we have a breaking update from the chopper."

"Yes, David. We're flying over the south wing now, where I can see FBI teams storming the building again. This time, it appears to be a full breach. Flashbangs are being deployed, and we can see smoke near the east entrance. The SWAT team is now moving in. Meanwhile, in the south courtyard, the lone agent who rescued those children collapsed, clutching his head, shortly after handing them off. He's now being treated by medics in a waiting ambulance for what appears to be a head wound."

"Turn it off." The president turned and headed for the door. Newtridge jogged to catch up. "I want that agent's name, who he is, where he lives, what he had for breakfast. Everything. Cancel the ambassador and get the chopper ready, we're going to Lilyfield."

✳ ✳ ✳

The flight to Lilyfield had been a masterstroke, a whirlwind of staged compassion and raw emotion. But now, twenty-four hours after declaring the siege over, the botched assault on the school was threatening to take away his headline. He had to maintain the momentum, bring the spotlight back where it belonged. President Carlton Crisp went over his notes with Press Secretary Lisa Manou before heading into the White House Press Room. Newtridge caught him on the way in.

"Nine points up," he said, grinning.

Crisp pumped his fist. "And Fox?"

"Gushing."

His trip to the siege site had given him exactly what he wanted; air time while the nation watched on. But that was yesterday; he knew all too well that if he didn't seize the moment, the story would soon wane. Families had welcomed his immediate response and thanked him for taking the initiative. He made sure that those thanks were captured on camera.

A sizable contingent greeted him as he stepped up to the podium. The rumble of chatter slowly faded. "My fellow Americans." President Carlton Crisp paused. He glanced around the press gallery, selecting a face to focus on. A young reporter took special pride in catching the president's eye. Laura French straightened her back and smiled in response. She suddenly wished she'd spent more time on her makeup that morning. From the President's perspective, she might as well have had a target painted on her face. Choosing a focal point, a trick he'd learned many years ago, allowed him to convey his words with greater sincerity.

"Yesterday, we were privileged to witness an act of bravery," he began, pausing for emphasis. "An act of extreme courage that saved the lives of sixteen of our nation's most vulnerable." His eyes roamed the room before returning to rest, always on the same young reporter. "When we, as a nation, first became transfixed by the events in Lilyfield, our hearts broke openly for the parents and families of those involved. We wept with them. We prayed with them. We asked for a miracle." He waited, allowing his audience to recall the images that had been broadcast into their homes. "When all hope seemed lost... when all hope seemed lost..." Crisp looked directly at the reporter, his eyes wide, piercing hers as though searching her soul for a response. "When even the brave amongst us faltered, that miracle arrived in the shape of an Angel. We all know by now that Angel was, in fact, Special Agent Raymond Waring of the Federal Bureau of Investigation."

The president appeared on television news reports throughout the school siege and leading up to its violent conclusion. His scathing attacks on the character of those responsible, along with his warning that he would deal with them ruthlessly, earned him widespread support in the polls. With each passing day, he rode the wave of public outrage, fully aware of the passionate emotions gripping the nation. Aligning himself with the hero of the day was a calculated move to boost his previously flagging popularity.

"Agent Raymond Waring and I share the same values. Life is sacred and must be protected at all costs. He's a man after my own heart. Raymond Waring is an American of the highest order, and my respect for him is boundless. While others stood by, his selfless act of heroism, undertaken without regard for his own safety, brought these children home to their loved ones." Crisp paused, grasped the lectern on either side, lowered his head, and remained silent for several seconds. When he raised his head again, he looked directly at the female reporter.

"This afternoon, I was briefed by the Chief Medical Officer at The Washington Hospital Center. At twelve-thirty last night, surgeons successfully removed bullet fragments from Raymond Waring's brain. However, while his injuries have been stabilized, our hero, ladies and gentlemen, is now in a new fight for his life." A low murmur rippled through the gallery. "Surgeons discovered a life-threatening condition, previously unknown to their patient. One that will require all of his strength to overcome." Hands flew into the air, and questions peppered the president, asking for more information about Ray's condition.

Crisp raised his hand to silence them. "Please, we must respect Raymond's privacy. But rest assured, Raymond Waring is in the best possible hands. As the leader of this great nation, I will say this: if the combined will of this people counts for anything, Raymond Waring will prevail through this ordeal. Ladies and gentlemen, our hero needs your prayers right now."

Prayers couldn't help an out-of-luck gambler, a thousand miles north, while Ray lay in the MTC.

The Neon lights of the Ojibwa West-Winds Casino flickered against the midnight sky. Brad Cover stumbled out into the cold Upper Michigan air. His pockets were empty, his head buzzed with cheap whiskey, and his last hand, a desperate all-in with a pair of deuces, had been crushed by a rivered flush. The dealers recognized his face, the pit bosses had long since stopped comping his drinks, and now, even the night seemed to reject him, the wind slicing through his thin jacket like a blade.

The power station sub-contractor made his way back to his temporary shelter, a dilapidated camper the casino rented out to seasonal workers like him. It was all he could afford, last-resort lodging for those who'd exhausted their cash and luck. He fumbled with his keys, his vision blurring. He heard the crunch of gravel. Soft. Deliberate.

The attack came from behind, a forearm, strong as an iron bar across his throat, choking his gasp into silence. A knee drove into his spine, sending him face-first into the caravan's aluminum siding. Before he could scream, a gloved hand wrenched his head back, and a rag, reeking of chemicals, clamped over his mouth. His vision tunneled. The world went black.

Consciousness returned in fragments. A site workshop; *his* workshop. Tools lined the walls, organized and labelled. The sting of duct tape biting into his wrists. The metallic tang of blood on his lips. The low hum of his generator outside. And then, the whine of a pneumatic nail gun, cycling with a hiss of compressed air.

A figure stood over him, face obscured by a ski mask, eyes glinting in the dim light of a single hanging bulb. Cover tried to beg, but the tape muffled his voice into a whimper.

The attacker leaned close. "You should've quit while you were ahead. Seems like you tick all the loser boxes, don't it, big boy." Crack! A three-inch nail pierced Cover's thigh. He screamed behind the gag, his body convulsing. The attacker watched, tilting his head curiously. Another sharp crack, the nail driven deep, this time through his shoulder.

Cover's vision swam with tears. He thrashed, but the bindings held. The attacker moved methodically, circling, choosing his spots. A nail to the hand. Another to the calf. Each one precise. Each one avoiding anything immediately fatal. Blood soaked his jeans, pooling on the floor. His breath came in ragged, wet hitches.

The attacker paused, took out a candy bar from his pocket, unwrapped it and slowly ate. All the time watching coldly as Cover wept, his muffled sobs a plea for mercy. The attacker stuffed the last bite into his mouth. "Mmm... I love them," he said, licking his lips. Then he resumed the torture with chilling calm. Finally, he pressed the muzzle of the nail gun to Cover's temple. "This one's for the house." An ear-splitting clap was the last thing he'd hear as the nail buried itself to the hilt in his skull. Cover's body jerked once, then went still.

The killer stepped back, admiring his work before disappearing into the night, leaving the nail gun's hiss and the stench of blood and whiskey behind.

Chapter 2

Ray Waring boarded the plane, ignoring the newspapers stacked at the gate. He'd spent six weeks recovering, ignoring the world, no news, no updates, no reminders of the things that nearly killed him. A single paragraph in the discarded *Washington Post* mentioned an unsolved murder in Upper Michigan. Ray never saw it.

The economy cabin seethed with irritation, exhaustion, and the reek of damp wool. Passengers struggled to find stowage space. Overhead bins groaned under the weight of overstuffed carry-ons; winter coats spilled out like lolling tongues. The recycled air carried the smell of wet scarves, stale coffee, and the metallic tang of anxiety. Every seat was filled; middle seats wedged with people still wearing their snow-dusted hats, faces flushed from rushing through the terminal.

Ray settled into his seat and watched the free-for-all. Elbows jostled for control of the armrests. Seatbacks leaned back a defiant inch, met with hissing protests. A woman stared blankly at the safety card. The engines whined, a high-pitched plea against the weather.

Across the aisle, a man in a salt-stained parka clutched his boarding pass so hard, it could have been a winning lottery ticket. With his eyes closed, he mumbled a litany to calm his nerves. Two rows ahead, someone sneezed. Outside, the wind howled. A man in the window seat wiped condensation from the glass to reveal wind-driven snow, falling in waves against the floodlights' orange glow. Baggage handlers loaded the last of the luggage, and the thuds reverberated through the fuselage. Somewhere at the front, a flight attendant forced cheer into her voice. "Ladies and gentlemen, we'll be getting underway shortly..."

Ray smiled at the elderly woman sitting to his right. She smelled of mothballs. A flight attendant knelt beside him and placed her hand on his arm, giving him that sympathetic look he had encountered so many times in recent weeks. He had no time for sympathy, for well-meaning kindness. The unwanted attention drained him. He missed being just another face in the crowd.

"The captain sends his regards, Mr. Waring. We have a seat available for you in business class, where you will be more comfortable, with our compliments," she said.

"No, thank you, I'm fine, really."

"It's no trouble, Mr. Waring. We would be thrilled. It's an honor to have you on our flight. I can help you with your cabin luggage," she insisted.

"I'd prefer to stay here."

She smiled again, her face annoyingly consoling. "Very well, Mr. Waring, but if there is any way we can make your journey more comfortable, please don't hesitate to let me know."

Ray sighed as she walked away. Out of the corner of his eye, he noticed the elderly woman staring at him, waiting for him to turn. Eventually, he did and saw the recognition on her face.

"You're him, aren't you?" she said.

"I guess I am," he replied, looking away to avoid further conversation.

Ray closed his eyes. He recalled the president's face on his visit to the White House, the big man positively glowing. The politician's handshake, delivered with such passion and the enthusiastic look in his eyes, told Ray he was there as part of the president's publicity campaign. The Oval Office was smaller than he'd imagined. The long windows, clearly made of bulletproof glass, made the room positively glow. Secret Service officers stood outside the door. Ray felt nervous, an unexpected reaction since he had little respect for Crisp. He tried to avoid this meeting with the president and would have preferred to fade from the public eye. Crisp's aides were insistent that he attend the ceremony in person.

Crisp had been a popular president until his extreme economic policies began to take effect. His trade conflict with Mexico and Canada had escalated into a full-blown trade war. Interest rates were at their highest in a decade, and rising gas prices were straining household budgets. The opportunity for Crisp to improve his shrinking fortunes through his association with Raymond Waring seemed almost irresistible. Ray saw a desperate man behind the flashy façade. He wondered how a bunch of actors, sports stars, and philanderers could consistently govern the most powerful nation on Earth.

"How are you holding up, Raymond?" The question, delivered with all of Crisp's well-honed sincerity, came across as shallow and insincere to Ray.

"I'm doing fine, sir. Just want to get home and get my life in order."

"That's great, Raymond. Have you been briefed on the schedule and what we would like you to say?"

Ray chuckled. The speed at which the Commander in Chief brushed aside his first question and his subsequent answer was as slick as the way he combed his hair.

"Yes, sir, your press secretary gave me a thorough rundown on what she wanted me to say. She put the words right into my mouth." Crisp caught the sarcasm.

"If you are concerned about the wording, Ray, I can assure you we only want to..."

Ray shook his head and smiled. "No, sir, everything is fine. Let's get it done."

Crisp sat on the edge of the desk. "You know, Ray, I have to confess I'm confused by your decision to forgo the surgery. You can tell me it's none of my business, but I believe you're making a mistake. I know Dr. Weinberger very well. He may portray the worst-case scenario, but he believes surgery could be successful."

Ray studied the president for a moment. If he were in Ray's position, he wouldn't want to be a vegetable either if things went wrong. The tumor discovered by chance during his trauma surgery was going to kill him unless it was removed. The problem was the risk associated with its removal.

"It's a personal choice, sir. With respect, I don't want to talk about it further."

A tap on the shoulder brought Ray back to his seat on the plane. A flight attendant offered refreshments from the trolley. He declined the evening meal and ordered vodka on the rocks. She poured him a double and set several bags of salted peanuts on his tray table before moving on. He took a velvet-covered box from his pocket and placed it on the tray table without opening it. The Presidential award, within, seemed a ludicrously small thing to show for his life. He reached into his jacket once more and pulled out a letter. Prescott Guziac, how long had it been?

Dear Ray,

I know you have a lot on your mind now what with all the television shows and newspaper interviews. You sure are a celebrity these days.

I saw you on channel 9 with the president and I couldn't believe it, my old buddy standing up there with Carlton Crisp, for crying out loud. Anyway, it got me to thinking about how long it's been since you and I got to talk. I sure would like to talk Ray.

They said on the news you had cancer and probably not got a whole lotta time left. Sorry about that, I thought that was a real shitty break. But if you want to, I would really like to see you again before it's too late. In fact there are a whole lot of folks would like to see you Ray, I bet they would.

Please write.
Your best friend,
Scottie Guziac

Ray chuckled at Scottie's blunt diagnosis. He was right, of course; declining the operation meant only one outcome. It was a matter of when, not if. He closed his eyes. The story of his life had come full circle. They shared the same maternity ward, the same school class, and the same carefree days of childhood. But their lives had diverged long ago. Scottie's unexpected letter became the final motivation for his return to Fowler. A bolt from the blue, this contact opened a door in his psyche that he had tried so hard to keep closed. In his mind, Fowler Sound was merely a bad memory, a place of nightmares too painful to confront. Now, he had resolved to face his past and the demons he had locked away.

He thought of Jess, the last time he'd seen her, and his heart raced. 'It's not your fault!' were her last words before he left. Clair's face surfaced unbidden. He recalled the accident, and his pulse hammered. Cold sweat formed instantly on his brow, and he quickly pushed the thought away. His thoughts returned to Scottie. They had grown apart long before he left Fowler. He remembered the letters he'd received during his first years in New York with the NYPD. Letters that stopped coming, most likely because he failed to reply. Scottie's enlistment in the Army had been the last news. He couldn't picture Scottie in the military. Rules and a regimented lifestyle didn't seem to fit him.

His decision to return to Fowler had come after reading Scottie's letter. 'A whole lot of folks would like to see you,' he'd written. That was a lie. But there were people he needed to see, whether they wanted to see him or not. A homecoming had been on his mind since Doctor Weinberger delivered the bad news; it was simply time to lay the past to rest and confront his worst fears.

He thought of Jess once more. There could be little chance she had forgiven him, no matter how many years had passed. He drifted back in time, recalling the long summer days and the laughter they shared. He visualized the happy, smiling girl who ran through the fields, the long green grass arching over her head, before she stumbled and fell, laughing until she gave herself hiccups. He saw himself tumble down beside her, kiss her on the cheek, and wished those days had never ended. Ray, Jess, and Scottie, three children who shared a bond so close that they once imagined it would last a lifetime.

Ray glanced out the window into the abyss, a harbinger, it seemed, of where he was headed.

Chapter 3

The descent into Gerald R. Ford Airport was a teeth-rattling crawl. Air traffic control had imposed limits on the number of flights landing due to severe snow squalls. Ray's flight was the final one allowed before the runways closed. He passed through the terminal and heard a barrage of angry outbursts as airline staff struggled to manage passengers' enquiries. Ray had anticipated the weather and made a hotel reservation earlier that day. His long journey north to Fowler Sound would have been impossible in the conditions. He hoped that morning would bring better weather. The satisfaction he felt at booking his accommodation soon faded when he realized he should have also arranged a car rental. He stepped outside, saw the long line of hopefuls at the cab rank, and resigned himself to a long, cold wait.

The sidewalk leading to the cab stand was a grim, slushy trench carved between walls of grimy snow. The streetlights cast a sickly yellow glow over the uneven surface, pockmarked with boot prints. Freezing sleet had started again, not quite snow, not quite rain, just enough to slick the pavement and make every step treacherous. The water seeped through his shoe leather, numbing his toes, while the wind sliced down the narrow gap between buildings.

Somewhere, a car horn blared, long and aggrieved, before fading into the general murmur of tires moving through slush. He heard the distant wail of a siren, the low, miserable muttering of those waiting, hunched against the cold. The sleet kept falling, large wet blobs, only to be pounded into gray slop by the next wave of slow-moving car tires.

It was the kind of night that made him question every life choice leading him here, shuffling forward, head down, shoulders tight, just trying to get home without breaking an ankle, or what remained of his spirit. The icy blast of wind on his face highlighted the reality; he had now arrived back on Michigan soil, and it cut him to the bone.

"Mister Waring! A word?" Ray turned to see a man with a microphone. His red beard held fallen flakes of snow, and the heavy-lensed glasses fogged from his breath. He waited for Ray to reply.

Ray's stomach churned. There had already been too many interviews. He pushed the microphone away from his face. "I'm sorry; I have nothing to tell you. I said all there is to say in the capital."

"But, Ray, you're a hero here in Michigan, won't you tell us your story?"

Ray looked for escape. "There's no more to it." He tightened his grip on his suitcase and wished he'd opted for a rental.

"I think there may be more to your story than you'd have us believe. Secrets you haven't told us about. What about Squall Lake?"

The question hit Ray hard, a punch to the gut. His fists clenched. Heads turned on bystanders. One young woman raised her phone to record a video. He shoved her phone away, screen flashing as it tumbled into the slush.

"Nothing you'd care to share, Ray? Were you the hero that day at Squall Lake? Perhaps you're not the hero you'd have us believe?" The man lunged with the microphone. Ray turned toward the terminal. A car horn blasted.

"Ray Waring!" He turned to see a silver Dodge at the curb. Its passenger door was open, tailpipe belching clouds of emissions into the chilled night air. A woman leaned across from the driver's seat and called out again: "Ray, can I give you a ride?" He recognized her face.

The reporter was approaching again, microphone held high in his hand. Ray thundered past, knocking him to the ground. He headed for the Dodge, pausing at the curb. The woman flashed a smile. "You look like you need to be rescued, Ray. Hop in." She popped the trunk, and Ray put his bags inside. She also had luggage. He noted a tag from the capital. The car was a rental. As they pulled away from the sidewalk, the reporter watched, his image soon disappearing as the snow fell around him.

The young woman leaned over and adjusted the heater. "Where are you headed?" she asked, wiping the windshield with the back of her hand.

She was young, maybe thirty at most. She wore a business suit and well-defined makeup. Ray figured she spent a lot of time in front of the mirror. "The Baymont, you?"

"Small world," she said casually. "Can you believe this weather?"

Small world indeed. Now he remembered her. *Out of the frying pan into the fire.* "You're a reporter, I saw you in Washington at the White House ceremony."

"Laura French," she said, acknowledging her blown identity. "We didn't exactly meet, but I followed your story for some of the independents. You must be tired of us all by now." She kept her eyes on the road. She struggled to follow the taillights ahead. The windows continued to fog, making it difficult to see. "I hate snow," she said. "I should have picked up a cab."

"If you had, we would still be standing in the cold, and I would be at the mercy of that guy back there. Just take it slow and do everything well in advance. Where are you headed, after the Baymont, I mean?"

"Home. Buffalo. My flight was diverted." A signal flicked to red, and she slammed on the brakes. The car skidded sideways. She yanked the steering wheel with no apparent effect on its path. They slipped into the intersection before coming to a stop with a thump in the snowbank. "Shit! Excuse my French. Are you alright? Well, there goes my excess."

"We're fine. I don't think there's much damage done. Why don't you get out? I'll drive." Ray jumped into the driver's seat as car horns honked around them. "We were lucky," he said. "Losing your excess would've been the least of your worries if something had been coming the other way."

She shook visibly; her hands trembled, and she fumbled in her bag for a Kleenex. "I'm sorry, I've never driven in snow before."

A girl from Buffalo who says she's never driven in the snow before. Something didn't figure. "What part of Buffalo are you from, Laura?"

She hesitated. "The east side. Have you stayed at the Baymont before, Ray?"

"Me? No. Where on the east side? Depew? Cheektowaga?"

"Not far from there, Cheektowaga."

"Cheektowaga?" Ray kept his voice light, but his eyes locked onto hers. "Funny, I've got a buddy there. Which diner's best, Louie's or The Towne?"

"Eh, either is good."

Ray did not let it go. "Near Fort Erie, right?"

She realized he was interrogating her, and her lips curled into a smile of acknowledgment. "No, Mister Waring, Fort Erie is on the Canadian side. But you're right, I don't live in Buffalo, I live in Los Angeles."

Ray smiled. "So why did you lie, or is that just something that comes naturally to you media types?"

"If I'm straight with you, will you talk to me?" Ray said nothing. "I'm here because you are. I have a commission for People Magazine. They want the human story behind the hero. I'll be honest with you, I wanted to get you talking over dinner, okay? I would have told you eventually. I didn't want to scare you off before we could get to know each other, that's all. I'm sorry I lied."

Ray stayed quiet. If she wanted to talk, she'd approached it the wrong way. But he wasn't about to get out and walk. Besides, she was cute, which gave her a pass. "The human story, what does that mean?"

"Just what it says. Everyone knows the story of the siege and your..."

"Condition?"

"Right, condition. What they don't know is *who* you are. What kind of man risks his life like you did for others? I promise, I won't write anything negative. And you'd rather I tell the truth than make it up, right?"

Ray sensed that she was somewhat desperate. He felt generous. Company for a late dinner might be what he needed tonight, even with the press.

"Dinner on you then."

She smiled. "Dinner on me."

A hot shower worked wonders for his aching body. He remained a physical wreck, even though the scars had started to heal. The bullets left their mark inside and out. On a positive note, his mind had cleared. There had been no dizzy spells or severe headaches for over two weeks.

Laura arrived at 9:00 p.m. sharp. Her face was scrubbed clean of makeup, freckles visible under the bar lights. She had swapped the business suit for a slim-fitting sleeveless dress that highlighted her figure.

"I'll have bourbon, straight, please."

Ray raised his glass. "Here's to dinner!" He took a long swallow of vodka. "Snow's letting up, should have blown through by dawn."

"That's when you blow through, right? Fowler Sound, a nice part of the world, I hear."

"It's pretty good if you like small towns and lots of winter snow." He eyed her bare arms, the California tan. "It's a comfortable town, uneventful with no extremes, except maybe the winter weather. Are you really headed for Buffalo, or do you plan on sticking around?"

"If I get my story, there's nothing that can keep me in this frozen hell a minute longer than necessary. That's a bit of an overstatement, I know, but give me LA any day. I have a cat named Katie, who's waiting for my return. And I'm desperate for fresh clothes. Who's waiting for you, Ray?"

The question twisted his gut into knots. He was slow to answer. "Folks I should have seen a long time ago. I'm looking forward to some good home-cooking. Sometimes in life, you just want to hang out with folks who care about you. Besides, I've been moving about for weeks, and I need somewhere to do some washing."

"Is that mom's home-made cooking?"

"Mom died when I was young. I'm going home to an aunt and uncle. Good, simple people. Not much of a story for you there." He felt a warm sensation at the thought of them. He wondered how they would look after all these years. A pang of guilt churned in his chest.

"And what about that dirty laundry?"

"Is that a metaphor?"

"Is it?" she fired back.

"Come on, Laura, you're better than that."

"Worth a try." A mischievous grin flashed across her face. "What was it like, meeting the president?"

He drained the last vodka from his glass and wondered whether he should tell her what he thought about meeting Crisp, or soften his words for the sake of her story. He cared little for Crisp and even less for her narrative.

"Crisp is a self-obsessed politician and not a very competent one. He should've stuck to hockey. At least he was good at that. The award was as much for his image as it was about me. A man like that has personal reasons for everything."

"Can I quote you on that?"

"Write what you want. It's your story."

"Why did you go in alone, when the order was to fall back?"

"Frustration. I'd seen it all before, the tragic results of indecision. The incident command was chaotic. Competing authorities confused responders.

We were going in, and counter-commands called for everyone to withdraw. I assessed an immediate threat to life and responded."

"There are those who portray your actions as reckless rather than heroic. Do you think you put the hostages in greater danger?"

He took a long moment to answer, ordering another round of drinks while she waited. "If you had seen those kids, you would've done the same." He swallowed hard. "As we were going in, one of the masked men opened fire through an open door. I was up front. I saw the boy behind him, his face all bloodied and bandaged, the rest of the kids all terrified and distraught. I kept moving, took him down. Once inside, I saw the big man, the one they called Seb, raise his gun, point it at that little girl, and squeeze the trigger. What kind of man would do that? I just let loose with the thirty-five, emptied it into him. He fell to the floor with that dead look in his eyes. But I made a mistake," he continued, "I knew right away. Emptying the gun was foolish when I knew three other hostiles were present. By the time I turned around, one of them had put one in me. I dropped to my knees, and he stepped forward. One of the kids screamed, took his attention for a split second, enough for me to take his weapon and kill him with it. The boy saved my life."

"Why did you empty your weapon into the first man if you knew better?"

"Rage, pure rage. I wanted to destroy him, take away his right to live for what he'd done to the children. Can you understand?"

"I can understand." She paused for a long minute. "So, the other gunmen, how did you manage to kill them when you were so badly injured?"

"They panicked, looked outside, and saw the team finally moving in. They threw their guns to the ground and raised their hands above their heads. I shot two where they stood. The last one dropped to the floor, grabbed his gun, got a shot off, hit me in the shoulder, and ricocheted, ending up in my head. I put a round in his heart before I dropped; automatic reaction, I guess." He saw she was troubled. "My shooting unarmed men bothers you?"

"Of *course*; they had already surrendered." She judged him without hesitation. "According to the law, you murdered them as surely as they would have murdered you. Do you feel any remorse?"

"Not then; now, maybe. Not because I feel anything for them, I don't. But maybe I let myself down."

"The investigation is going to show that you executed them."

"I'm ready if they come for me."

"So why are you telling me all this?"

"I have nothing to hide. If you decide to tell it the way it was, it's only the truth. And to be honest, it's the least of my worries."

*   *   *

Laura French had reached a crossroads in her life and career. She knew this story was make or break. If it weren't received favorably by her editor, her last chance would be over. Nothing had gone right for her recently. Being bumped from the previous edition had her seriously considering a career change. Her editor had told her as much.

The bourbon went down easily, and her mind wandered. She watched Ray and wondered what it would take to get him into bed. He was handsome, though a bit rugged for her taste. But beggars can't be choosers. He had started growing a beard, and the stubble made him look older than he had appeared in Washington. He had an unusual combination of jet-black hair and blue-gray eyes. The dark hair color accentuated his eyes, making them striking, like those of a bird of prey.

"How do you feel about dying?" She asked the blunt question, watching him closely for the telltale signs of fear and anxiety in his response, but there were none.

"It's not an issue. We all have to go sometime. I need to wrap up some loose ends, then I'm good to go."

"Good to go?" She felt suddenly sad for him. Not in a pathetic, sympathetic way, but sad that he would give up so easily. He seemed more stoic than that. "The prognosis was emphatic then?"

"The surgeon laid out the risks. I could end up in a wheelchair with spittle running down my face, and I couldn't handle that."

"But you can't go on indefinitely without help. I did some research; if you don't receive treatment, you could have a major seizure or a stroke without warning. What about pain?"

"Doc said that with this type of tumor and its position in the brain, I can probably go about things as normal until... well, until I drop dead, I guess."

"What if..."

"Can we change the subject, please, and talk about you for a minute? You need this story pretty badly. Why the desperation?"

"You think I'll sleep with you to get what I want, don't you?" She paused, glanced around the room, then refocused on him. "Well, you're right, Raymond Waring, big shot hero." Her stomach churned. What the hell. She had nothing to lose. Her heel brushed his calf under the table. "Give me your story and we'll let the night go wherever you want."

❄　❄　❄

Ray took a drink and considered the unexpected offer, though he had to admit the thought had crossed his mind. When he studied her face, he saw many regrets. Perhaps her offer was not just for the story. Maybe she was lonely, looking for comfort on a cold night in a city far from home. "I'll tell you what; you do what you have to with my story, I'll tell you everything you need to know, no expectations in return. But sleep with me because you want to, not because you think you have to."

She looked for a moment as though she would cry. She staged an act of searching through her purse. Her lip quivered. "You know, it's getting late, and my appetite has gone. I..."

He placed his hand over hers, causing her to pause before she could speak further. She examined his face. Her expression softened into a tender smile. "The answer is yes; I want to."

Chapter 4

The Greyhound groaned up the rise, halting at the escarpment lookout. Beyond it, Fowler Sound glittered under fresh snow. An elderly couple moved to the door, while the driver went to retrieve their luggage from the hold. Ray took the opportunity to stretch his legs. The lookout offered a birds-eye view over the town, nestled at the mouth of the river under the escarpment. Two large grain silos towered over the east end, and two grain ships lay tied up beside them. Iced in tightly, the vessels had been overwintered until the spring thaw. He spotted the church steeple near his home and traced the river up to the falls. It felt good to be home, seeing his hometown like this in all its winter magic. He took deep breaths of the cold, crisp air and, for a moment, his dread faded.

Aunt Eadie shuffled into the lounge on swollen legs. Ray watched with sadness. Nearly twenty years had passed since he'd seen her, and time had taken its toll. Sunspots dominated her wrinkled face, and her hair had turned pure white. "Give me a minute to catch my breath, love, and I'll make you some lunch. Arthur's having a nap." She filled Ray in on Arthur's decline. Dementia had stolen him piece by piece over the years, leaving only flickering moments of clarity in its wake. "Some days he's still our Arthur," she said, her voice catching. "Then he's gone again. Strange really."

Eadie and Arthur had been a constant presence in his life throughout his growing up. Even before his mother passed away, they shared the responsibility for his education and well-being. Coming home to face them after so long took all his strength to overcome his shame. Until now, they had never judged him for staying away. They didn't need to; he felt enough guilt of his own making.

Ray stepped out onto the back stoop while Aunt Eadie made lunch. He closed his eyes and heard the laughter of children in the street. He thought of his childhood and recalled the kids who had played in the yard. In his mind, he saw their faces. He saw Jess, a ten-year-old. He could almost touch her. *Jess*. What would he say to her, right now, right this minute? His breath faltered as the thought swirled. A black squirrel emerged from hiding, hopped along the fence, and dropped into the snow. It climbed the bird feeder, black eyes staring, wary of his presence. "I know how you feel, buddy."

"Everything's up there, Ray; we threw nothing away. Kept all your stuff too," Aunt Eadie said as Ray made his way up to the attic. The room was cold and musty, so he slid the grill on the heat vent, sending a cloud of stale dust into the air. His old bed looked small now. He ran his hand along the wall and felt a cold chill. A room filled with memories. He heard the echoes of his mother gasping for breath in the room below, her coughing and crying ringing in his ears, silenced only when she passed away.

The room now served as a storehouse, filled with dust-covered boxes stacked high to the ceiling. Thick black writing described the contents: *Ray's old school books, Ray's baseball glove, Ray's trophies*. He moved the box labeled *Shoes* and set it aside. He opened the flap on a box that said, *Anna's stuff*. His throat tightened at her name. He saw a bundle of letters, wrapped in a thin red ribbon, all addressed to Anna Shevchenko, his mother's maiden name. He left them unopened; too personal, sacred keepsakes meant only for her eyes.

He picked up a tired-looking chocolate box. A rubber band held the lid in place. The corners were torn; the box heavy with memories. Inside, he found labels, tags, and greeting cards, every card he ever gave her. Inevitably, he came across the photographs. Every print kept, regardless of quality. His mother never found the time to mount them in albums.

He browsed through the images, trying to put names to faces. Most were strangers to him; their identities gone forever, lost in his mother's past and buried with her memory. People she once knew and loved, he supposed. She looked happy in her youth. Her face told a story of passion for life, a carefree exuberance radiating from her smile. She'd deserved more than those final years; her life measured in cigarette packs and pain. In almost every photograph, he saw the cigarettes that killed her.

Dust swirled as he lifted an empty picture frame. Beneath it, his younger self grinned, a stranger frozen in time. Below that, a hundred more. He flipped through them slowly. He remembered them all as if it were yesterday. They looked so happy, he and those children from his past, with their grinning faces and radiant smiles. Scottie and Jess, always at his side in those early years.

Graduation. Jess in violet, him in a rented tux, their futures bright as the flashbulb. *God, we looked good together; we felt good together*. He stared for a while, then closed the lid. Was it so long since he had run out on everything he cared about, everything he loved? It seemed that a lifetime had passed him by.

When he awoke, the light had faded from the window. He made his way down to the lounge, where Arthur had fallen asleep yet again in the fireside chair. Aunt Eadie sat in a kitchen chair, picking the lint from an old sweater spread out across the table. "I thought you'd gone to sleep up there, you've been gone so long."

Ray rested his hand on her shoulder and kissed the top of her head. "I did actually; must have been tired after the journey."

"I'll fix you something now, love; just let Arthur sleep a little longer." She watched as Ray approached the bookshelf and picked up a framed photo of his mother. He replaced it and grabbed another, where he was with Jess, by the lake.

"She missed you badly, Ray; it took a long time to get over it. Jess used to call on us just about every day, waiting for news and hoping you would be back. Still, you had your reasons; everyone has to do what's in their heart." She paused. "Even if it means breaking someone else's." The remark stung, even if it wasn't meant to.

"A reporter called in to see you." Ray felt a tug in his stomach. "I sent him away, figuring you had all the television and newspaper people you could handle. It's rest you need. I thought you would end up on Oprah or one of those shows, though I do like Oprah. I'm sure she would've been nice to you."

"What did he look like, this reporter?"

Eadie shuffled to the kitchen before she replied. "Ginger top. Funny-looking turkey, bushy red beard, thick glasses. Looked half blind behind those lenses. Looked like his false teeth were falling out, too." She laughed. "Goofy looking fellow, that's for sure." She laughed again. "Said he'd be back, and I expect he will."

*　　*　　*

The orange lipstick slid across his lips with a familiar sense of pleasure. It always gave him great satisfaction to become a woman, to violate their world unnoticed, as if he truly belonged. They didn't even realize he'd invaded their personal space, mingling among them undetected. He leaned close to the mirror and spotted a blemish on his nose. The line he carefully traced around his eyes appeared particularly fine, he noted. He stepped back to examine his figure and observed his protruding stomach. The pantyhose accentuated his extended abdomen, he admitted, as he slipped into a knee-length green dress. What was it about green that seemed to age you?

"So, Raymond, I can call you Raymond?" His voice, high and effeminate, wavered to the point of breaking. "You have been away a long time, Raymond; we missed you." He walked around the room twice before stopping to see his reflection in the mirror. "Tell me, Raymond, why did you leave our beautiful town for the bright lights of the city? Why did you leave your friends without a word, discarded playthings, like we were worthless pieces of crap?" He paused, tilted his head back, and watched himself, turning his head from side to side to take in each angle. "To say that you hurt us would be an understatement," he said, almost a whisper now. "We trusted you, gave our love. But I don't think that was of consequence to you, was it, Raymond?"

He moved to the mirror and ripped the wig from his head before throwing it at his reflected image. He wiped the lipstick from his mouth using the back of his hand. Colored grease paint smeared his face in a broad curve toward his left ear. The resulting image took on a surreal appearance, as though part of his face had been wiped away. He looked like a clown. What was that movie with Joh... Phoenix or something? *The Joker*. Yes, that was it; he looked like the Joker. He never liked that actor. Too smug. But there could be worse characters to base his own on than the Joker. After all, every great actor needs a muse. His attention returned to Ray.

"You think you're some hero, don't you, Raymond? Well, I've got news for you; we're going to see how big you are." He turned to the bundle of newspapers spread across the bureau. The articles detailed Raymond Waring's rise to glory. The headlines and photographs, the drama, sprawled across the pages for the entire world to marvel at. The thought made him sick.

FBI HERO RESCUES LILYFIELD SCHOOL CHILDREN. FBI HERO IDENTIFIED AS SPECIAL AGENT RAYMOND WARING. RAYMOND WARING CLOSE TO DEATH. PRESIDENT'S HERO OUT OF SURGERY. SHIELD OF BRAVERY FOR SUPER HERO AGENT WARING.

And then the worst of them all: SPECIAL AGENT RAYMOND WARING TO BE IMMORTALIZED IN NETFLIX PRODUCTION.

"Not to worry." The man picked up a tissue and removed the remaining makeup from his face. "You're back home now, and that's all that matters. We did miss you, Ray." He chuckled as his voice returned to a standard pitch. "We're going to have some fun, Ray. It will be like old times. Remember how we used to skate on the river? Hell, I miss those days; I bet you do too. You always had to show off, though, making a fool of your friends. I remember that, Ray, the way you showed off, making me look foolish. You used to be so fast, but that was on account of my knee; you were faster because I had a knee injury. You never did admit that, Ray; never did admit I had an injury; it wasn't a fair contest."

He continued to study his face in the mirror. He was getting better-looking every day, he thought. "Bet you never expected to start fading before the rest of us, did you, Ray? But I promise we'll have a blast before you croak." He ran his fingers over his chin and felt the oily smoothness of his skin. "You sure are going to have a good time with your old pal Scottie, Ray."

Chapter 5

Two days after getting into town, a visit to the yard on Seventh had Ray complete a deal on a carousel red '73 Pontiac Firebird Trans Am. According to the salesman, the mint-condition classic had been wrapped in cotton wool since the 1970s. "A prize winner at cars-and-coffee meet-ups around the country," the salesman said, stroking the vehicle as though it were alive. The clock had just rolled over 74,000 miles, a genuine reading according to the same salesman's pitch. Ray had no problem believing him. The Firebird gleamed like she'd rolled off the line yesterday, the orange-and-black hood emblem begging to be unleashed. The purchase was an indulgence he hadn't intended in his quest for a mode of transport. But seeing the bird in the dealer's showroom had turned his head. He'd just cashed in his pension, and he had money to burn. After all, it wasn't like he would get to spend it elsewhere.

Ray pulled out of the lot to the comforting growl of the 455 V8. She gripped the salty ice, spinning her wheels and fishtailing onto the road. His heart fluttered at the sensation; she was raring to go. To Ray Waring, all cars were female but came without the complications of their human counterparts.

Cruising toward the harbor, he adjusted the rearview mirror and noticed a brown Buick pull out behind him. He watched the car follow for two blocks before it turned onto Third Avenue. He took a ride through downtown, across the river, and alongside the railroad tracks, turning down First Avenue, then past the ferry terminal. Boats lay at anchor next to the wharf, already encased in winter ice. The Firebird's eight cylinders roared to life as he pressed the pedal to the floor while speeding past the towering grain silos. The winter tires fought for grip but slipped on the icy road. Instead of easing off the accelerator, Ray spun the wheel and gunned the gas, making the car perform a doughnut. He smiled, turned back to town, and headed for Prescott Guziac's house.

Scottie's home stood on a sprawling lot on the east side of the river. The Romanesque mansion was once the residence of Maria Steelton, a millionaire chain store owner and Scottie's stepmother. From the street, the house projected an image of wealth and power. The three-story late nineteenth-century home resembled a castle more than a family residence. Its rough-hewn stonework and roof parapets conveyed a solid sense of permanence. But first impressions were deceptive.

Ray climbed the steps and saw that the building needed repair. Peeling paint seemed the least of the issues. There were obvious signs of rot in the woodwork. Several windows were cracked or entirely broken. Shutters hung precariously from rusted hinges. Rotten pieces of the window frame lay on the ground.

His breath caught in his throat as he stood frozen in the open doorway, eyes widening in disbelief. The mansion loomed before him, not as the proud relic of old wealth he'd seen in his youth, but as a corpse of its former self, decayed, violated by time. His stomach twisted as the stench of damp rot and stale air rushed over him, thick enough to taste. *What the fuck, Scottie?* His fingers tightened around the rotting doorframe, the flaking paint crumbling under his grip. Everywhere he looked, ruin stared back.

"Scottie!" he called out. Silence.

His boots crunched over debris. The parlor was a nightmare of neglect; a velvet sofa split open like a gutted animal, its innards spilling out in clumps of mold and horsehair. He entered the dining room and reached out, brushing a finger against the dining table, only to recoil as a layer of grime came away, sticky and black. His pulse pounded in his ears. This wasn't just neglect. This was violence, the slow, merciless kind, inflicted by years of indifference.

"Scottie, are you there?" The sound echoed in the deadly silence. A thick mustiness, damp wood, mildewed fabric, and the sour tang of decay drifted through the house like poison. Beautiful once, all evidence of the vibrant days of Maria Steelton appeared now long gone. Amid the peeling wallpaper and falling plaster, only ghosts of the life once lived remained.

Scottie's birth mother abandoned him shortly after giving birth. His father, Peter Guziac, struggled to cope until he fell in love with Maria. The wealthy businesswoman had hired the handsome Polish immigrant as a gardener. They married after only a month, and Peter Guziac moved into Maria's grand residence with his son Prescott.

Their whirlwind romance ended in bitter fights over Guziac's drinking, culminating in an acrimonious split two years later. He moved into a crumbling west-side townhouse with four-year-old Scottie, a stark contrast to Maria's mansion. Their pre-nup agreement left Guziac with nothing. Maria set up a meagre allowance for him and a trust for Scottie's upkeep, most of which fueled Guziac's addiction.

Ray remembered Scottie's early years in near-poverty, just blocks from where he now stood. Though Scottie claimed he didn't care, Ray saw the resentment festering through childhood. School kids mocked his threadbare clothes and shoes, taunting that his stepmother had abandoned him like his mother. Scottie fought back, but often, it was Ray who defended him.

Ray stopped before a stained and grubby portrait of Maria, hanging above a blackened fireplace. Her face, half-melted by moisture, seemed to glare at him in accusation. She looked down from her canvas with a condemning stare. Ray suspected Scottie would cower beneath her image every time he walked by.

"She never changes, does she, Ray? Still judging us from the grave."

Ray turned to see Scottie in the doorway. "I always felt she could see inside my head, knew what I was thinking."

"And what if she could? What would she see now, Ray? Probably the same dirty thoughts you had when you was younger, I imagine."

"I like what you've done with the place. *What the hell, Scottie?*"

Scottie grinned. "Yeh well, you know me, always was houseproud."

"She'd turn in her grave if she saw it."

"Nah, I drove a stake through her heart. She won't be turning anytime soon. How have you been, you world-famous son of a bitch?"

"You know, keeping out of mischief."

"Look at you, humble hero, Raymond Waring. Come here, let me see what the years have done."

Scottie extended his arms and walked across the room to where Ray stood. He pulled Ray into a strong embrace that caught Ray off guard. Ray patted Scottie awkwardly on the back. Scottie held Ray for several long seconds before stepping back to take a look at him.

"Haven't changed a bit, 'cept for that ugly face of yours. And we've seen enough of that lately. Well, well, Ray Waring. You've finally come back to grace us with your presence." Scottie's expression shifted. A serious frown replaced the welcoming smile. "Better late than never, I suppose."

Ray didn't answer, and turned back to Maria's portrait. "She left you the house and everything?"

"Surprise, huh? But not everything; she left the business empire to some faggot who'd worked for her for thirty years, her right-hand, she called him in her will. Still, I don't give a shit; what would I do with a bunch of stores anyways? She left me with plenty."

"Wouldn't hurt to spend some on keeping the place up a little."

Scottie pondered for a moment and then smiled. "Nah! I like seeing it rot around me and knowing the sight would give her the shits. I look at that picture there and imagine it's her looking on from the grave; I drop my pants and give her the eye."

"You're insane. You do know that, right?" Scottie shrugged. "You can't actually live in this hole?"

"Mine's upstairs. Let's go get us a brewski."

Logs crackled in an oversized fireplace. Scottie flipped the caps off two bottles of Bell's with his belt buckle, handed one to Ray, and flopped into a voluminous lounge chair, his legs swinging over the armrest like a teenager. A kicked-off boot sailed past Ray's head and thudded against the wall. Scottie laughed. "It's the best, isn't it, us here like this?" He took a slug of beer and threw his head back. "Remember when we used to come by here on a winter's night; throw rocks at the windows and doors and then run like hell, disappearing into the dark?"

Ray remembered well. Scottie did most of the throwing. He recalled one Halloween when Maria Steelton decorated the veranda with two dozen carved pumpkins. Scottie went on a rampage, smashing them to pieces. Ray had never seen such rage build in someone so quickly.

"I used to imagine her holed up in here like some old witch, watching us from the windows. Then other times I'd think about her sitting by the fire with a book, and I used to think how good it would be to be sitting in here next to her." Scottie seemed to fall into deep thought for a few moments, then shook his head and snapped out of it. "Bitch knew I was out there watching I reckon." He sighed. "Anyway, Ray, we're in here now."

Ray studied Scottie and saw the lingering sadness of a child who had been rejected. "Hey, you had the last laugh. And you deserved better from her."

"Don't give a shit, Ray. I never really wanted anything from that woman." A long silence followed. Ray let it simmer until Scottie said, eventually, "Thought you would've been round before now."

"Give me a break. I had to catch up with Aunt Eadie and Uncle Arthur first. Haven't seen them in years."

"And whose fault is that?"

Ray took a mouthful of beer. "I was wrong to stay away for so long; they deserved more from me."

"We all deserved more, Ray."

Ray wondered why Scottie would care. They had drifted apart long before Ray left for New York. Their childhood friendship had soured over time, marked by a chip Scottie always seemed to wear on his shoulder.

"I saw that reporter sniffing around looking for a story," Scottie said, changing the subject. "I told him nothing, said I wouldn't talk on account of you being my best friend and all. Think you'll have to be careful of that one, though; reckon he's a real news hound. Seems kind of smart and determined, too."

Ray pictured the reporter with the red beard, and his stomach twisted. He'd been hounded for weeks by one reporter after another since the siege. When Ray took matters into his own hands live on television and nearly died in the process, he became a household name overnight. Then, when news of his illness broke, the result was a media feeding frenzy. Now it looked like they were showing up in Fowler.

He thought of Laura French and couldn't help smiling. He wouldn't be troubled if she came to town. There was something about her that intrigued him, and it wasn't just her free-spirited love-making. She'd surprised him with that. But she was a paradox. Smart, independent, and strong on the outside, yet there could be no mistaking her vulnerability, the unhappiness behind her breezy exterior. She hid behind her self-confident persona. What she hid from, he would never know. She was like him in so many ways.

"What was it like, killing all those men?"

Ray snapped back to the present. Scottie was eager for the gory details, his curiosity buzzing. But Ray had no time for such questions. The terrorists were the first people he had ever killed. When he awoke from an induced coma in the hospital during his second week, his only thought was to return to work and confront more like them. But as time passed, their deaths began to weigh on him. Like shadows from his past, the recollections lingered, haunting him even in sleep.

"They said you took them out like a man possessed, like a one-man army. Shit, Ray, they said you left only blood and bones when you were done." Scottie laughed and popped the tops on two more beers before handing one to Ray. "Heard you blew one's head clean off! Fuck, wish I'd been there; we would have made a team you and me, Ray, fucking A Team." Scottie seemed to be acting out the image in his head. He used his fingers to symbolize an automatic weapon and sprayed the room with imaginary bullets. Beer spewed from the bottle in his hand.

Ray watched as Scottie settled into his chair, a distant look in his eyes. He recognized that expression from their youth. Scottie Guziac, the eternal daydreamer. Ray recalled their teenage years and the embarrassment he often felt when Scottie told outrageous lies. Everyone knew he was just big noting himself. Conversations halted when Scottie entered the room, and people snickered behind his back. If not for Ray's loyalty, Scottie would have had no friends at all during high school.

"I can't talk about it, Scottie, there's an ongoing investigation," Ray answered eventually.

"Whatever." Scottie scowled, annoyed by the snub. He sucked his teeth and picked at a thread on his jeans, pouting like a child.

Ray let the silence linger, studying the room for insights into Scottie's life. The spacious second-story room seemed to have once served as a function room, possibly even a small ballroom. Scottie's possessions were scattered about in a chaotic arrangement. It was a bachelor pad on steroids. Musical instruments—guitars, keyboards, and drums—sat unloved. The strings of the guitar were broken, and the bass drum had a large hole in its skin, which looked to Ray as if someone had kicked it. Jumbled clothes were strewn across the floor, draped over furniture, or tossed into corners. Empty food containers and beer bottles completed the scene of disarray. A large flatscreen sat on a stand in one corner, surrounded by gaming paraphernalia: steering wheels, controllers, and joysticks. A second, damaged screen sat propped against a pinball machine. A cocktail bar occupied half of one wall, offering a smorgasbord of liquor. A dartboard had someone's photograph pinned to the bull's-eye.

Ray broke the silence. "How was your time in the Army? And what's all this crap about you being an actor now?"

A broad grin replaced the frown. "Special Forces, made Weapons Sergeant."

"How long?"

"Six years. It was a blast, for a while. But who wants to be in an army and never fight? Other units were doing tours in Iraq and Afghanistan, frontline stuff I trained for. Where did I end up? Chad for fuck's sake. Uganda and then Cameroon. Intelligence sharing and combat overwatch, they called it. What do I look like, a zookeeper?"

"You didn't see action?"

"Never. That's why I left, that and me suddenly becoming a multimillionaire," he added, laughing hysterically. "I had this commanding officer, he said I'd gone as far as I ever would in *his* army. Called me a wannabe soldier. Can you believe that? Me? I remember his face when I told him; *Sir, my stepmom just dropped dead and left me a fortune.* It was priceless! Bet that motherfucker still gets up at four in the morning for chump change and thinks of me tucked up with my millions."

Ray chuckled. "You got any good vodka in that overstocked bar of yours?"

Scottie beamed. "Hell, I got every lethal cocktail known to man, buddy! Throw another log on that fire and let's get shit faced, *woohoo!*"

"So, Scottie Guziac, the actor," Ray said as Scottie went for drinks. "Have I seen anything you're in?"

"Just finished filming and now I'm assessing offers. Can't say more than that, Ray."

"Filming what?"

"Like I said, I can't tell you. Studio clause in my contract. Top secret until the premier."

"Sounds exciting."

"Yeah, well, there's talk of..." Scottie acted as if accepting an award, big cheesy grin running ear to ear. "No one likes to say it out loud, bad luck, but that little gold guy could be heading this way next year. But keep that to yourself."

Ray had doubts about the Oscar. Nevertheless, he was glad things were going well for Scottie. As the hours went by, they both became slowly and deeply intoxicated, just as they had intended. They reminisced about childhood memories until the subject came to its logical conclusion.

"Does Jess know you're back?"

Ray tipped the empty vodka bottle, releasing a single drop into his dry glass. "I don't think so."

"Have you tried contacting her?"

"No. She'd probably hang up if she knew it was me." He grinned stupidly as the alcohol buzzed his brain. "Little Jess Moran, one of a kind!" He raised his glass and laughed. "Think she'd spit in my face or just slam the door, Scottie?" he scoffed. "Jess, oh, Jess, oh, Jess. That girl must hate me passionately."

"You can count on it, Ray. And it's Fischer now, Jess Fischer. She's married to some German geek. Looks like an Alien with big bug eyes and Spock ears. What she saw in him... Money, I expect. It's like beauty and the beast. 'Cept, she ain't so beautiful these days, not with all them wrinkles. Not when you get up close anyways."

Scottie rambled on, but Ray ignored his mindless chatter. Instead, he recalled the face of the girl he adored. The last time they spoke, it had been a heated and raw conversation.

"The day of the accident, do you remember it? Still think about it?" Ray said eventually.

After a long wait, Scottie finally answered. "Sometimes, not very often."

"I do. Every day, I think about it. I think about Clair. I have night terrors about her. I see her face under the ice. I wake up screaming, trying to break the ice with my fists until they bleed. Sometimes she's struggling deep underwater, trying to swim to the surface, and I'm trying to reach her. But I can't; she slips away, down into the blackness."

"Shit's passed, Ray. Leave it there. Nothing you do's going to bring her back."

"No, it won't. But I can't leave it there, Scottie. Not any longer."

"Walt never did get over it. I'd sometimes go fishing up there at the lake. I'd find him sitting there, just staring at the water like he was in a trance."

"He blamed me. No one else said it out loud, but Walt did. I remember his eyes. The pure hate in them whenever he saw me after that."

"I remember, too, when he came at you at the funeral. Took six or seven guys to pull him off. Never seen a man with such rancor."

They sat silently for a long while. Each was deep in thought until Scottie continued. "He spent years in a psycho unit; everyone thought he'd lost it for good, but he came home eventually."

"I didn't know."

"Yep, poor old Walt was a nut job right enough. Never thought they'd let him back on the streets. But they did. He works at the raceway on the maintenance crew. Poor bastard never will be quite right though." He paused for a long moment, as if considering his next words carefully. "When I found her, it was like she was only just gone. Like if I'd been there two seconds earlier, I could've saved her. Remember, I jumped in? I got to her, and I swear she'd just stopped breathing. I worked on her until help came. But..."

Ray broke out in a sweat, words echoing in his brain. His stomach twisted, his throat swelled. He rose to his feet, his head spinning, his vision blurry. He reached for support, but he missed the arm of the chair and collapsed in a heap on the floor.

Ray woke to the crackle and pop of Scottie tending the fire. For a long moment, he was disoriented by his surroundings.

"Thought you was a gonna for a moment," said Scottie.

"How long have I been out?"

"Half an hour just about. Wasn't sure if you was just drunk or that thing in your head exploded. Then I thought, drunk probably. Let him sleep it off."

"And if my brain had exploded?"

Scottie didn't answer. Just grinned stupidly, as though he found the idea funny.

"You're a prick."

"You know it." Scottie threw a log on the fire. "Don't want to start you off again, but while you was out, I heard something outside. It sounded like a raccoon trying to get at the trash can. Last week, I caught one in the den eating leftover fried chicken. It turned out there was a whole bunch of them getting in through the basement window. So, I went and took a look around. I noticed footsteps in the snow. As far as I know, those little trash bandits don't wear size ten boots. So, I went and got my Sig. I checked the grounds and found this on your ride. It was pinned behind the wiper."

Ray read the crumpled note. Scrawled in pen, the ink bleeding into the damp paper. *Big mistake coming here. You should have died in that school.*

❄ ❄ ❄

Scottie watched Ray drive away from the window. It felt strange to see him now, hurt and confused. Probably wallowing in self-pity, Scottie thought. It was an unexpected turn of events. When he had asked Ray why he had come back, Ray cited Scottie's letter as the final prompt. He said it had triggered a need to return and make things right. *Make things right? A bit late for that now, Ray...* He looked older than he'd imagined, gray in the face, a little beaten perhaps. No, not Ray Waring, not beaten; that was unlikely. He would be disappointed if his old friend showed weakness in the face of death. Beaten? Not Ray Waring.

Chapter 6

Same old Scottie. A few hours with him had revealed the same manic grin, same lies dripping like syrup. Irritating. Ray wondered why he'd bothered. He shifted into fourth. The Firebird snarled as he punched the gas, fishtailing onto Ninth Avenue East. He glanced at his rearview mirror and noticed a Toyota Land Cruiser closely tailing him. Ray coasted for three blocks before making a right onto Sixth Street. The Land Cruiser continued to follow for two more blocks. Ray took a sharp left and pressed down on the accelerator. The Toyota mirrored his movement. Ray activated his blinker and gradually pulled into the Shell forecourt, gliding past the pumps before parking outside Subway.

Without glancing back, he exited, locked the car, and walked inside. The aroma of freshly baked bread filled the air, and his stomach rumbled. Ray ducked past the counter, the restrooms, and out the side door, the clerk's 'Sir?!' lost in the hum of the soda fridge. A cautious glance around the corner of the building allowed him to spot the Firebird. The Toyota had parked alongside, and the driver, an older, stocky man, stood between the two vehicles. He had his back to Ray, and he seemed to be examining his phone, alternating between the device and Ray's Firebird, possibly taking photos.

Ray approached carefully, trying to avoid the crunch of frozen snow beneath his winter boots. He froze when the man crouched down, his hand resting on the bird's rear wheel. Ray lunged, grabbed the man's collar, and slammed him into the Firebird. Skull met fender with a crack that echoed off the pumps. He seized the guy's right arm, pulling it behind his back and using his body weight to pin him against the car. The man stumbled sideways, clawing at the ground with his left hand. Ray pressed his knee into the man's back.

"Alright, alright. I was just looking for chrissakes."

"Looking for what?"

"Looking! I'm a car guy. Hey, mister, can I get up? I didn't mean to harm the car. God knows I wouldn't. It's the best I've seen in a long while."

"What did you hope to find? Or were you leaving something behind?"

"I honestly don't want any trouble. Please, let me up."

Ray cautiously allowed the man to stand. He maintained a firm grip on the guy's arm while slipping his hand into his inside pocket and pulling out his wallet. He flipped it open to reveal his license. "Alexander Cummings?"

"Right you are. That's me, friend. Now, please, can we just calm down and talk?"

Ray released his grip, allowing Cummings to gather himself. He brushed the dirty snow off his clothes and sighed, shaking his head. "I didn't expect that little dust-up," he said, trying to force a smile.

Ray saw that Cummings was shaking. "What were you doing under the car?"

"I wasn't exactly under the car. Though my wife would say she wouldn't be surprised if I had been. I saw the Firebird and wanted a closer look. Don't often see one out and about in the winter. Especially one so mint. It really is a beauty. I'm travelling up from Minnesota on business. I saw..." The man wheezed, fishing out a business card with shaking hands. "Prairie Wheels Vintage Motor Club. Treasurer. We host a show in Duluth every July." Cummings offered his hand. "As I said, I was passing through. I saw your motor and I just had to take a closer look. I was a bit shocked to see it go by, covered in slush and salt crust. Not that I'm criticizing, you understand."

Ray glanced at the car. The Firebird's hood was now streaked with road salt; its carousel red dulled to corpse-gray. He handed Cummings his wallet and apologized. "I'm sorry. Just a bit jumpy, I guess. I thought you were... You know."

"Well, okay then. I'll... Say, aren't you that fella... You are! You're that Fed who rescued those kids. Well, let me shake your hand and thank you for your service, sir. We could do with more heroes like you."

Ray pulled out his phone and snapped a photo of the license plate as Cummings pulled out of the lot and headed south. His phone buzzed in his hand. He answered on the third ring. "Waring."

"Ray, it's Carrigan."

Carrigan was Ray's partner at the bureau. He was the closest thing Ray had to a friend. "Shawn, what's up?"

"How are you, Ray? I thought maybe... How's the eh—"

"I'm kind of busy, Shawn," Ray interrupted. "What's this about?" He wanted to avoid small talk, and he had no intention of talking about his medical condition.

"Okay. Sorry. I know you're not... Well, you probably have other things on your mind right now. I just wanted to give you an update. Keep you in the loop. A heads-up on the investigation."

"Go *on*."

"The group was once associated with the Outlaws motorcycle gang, organized crime, that sort of thing. A few years ago, they had a falling out with the gang and formed Brothers for America, right-wing troublemakers. They market themselves as patriots. Very anti-immigration, even as half of them, including the leaders, come from immigrant families. We've managed to pull in seventeen members so far. Finnis O'Brien was Sebastian Ramos's right-hand man. O'Brien ran the group's social media. The political voice of the right-wing organization. But in reality, just a racist thug with previous. He says Ramos concocted the whole false flag idea."

"Where are you going with this?"

"Sebastian has a twin, Mateo Ramos. Even crazier than his brother. O'Brien says he's out there looking for revenge. With Sebastian lying in the morgue, Mateo wants blood. Especially yours, Ray. We have a nationwide out for him, but he's gone dark. We raided his home. Guns. Ammo. Explosives. These guys weren't playing around, Ray. They were planning a massacre."

Ray considered the threat, remote since a manhunt was underway. Ramos would more likely be worried about getting caught than seeking revenge. "Thanks for the caution, Shawn. I'll stay alert. Oh, and before you go, can you run a name through the system for me, Shawn? The name's Cummings. Alexander Cummings." Ray gave the details and hung up. Across the street, a figure in a Silverado watched. He flicked a cigarette butt out of the window and lifted a phone to his ear.

Chapter 7

What was he thinking? One night with Scottie was exhausting. So why had Ray agreed to this? Hadn't one night been enough? He was drunk, he told himself, and the invitation seemed appealing at the time. Now, in the cold light of day, agreeing to go snowmobiling with Scottie was what it was, a bad idea.

Scottie had always been an oddball, but he had to admit, he was more than troubled by the state of the mansion and his bizarre ideas about getting back at his stepmom. Scottie had moved upstairs, turning it into a self-contained apartment, leaving the rest of the house to rot and ruin. It was strange at best, freaky even. What was going through his mind? Not much, thought Ray. He stood at the edge of the frozen bay. Scottie's Ram truck was nearby. A trailer hitched to it carried one Polaris snowmobile. Tie-downs on the trailer indicated that a second machine had been taken to the lake. There was no sign of Scottie.

Scottie's invitation had forced him to get off his butt and head down to the bay he loved so much as a boy. The sight was enough to lift the spirits of even the most desperate soul. Warm clouds of breath condensed into wisps. It was good to be out in the cold, crisp air; the kind of air that sharpens the world into crystal clarity. Before him, the bay lay frozen beneath a flawless sheet of ice, smooth as onyx, a pale blush reflecting the azure sky. The water had surrendered entirely to winter's grasp, its murmurs silenced beneath the ice. On either side, the dolomite escarpments rose like ancient sentinels, their rugged faces dusted with snow. The stone, usually a warm gray, now wore a frosting of white along its ledges and crevices, where the wind had caught and gathered the powder. Beyond the bay, the sound stretched away, a narrow passage between the cliffs, its far end lost in a soft haze where lake and sky blurred together in a milky mirage. It was a day of perfect stillness, untouched and serene, as if the land itself was holding its breath beneath the weight of winter's beauty.

Ray observed fishing huts scattered throughout the inner harbor, where the ice was thickest. Wood smoke wafted from the tiny cabins, and he knew that diehard anglers inside had already dropped their lines through the ice for a day of fishing. A small black dot on the horizon carved circles across the lake; he watched as the specter turned toward him, gradually growing larger as it approached the shore. He followed its approach and spotted the glint of shiny paint reflecting the early rays of sunshine. As the oncoming vehicle swerved in a wide arc, the low morning sun caught the frozen snow, prompting Ray to squint against the glare. In that moment, he heard the drone of a high-powered snowmobile escalate into a full-volume roar, and in less than an instant, he opened his eyes just in time to see the machine speed past within inches, skidding to a stop next to the truck. Ray stumbled backward, fell on his rear, and cursed. Scottie removed the helmet from his head and beamed with satisfaction. Clouds of steam rose into the air from his gaping mouth.

"Sidewinder SRX 998 Genesis Turbo," he exclaimed proudly. "Shit, this baby flies, Ray."

"You almost hit me." Ray picked himself up off the ground. Already, he regretted the arrangement. They set about unhitching the Polaris from the trailer. Ray watched Scottie stow the lashings. He wore that awkward smile he knew so well. For a moment, he saw him as a child again. The hours and days they spent in each other's company were etched deep in his mind.

Scottie's smirk brought those memories rolling back to life.

Ray climbed onto the machine and attached the kill switch tether to his harness.

"Planning on taking a tumble?" Scottie laughed and pulled the visa across his face.

"Where are we headed?"

"We'll take the train line up through the cutting and out past Chippewa Creek, then take the trail out over the escarpment."

Ray frowned. The single-track freight line wound its way around the edge of the bay through a narrow cutting before heading south in a steep decline toward Grand Rapids and eventually Detroit. "The train line?"

Scottie pushed the visor back up and grinned. "You're a bit skittish for a genuine FBI man, Ray! Don't worry, buddy, the track isn't used but only twice a week these days. Only haul freight up from Grand Rapids if it's essential during the winter." Scottie's sled jerked into motion, leaving a spray of powder in its wake to rain down on Ray.

Ray flicked the key and felt the engine's buzz beneath him. *So, you want a race, eh, Scottie?* He took a deep breath and swerved out over the road onto the tracks where Scottie had already vanished into the distance.

The last time he rode a snowmobile, he was sixteen years old, and the machine was an old Ski-Doo that had been rebuilt during the summer in the school's motor shop. Noisy as ever, she was a hefty beast with limited power. He recalled how Jess and he had taken the trail out to the falls on a bright winter day, only to break down halfway there. He remembered the long trek back through the snow to get help and Jess's insistence on singing Christmas songs the whole way home. He chuckled as the memory vividly surfaced in his mind.

The monster beneath him now, a Polaris Switchback Assault, boasted a 180-horsepower engine and handled like a Formula One race car. His cautious use of the throttle soon gave way to his competitive instincts. He twisted his grip and dialed it up, making the front end rise under the thrust. Scottie's lead had shrunk to ten feet. Ray maneuvered his machine between the tracks. He felt the undulations batter the skis, sending shockwaves through his arms and wrists before the track leveled out on some hard pack. Snow piled up in banks on either side, where the plow had dumped large mounds in curls of solid ice, sometimes towering over the riders beneath high frozen walls. The two snowmobiles tore through the cutting, their engines snarling in the frigid winter air.

Ray began to feel a rush of excitement building inside him. He now trailed Scottie by less than a yard, reaching speeds over seventy miles per hour on the straights. "Move over, Scottie, let a man show you how it's done," he shouted over the roar of his machine, his breath pluming in the cold. Ahead of him, Scottie leaned low over his handlebars, his black snowmobile a ghost in clouds of powdered snow. He glanced back, his visor flashing in the sunlight, then yanked his sled into a sharp turn, sending up a spray of powder and jumping the steel track.

Ray cursed and swerved, his skis clipping the rail and bouncing him back between the tracks. The snowbanks grew taller, and he lost sight of Scottie, then plowed through a drift. In places, the banks reached ten feet high, towering above him. Then came a break in the wall, and Scottie hurtled onto the tracks once more. Adrenaline pumped as the pair crouched low in their seats to gain a streamlined advantage. Between the walls of ice, like competitors on a bobsled run, they navigated the curves with ease. They rattled down the straightaways, picking up speed as they went. The track split to the left into a siding where trains could pull aside to pass. Ray seized the opportunity to break in front. A split second was all he needed. He rode the hump between the tracks and landed in front of Scottie with a thump. He felt a thrill at the moment and noted the smile that stretched from ear to ear beneath his helmet. He wanted to laugh, and then he did. How long had it been, he wondered, since a smile like this had graced his face?

A thud from the rear snapped his head back. Scottie's nudge sent him slewing into the snow bank before he bounced back into the middle of the track. He twisted the grip and surged the machine forward, only to feel Scottie ram into him once more from behind. The shiny fiberglass body scraped against the bank, sending shards of snow and ice curling in his wake. He let out a whoop, twisted the throttle, and let the machine take off. He glanced over his shoulder at the receding outline of Scottie's Yamaha. He saw Scottie wave to concede victory, but the wind carried away his words.

Ray eased off the throttle. He looked back and saw Scottie pull off the track. He couldn't help but laugh. *Winner, winner, chicken dinner. Got you, Scottie.* As he slowed, his first thought was that it was the wind in his ears, but it wasn't. The rails hummed. A deep, shuddering vibration pulsed through the ground. *Train!*

Around the bend, a massive freight locomotive plowed through the snow, a steel avalanche, its plow blasting a tidal wave of white into the air. The trees swayed violently on either side of the tracks. Caught in a trap, Ray had no time to second-guess. He gunned the throttle and headed toward the onrushing giant. The vast bulk of the diesel, with its brilliant white headlight, seared his vision, its appearance surreal and unimaginable. The monster carved its way forward, terrifying, like a charging bull. Ray had nowhere to go; the banks were too high. *Move!* He hit the throttle again, surging forward. The train driver tugged on the whistle. At the last second, Ray yanked his sled sideways, launching off a snowbank, and for a heart-stopping second, he was airborne, his machine soaring clear over the plow's arc before slamming back down on the other side.

He swore and ducked low, threading the needle between the train and the rocky cutting as snow pelted his visor like buckshot. The locomotive's horn bellowed as it thundered past. At first, he thought he had struck the plough. He caught a glint of steel as he flew through the air and felt a sudden pain; the handlebars had hit his chest, driving the air from his body. The machine came to an abrupt stop, and the left ski crumpled under the impact. He glimpsed an inverted image of the receding train as he somersaulted over the handlebars, landing with a soft thud in a drift of snow.

The tether cord did its job, cutting off fuel to the engine. The crippled machine lay silent. Ray was stunned. His chest heaved, and his breathing was heavy. He heard the rumbling locomotive and its fading siren disappear into the distance. Silence. He slowly pulled the helmet from his head and lay back in the snow, the pounding of his heart the only sound that remained in his ears. Everywhere was now at peace. He picked himself up slowly from the ground and gazed down the railroad track and beyond to the bay. Scottie was nowhere to be seen. He took time to regain his calm, replayed the narrow escape in his mind, and then chuckled at his lucky break.

Ray inspected the machine. The left ski was bent, not broken. He took a tree branch from some blowdown and wedged the thickest part between the stays and the sled body. He applied strain, placed his weight against the bent strut, and pulled it roughly back into line. Not perfect, but it would do. He turned the key with relief as the motor kicked over with ease. Almost simultaneously, Scottie's Yamaha cut through the soft snow toward him and came to a halt ten feet from his machine.

"Figured you was quicker than that, Ray! Shit, I thought you was a goner for sure when I saw that big old beast bearing down on you. I was waving like a crazy man." He laughed loudly, then twisted the throttle to rev the idling motor. "I swear, Ray, I think you rode right up the blade of that there plough like it was a ski jump. A real O-lympic performance. God damn it, I never had so much fun in years. Just like old times, eh, buddy?"

"What happened to twice a week? You said the train only pulled through twice a week!" Scottie's laugh rang in his ears, and he felt a sudden rush of anger build within him.

"Didn't say when it was due, did I? Figure you needed a shakeup, Ray, something to make you feel alive before you go dying on us. Anyway, I thought you FBI types liked surprises." Scottie eyed Ray's machine and snickered. "Come on, Ray, admit it, you're having the time of your life, a regular Sled Head." The noise from the Yamaha drowned out Ray's reply. Scottie released the clutch and sped into the forest. Seething, Ray jumped onto his snowmobile and gave chase. Anger surged through him. He dodged trunks and blow-downs, ducking under low branches to avoid collisions. Scottie glanced over his shoulder and veered his sled onto a logging trail before speeding off again. Ray relished the chase. Playing cat and mouse was the ultimate adrenaline rush. Scottie was right. It felt good to be alive.

The forest was a blur of shadows and snow, with the trail narrowing into a treacherous gauntlet of roots and ice. Scottie hit a fallen log at full speed, launching into the air, and for a heartbeat, he was flying. He landed with a jolt, skidding sideways before regaining his balance and darting down a slope. Ray took the jump next, his stomach lurching as the world dropped away beneath him. He landed hard, his teeth rattling, but he didn't slow down. Ahead, the trees thinned, revealing a frozen river, a straight shot to the old bridge.

"Now or never," Ray muttered.

Scottie hit the ice first, his track spinning for traction before finding grip and rocketing forward. Ray followed, the wind howling past his helmet. The bridge loomed, collapsed in the middle, a jagged ruin of splintered wood. Scottie wasn't stopping. Ray's pulse raced. "You're insane!" At the last second, Scottie angled toward the bank, his sled skimming the edge of the wreckage. Ray made his move, cutting inside between ice and debris. For a moment, they were side by side, close enough to lock eyes. Then the world exploded in white. A snowdrift tumbled from the branches above, burying the trail in a powdery avalanche. Ray wrenched his sled sideways, skidding through the chaos, but Scottie disappeared into the cloud. He emerged on the far side, his sled coated in snow but still moving. He raised a gloved hand in a mocking salute before vanishing into the trees.

Ray grinned. "Oh, it's on."

He revved his motor and gave chase, the forest swallowing them both once more. The two machines brushed against each other as they rode the narrow track. Ray's sled was constantly pulled to the right as he struggled against the misalignment of the damaged ski. All trace of anger had now faded, replaced once again by the thrill of the race. Scottie clipped a stump and swerved ahead. "You're done, Ray!" he roared over the scream of his engine. Ahead, Scottie leaned into a drift, kicking up a rooster tail of snow as he cut dangerously close to a maple. He shot a glance back, smirking, before gunning it harder. Ray took a detour, rounding a stump and running parallel to Scottie. He realized that the smile had returned to his face. Scottie was already pulling ahead again, weaving through the skeletal trees lining the trail. But Ray wasn't giving up. He spotted his chance. He veered off through a drift, his sled bucking over an unseen log before rejoining the trail just in front of Scottie. *To the victor go the spoils*, he thought as the track narrowed.

The narrowness of the trail between the trees heightened the feeling of speed. Scottie's sled rounded a trailside stump, rebounded off the ice, and struck Ray's ski as it did so. He twisted his throttle to the stop, pulling alongside Ray. With a grunt, he kicked off his sled, launching himself across the gap, and slammed into Ray, tackling him off his snowmobile. They hit the snow in a tangled roll as Ray's abandoned sled plowed on. Ray's knee caught Scottie's helmet; he cried out in pain.

This time, there was no tether to cut the power. Ray watched the sled careen onward, out of control. Rage reignited, he grabbed Scottie by the jacket, yanked him to his feet, and slammed his fist against Scottie's unyielding helmet, futile, hurting his hand in the process.

"Take it off! Take the fucking thing off so I can beat the shit out of you!" Ray screamed.

Scottie pushed his boot hard on Ray's chest and kicked out violently. Ray fell back, regained his balance, and sprang at him like a man possessed. They fought like children, slapping at one another with gloved hands. Neither landed a telling blow, each shielded by the hard-shell helmets, cushioned by the bulk of their wilderness suits. Eventually, they both dropped exhausted to the ground. Their chests heaved as they fought for breath, their bodies fatigued by the heat of their protective clothes.

"Could... Could have let you go, Ray," Scottie said, breathing heavily. "Take a look; could have let you go, man!"

Ray lifted his head and followed the tracks left by his runaway snowmobile where they cut through a large drift. He shuddered at the sight, and a sharp jolt ran down his neck. Above the tracks made by his snowmobile, he noticed a single twisted strand of rusted barbed wire. Taut and straight, it formed a stark line against the white expanse of snow. A clump of snow suddenly fell from the wire, revealing a sign. KEEP OUT. At head height, the wire would have sliced through his neck like taking the top off a carrot. The papers reported such incidents every winter season. Accidental decapitations frequently made the headlines, detailing unwary riders who had ignored property boundaries.

"Saved your life, Ray; saved your life, man!"

Scottie dropped the hood back over the crumpled front end of Ray's snowmobile. "Looks like we leave the bitch here and double up, buddy." He pulled a flask from his suit pocket and flopped to the ground beside Ray, who was still processing the near miss. "Here, buddy, take the chill off with this," he said, handing Ray the flask of bourbon.

"Sorry!" The single word was all Ray could muster. Prescott Guziac remained the most annoying idiot he had ever known. But he had probably saved his life. Ray chuckled. This would only serve to make him more unbearable. He had to admit he'd enjoyed himself up to this point. Hell, what a ride they'd managed to have together, truly like old times. Looking back on their childhood, they'd always taken things too far. The friendliest football game, the simplest game of tag, it didn't matter what they did, things always ended in a fight to the finish, with a bloody nose or a blackened eye. In a way, they were more like brothers than friends, competitive siblings in a struggle for dominance. Ray watched Scottie screw the cap on the flask and belch. Why did he irritate him so much?

"Apology accepted, Ray. No sense in brooding over you doubting me like that. I was just hurt, is all, you thinking I was trying to injure you or something." He laughed. "Shit! I don't know what old Aunt Eadie would have said, though, me turning up on the doorstep with your head in a paper bag. *Sorry, Eadie, I gave him a head start, but he lost it! Ray thought he was a race winner, and it went to his head!*" He snorted out another chuckle, then continued. "She would have looked in the bag, seen your head, maybe still in its helmet, and said, *Shit Scottie, I thought you was bringing me cookies!*" He snorted again and took a tug on the flask. Ray shook his head. He couldn't help laughing fondly at the fool before him. There followed a long silence.

"Do you ever think your life has been wasted, Scottie?"

"Wasted?"

"Like you've wasted all your time when you should have been using it better. Suddenly, you find it's too late. Your chance at living a good life, a meaningful life, has passed you by."

"Don't know what you're getting at, Ray. My life's been meaningful. You think I did nothing? Wasted my life?" Scottie's glove clenched around the flask.

"I'm talking about me, not you. I'm the one ... Doesn't matter. Forget I brought it up."

"Well, sounded a lot like you was getting at me, Ray. I may not have been up there with President Butthead, but I've done things. You think saving your ass was my first rodeo? Hell, Ray, you don't know half my stories." Scottie's indignant expression was more like a grimace.

Ray didn't respond, and a long silence passed.

"I thought you was resigned to it anyway. Dying n'all."

"I thought so too. So why am I so relieved to be sitting here? I look at that wire and think how lucky I was that you saw it first. I should be mad at you for prolonging the process. At least it would have been quick." He turned to Scottie and saw a blank expression. "Maybe I'm not ready, Scottie. That's what I'm getting at. I thought I was, but I'm not." He paused. "I'm not. I need to do things. I need the time I've wasted."

"The Lord works in mysterious ways, Ray. You may *wish* you went through that wire before you're done. Only He knows what He's got in store for you."

Scottie jumped to his feet and brushed the snow from his pants. "Hey, I forgot to tell you. I made my own list!"

"List?"

"You told me you had a list of things to do before you croak. Got me to thinking. So, I made one too. Things to do before I die, just like you, Ray. I made a list of all the things I have to do, 'cept I ain't waitin' around 'til some old tumor pops up in my head. Shit, it's amazing how many things there is when you sit down and think about it. Good idea, Ray, good idea of yours." He patted his right breast as though he had the actual list safely tucked away there.

"That's great, Scottie, it helps crystallize things. Focuses you on what you have to do with your life. It's a positive move."

"Yeah, crystallized and focused, that's me, Ray, crystallized and focused."

"So, what's first on your list?"

Scottie squinted at the sun and pulled the padded gloves back over his hands.

"Well, I could tell you, Ray." He grinned stupidly. "But then I'd have to kill you."

Chapter 8

Sell up, grow up, and shape up; that's what should be topping Scottie's list. The newly salted sidewalk crunched beneath Ray's boots. Scottie loomed large in his thoughts. He'd replayed the snowmobile chase a dozen times since, and still he felt the buzz. They'd had the best day despite the almost fatal challenges. One thing you could always count on was Scottie's gift for chaos. He wondered if Scottie truly had a list and if anything would change if he did. He doubted it. He'd thought about giving advice, but thought better of it. Scottie needed to sell the big house before it fell down, get himself an apartment, take some responsibility. The guy thought he was still a kid, playing with his expensive toys.

Why am I even thinking about Scottie?

A snowplow rumbled past, its massive blade skimming the pavement and scraping a thin layer of slush into the gutter. The town had changed since he left. Fast-food joints had appeared along the boulevard. Vern's café, once his favorite hangout, was now a Starbucks. Next to it, a Pilates studio replaced the old Dairy Princess, where he took Jess on their very first official date.

He wandered past the old hardware store; at least that was still thriving despite the big-box stores that lined the boulevard. A town with a population of just over twenty-five thousand, Fowler Sound struggled to maintain a small-town feel. He observed the people on Main Street, heads bowed and focused on their cellphones. Once a thriving timber town, Fowler's Great Lakes harbor had previously served as the export center for a logging trade that stretched across the upper Great Lakes. A collection of faded photographs adorned the walls of the old post office. Carpets of floating logs covered the bay from one end to the other.

Ray skirted city council workers raising a thirty-foot spruce in the square at Town Hall. The event had become a major operation, closing the street to traffic and drawing a crowd of onlookers. Ray stepped off the sidewalk and pushed through the crowd. The interaction was a brief bump, just a moment of contact. He turned to apologize and froze. His breath faltered. His pulse spiked. *Jess?*

She stared at him; her shock seemed greater than his. For a long moment, she didn't speak. Then, barely audible: "*Ray?*" Her voice splintered. "*God, Ray!*" She shook her head, as if disbelieving her own eyes. Then, slowly, the ghost of a smile touched her lips.

"Jess." He'd rehearsed this moment a thousand times, but now every word deserted him. She was even more beautiful than he remembered, her hazel eyes, the curve of her cheek half-hidden by a purple scarf. A shiver ran through him. "How are you?" The words sounded hollow. Pathetic. After all these years, after vanishing without explanation, that was all he could muster?

Jess exhaled sharply. "Ray," she said again, her voice unsteady. "What...?"

He wanted to reach for her. Instead, he tucked his hands in his pockets, and glanced around the crowd, trying to think of something to say. "You didn't know I was coming home?" His hands came out, fidgeting, restless. He wasn't ready for this. "Of course you didn't, how could you?" She kept staring, mouth agape, also struggling for words. "You look amazing, Jess. Really." Still, she seemed stunned. He clapped his hands, tapped his feet, and grinned. "Forgot how damn cold Fowler gets."

Jess's shock softened, slowly replaced by a look of concern. "No, I didn't know you were back. Ray, I'm so sorry about..." She paused. "How's the treatment going?"

He deflected with a grim joke: "Tumor's thriving. Brain's a lost cause."

She winced. "Oh, Ray."

"Sorry. Bad taste." He straightened, desperate to shift the subject. "Aunt Eadie says you've got two kids now? A boy and a girl?"

Her face lit up. "Abbie and Brighton. They're chaos." She checked her watch, hesitated. "I'm late getting them. Are you headed this way?"

"Bank first," he lied.

Her hand brushed his, warm, fleeting. "It's good to see you." She stepped back. "I've really gotta run. I'm so sorry."

"Go," he said, relieved. "Take care."

She turned, then stopped. Swung back. "Are you free tonight?"

"Aunt Eadie's got a roast planned."

A beat of awkward silence followed. "Right. Well... see you around." She started to leave again.

"Tomorrow?" The words slipped out.

Jess turned back, grinning. "Supper. Our place. Eadie knows the address." With that, she hurried off, nearly slipping on the slick, icy pavement before disappearing down the sidewalk.

Supper. At her place. With her family. His stomach twisted. He'd wanted to talk to her alone, needed to. Now he'd have to face her husband. Her kids. Small talk. And the weight of everything left unsaid.

*   *   *

Jess Fischer made her way to her babysitter; her mind fixed on Raymond Waring. Her body tingled with excitement, and her head swam in a sea of dazed confusion. She had no idea he would come home, and kicked herself for not anticipating it. It was only natural he would return for what could be... Her stomach turned. What was she thinking? She was acting like a hysterical schoolgirl. How could she be excited about his homecoming when he might be home to die?

Her initial surprise at seeing him soon gave way to a surge of forgotten feelings, and dark memories loomed. She thought of the days and nights she'd waited to see him, how the years had passed without a word. Her disappointment had turned to anger, then resignation. He was never coming back.

He'd caught her off guard, appearing out of the blue as he did. Why had she invited him for supper? What would her husband think? She was a mess of thoughts and second thoughts. She saw his face again, the shock at seeing her. Then the excitement returned, and a burst of laughter escaped her. *Ray Waring, my God!*

❄   ❄   ❄

Ray walked through the Dollar Store and aimlessly browsed the shelves. Adrenaline surged through his veins. His thoughts were chaotic. The surprise encounter with Jess had rattled him. Eventually, he returned to the street, the image of Jess still swirling in his head.

He soon became aware of a man watching him. He wore a green jacket and a black woolen beanie. Ray did a double-take. "Walt?"

If this had been Walt Callus's grandfather, Ray wouldn't have blinked. But the brash college kid he'd once known, the one everyone swore would conquer the world, was gone. The man standing in front of him looked like a hollowed-out stranger. Gray stubble, sunken cheeks, eyes as dead as a corpse. *Jesus. What happened to you?*

Walt's lip curled. "So it is you. Thought I caught a whiff of something rotten."

"Walt. We need to talk." This was the last thing he needed right now, fresh after seeing Jess. Who else would pop out of Fowler's woodwork?

Walt didn't move. "I've got nothing to say to you. You don't belong here."

The last time they spoke, the day before Ray ran off to New York, Walt told him he was dead to him. 'You killed her.' Those words had been the final push that forced him out the door.

Ray stepped closer, hand outstretched. "Walt, take my hand. Come on, buddy."

Walt held his stare. A beat too long. Then, flatly said, "I talked to her last night. We don't want you here."

"Who? You talked to who?"

"She sees what you are." He turned away, shoulders hunched. Over his shoulder, barely audible, he added, "Stay away from me if you know what's good for you." And Ray thought he heard him say, but could not be sure, "Stay away from Clair too."

Chapter 9

The sight of Jess still fresh in his mind, Ray made his way back to the attic. Earlier in the day, Aunt Eadie had reorganized the room in preparation for his return to the boxes. Heat burst out when he opened the door; the room was an oven. He smiled at the sight of the made bed and the new reading lamp on the bedside table; just in case he fell asleep again, she told him. Two new empty cartons, one labeled 'garbage' and the other 'to keep,' sat waiting by the bedside.

He emptied a box labeled 'Kids' Christmas decorations' onto the floor. The sight of handmade trinkets brought a flood of memories. He picked up a simple tinsel star and remembered his mother's hands guiding him as they made it. Her patience seemed endless. Christmas was a difficult time. Ray had just turned four when his father died in an industrial accident just weeks before the holidays. He recalled his mother's strength as she masked her grief to make Christmas special, Aunt Eadie by her side.

When Connie Waring lost her fight with lung cancer eight years later, Aunt Eadie carried Ray through the grief. That first Christmas without his mother, they turned mourning into celebration, singing her favorite carols loud enough to shake the rafters. She had stepped into his mother's absence without ever trying to replace her. A guiding hand for him as she had been for his mother. And he'd repaid her by leaving when he needed her most. He'd failed them both. They'd raised him better.

The photo carton sat at the foot of the bed. His mother's face looked up from the open top. He lifted her picture, pressed it to his chest, and exhaled. Flipping through the stack, he froze at a teenage Jess, all wild hair and mischief. Then another, the two of them, flushed and grinning after a Bayside Arena hockey game. A third showed their friends mugging for the camera. Jess had stuck out her tongue, eyes crossed. Walt loomed behind him, an arm slung over his shoulders while dangling bunny ears over his head, sombrero jingling, that cocky grin plastered across his face. The crowd around them roared with laughter, others whose names had blurred with time.

But not Scottie. Perched alone in the background, Scottie watched the fun with quiet eyes. Ray's thumb hovered over the image. He was unreadable. *Had he ever really seen Scottie back then?*

His phone buzzed, and as if on cue, Scottie's name flashed up.

"Scottie, I was just thinking about you. Looking through a bunch of old photos, and there's your pretty face."

"Yeh? Well, I always was the good-looking one."

"There are loads of photos here, when we were kids, school events, hockey."

"Hockey? I was wondering when you would get around to hockey. Hey, remember when Sherman and the team came down to the Bay to play a charity game with the Bucks? We were in the front row 'cos my stepmom sent us tickets for my birthday, do you remember?"

"Course I remember."

"Who would have thought then, watching Crisp slugging it out with Rosinsky, remember, gloves dropped, blood everywhere. Who would have thought he'd be the fucking President of the United States of America. And no way I'd have guessed you'd be standing up there with him on television? Shit man, no way I would've dreamed it up, no way."

Ray smiled at the thought. Crisp was a fighter, a dirty one. He never backed down from a brawl, ever! "You had a poster of him and Sherman on your wall. I remember that." There was a long pause. "Scottie, are you still there?"

"Yeh, I'm here. Do you remember Sherman, that arrogant son of a bitch? We were waiting to get some autographs, and you had just gotten Crisp's on your cap, lucky bastard. Sherman came out of the dressing room. I rushed up to that fucker like he was Santa Claus. And what does he do? He brushed me aside like some pesky fly. I fell against the wall, remember? Shit, Ray, he never even gave me a second look, not a, *oh, sorry kid*, nothing! When I got home, I ripped that fucker from the wall and cut him into little pieces. Saved his eyes though."

Ray remembered. "He's still an arrogant son of a bitch."

"Want to take in a game on Saturday, Ray? The Bucks are playing a home game; be like old times, me and you."

"Let me take a rain-check on that one." He wasn't ready for another evening with Scottie. "I just got back and... You know how it is." Another long pause.

"Yeah, I know how it is, Ray, you got things to do."

The Fischers lived in a detached pre-war brick veneer, surrounded by mature maples and a grove of blue spruce. Christmas lights had already been strung along the front porch, and the tallest spruce sparkled with colorful bulbs. A seasonal wreath welcomed him at the door, and a small plaque reminded Santa to stop by. Ray hesitated before knocking.

Alan Fischer opened the door, wearing an apron with the statue of David's torso emblazoned up front. The illusion took him by surprise; Ray had to do a double-take as Fischer reached out a hand to greet him. Ray felt a strong grip, as if it were meant to send a message. They held the grip for a long moment until Jess appeared in the hallway, and Ray's stomach did a flip at the sight of her. Fischer let go of the hand and turned to Jess. She squealed, "Oh my gosh! Alan. I'm so sorry, Ray. He got that apron on our trip to Italy two years ago. I threw it out twice, but he keeps bringing it back."

"What?" said Alan. "I'm sure Ray has seen the naughty bits before. Isn't that right, Ray?"

"I'm sure he has. But it's still no way to greet a guest," she said, laughing. "Alan's been in the kitchen helping me with supper. Come on in, Ray."

Ray took off his boots at the door and handed Fischer a bottle of red wine, his contribution to the meal. Fischer thanked him for the gesture but told him he shouldn't have bothered. He didn't drink alcohol. The remark seemed rude.

"Hey, there's more than you in this house, mister perfect! Welcome, Ray, and thank you for the thought. Don't mind him. My saint of a husband thinks nobody should drink alcohol, just because he chooses not to."

Fischer raised his eyebrows in mock indignation. "Come on, that isn't true. I just thought in Ray's... anyway." He laughed, pulled Jess in close, and planted a series of kisses on her lips.

Ray felt the display was meant for him, a declaration. Like the overly firm handshake, Fischer was marking his territory. He noticed a hint of unease on Jess's face as she pushed her husband aside. She laughed awkwardly and invited Ray into the family room. The room felt cozy.

"Would you like a drink while we're waiting to eat, Ray? I'm running a little behind with the casserole." While he wanted to say yes and ask for a large one, he remembered Fischer's comment and told her he would wait until they were eating. "Well, I'm having one even if you won't, but I hate to drink alone."

"In that case, I'll join you. Vodka would be great if you have any?" Vodka had always been their liquor of choice. He noticed the unopened bottle and wondered if she'd bought it especially for him. She poured two. They clinked their glasses and toasted their reunion while Alan looked on.

"So, Ray, you must find Fowler pretty dull after Washington and New York. Meeting the president and getting all that publicity. And now you're here in the land of the normal. Must make you crave the big time." Ray sensed more than a hint of sarcasm. A reluctant host, perhaps. He wondered how Fischer had reacted to Jess's supper invitation. "How long will you be staying?"

"Well, that depends, Alan. How much time would you give me?" The sarcastic tone in his voice betrayed him. He regretted it instantly.

Jess jumped in before he could apologize. "The kids are in bed, Ray; I'm sorry you missed them."

"I'm sorry too, Jess. Aunt Eadie said they're great kids. You must be very proud, both of you. You're a lucky man, Alan."

"Thank you. I know that."

Supper crawled. Polite chatter sparked, then died as Fischer steered conversations into shallow waters. Stories of the past surfaced like drowning men, gasped, then pulled under again. Ray and Jess danced around their history, speaking only in glances. Each look held entire conversations. Each averted gaze confessed everything. Ray measured his attention carefully. Never too long. Never too obvious. But he was sure Fischer noticed.

When the plates were cleared, Ray declined coffee with the excuse of exhaustion. He shook Fischer's hand, firm, impersonal, but didn't trust himself to touch Jess. Not even a brush of fingers. Not when every nerve screamed to pull her close. The night air hit him like relief as he stepped off the porch. One last look back caught Jess turning away, her profile tense in the doorway light.

The short drive home required caution. The roads had iced over, and the salting trucks were not yet out of the pound. Ray drove two extra blocks because the headlights of a late-model Silverado appeared too close in his rearview mirror. As he began a second circuit, the truck peeled away, and Ray watched its taillights ascend the western hill before stopping just short of the crest. He waited several minutes until the car finally moved on and disappeared over the hill.

The Silverado had spooked him. He'd always had a keen instinct for trouble. Since arriving home, he'd had an uneasy sensation that someone was tailing him. The appearance of the truck only fueled his suspicion.

Aunt Eadie and Uncle Arthur had already gone to bed. He noticed a light in their bedroom and guessed Aunt Eadie had stayed awake until he arrived home safely. He poured himself a large vodka, dropping three cubes into the glass before taking a big gulp. The cold liquor felt good on his dry throat. He carried his drink to the family room and placed it on a side table along with the bottle. After two more glasses, his eyelids began to droop.

Just as he was about to succumb to sleep, a shadow darkened the frosted glass door panel. Ray's hand shot to the lamp. Darkness. His pulse hammered. He envisioned his nine-millimeter locked in the bedroom, his service revolver surrendered in D.C., and felt exposed. He dropped into a crouch. A silhouette loomed at the door. Ray waited. The figure turned away, and Ray ghosted to the window. One glimpse, a retreating back. The doorknob turned silently under his palm. Cold air kissed his face as he slipped onto the porch, and the figure stepped off the stairs.

The figure pivoted. Ray moved. Three explosive strides, then his foot skidded on icy wood. He launched into empty air, limbs windmilling, and face-planted in the snowbank just shy of his target. Muffled laughter rang out above him. "Christ, Ray!" Ray spat snow. He knew that voice. "What are you doing? Are you alright?" Jess looked down at him, astonished by his dramatic appearance. "I saw the light go out as I was about to knock, and thought you must have gone off to bed. I decided it wasn't such a good idea after all. I should have called you first."

Ray slowly got to his feet. The light from a streetlamp fell on Jess's face. "Just doing my late-night workout," Ray said, brushing the snow from his clothes.

Jess put a hand to her mouth and giggled. "Is that what it was? I thought for a minute you were reaching for a basketball hoop."

"I was just going to bed when I heard someone on the porch." He looked back at the slippery steps. "I slipped."

"I can see that."

"What are you doing here, Jess? I didn't expect to see you again so soon. Is something wrong? It's after twelve."

A heavy silence stretched between them. Jess opened her mouth, then shook her head. "You know what? I shouldn't have come," she muttered, pulling her coat tight. "I'll call you." She turned toward her car, lights flashing as she unlocked it.

"Hey, Jess, come on, talk to me."

Her hand froze on the door handle. "Why are you here, Ray?"

Thrown by the question, he snickered. "Here? In Fowler?"

Her eyes flashed. "Yes, here in Fowler. Why?"

There was no mistaking her harsh tone. He struggled to make sense of it. Two hours ago, she'd been smiling, telling him how good it was to see him. It was everything he'd hoped for. Now, out of the blue, her voice cut like glass. "I don't understand."

"Jesus Christ, Ray! You can't just pick up where you left off. It's too late for that."

"Hold on, I'm not trying... I came to settle things, Jess. I came back to make things right."

"Make things right?" She laughed, sharp and hollow. "You disappear for years, then waltz back in expecting what, forgiveness? Do you have any idea what you did to me?"

Ray recoiled. "You seemed fine earlier, I thought..."

"*Fine?*" The word exploded from her. "Oh my God. Fine is for the weather forecast; fine is for a fine time. Did you really think it was all hunky dory between us?"

"Why did you invite me then?"

She choked back a laugh. "Because I was in shock; I don't know. I wasn't thinking straight." She looked to the sky and exhaled. "*Jeez* I'm so mad at you. You have no idea what your leaving did to me back then. I was eighteen, Ray; ready to spend my life with you. I spent years wondering what I did wrong, praying you'd come back so I could apologize. *Me, apologize*, for whatever drove you away! I must've been crazy." Her tears came now, furious and hot. "I offered God everything, my soul, my life, if He'd just bring you back. But you weren't coming back. You were never coming back."

Ray reached for her. She slapped his hand away. "Don't you dare," she snapped. "I have a family now," she said, wiping her face with shaking fingers. "A husband who loves me. Children who need me. A life without you. That's what matters."

"I don't want to take that from you."

"Good. Because you can't." She yanked the car door open. "It was stupid of me to invite you. I don't know what I was thinking. After you left tonight, I realized how dumb the idea was. We can never be friends. So, I had to put an end to it, say what needed to be said. And now I've said it. That's why I came." She took a long moment to look into his face, her eyes full of pain. "Alan knows I came here tonight. It will be the last time. Don't contact me again."

She turned the ignition as Ray stood numb, the weight of her words crushing his chest. What had he expected? Forgiveness? Absolution? Her headlights washed over him, a disorienting light. He imagined her sitting behind the wheel, anger raging across her face. Then he swayed. Pain exploded behind his eyes, vision blurred, and the world went black.

Chapter 10

Y ou need to think about going into a hospital facility, Raymond. This is likely to happen more often as time goes by." Doctor Galway, a balding, portly man in his late sixties, packed his instruments into a black leather case and placed the prescription on the coffee table beneath the lamp. "You'll need more than Codeine before long, Ray. Are you sure about the Tramadol?"

"I'm sure. The last thing I need is to start on the hard stuff."

"Well, let me know if you change your mind. The surgery you refused back in Washington, will you reconsider? It could save your life."

"I'm not sure I want a robot poking around in my brain, Doc. Anyway, Doctor Weinberger says there's no guarantee that it'll work. I could end up like a zombie."

"No guarantees? There's one guarantee, Ray. You'll die if you don't have surgery. I don't mean to be callous, but that's the reality."

"I know, Doc. I'm still considering it."

"Okay then. Come and talk to me when you're feeling stronger, we need a long chat."

Ray thanked the doctor for coming out. It was a house call he could never receive in the city. Now long past retirement age, the old-fashioned physician knew the intimate details of every patient under his care. Galway had been the Waring family physician long before Ray was born. He cared for Connie Waring through her cancer and was there when she passed. From birth to the grave. Would he be there at Ray's passing?

Doc Galway had only been gone for ten minutes when Ray's phone vibrated on a table in the family room. Eadie answered it. She took the phone to Ray in the bedroom, worry etched in her expression.

"I don't want to bother you, son, but it's Scottie, he seems upset; he's crying."

Ray took the phone. "Hey, Scottie, what's going on?"

Scottie wept into the phone. "It's my pa, he's dead, Ray." It took Ray a moment to realize what he had said. "Killed himself, Ray, took his own life."

Peter Guziac cast a long shadow in Ray's childhood memories. Drunk most of the time, he lived unemployed, consuming hard liquor and chain-smoking cigarettes. Ray intensely disliked him, primarily because of how he treated Scottie. Bitter and twisted, Guziac saw himself as a victim of his circumstances. He blamed everyone but himself for his misfortunes, particularly his only son, Scottie. Ray never witnessed Guziac strike Scottie, but the evidence of such attacks was apparent in the bruises. Connie Waring had reported him to child protection more than once. It was Scottie himself who denied the abuse, steadfastly insisting that the bruises were self-inflicted. Throughout all the years Ray had known him, he had never seen Scottie show affection for his father. To hear him weep like this at his passing was a complete surprise.

The drive to Traverse was an uncomfortable journey. Ray tried to start a conversation, but Scottie mostly stayed silent. Ray had offered to go with Scottie to identify his father's body when Scottie said he couldn't face it alone. They were scheduled to meet Detective Carson at Guziac's apartment, the place where he died.

Peter Guziac had moved to Traverse City ten years earlier. He met a woman in a local bar and moved in with her. Their relationship lasted only a few weeks, even though they shared many similarities, including their addictions to alcohol and cigarettes. What appeared to be a perfect match unraveled when they argued over rent money. She moved out.

Local police had set up a crime scene at the rented apartment. A police officer stood guard at the door and told them to wait. A detective called them inside.

Unkempt and dirty, calling the apartment a home was a stretch for anyone's imagination. Bereft of possessions, the slovenly interior was a direct reflection of the man, Ray thought. Ray considered Scottie's house; the similarities were striking, even if the scale of the shambles differed.

"Carson." The detective shook Ray's hand with both of his, holding them reverentially like a priest greeting the Pope. "I can't tell you what a pleasure it is," he gushed. "Wait 'til I tell my wife." Scottie watched, seeming bemused by the detective's enthusiastic greeting. "We're all fans here in Traverse."

Carson ignored Scottie, guiding Ray into the small living room. Scottie followed. A forensic technician took blood samples from a pool on the floor. Two others, dressed in blue coveralls, worked throughout the room. One man handed out disposable foot covers. As Scottie slipped his on over his boots,

Carson seemed to notice him for the first time. "And you are?"

"Detective, this is Prescott Guziac, the victim's son," said Ray.

Carson gave Scottie a long, curious glance. No condolences were offered. "Your father lived here alone?"

"Yes, sir."

"When did you last speak with him?"

"Oh, I don't. Didn't. We haven't spoken in years. The fact is, my daddy and I never quite saw eye to eye on things. Ain't that right, Ray?" Scottie scanned the room with an air of disdain, seemingly oblivious to the remnants of death. Blood and brain matter sprayed across the wall like graffiti.

"Was there anyone else in his life that you know about?"

"I know it's hard to believe, Detective, but my daddy could pull the ladies like flies at a hog roast supper; must have been those family good looks. Course, he never kept the ladies long. I believe he moved in here with some deadbeat slut from the city. But she left him like everyone else in his life." Scottie paused, sneering at the wall. "Guess she broke his heart and he decided to go out with one last bang."

Carson squinted, unsure if he had heard correctly. "Just to be clear, we're not looking at suicide here. This was just a clumsy attempt to make it look that way." He turned to Ray. "The killer made little effort to hide any tracks. They either panicked or they didn't care." He then turned back to Scottie. Ray could see the wheels turning in his head. Scottie's tone had been far from mournful. The grief-stricken performance of the previous night was nowhere in sight now. "Sounds like there was no love lost between you and your father?"

"It's like I told you, Detective, we didn't see eye to eye. My daddy was a mean old man who reveled in the filth of his miserable life. I make no excuse for the way I feel about him. He made us both the way we are."

"Where were *you* yesterday evening, Mr. Guziac?"

"Oh, I was home feeding my goldfish, Detective Carson."

"Anyone can attest to that?"

"Not unless you count the fish. You could try grilling them for answers, Detective." Scottie snickered at his joke, looking to Ray for applause.

Carson shook his head in disbelief. "I think you should wait outside while Mr. Waring and I talk." Once Scottie had left the room, Carson turned to Ray. "What's with this guy? Is he for real?"

"Scottie's one of a kind. You have to understand he had a tough relationship with his father. That doesn't mean he would kill him."

"I'll take your word for it. But he doesn't go anywhere 'til he answers some questions." Carson pointed to the crime scene. "Do you mind? What do you think?"

"Detective..."

"Larry, please."

"Larry, I'm no longer with the bureau. I'm not sure it's right for me to get involved. I came here to support Scottie, nothing more."

"Humor me, please."

Ray sighed and reluctantly studied the room. A kitchen chair with a vinyl seat stood in the corner of the room near the wall. Blood spatter covered the wall in a large halo that spanned both walls and the ceiling for ten feet. Congealed brain matter and bone particles adhered to the vertical surface where the gunshot had blasted it. "Weapon?"

"Smith and Wesson revolver, .357 Magnum, Hornady hollow point. Made a mess of the vic; you don't want to see him before dinner. Back spatter on the hands tells me the victim didn't fire the fatal shot. Confirmation from the lab is pending."

A large ring of dried blood covered the floorboards beneath the chair. The loose-fitting boards allowed blood to drain beneath the surface. A strong smell of urine mingled with the metallic tang of blood. The outlines of two shoes were visible next to each chair leg where Guziac's feet had been. Blood spatter on the right wall was interrupted by a clean silhouette where someone had stood.

"Witnesses?" he asked without looking at Carson.

"Still conducting a door-to-door, but one neighbor says she saw a woman leaving the apartment. She couldn't say when."

The floor near the door had been only partially wiped clean of bloody footprints. The print powder on the door handle showed no signs of fingerprints. The handle had been cleaned thoroughly. Ray shook his head. "Doesn't make sense. Why bother cleaning up at all if you're going to leave so much behind?" Carson didn't answer. He watched Ray move through the apartment.

A well-worn La-Z-Boy marked Guziac's seat in front of the television. Beside the chair, a coffee table held a two-thirds empty bottle of Kapitanska Polish Vodka; next to it sat a half-empty glass and an ashtray overflowing with cigarette butts. Dirty plates, cups, cutlery, and pans cluttered a rickety dinette table. One plate, a knife, a fork, and a coffee mug had been washed clean and stood drained in the sink.

Ray observed a variety of magnetic novelties adorning the door of the fridge, peculiar decorations for the man he knew. Several of these held a selection of children's drawings. They depicted scenes with matchstick figures, shining yellow suns, and multi-colored rainbows. A postcard from the Caribbean extended greetings from the land of sea and sand. A handwritten reminder, secured in place by a bright red ladybug magnet, read Garbage Day. Get rid of the trash.

"May I?" Ray asked, pointing to the postcard.

"Be my guest." Carson watched as Ray removed the card from the fridge. "So, how come you and Guziac know each other?"

"We grew up together in Fowler Sound. We're not so close now," he added quickly. "But he doesn't have anybody else who can... You know?"

Ray turned the card. Addressed to Christie from Mommy, the writer was enjoying the sunshine and promised to bring Christie a special gift from Jamaica if she behaved well for her brother. He checked several pictures decorating the fridge door and noted the young artist's name as Christie. A star magnet held in place a drawing of four people, each with a name underneath: Mommy, Christie, Charles, and Peter. Ray turned to Carson, but didn't need to ask the question.

"Amelia Cain, her son Charles, and daughter Christie live next door. Seems Amelia has been caring for Guziac over the last three years." Ray made a show of scanning the unholy mess. "Yeah, I know. But she ran errands, bought his groceries, and so on. Just out of neighborliness and a kind heart, she was keen to emphasize. Guziac had a stroke a while back and became partly paralyzed down the left side of his body. Sat and watched TV for most of his days, just taking his pleasure from drinking and smoking. Mrs. Cain says he was happy enough in his misery. Never offered any thanks for what she did for him, she took pains to tell us, though she does believe he appreciated her kindness in his own way. The only time he smiled, she said, was when Christie talked to him; says Christie was the only one who could reach him."

"Did she hear the gunshot?"

"No, she said, they were all out at her sister's place and returned late. She dropped in to turn off the light, and that's when she discovered Guziac's body. Traverse is generally a safe city. But people keep to themselves in this neighborhood. Nobody hears nothing. In apartment buildings like this, most people sit behind the doors of their units like cons in a cellblock. Even if she heard the gunshot, I doubt she would tell us."

Ray replaced the card on the fridge door. "How did she take it?"

"She's pretty shaken up, though the son seems pretty cool about it. My partner is next door, taking a statement. I'm heading in there now if you want to tag along."

Amelia Cain sat quietly on the sofa. She was a middle-aged African American woman with a healthy build and a warm face marked by soft features. Charles Cain stood behind her with his arms crossed over his chest. He was a large eighteen-year-old who seemed worn out by the implied accusations. Samantha Riley, the detective asking tough questions, was a white veteran of homicide with over twenty years' experience. She knew exactly what to ask and how to press to get a reaction. Her questions made it clear that the Cains were suspects unless proven otherwise.

Ray observed the furnishings and cleanliness, concluding that Amelia Cain maintained a proud home. She held a well-worn Bible in her hands as the detective posed her questions.

"Mrs. Cain," the detective said, "did you shoot Peter Guziac last night?"

She asked the question aggressively, considering Mrs. Cain's gentle demeanor. The accusation and the detective's harsh tone clearly shook Amelia Cain. All kinds of people commit homicides, and Ray had seen them come from all walks of life, but his instincts quickly led him to conclude that Amelia Cain was not one of them. Ray was irritated by Riley's approach. Charles Cain dropped his hands to his sides and clenched them into fists at the last question.

"Momma didn't kill no one!" he yelled. "She cared for that ungrateful pig without anything to show for it. He lived like a pig and he died like one!" Amelia turned to her son; tears rolled down her plump cheeks in rivulets and dropped to her lap.

"You wash your mouth out, boy. You talk like that, I'll give you a hiding, so help me I will."

"Well, they got no call, Momma, accusing you like that when all you ever gave was good love to that man. He had no one but you, and now they say you shot him dead."

Amelia wiped her face with a clean white cotton handkerchief and turned to the woman detective. "He don't mean nothing, he's just upset that's all. No ma'am, I surely would not shoot Mr. Guziac. I cared for him like he was family."

"Is that why he lived in squalor?"

Ray stood by the door to avoid intruding on the interview. He took in the room and its simple hominess. This was a good woman. He noticed Charles Cain and his uneasy demeanor, along with his defensive posture. Ray figured he was capable of killing if the circumstances warranted it; he saw no fear in the young man's eyes. But Charles Cain appeared to him like most kids his age. He was your typical, everyday angry young man.

While Riley grilled the Cains, Carson wandered the room. He picked up a handful of unopened letters from the entrance table. As he leafed through them, he turned them to Ray. Three were addressed to Mrs. Amelia Cain, accompanied by two printed flyers. However, there was one sealed envelope addressed to Mr. P. Guziac. Carson flipped the envelope over and read the return address: Herbert & Lang, Attorneys at Law, Box 1256, Grand Rapids, Michigan. Carson raised his eyebrows and smirked at Ray.

"Mrs. Cain, are you in the habit of collecting Peter Guziac's mail?"

Mrs. Cain let out a deep sigh at the question and glanced at the Bible in her hands. Ray noticed a fearful look directed at her son before she replied.

"Mr. Guziac received a generous monthly allowance from his ex-wife's estate. He was unable to leave the house to cash this allowance at the bank, so he signed the checks over to me when he became sick so that I could cash them for him."

Carson exchanged a glance with Riley. Ray imagined they'd sensed a breakthrough. Carson took the lead from Riley, sitting close to Mrs. Cain. An intimidating posture, Ray thought, was unnecessary.

"You seem a little uncomfortable, Amelia. Did Mr. Guziac know he was signing his allowance over to you, or did you take it on yourself to take advantage of his condition?"

Amelia fidgeted, squeezed the book, and lowered her eyes to the floor in shame. Carson had taken all of twenty seconds to break her.

"I started out spending it all on him," she began.

Charles panicked, reached over, and gripped his mother's shoulder. "Momma!"

She placed her hand on his and smiled. "It's alright, son; it's time I face the consequences." She paused for a moment and gathered herself before continuing. "He just sat staring at that TV, day in and day out, never opened his mail. He liked a drink and a cigarette; I knew that, so I bought them for him regularly. I bought him food and cooked it for him, purchased his personal needs, and the like. I didn't begrudge that, you understand; the Lord says you should help thy neighbor. But times are tough for us without a husband and father, and it was a stretch to keep meeting his needs out of my own pocket.

"I saw the letters piling up and read that they came from lawyers. I worried they were chasing him for something. So, one day I opened one, and there it was; a check for six thousand dollars." She laughed and waved her hand like a fan across her face. "I only wanted to take what was owed, what was spent on his behalf. But the Devil sits on all our shoulders, Mr. Carson, and I borrowed a little, then a little more."

"Mrs. Cain, I think it would be wise to consult a lawyer," Ray interrupted. "I'm sure Detective Carson was just about to read you your rights. Isn't that right, Detective?"

Carson and Riley both turned and shot Ray a look that could kill. Ray knew he had crossed a line, but he didn't care.

"That's right, Mrs. Cain. Riley, will you read Mrs. Cain her rights while I take Agent Waring outside for a word?"

Before he could say more, Amelia Cain spoke. "Oh, I don't need a lawyer, Detective Carson. I want to get this off my chest now, please."

Carson couldn't hide the smile on his face. "You're sure about this?" Amelia Cain nodded. "Go on. Please."

Mrs. Cain dabbed he face and continued. "Mr. Guziac didn't seem to care about his checks. As long as he got his favorite vodka and his cigarettes, he was happy. I only wanted to make things easier so I could continue to help him."

"The Caribbean holiday sure made things easier," Riley said sarcastically.

"Oh, you already know about that?" Amelia smiled and turned to her son.

"We saw your postcard. Very heartwarming," Riley said, smirking.

"That was Charles' idea, only thinking of me and wanting me to have a birthday treat. He brought all those colorful brochures home, and we sat for nights on end just looking and dreaming. I truly believe that was the finest birthday I ever had, yes, sir." She paused, and her face turned somber. "I knew it was wrong. I told myself I would pay him back one day; I believe I would have in time."

Ray scanned the modest home and discovered nothing to suggest she had lavish tastes. He moved forward and spoke, much to Detective Riley's irritation.

"Mrs. Cain, six thousand dollars a month is a lot of money; I don't see a lot to account for that kind of money."

She reacted indignantly. "Oh no, sir, I only spent a little. Most is put aside for Mr. Guziac." She stood and walked to a side cupboard, opened the drawer, and took out a small bank passbook. She handed it to Carson, who immediately flicked to the current balance.

"One hundred and eighty-four thousand, two hundred and twenty-three dollars, and sixteen cents. That's a tidy sum, Amelia; *worth killing for?*"

Outside the Cain residence, Carson pulled Ray aside. "Where do you get off jumping in on my investigation, Agent Waring?"

"You asked me in, if I'm not mistaken." Ray paused. "Sorry if I stepped on your toes, but come on, Larry, you know she has a right to a lawyer. Maybe she did the wrong thing borrowing Guziac's money, but..."

"Stealing it. She stole his money."

"I don't see her for his murder. With Guziac alive, she had a steady flow of income for herself and her family. The idea that she would kill the golden goose makes no sense."

"What if Guziac discovered the theft of his money and threatened to turn her in? That would give her motive, and the boy seems more than capable of doing the deed for his mother."

"Maybe you're right. But what about the woman seen leaving the apartment?"

"Could have been Mrs. Cain."

"I don't buy it. People would recognize her; know it was her."

"Let's see what the lab brings back. We'll take the Cains in and run DNA and PRT. If it were either of them, we'll find evidence, blood, and powder residue. I guarantee it."

A young uniformed officer clutched his notepad, gave Ray a curt nod, then turned to Carson. "I took a statement from Prescott Guziac, sir. Claims he hadn't seen his father in months, maybe years." He thumbed the edge of his notepad, voice low. "Says he was home alone last night, rented a Disney movie, no alibi. Also confirmed his father owned a thirty-millimeter handgun, same as the one near the body."

A beat of silence. The officer glanced at Carson, gauging his reaction, then flipped a few pages. "Claims his father had plenty of reasons to kill himself. When I corrected him, told him it was a homicide, he just laughed. Said, 'Then he probably had it coming.'" The officer exhaled sharply. "Kid's got venom for the old man. Said, 'If I wanted to kill that son of a bitch, I'd have made him suffer first.'" He snapped the notepad shut. "Cold thing to say about your own father. Even if he was a bastard."

"What was the movie?"

The cop frowned. "Movie?"

"What was the movie? The movie, the one Guziac rented?"

The cop stuttered, taken off guard by the question. "Movie? I didn't ask."

"Then go and find out, kid." The youngster seemed confused; he stood and waited for further instructions. "Now, kid!"

As he walked away, Ray turned to Carson. "Scottie, a suspect, Larry?"

"Just covering my bases. But he doesn't seem too shook up about this." There was a long pause before Carson continued. "I guess you know him better than me. What's your take on his reaction?"

Scottie stood near the police cruiser, talking to the young cop. Ray watched him joking with the officer, laughing out loud. Perhaps it was just the initial shock of hearing the news, but Scottie genuinely seemed to be all torn up when he called Ray for support. Now, here he was, a day later, as if he didn't have a care in the world.

"Scottie's a complicated character," Ray said, trying to imagine what Scottie was thinking. "Who knows what's going on in his head. Damned if *I* do."

Chapter 11

Jess Fischer's day mirrored her sleepless night; a relentless loop of Ray, past and present. What she'd said, what she should've said. *Why can't I shake him?* Forgotten feelings, buried for years, now clawed their way to the surface. *Damn you, Ray.*

She folded laundry with rough, distracted motions, tossing shirts into haphazard piles. The mess glared at her. With a growl, she swept the clothes to the floor. "What are you doing to me?"

Get a grip. His choices were made long ago; let him live with them. He chose silence instead of trust; solitude instead of her. He was selfish, cruel; he hadn't given her a thought. She'd waited like a fool, *'Give him time'*, while he vanished. He wasn't coming back, so she'd picked up the pieces alone, built a life without him. He didn't belong in her heart anymore. So why did it ache like a fresh wound?

The house held its breath, Abbie at school, Brighton napping, but the quiet only amplified the storm inside. Family photos lined the mantel, proof of the life she'd forged. Yet all she saw was *him*. Her pulse roared. She snatched her phone, thumbed his number. Three times she hesitated. The fourth, she let it ring.

"It's Jess." A beat of silence. Then, barely audible, "I wanted to apologize for the other night."

"You don't owe me that." Ray's voice was gravel. "After what I put you through, I understand why you hate me."

"I don't hate you." *How could I hate you? How can I still love you? Shit, what am I doing?* "But it was a mistake trying to sweep the past under the carpet. My fault, not yours; I shouldn't have been so impulsive."

She blamed the shock. Seeing him after all these years, his *dying*; it had short-circuited her logic. Supper invitations, Alan's feelings, her own, none of it had registered as rational thought. Absurd, how they'd sat there like old friends, the past erased.

Her fingers tightened on the phone. She spoke quickly before doubt could stop her. "There are things I have to tell you, questions I need answered. Can we meet? I'm taking the kids to the park later this afternoon. Meet me at the kiosk for a coffee."

Ray's phone rang three minutes later, Jess still dominating his thoughts. It was Shawn Carrigan from the Bureau. "I ran that check on your guy from Minnesota. Alexander Cummings. He's legit, Ray. A farm machinery rep. He's the cofounder of The Prairie Wheels…"

"Vintage Car Club," Ray finished for him.

"That's it. If you need anything else on him, let me know. Did you hear we got two more members of the group?" Ray hadn't heard. "Holed up in Des Moines. Big fish. We called a number from Ramos's phone, and some dipshit answered. We had him on the line long enough to trace it. He was just a gopher, but when we raided the premises, two of the group's leaders were there. O'Brien ID'd them as principals in the planning. They run a podcast under the aliases Smith and Jones. Real shit stirrers. Conspiracies galore. They're keeping shtum, though, all lawyered up. No sign of Mateo Ramos or his sidekicks. It could be they regrouped and headed south of the border."

"I've seen a Chevy Silverado cruising through town. I think it had Kansas plates, but I didn't get a good look. Not enough to get a registration anyway. Maybe just my imagination, but it could have been following me. I'm starting to see the bad guys on every corner. Gotta get my shit together."

"You be careful, Ray. If you need, I can have a couple of guys come up there and keep an eye on you."

"Thanks, Shawn, but I'm okay. I'll let you know if I see them again."

Harold Park glittered under floodlights, skaters carving arcs across the ice. The Kiosk, once a humble stand, now a sprawling lodge, hummed with families warming by the fire. Ray spotted Jess through the window, herding Brighton inside while Abbie was glued to her iPhone.

Greetings were awkward. They settled into mundane chatter, Ray quizzing Abbie unsuccessfully about her day at school. They all ordered hot chocolate with a brownie for Brighton, which he smeared across his face like war paint. Half an hour later, Jess dabbed him clean and bundled him into his coat. "Let's check out the rink," she said, but her eyes told Ray: *Talk.*

They claimed a bench. The park was a snow globe of nostalgia. Choir carols from the bandstand, the scent of woodsmoke, the scrape of blades. Jess convinced Abbie to go make a snowman for her brother. She complied reluctantly. Nearby, three boys played with a puck, slapping it toward their makeshift goal of hats and boots.

"Remember when we used to do that?" Jess nodded to the boys shoving each other, mimicking the behavior of their professional heroes. "No one wanted me to play, but you always said I could."

Ray laughed. "You were better than most of us; that's why they never wanted you to play. No one wanted a girl to show them how it was done." He paused for a moment, allowing the memory to linger. "We were close, weren't we, Jess? Closer than most would believe." She didn't answer, simply gazing solemnly at the people on the ice.

Eventually, Ray found the courage to say what he needed to say. It didn't come easily. "I know there's no way I can make up for leaving. I was in a bad place. I know that's no excuse, but…"

"We were all in a bad place, Ray."

Ray said nothing in reply. He knew she was right. "When the doctors told me I had cancer," he said eventually, "my first thought was to put a bullet in my head."

Jess flinched. She let the words hang. "What changed your mind?"

"You did, Jess."

"Don't. Don't lay it on me, Ray. That's not fair."

His throat tightened. "I owed you the truth; I owed everybody. I couldn't go out with so many loose ends. But now I'm here, how do I explain why I left?"

"Loose ends? Is that what I am?"

"That's not what I meant, Jess. I want you to understand."

"Start with *why*." Her voice sharpened. "Why abandon everyone who loved you?"

"Fear." The admission was raw. "Of facing you all. Knowing I failed everyone I loved."

"We *both* failed Clair." Jess's knuckles whitened. "You don't get to martyr yourself alone. What do you think I was going through?"

"No. It was all on me. Walt left her with me. It was my responsibility alone. You didn't need to feel guilty."

"No need? We were both to blame for letting her out of our sight. We were too busy making out to see any danger. We were adults, and she was just a kid. We had a duty to put her first, and we didn't. But it's on both of us, Ray. It always will be."

"I know you're trying to help, Jess. But you can't know what it did to me."

"I know, Ray. I know it hit you hard. But Clair wouldn't want you to live a life of guilt. She loved you like a brother. And you treated her like a little sister. One mistake doesn't change that."

"I didn't want help, didn't deserve it."

"God, you make me so angry. You had no right to stop those who loved you from helping!" Her tone was fierce once more, but she quickly softened. "So, this life you made away from us all, was it worth it?"

"It wasn't a life, not really. I immersed myself in work. Avoided friends, anything that involved a relationship. I was good at my job. Eventually, it took over everything. It helped me block out thoughts of home, of you. I don't want to go without making peace, Jess."

"It's not Clair, not to me, Walt, or anyone else with whom you need to make peace, Ray. Stop torturing yourself and start forgiving yourself."

"Forgive myself?"

"It's never too late."

Jess placed her hand on his and ran her cold fingers across his knuckles. She took his hand and cradled it. For one heart-stopping moment, they looked into each other's eyes, and there it was, undeniable; they loved each other still. He squeezed her hand, and they both shared a sad smile of regret.

There came a sudden swoosh of skates cutting ice, so close it brought them both back to reality. "Hey buddy," Ray called after the skater. "Not so fast. There are kids on the ice."

Jess laughed as the skater carved toward the far end of the ice. "What an idiot. Have you ever seen anything so ridiculous?" Her beaming grin was infectious, and Ray found himself smiling despite his mood.

The man was a spectacle, tartan kilt flapping, feathered Glengarry hat tilted at a jaunty angle, his bushy gray beard and John Lennon sunglasses completing the absurd ensemble. Silver buttons gleamed on his black tunic as he wove through the crowd like a rogue highlander on blades.

"Must be a little chilly, don't you think?" Jess said, and they both laughed as the man weaved in and out of the increasing number of family skaters.

"He needs to slow down. He almost clipped us when he went by."

"I hope he doesn't fall over, or if he does, let's hope he's wearing boxers," Jess said. They laughed some more before falling into a long silence.

"It's good to see you laugh, Ray."

"We used to laugh all the time."

They chatted freely for a while, memories, mostly, becoming more relaxed in each other's company as lighter subjects took over the conversation. Twenty minutes passed quickly.

"Probably time to get going; Abbie's got school in the morning. Maybe we can talk some more."

"I'd like that."

Jess glanced across the ice and saw Abbie sitting on a bench with a school friend. They were laughing at something on their phones. She scanned a group of nearby kids, knocking down a snowman. She couldn't see Brighton.

"Abbie! Abbie!" she called out. "Where's your brother, honey?" Abbie shrugged and turned back to her friend, peering over her shoulder into the phone as she giggled. "Abbie! Where's Brighton?" Abbie looked around and shrugged again. Jess stood to get a better view.

"I can't see him. Can you see him, Ray?" Ray saw a mother's panic spread quickly across Jess's face. She moved urgently to where Abbie sat and took her roughly by the arm. "Where is your brother?" Abbie looked suddenly alarmed by her mother's reaction.

"I don't know. He was here playing with the snowman." Abbie got to her feet, scanning the crowd for her brother, mirroring her mother's panic.

Jess started running, desperately raising the alarm among the other parents in the park. Her anxiety soon spread to Ray.

"I'll go to the kiosk in case someone's reported him lost." As Ray jogged toward the lodge, he saw the Scot watching the chaos unfold from the ski trail. Now on cross-country skis, his skates were slung over his shoulder. He looked over to Ray, raised his arm above his head, and waved. Ray called out, "Have you seen a little boy?" The man didn't reply. "We've lost a little kid.

Blue snow suit. Have you seen him?" The man stood grinning.

As Ray got closer, the guy started laughing. His deep cackle cut through the cold air, taunting, deliberate. A terrifying thought hit Ray hard. *He's part of this.*

Ray lunged forward, boots sinking into the snow as he fought for traction. The stranger planted his poles and glided effortlessly down the trail.

"Stop!" Ray's shout ripped from his throat.

The man slowed. Turned. Tipped his hat in a mock salute, then vanished into the gathering darkness.

Ray rushed to the kiosk and found Jess inside, yelling hysterically at a girl behind the counter. A group of concerned patrons gathered. One woman tried to calm Jess, putting her arm around her shoulder, but Jess shrugged her off. Two teenagers held up their smartphones, filming the fracas. Jess lunged at one, reaching for her phone as the other teen pulled away. "Get off your damn videos and someone call the police, for God's sake."

"Look, Mommy." Everyone turned at the sound of his voice. Jess pushed past the bystanders. "Here, Mommy." Jess spun on her heels as the crowd shuffled aside. Sitting at the first table in the restaurant, Brighton clutched a large red and white striped candy cane. He held it proudly in the air for his mother to see.

"The guy said you would be here to get him in a few minutes. He gave me a couple of bucks and asked if I could watch him until you arrived," the waitress said, horrified by the commotion.

"What man?" Ray demanded.

"The guy in the kilt. He bought the kid a candy cane and sat him at the table, said he had to go to the car for a minute, and that the kid's mother would be here by the time he got back." Everyone stared at the waitress. "Hey, it's not my fault, ma'am. I was doing him a favor. *I'm* not responsible for your kids!"

Chapter 12

Ray slept fitfully; thoughts of the kilted stranger and the chaos he'd unleashed disturbed his rest. That mocking salute was a message meant for him alone. This wasn't about Jess or her kids. But what *was* it about?

Dawn's light brought relief. He dug his old skis from the basement and took to the falls trail, letting the rhythmic glide soothe his nerves. Snow sparkled under his skis like scattered diamonds. Cedar boughs sagged under their white burdens, framing the trail in postcard perfection. A lone aspen clung stubbornly to a few of last autumn's leaves, its gold defiant against the monochrome. He paused as a snowshoe hare startled across his path, then watched a buzzard carve slow circles overhead.

At a familiar bend, he stopped for a breather. A long-forgotten image materialized as he traced a set of initials on a gnarled maple. Time had blurred the carvings, his now illegible, Jess's J and M fused into a single character, Scottie's PG warped into a lopsided grin. The memory rushed back; Jess sprawled on sun-warmed rock, Scottie heckling as he carved, their laughter threading through the trees. For a moment, he could almost hear it.

The climb had taxed him more than expected. A rockfall forced careful navigation, and he almost slipped into the gorge. This trail had always been rugged, long abandoned for gentler routes. The real thrill lay in the descent; the heart-stopping plunge past the falls, through tight tree-lined turns, only for the bold.

Breath clouded before him as he crested the ridge. Below, the frozen falls clung to a last silver thread of flowing water, winter's grip tightening by the hour. Suddenly, twelve-year-old Jess and Scottie materialized in his mind; Jess shrieking as his snowball found its mark, Scottie volleying curses that would make any sailor blush. Back then, they were invincible. Before high school, before fractures.

The lake was three miles ahead via the direct path. He chose the eight-mile detour instead; the groomed trail that steered clear of the far shore, where Clair had died. His chest tightened. *Not today*. Today was for happier ghosts.

The 'NO TRESPASSING' signs were new. Ray rounded the bend, nostrils flaring at woodsmoke, a scent that conjured decades of campfire memories. The shack emerged through the pines, its cedar siding weathered but standing. Smoke twisted from the chimney until the wind shredded it in an angry swirl.

Little had changed, save for the rusted Chevy buried in snow where Waagosh's old Dodge once sat. Ray closed his eyes and saw the Chippewa man mending canoes, hawking bait and maple syrup to summer tourists. Now, the boat shed's roof sagged like a broken spine. Rotting clinker hulls littered the shore. 'TRESPASSERS WILL BE SHOT' signs replaced the welcome mats of Ray's youth.

His boot scuffed the half-buried 'WORMS & TACKLE' sign. The deck where he'd shared sodas with Jess still stretched before the door. The empty dog run yawned, once home to six howling Malamutes who'd announced every visitor.

How many firsts happened here? First cigarette behind the shed. First warm beer by the creek. First kiss with Jess, her lips tasting of cherry soda. The ache settled deep.

A row of white beehives stood sentinel. Ray imagined Waagosh harvesting honey while bees swarmed his face, the same man who'd enchanted them with Chippewa legends, taught them to track deer, fish, and read the stars. Uncle Arthur had called him an Elder, a medicine man. To Ray, Waagosh was a calm, soft-spoken man, friendly, sometimes mystical in his demeanor. He carried with him the wisdom of his ancestors. A teacher of legends.

Waagosh had a special fondness for Ray, Jess, and Scottie. He and Uncle Arthur would fish off the jetty while they played freely around the property. When they were old enough, they would come up to the lake on their own. They came to see the boat shack as a home away from home. Waagosh never seemed to tire of their company. He'd seen Ray and Jess grow into young adults and watched as they fell in love. After so many years as playmates, the old man must have found it amusing to see them become lovers.

Ray felt something sharp against his back. "Don't move. What do you want here?"

"Waagosh?"

"Who wants to know? This is private property," the old man countered.

Ray raised his hands in surrender. "An old Indian told me once: 'It is not man who owns the land; it is the land that owns the man.'"

Silence. Ray turned. Waagosh held a gardening tool in his hand. The old man squinted. He reached into his pocket, retrieved a pair of spectacles. Slowly, a toothless grin spread across his curious expression.

"Raymond?"

"Nice of you to remember, sir, considering the reception you just gave. I thought I'd come to the wrong lake."

"Things change like the shifting seasons. Did you expect a welcome song after neglecting me for so long? Did you think you would return and find things as you left them? Come, Raymond, we can talk inside. This wind chills my old bones."

Finding the old man well, with his memory intact, gave Ray a warm sense of satisfaction. He had considered Waagosh to be an old man twenty years ago. Yet age and time had not brought him down. Ray sat at a table near the window, gazing out at the lake, while the old man hung his coat on a peg by the door. The interior of the cabin, a jumbled collection of belongings, seemed in need of a thorough cleanout. In the past, it had been an orderly place. The open-plan room housed an impressive collection of books and collectibles, but it seemed to Ray that the old man had become a hoarder, given the abundance of items. Dozens of dreamcatchers hung from the ceiling. The old counter, where Waagosh once served customers, sat beneath a dusty collection of unused fishing tackle and snow gear. A cigar store Indian stood sentinel near the door, an odd addition to the décor, Ray thought.

"I thought these were taboo. Inappropriate."

"I rescued it. To my eyes, it is a strange thing, a shadow of our people, frozen in silence. But I like its colorful carving."

"You look so well, sir. It must be all the honey you eat. I see the hives are still there."

"Thank you, Raymond. But you can stop with that 'sir' nonsense. You know my name. Or have you forgotten?"

"I remember; how could I forget, Henry?" Waagosh had encouraged the kids to use his simple American name, Henry. He once told Ray it was a middle name given to him by his mother because she loved Henry Fonda, and he was fond of it.

Henry grunted as if he shouldn't have had to tell Ray. He moved slowly through the cabin, and despite his defiance in the face of time, Ray now saw that, like his Aunt Eadie, life had taken its toll on his old body. He pulled two tin mugs from a shelf on the wall and set them on the little wooden table, wheezing at the effort. "I need some new mugs." The chipped enamel left jagged edges on the mug rims, and Henry rubbed them with his thumb as if he were trying to wipe them away. He pulled a large jug from under the table and poured two measures of honey wine. He added hot water from a steaming kettle that had been percolating on the woodstove; a sprinkle of spices completed the brew.

"A little early for a drink, Henry."

"Never too early at my age. Anyway, it is medicine." Eventually, Henry joined Ray and sat at the table. He beamed a mouthful of blackened stumps where teeth once stood. His thick glasses magnified his eyes out of all proportion, resembling fish eyes in a fishbowl. "Welcome home, Raymond." They clinked their cups and drank, allowing the warmth of the drink to settle comfortably inside.

"It's good to see you, Henry," Ray said fondly.

"So, where you been, Raymond? Why didn't you come see an old Indian once in so many years?"

Ray felt a pang of guilt. "Are you keeping well, Henry?"

The old man let the unanswered question go with a shrug of his shoulders. "I'm about as well as I should be. Better than dead people anyway. I could do without the arthritis, and my eyes aren't so good. But I cannot complain. The ancestors wouldn't hear of it, even if I did. What do you think about what I've done to the place? Good, yes?"

"Looks great."

"When did you become a smartass?" Henry responded. "The place is shit."

Ray spluttered and almost choked over his wine. "It is a bit out of hand."

"I would tidy up the place if I could be bothered. But who's going to see it? You're my first visitor since the police came. They thought I should be in a nursing home for old people. Me, old, do you believe that?"

"Police?"

Henry grunted. "I've been having people come to the cabin. Causing a ruckus on the lake and stealing things from the boat shed. Doing damage for no good reason. I had a fall last summer, and they came inside while I was in the hospital. Look what they did, those troubled souls." Henry pointed to a wall, where, almost hidden by junk, someone had spray-painted a slur against his people.

"Kids?"

"Grown men, not kids. Usually, four or five of them. Always the same ones."

"That's why the *no trespassing* signs. What did the police say?"

"They said they would ride by now and then. I told them, so does the wind. But the wind cannot hang around and watch over me forever. I'm a peace-loving man, Raymond, but they keep coming back. One day, one of them pushed me to the ground after I tried to stop him from walking off with a full can of gasoline. They tried to steal my Ski-Doo in there. Couldn't get it started. It's as old as me." Henry paused a moment. "But I'm ready for them when they come again," he said defiantly.

Ray was worried about the old man. "Ready how? Don't be doing anything rash now, Henry."

"I don't do rash, Raymond? But I can still hold a rifle, and you know I'm not scared of using it."

"What happened to the man who taught me to turn the other cheek?"

"You are right, Ray. I taught you well. The way of violence is a path that, once walked, cannot be easily left. These bullies strike from a place of weakness, not strength. A truly strong spirit doesn't need to harm others. But there comes a time when turning the other cheek only invites more harm, not just to you, but to others who may suffer after you. If a bully will not stop, if he seeks to break your spirit or harm those you protect, then you must stand like the oak."

"Just the same, let me talk to the local police and see if there's anything they can do. Like it or not, Henry, you're an old man and these men are young. I don't want you to get hurt."

"If it eases your mind, know that I will meet their violence only when there is no other path."

They sat in silence for a while, then Henry said, "You're a hero, I see."

"You heard about it, out here?"

"On my television before those men stole it. I have a satellite dish."

"They stole your TV?"

"It was a curse. But I miss Judge Judy."

"I'm dying, Henry," Ray said without warning.

Henry stood up and shuffled to the woodstove. He added a log and poked the fire, sending sparks up the flu.

"I'm dying," Ray repeated.

"I heard you. But sadly, we're all dying." Henry straightened up, holding his back. "Are you afraid of dying, Raymond? A man should not be afraid of death. No more than he should fear the sunset. It's the natural way. Our bodies will return to the earth, our breath to the wind. This I know as surely as I know the seasons turn. Are you sick?"

"Brain tumor," Ray said, almost matter-of-fact.

"Your brain was always too big for your head, Raymond." Ray laughed. "You are a lucky man."

"How do you figure that?"

"Death's shadow is what makes the sunlight precious, the bloom more fragrant. Ask yourself two questions: Did you live well? Did you love well? If you can answer yes, then you will go like autumn leaves, letting go gently, having first turned beautiful colors." Henry returned to the table, where he allowed the silence to hang between them for an age before he spoke again. "My heart tells me you carry an even heavier torment today. Is it the child's death that makes you ponder your own end?"

"You asked if I was afraid of dying. I'm not. For a long time now, I couldn't care less if I lived or died. But now I come home to die, I find I need more time. I think I fear dying too soon, before I get the chance to make amends. I've wasted my life, and ruined everyone else's."

Henry contemplated for a while. "You didn't come home to die, Raymond," he said eventually. "You believe you did that already, when the child died. But you are wrong. I hear hope in your despair. When will you say her name? Isn't that why you are here at the lake, to look for her and seek her forgiveness?"

"How can I do that? She's gone and it's my fault."

"What you speak of is a terrible sorrow. A life so small, so sacred, gone too soon. The pain of that day lives in your bones, and no words can lift it from you entirely. But hear me when I say this: guilt is not a place you must live in forever. In the words of the ancestors: Even the deepest grief must one day let the light back in. The child's spirit knows your remorse, just as she knew your love before the ice took her. Children who go to meet the ancestors are pure; they do not carry anger, only the hope that we will learn from their leaving."

"I want to believe that."

Henry placed a gnarled hand on Ray's and squeezed. "Listen to an old Indian whose wisdom you may think of as bulldust; the rantings of an old man. But these words I share are born of experience. Forgiveness cannot be rushed like a river in spring. You must earn it, not just from the child's family or the Creator, but from yourself. You must face your fears head-on. Honor her memory by speaking her name aloud so she is not forgotten. Carry her in your heart, but not as a burden; she is a teacher.

"You are still here. That is not an accident. Do you think saving those schoolchildren was an accident? During the time you have left to grace this world, the world needs your hands to mend what you can, your voice to warn others of thin ice, and your life to prove that even the darkest mistakes can grow into wisdom. That young girl died, but she sits on your shoulder, not to haunt you, but to guide you. I hear the sorrow in your voice. You hold this guilt close, as if you are carrying a stone in your chest. It does not honor the past; it only steals from the present. The ancestors see your struggle. They do not ask for perfection, only for you to rise each day and try again. That is enough."

Ray and Henry sat together, contemplating. Eventually, Ray thanked Henry for his wisdom and said goodbye.

"You and Jess, you never stuck together?" Henry said as they stepped out into the snow.

"You know how it is, Henry, life took us on different paths; it wasn't meant to be."

"No, I don't know how it is. You two kids were made to be together. Different paths? We both know you chose the path and left her wondering why. But I think we have said enough. I know you are ready to heal this mistake, too."

"She's still beautiful, Henry."

Henry grunted. "Of course she's still beautiful, she'll always be beautiful; my sweet daughter of the lake."

Chapter 13

Celine Bird peered through the drapes to the road. She watched the snow fall heavily and worried about the sidewalk. She planned to find Martin Shaw's phone number and have him clear the path once daylight came. The consequences would be severe if someone slipped on the sidewalk or the path to her door.

She mixed some hot chocolate in a mug and then added two heaping spoons of marshmallows to the mixture. She thought about getting her bag ready for school, just in case they called her to substitute in the morning. Some teachers might not be able to make it through on the roads. Of course, they never called on her these days. They said she was too old and that "things had changed" since she taught class. What could have changed, she wondered, about simple arithmetic and the English language, other than the lazy teaching practices of an undisciplined faculty? Still, they might call her this time if the snow blocked the roads from out of town. She hoped there would be no canceled classes. She thought they canceled classes far too easily these days.

The old woman prepared to turn off the lights and go to bed, where she would drink her hot chocolate and finish her book. As she reached for the switch, a face appeared at the window, startling her. When she looked again, no one was there. The apparition must have been a trick of the light reflecting off the blowing snow, she decided. She turned toward the stairs and then heard the creak of old boards on the porch. Who could that possibly be at this time of night? A tap on the front door confirmed she had a visitor. Her aging hand unhooked the chain and turned the door handle. She felt a cold blast of air on her face and legs as the door swung open.

"Whatever do you want at this time of night? You look terrible; is something wrong?"

＊　　＊　　＊

The drive through town took Ray past the McDonald's and the Big Burger, past the mall, and up to the raceway. High-performance snowmobiles were warming up for the annual Ski-Doo Grand Prix weekend. Ray pulled into the parking lot and watched them go through their paces. The cold air carried the high-pitched whine of engines as snowmobiles darted across the groomed raceway. The machines, sleek and aerodynamic, carved sharp lines into the packed surface. Riders, dressed in brightly colored suits and helmets, crouched low over the handlebars, their bodies shifting in sync with every turn, their movements almost dance-like in their fluidity.

The track itself was laid out like a winding ribbon of snow, bordered by tall berms, sharp hairpin turns, and straightaways where the snowmobiles reached blistering speeds. Snow sprayed in broad arcs as the riders leaned hard into corners, their studded tracks gripping the ice. The roar of the engines rose and fell in a rhythmic chorus, punctuated by the occasional burst of acceleration as a rider gunned the throttle out of a turn.

Ray had fond memories of the raceway. The highlight of each summer was the Smash-Up Derby, when the motor circus came to town. He recalled the thrill of high-speed racing and the stunt drivers with their outrageous performances. He thought of his mother and the big bag of popcorn she bought for him as they sat in the bleachers, cheering the antics of a daredevil clown dodging the cars to the delight of the crowd. Good memories.

Ray glanced at the mall. Christmas music floated out to the raceway, and he saw the parking lot was crowded with seasonal shoppers. Bargain hunters seeking deals, no doubt. It seemed they started earlier every year, so that by the time Christmas arrived, everyone was tired of it. He looked back at the raceway and sat there for five or six minutes. He was procrastinating. Walt Callus was somewhere inside, working. Ray knew he would be unwelcome, but it was now or never. He got out and walked onto the grounds. A guy in coveralls was on a ladder fixing a Tannoy speaker to a steel post. The big guy turned as Ray approached. He smiled. "What can I do for you, friend?"

"I'm looking for Walt Callus."

The guy paused momentarily, then a shadow crossed his face. It was a dark expression Ray had seen before. "You're Ray Waring."

"I am."

The guy turned back to the task at hand and remained silent for a long moment. "Walt doesn't want to see you," he said eventually. "I know what you want with him, but he's not interested."

"Where can I find him?"

"I don't think you heard me right. I said he doesn't want to see you."

"He told you that?"

The guy set down his tools and stepped off the ladder. "He doesn't need to tell me. I know the story. It nearly killed him to lose his sister. Leave him alone. There's nothing for you here."

Ray didn't respond. Instead, he walked toward the outbuildings in search of Walt. The smell of gasoline and hot metal filled his nostrils. Occasional clouds of exhaust fumes hung in the air before dissipating as mechanics tinkered with their machines. He paused at what had become the temporary pit stop. Coaches and teammates watched their riders, analyzing every move and shouting feedback over the din. The snowmobiles blurred past in flashes of vibrant color, their headlights cutting through the winter haze. Heads turned to him briefly, but they ignored him as he searched for Walt in the crowd. He noticed a plume of snow high in the air; someone was blowing out the paved area behind the stand. Ray turned the corner, saw it was Walt, and approached. Upon seeing Ray, Walt stopped the machine, removed his ear protection, and waited for Ray to speak. The years had etched new lines into his face. His eyes were hollow and dead, the kind that told of too much pain and loss, the sort of eyes he'd seen in addicts.

Ray hesitated; the weight in his chest was heavy with trepidation. It wasn't a fear of physical harm, although Walt was a big man who could inflict serious damage, but rather the fear of the rejection he anticipated.

"Can we talk?" Ray said.

Walt's mouth twisted. "There's nothing we need to say."

Ray moved in closer. The silence between them was a living thing, thick with all the words Ray had never said. He imagined Clair standing beside Walt, her hair catching the sunlight.

"I'm dying," he said. It wasn't a plea, just a fact.

Walt's knuckles whitened. "Good."

The word hung there, brutal in its simplicity. Ray had anticipated this, yet something inside him still flinched.

"I didn't come for forgiveness," he said. "I know better."

"Then why?" Walt's voice was low, dangerous. "You think you can just show up after all these years and…"

"No." Ray exhaled. "I just wanted to see you. To say it to your face. That I'm sorry."

Walt laughed then, a sharp, jagged sound as the laugh transformed into a bitter snarl. "Sorry doesn't bring her back."

"No." Ray met his gaze. "But neither does hating me. It only hurts you, Walt."

For a moment, something flickered in Walt's eyes, not softening, not exactly, but a crack in the armor. Then it disappeared. He leaned forward, his voice a venomous whisper. "You don't get to do this. You don't get to die and leave me with nothing but your apology."

"It's all I've got left."

Walt edged closer to him, forcing Ray to step back. "I imagined what I'd say if I ever met you again. In my mind, I've said it all. But know this; When I look into your face now, I see nothing, nothing of the friend I once knew. I see only a coward who killed my Clair and ran like he was the one in pain. Get out of my sight. I don't know you. I don't ever want to set eyes on you again."

Ray didn't answer. There was nothing left to say. He raised his hands in a show of submission. "I tried," he said softly. Just as he turned to walk away, a heavy jolt in the back sent him sprawling to the ground. Walt stood over him, pointing a finger.

"I see you again, it *will* be the last."

Ray picked himself up and brushed himself off as Walt walked away. He went back to the parking lot and saw a black Chevy Tahoe parked next to his car. He recognized the grill lights and knew it was an unmarked squad car, with the man in the driver's seat being a cop.

The vehicle had local plates. As Ray neared his car, the driver got out of the Tahoe and introduced himself.

"Barnabas Lawrence; most folks call me Barney."

Barney Lawrence was a large man, weighing about two-fifty pounds, half of it around his belt. His cheerful face presented an unthreatening appearance, and he looked like the kind of guy you would go to a game with or share a beer on the patio. Lawrence's hair glowed yellow in the afternoon sun, but only thin gray strands covered his balding scalp. Ray took his hand, shook it, and managed a friendly smile in return for Lawrence's broad grin.

"I couldn't help notice the bird sitting here in the lot. She's a beauty, that's for sure."

"So everyone keeps telling me."

"Looks like you've got a flat tire, two in fact," Lawrence said.

Ray glanced at his rear wheels and sighed. He scanned the parking lot and noticed the maintenance guy observing him with a smug grin. "Son of a bitch," Ray muttered.

"Do you know that car sat in the showroom window for two years before you bought it? I used to drop by every so often to drool over it. It's a shame to see it covered in crud like that."

"Again, so everyone keeps telling me."

"You're Ray Waring." It was a statement, not a question. "I heard some of the guys in the unit say you were driving this babe around town. Not like you came home keeping a low profile. Superstar all the way."

"It's just a car."

"Hmm. They say you're back home because you had to bow out of the Bureau." He tilted his head and stared at Ray's forehead as if searching for something to mark the spot. "Too bad about the brain thing. Sure is a bitch." He looked absently in no particular direction and spoke into the air. "So, you retired completely?"

"No choice. Like you said, I had to bow out. Incapacitated due to health-related issues, the discharge papers said."

Lawrence grunted. He looked like a man with something to say. "Too bad, really. I mean, all that experience in the Bureau, it's a shame to waste it, to hang up the gloves."

"What's on your mind, Lawrence?" Ray went to the trunk to look for the spare, a useless endeavor as he needed two.

"Don't get too many homicides in Fowler, you'd probably know that. It's been twelve years since old man Peerce cut up his wife with a hacksaw and dumped the pieces in the Salvation Army clothes can." Ray nodded; he'd read about that one. "Tell a lie, there was the kid from Rapids who held up the Shell on Seventh and shot the attendant with a BB gun. When the attendant laughed at him, he beat him to death with it. Caught him same day trying to steal a book from the library, go figure."

"What was the book?"

"How to win friends and influence people," he said quickly with a smile. "It was actually a copy of the *Popular Mechanics Handbook*. He said he wanted it so he could fix his mom's old Chrysler. He said he loved his mom."

"Get to the point, Lawrence."

The big man stood next to Ray and leaned over the trunk. He breathed hot chili as he spoke. "Got a homicide on the hill, retired schoolteacher by the name of Celine Bird. Thought you might like to take a look, share your expert opinion."

"I know Celine Bird; she taught me at Myerson." Ray saw her face immediately and heard her scolding voice. A tyrannical woman, feared by all of her students; he could count a thousand kids who had once wished her dead, including himself. "Like I told you, I quit the Bureau; you don't need me poking my nose in."

Lawrence smiled. "You didn't exactly say you quit, Ray. What you said was that you had no choice. Maybe it's what you need to take your mind off things."

Ray searched for the jack, but there wasn't one. He sighed. "What I need, you can't give me, Detective, unless you've got a jack and a spare wheel?"

Lawrence ignored the question. "Neighbor says he saw a woman on Ms. Bird's stoop late yesterday evening; we're chasing that one down. But this wasn't the work of a woman. Believe me."

"Do you have any suspects?"

"No, I..."

"So why assume this woman's not your killer?"

"The victim was badly beaten. Humiliated. Seems to me it's got a male perp written all over it. Woman on the stoop doesn't fit the profile."

Ray couldn't resist a smirk. "Believe me, Detective, it takes all kinds to kill. Women were involved in some of the worst cases I worked. Bird was what, eighty?"

"Eighty-three. I know, what twisted fuck would want to kill an eighty-year-old bag of bones, right? Look, all I ask is that you take a look. Meanwhile, I'll get one of the guys to come up here and change your wheels. What do you say?"

Ray exhaled and slammed the trunk shut.

Chapter 14

Celine Bird's home, an elegant red brick veneer with a porch that extended across the entire front, was situated in a leafy neighborhood on the west hill. A giant rock maple loomed over the property, its massive roots pushing up through the driveway and lifting two large paving slabs into a pitched roof, making it impossible to drive a vehicle onto the property. The garden had long since fallen into decay. The path to the front step lay deep in fresh snow, but the front lawn had been heavily trampled by personnel who had swarmed over the property.

Several squad cars were parked behind the medical examiner's van. A local television crew had set up a satellite truck, and they gathered on the sidewalk opposite. A reporter practiced her script, unaware of the national celebrity accompanying Barney Lawrence into the victim's home.

Inside, Ray scanned the room as he always did before a closer inspection. He preferred to get the overall view in his head before the picture became clouded with too much detail. The entrance hall showed no signs of unusual activity. A large steel grate in the wooden floor marked the return grid for the old-fashioned furnace in the basement below. An arched walkway led to the left and into the main living area, with the kitchen at the rear. Floral prints adorned the walls. From the old-fashioned wallpaper designs, he figured they could even be original to the house. The furnishings, as he would expect from Celine Bird, were expensive, original pieces; high-quality antiques rich in dark wood grains, perfect for the formal setting. Starched white, handmade lace, covered tables and other horizontal surfaces, serving as foils for the many porcelain collectibles she had acquired over the years of her life.

Two morgue technicians were preparing to remove the victim, now wrapped in a body bag, lying on a gurney. Ray imagined Celine Bird inside. He turned and bristled at the sight of the straight-backed dining chair that stood in the center of the room. Both front legs had the remains of duct tape attached near the floor. An evidence card with the number 2 lay next to the chair leg. Fine blood spatter covered the pale Persian rug, the sofa, and one lounge chair.

"This is where she died?" he asked.

"She was beaten over there by the table, then dragged over to the middle of the room and tied up. We figure she was beaten with that willow switch for several minutes before he took to her with his fists." Lawrence pointed to the thin wand of leafless willow, lying in a corner of the room and marked with a number 5. "She was probably unconscious when he tied her to the chair with duct tape. She had her underpants over her head and was strangled with a pair of woolen tights. It looks like she fought off her attacker for a while, but she was elderly, didn't stand a chance."

Ray remembered Celine Bird; tough was not an adequate word to describe her. She was the most feared of all schoolteachers, the classic teacher from hell. She would have fought for her life no matter how old or frail she had become.

"Eventually, he took a toilet roll from the closet and stuffed the paper, piece by piece, into her nose and mouth. She died of asphyxiation. This was cruelty for cruelty's sake."

Ray couldn't help the nauseous reaction to the account of her death. "Sexual assault?"

"Thankfully not. However, the mere act of having removed, or having her remove her underwear, raises the question of a sexual component. But I'd say he did it for kicks. He ransacked the place: drawers emptied, contents tipped out, and trashed. We can't rule out robbery entirely, but there's a heap of jewelry spilled onto the dresser in the bedroom. He left it all, along with a small amount of cash in her purse." Lawrence waited for Ray to comment, but he said nothing, browsing the room, seemingly searching for clues.

"He wanted to humiliate her, show his power over her," Ray said, as he stooped close to the chair to examine the ligatures.

"What feeling of power can someone get by beating up on a helpless old lady?"

Ray answered without looking at Lawrence. "She was not helpless in his mind; she was a tyrant."

"You think she knew him?"

"DNA?"

"That's the thing, we've got more evidence than you could shake a stick at, no pun intended. This psycho had no intention of covering his tracks. What do you mean, she was a tyrant?"

Ray examined the willow switch. Red blood stained the shiny brown bark.

"She used to wave a stick like this in class, always threatening to do you harm with it. Of course, she never actually used it, but all the kids lived in fear of her, no matter how well-behaved they were. She didn't discriminate between the good and bad kids in class; she terrorized us all."

"Still, it's not a reason for murder, is it? Weren't we all traumatized by school?"

"Probably, but she was one of a kind. I could think of a dozen kids who talked about doing this to her, killing her in some cruel, drawn-out way. She was hated. It became a competition to see who could imagine the worst fate for her; that's how bad she was."

Lawrence creased his eyes and studied Ray. "What kind of end did you dream up?"

"Can I see the bedroom?"

Lawrence guided Ray to the bedroom. The room had clearly been ransacked. Ray examined the jewelry scattered across the dresser. "This is all of it?" Lawrence nodded. "Was she wearing a ring when she died?"

"I believe she *was* wearing a ring. Why?"

"She used to wear a big ring on her right index finger; a large diamond and sapphire cluster set in white gold. She would slip it down to the middle of her finger and press it into your arm if you misbehaved. It wasn't enough to leave a mark for more than a few minutes, but it was enough to make you feel her wrath. She got away with it for years without being called out on it."

"I think the ring she wore was a plain gold band, but I'll check. Do you suspect he stole it, this ring you're talking about? Like a trophy?"

Ray shrugged. "What about the woman who was seen at her door? Are there any security cameras on neighboring houses?"

The detective shook his head. "We're following up on it, but have nothing yet. There was a camera two doors down, but the snowfall was too heavy last night to get anything here. It could have been a friend or neighbor visiting. We're checking with the people she knew. The way you asked those questions, you think this is an old classroom vendetta, a score settled?"

"Detective..."

"Come on, Ray, call me Barney, everyone does."

"Barney, why did you ask me over here?"

"Isn't it obvious? You're a legend here, Ray. Like I said before, we don't get many homicides here in Fowler, so I figured you being in town and all, you could show us hicks a thing or two about tracking this piece of crap down. You have a reputation. But to be honest, I thought you'd want to take your mind off the other stuff, help us old town boys clean up Dodge before you hit Tombstone."

He grinned and slapped Ray on the back. Ray chuckled. He found it refreshing to have someone who didn't tiptoe around the subject of his approaching fate.

"There's two long blonde hairs stuck to the duct tape on the chair leg."

Lawrence nodded at a forensic technician who was processing the scene. The tech responded, irritated by the interference. "I see it. Just haven't got that far yet."

Chapter 15

Jamie Carriger had just called to update Ray on the search for Ramos and other members of the far-right group. The whereabouts of Mateo Ramos remained unknown.

Eadie's high-pitched laugh and the sound of loud voices drew Ray from his room, just in time to see Prescott Guziac kick the snow from his boots. He pulled off his winter boots, leaving the removable linings on his feet like big woolly slippers. His face was flushed red from the cold. He slipped his parka off his shoulders and hung it on a peg near the door.

"Aunt Eadie and I was just saying how you ain't got time for your old buddy with all that high-powered detective work you've been doing. Seems you can't leave it be, don't it, Ray?"

Eadie looked at Ray defensively. "I didn't say anything!" she said, raising her eyebrows in a show of indignation.

"Aunt Eadie tells me I'm just in time for lunch. Boy, I miss your good cooking, Aunt Eadie, there ain't none can cook like you."

Eadie scoffed. "Don't think I don't know when someone's trying to sweet-talk me, Scottie. Perhaps you're feeling guilty. You might want to ask yourself why you waited until Ray returned before giving me so much as a howdy doo." Eadie shot a glare at Ray as though it were his fault Scottie had arrived for lunch unannounced. Then, she disappeared into the kitchen.

"It's all over town, Ray, you helping out the local boys with your expert knowledge of criminals. Old Tweety Bird, plucked and fucked, eh? 'Bout fucking time I say?"

Scottie's remarks reflected the typical behavior of the boy Ray had grown up with. Ray had heard it all, and worse, but these comments disgusted him in a way they never had before.

Aunt Eadie called out, "Keep the language down, Prescott Guziac. You're not too old for a slap on the ear."

Ray closed the kitchen door and walked to the lounge. Scottie followed, giggling like a mischievous schoolboy.

"So, what you find out, Ray? Do you have a suspect, a motive? What did the CSI boys come up with?" He seemed unable to contain his excitement. He wanted all the details, especially the gory ones.

"I can't talk about the case, you know that. And let's show a bit of respect, Scottie."

Scottie sneered. "What are you saying, Ray? Suddenly that old bitch deserves respect?"

"She was eighty-three years old, for crying out loud. She deserved more than to end her days like that." Ray eyeballed Scottie to make his point. "I've seen too many innocent people hurt in ways you can't imagine, ways that beggar belief that one person can do such things to another. We were kids when she had us quaking in our boots, man! I left those grudges behind long ago."

"I wasn't quaking."

"Well, I was. And I remember a certain... Never mind. She wasn't your average Mary Poppins, granted, but we all survived. Maybe we benefited in the process. Life's not so kind. We learned some valuable lessons from Bird on that count. So, she didn't think much of you when you were still a kid; get over it! She was an old lady, and now she's dead because of this psycho lowlife, someone she probably tried to help once."

A moment of silence accompanied the exchange of confrontational glares before Scottie finally relaxed.

"She won't get no tears from this boy, Ray. Whoever done this to her may be psycho, but she got what was coming in my book."

"Where were *you* yesterday, Scottie?"

Scottie laughed. He had a habit of snorting when he did so. "The bigshot FBI hero got this case broke already, huh? Why, you sure are a fast worker, Ray. Don't know how these local boys managed to go to the can without pissing on themselves before you arrived in town. Still, I give up, Ray, yes, it was me, I killed that old bird, I swear on Eadie's blessed life I done it." He held his wrists together outstretched before him. "Lock me up, oh mighty hero! Gotham City is safe once more."

Ray turned away and walked to the liquor cabinet. "Want a bourbon?"

"Is that okay for a condemned man, Ray? I mean me being a full-on psycho murderer an' all." He giggled stupidly.

"Give me a break, Scottie. Do you want one or not?"

Scottie accepted the offer and sprawled out on the sofa as if it were his own. "Them Traverse cops say my daddy was murdered; they have suspects. Them neighbors was robbing him too. Can't trust no one these days." He took the glass from Ray and swilled it in his hand. "Do you think it was them that killed him, or that mystery woman who went to his apartment?"

"Who told you about the woman?"

"That young cop who interviewed me. He said, and I quote: "A mysterious woman was seen leaving the complex shortly after gunshots were heard." I expect they'll be trying to track her down." Scottie snickered. "That bitch is probably in Mexico by now."

Ray studied Scottie's face and suddenly saw the boy in him, a complex, crazy fool. No one could ever get inside his head and understand his thoughts. If he was truly upset about his father's death, he no longer showed any signs; the door had closed. He might as well have been talking about a TV show, not the killing of his father.

"They'll get whoever is responsible. Most killers don't kill at random; they either know or are intimate with the vics."

"I saw Walt over by the school today." Scottie sat up, swung his legs around, and put his feet on the coffee table. "I heard he quit his job at the raceway on account of a set-to with the boss. Seems he was told to clean up the restrooms and got the shits. Not literally," Scottie added, scoffing. Ray noticed the way Scottie's fingers tapped restlessly on the arm of the sofa, leg bouncing up and down. Ever on the move, he twitched and fidgeted constantly.

"Walt has a temper."

"Yes, he does. Apparently, he lost it and told his boss where he could shove it, turned into what you law enforcement types call a *violent altercation*. I tell you, Ray, something will never be the same in old Walt's head. If I were that boss of his, I'd be watching my ass, I can tell you that. Shit, old Walt is just about crazier than a dog with a flea up his butt."

"Flea in his ear. The saying is flea in his ear, not up his butt. At the school, you said?"

"Castle Street, where Jess's little one goes to preschool. Figured he was fixing to meet someone the way he was hanging around there."

"You talked to him?"

"No. I just figured he was meeting up with someone."

"So, how'd you know about his bust-up at the raceway?"

Scottie got to his feet and walked to the kitchen, calling out, "Smells good, Aunt Eadie." He returned and sat down again, this time in an armchair. "Must have been Kiel Seedorf. Yeah, I saw Kiel, and he must have told me. He sure is a screwball, Walt. I'm so hungry I could eat a horse. How 'bout you, Ray?"

Chapter 16

Doctor Galway pushed air from a syringe, sending a short spurt of liquid into the air from the needle. "It's only going to get worse, I'm afraid, Ray. At the risk of sounding like a broken record, maybe it's time you thought about what will happen when it does." Ray winced at the brief jab and tried to focus on the computer screen in Galway's office. His file, along with his medical history, appeared on the screen, revealing the details of his illness and the treatment prescribed. A call came in for Galway, and he excused himself. Ray took the opportunity to turn the monitor and skip through the notes.

MRI Report – Washington Hospital Center
Patient: *Waring, Raymond.*
Findings: *A 4.8 cm midline mass between pons and*

cerebellum. Consistent with glioma (likely Grade 2/3) Definitive grading requires biopsy.

Ray moved quickly to treatment options:

Robotic-Assisted Neurosurgery (Preferred) *Stereotactic biopsy/partial resection using intraoperative MRI guidance.*

Risks: Ray zoomed in on key words. *CSF leak, hemorrhage, vision loss, cranial nerve damage, residual tumor.* **Galway was coming back down the hall.**

Adjuvant Therapies: *Radiation for unresectable portions. Chemotherapy if high-grade.*

Supportive Care: *Corticosteroids (edema). Anti-seizure meds. Pain management, opioids.*

Prognosis: Ray's stomach turned. *Average survival time, 12-18 months.* **Ray's vision was blurring just trying to read it.** *Only 25% of patients survive more than one year, only 5% of patients survive more than five years. See also tumor grade, resection margins, and molecular markers.*

Note: Preliminary assessment

The report writer added a note in brackets:

(Hi Vincent. Thanks for the referral. Without preempting next steps, I've seen dozens of glioblastomas like your boy's. Six to twelve months without treatment. Time's critical here. Wienberger's your best bet. Let's play a round when the snow clears. Cheers.)

The note's urgency clashed with its casual tone—golf plans sandwiched between a life-and-death prognosis. Yet Ray recognized his own detachment when he'd first received the diagnosis. The clinical terminology had obscured the simple truth: *You're dying.* His initial reaction had been relief, even anticipation. Then Scottie's letter, as though it were a call to arms. He'd started thinking of all those he would leave behind, all the words that would be left unsaid. It had shaken him from his fatalism, sending him on this final mission to settle accounts.

Now the numbers burned behind his eyelids; *Six to twelve months.* A wave of panic hit him, dizzying, visceral. For the first time, he desperately wanted those stolen years back. Sweat prickled his skin as his hands began to tremble. His vision clouded. The room swirled.

"Ray!"

Ray stared blankly at the elderly doctor. His rotund, bespectacled face, topped by a shiny bald head, drifted in and out of focus as Ray returned to reality.

"Ray, I asked if you were alright. I think you blacked out for a moment."

Ray nodded absently, rolled down his sleeve, and walked to the door. "Thanks, Doc." Then he left without another word. The concerned doctor looked on.

Ray stood on the sidewalk. The wind whipped up a cloud of powdery snow. It curled in the air, driving tiny shards of ice to prick his face and chill his flesh. But a different kind of cold now gripped his mind. A cold sense of death. It alarmed him more than he could have ever imagined.

He walked three blocks from Galway's practice, dazed and confused by his response to the report. He slumped onto a wooden bench at the bus stop and tried to find thoughts that could comfort him, but there were none. He was afraid. For the first time in his life, he was terrified of what lay ahead. He heard Henry's words: "Death's shadow is what makes the sunlight precious." Ray looked up at the sky, where the clouds cast a milky haze across the sun. He knew he wanted to live.

❅

Chapter 17

The Washington trip had drained him. Three days of scans, needles, and grim-faced consultations left him hollowed out. Yet in the sterile anonymity of hospital corridors, where no one recognized the 'Hero of Lilyfield Elementary School', Ray found something unexpected; clarity.

Fowler had become a circus, just like before in Washington, his notoriety growing with each news cycle. But here, just another patient in a paper gown, he could finally think. The medical purgatory gave him space to plan his fight.

Weinberger's tone had shifted; cautious optimism replacing clinical detachment. 'Time isn't our friend,' the neurosurgeon warned, pushing for immediate surgery. Ray delayed. There were things to settle first. Loose ends to tie, in case the knife stole more than the tumor.

He would return to Fowler with two certainties: he would fight, and he would do it on his terms.

Ray's phone rang. His mood lifted at the sound of Jess's voice. He avoided mention of the hospital visit. "It's good to hear from you, Jess."

"I've been thinking hard about things; you and I, how we should move on from here." Her voice was tentative. There was a long pause, when all he could hear was her breathing. "I can't get these thoughts out of my mind," she said eventually. "Not for a minute. I spent the whole day yesterday in a zombie-like state. I can't concentrate. I'm neglecting the kids. The fact is, I'm a mess, Ray. What kind of mother doesn't even know her kids are screaming for lunch and it's half past three in the afternoon?"

"It's my fault, I've turned your life upside down."

"No, it's not your fault, Ray. It's about you, but it's not your fault. I can take responsibility for my own actions." There was another brief silence. "I need to see you again. Alan is taking the kids to see his mom in Detroit this afternoon. He wants to take them to a Red Wings game. Brighton is only three, for God's sake. He's too young to sit through a whole game." Another pause. "Anyway," she said at length, "they're going to spend the weekend there. You can come for supper if you want; we can talk again without distractions."

Ray took a long time to shower and shave. The pain had returned to his head, causing his hands to shake like Jell-O. Each stroke of the razor took away pieces of flesh. When he was finished, he looked like a prizefighter after a losing bout. After stopping the bleeding, he'd had to lie down, and he fell asleep. He showed up at Jess's door two hours late.

"I thought you changed your mind," she said as she closed the door behind him. "What happened to your face?"

Ray laughed. "Cut myself shaving!" He decided not to explain the full story. *Who cuts themselves a hundred times shaving?*

Jess hadn't dressed up this time. Faded jeans hugged her hips, fuller now, but still shapely, while a crisp white blouse with rolled sleeves revealed olive-toned arms. The minimal makeup she wore did its work too well, accentuating the bow of her lips and making her eyes glow like sunlight through whiskey. She was both familiar and new, this woman who carried twenty years in the sway of her hips yet remained undeniably Jess.

When she turned away abruptly, Ray wondered if she'd sensed his thoughts, the sudden, visceral memory of how she'd fitted against him. That white cotton might as well have been a spotlight, illuminating every curve he'd once traced with his hands.

Then she turned back. No words passed between them. He felt an urge to hold her, to pull her close, just as he had in the old days. In the end, he didn't have to. She reached out for *him*. Tears pooling in her eyes said everything.

"I can't help it," she croaked. "Look what you've done to me." Tears streamed down her cheeks. He could feel her pain, and it made him ache for her. She took his hand, pulling him close to her. Hurt and vulnerable, the face among the tears was now that of the child he knew so well. But she was no longer a child, and the pain was no longer in her bruised knee. It was evidence of a deep and painful scar in her heart.

"I'm sorry," was all he could say without breaking down.

"I still love you, Ray; I never stopped loving you. I want you every minute of every day, every waking moment, and every sleeping hour. I want you beside me and inside me. I never want to be without you as long as you are walking this earth. Be it for a week or a year, it would be a lifetime to me, a lifetime to spend at your side. Please hold me. Hold me tight like you used to, as if the years apart never happened."

He lifted her from her feet, feeling the lightness of her frame and the warmth of her body. He pushed his mouth to hers and felt the overwhelming rush of love course through him. His world, with all its hate and violence, all its negativity and drama, the hunger for death, and the fight for survival, meant nothing to him now. At this moment with the woman he loved, the years of depression and self-degradation faded from his mind, along with all sense of reality. Now was the only reality.

✳   ✳   ✳

Jess wrapped her arms around his neck and crushed her lips against his. She felt the muscles in his neck go taut, the brief resistance before he surrendered. Without a word, he lifted her, carrying her up the stairs past the open doors of the kids' bedrooms. She stayed silent, eyes locked on his as he found her room, sidestepping the pile of clothes and toys she'd meant to put away.

He laid her on the bed; the soft flesh of her belly was exposed. A quiver ran through her as his touch traced her skin, so deliberate, so knowing, and she gasped, her body arching into him. His lips returned to hers, and when he nipped at her lower lip, the familiar tease sent a thrill through her.

His mouth moved lower, kissing the swell of her breasts, each press of his lips leaving fire in its wake. She writhed as he trailed down, circling her navel, his hands already at her jeans. The zipper slid down, and she lifted her hips, helping him peel them away before they were tossed aside.

Now, naked beneath him, she burned with need, shameless, aching. His fingers explored her with torturous gentleness, and she whimpered, her hands now frantic as she pulled at his clothes, desperate to feel his skin to skin. This was more than want; it was a claiming, a desperate reunion after too long without.

When he finally entered her, she clutched him tight, the emotion so sharp it threatened to shatter her. In this moment, nothing else mattered: no past, no guilt, only the two of them, lost in each other, as if time had never stolen them away.

* * *

Ray drank in the sweetness of her breath, filling his lungs with it as if it were the very air he'd been starving for. Her fingers traced his back, light as feathers yet burning where they touched. Every gasp, every frantic shift of her body screamed urgency. But when their eyes met, he saw more than need. He saw *her*, laid bare: the longing, the years of absence, the unspoken *why*.

The world fell away. No rush, no force, just the two of them, fused. She clutched him tighter, her thighs trembling around his hips, and for the first time in years, he felt whole.

But then the weight of it all crashed down on him. Tears came without warning, his breath fracturing into a sob against her neck. How had he abandoned his life with her? Her face was wet, her cheeks slick where his lips brushed them, their tears mingling together in salt and sorrow. He didn't just move within her; he worshipped her, every thrust a plea for a past they couldn't reclaim. When release came, it was an unraveling, their bodies shuddering with the sheer, brutal truth of what they'd lost.

Afterward, they lay tangled and silent. Words would have cheapened it. Her fingers curled into his hair, and his palm pressed over her racing heart. There was no separating where he ended and she began.

Only after the storm between them calmed did she speak, her voice soft yet unwavering. She shared with him the hollow nights, the heartbreak she experienced when he left, and the emptiness of her life without him. All traces of bitterness had vanished from her voice as she recounted her sadness and descent into darkness. His apologies could not excuse his mistakes. He still felt deep regret, yet he finally accepted her forgiveness and believed in its sincerity.

✳ ✳ ✳

The bed, *his* bed, their bed, still smelled of laundry soap and Al's cologne, but she refused to acknowledge it. *Not tonight.* The framed smiles on the nightstand, the studio portrait on the wall, the life she'd built without him, all of it faded into insignificance. There was only Ray.

The weight of his body against hers, the heat of his skin, the way his breath quickened when her fingers tangled in his hair, this was real. This was the world she chose now, if only for a stolen hour. She clung to it greedily, memorizing the curve of his shoulder beneath her palm, and the way his pulse jumped when she kissed his throat. Reality could wait. Guilt could wait. She would not think of the ring on her finger or the promises she'd made to someone else, promises that now felt like shackles. Tonight, she would be selfish. Tonight, she would pretend this was hers to keep. And when dawn came, she would let go. But not yet.

❄   ❄   ❄

Ray lay against the headboard as she settled under his arm, resting her head on his chest. She casually stroked his body with her fingers. They remained there in silence for a while until she eventually asked, "Why did you choose law enforcement?"

He reflected on when he'd arrived in New York, bewildered and lost, with no place to stay. "It was a billboard advertisement, a recruitment drive by the Nassau County police. I needed a job. It was an impulse."

"And all the dreams, med school? Forgotten?"

"Eventually. But police work suited my immediate needs. My partner, Byrne, was a hardened vet who schooled me in survival. 'Partners are a distraction,' he'd growl. 'Like wives, kids, friends, just more ways to get you killed.' The old bastard preferred working solo, tolerated me as a necessary evil. Didn't matter; his philosophy matched mine. Isolation wasn't just safety; it was my penance. I figured if I focused on the job, I'd keep the past out of my mind. So, I worked every hour I could. Double shifts when I could. I didn't socialize or make friends. I ate, slept, and worked, nothing else. It had the desired effect for a while. I found myself enjoying the job. I relished the next watch, the next patrol. But dark thoughts were always just a nightmare away."

"And the FBI?"

"Recruited. My single-minded focus on work brought me attention. Other cops didn't appreciate my work focus; they thought I was trying too hard, but the brass saw it. So did a senior FBI agent who worked on a case with us. Once I joined, I lived by the same code of conduct: head down, hard work. No room for any other thoughts. No room for anyone."

Jess shifted the conversation to lighter topics. In the hours that followed, they shared memories. Yet each joyful memory only highlighted their loss, causing them to oscillate between happiness and regret with every warm recollection.

"I went up to the lake a few days ago, spoke to Henry."

"No way!" she said excitedly. "I wasn't sure if he was still alive. Did he remember you?"

Ray smiled. "He has a better memory than I do. We talked for hours about the times we spent at the lake. He seemed to recall the tiniest details, things I'd forgotten. He called you his 'sweet daughter of the lake.'"

"Oh, now I feel terrible for not going out to see him. I thought about him so many times. He has to be the most gentle, wise old man I've ever known. He'd have to be in his nineties."

"I think he must. He's certainly still dishing out the wisdom, but the gentle side has gained an edge over the years." Ray told Jess of Henry's problems with intruders. "He's got his rifle standing next to the door, and I think he could use it if they push him any further. I'm a bit worried about him, to tell you the truth."

"We should go up and see him, together. I can't believe he's still up there."

They lay in silence once more until Ray mentioned Scottie. Jess grumbled at the name, but listened quietly as he recalled their reunion. "I can't get my head around him being an actor. He's got a big movie coming out."

"Oh, please. You don't really believe that, do you? Scottie Guziac couldn't act his way out of a wet paper bag. He had a small role in a soap which was set in Indian River. He was written out after the first episode. He became a laughing stock, Ray. I think he appeared in one or two ads for a hardware chain on WPBN, but that's about it. After that, he tried out for the stage, and when he couldn't secure a part, he bought the local theater. That was the last time it operated because no one would work with him. It's been left to fall apart just like that old house he lives in. And by the way, the word is, from Carmen at the bank, he's now about to go bankrupt. He'll lose that house too when the bank forecloses."

Ray was left stunned. "So, none of it was true?"

"He's no actor, Ray."

Now that Ray had given it some thought, he wasn't surprised by Jess's information. Scottie was a pathological liar. "You're right about the house. I couldn't believe the condition inside. It's... Well, let's say it belongs in one of those movies he can't get into." Ray went into details. The shock still haunted him. "Did you know his father died?"

Jess had heard. "I was sorry to hear that, I guess. But he was a horrible man. And Scottie's just like him these days. He gives me the creeps, to be honest."

They lay silently for several more minutes, each deep in thought. Eventually, Jess rolled the palm of her hand across his chest, then slipped it down to his legs and groin. Thus began the chain of passion that would carry them through the night until dawn

Chapter 18

They had a hurried breakfast of toast and coffee. Ray sensed Jess wanted him gone early, though she didn't say as much. She appeared nervous, constantly glancing at the door as though she expected her husband to walk through at any moment. Al and the kids would be gone until late afternoon, but he sensed her anxiety about a possible early arrival.

In a fleeting facial expression, he thought he saw regret when she glanced at him sitting at the table. It was as if she were experiencing a moment of shame. He quickly finished his coffee, kissed her on the cheek, and turned to leave.

"Wait," she said, almost in panic. She grasped his arm, pulled him to her, and pressed her lips against his.

They held each other close for several moments, then kissed again, and he left with a simple, "I'll call you." As he walked through the door, he wondered what lay ahead for them. The uncertainty twisted his gut.

Ray drove across town, heading to the Municipal Police Department. He felt exhilarated, more alive than he had in years. The cold, clean air infused a sense of purity into the world on a day when the sky, clear of clouds, appeared more intensely blue than he had ever seen.

He paused to take it all in by the river, pulling over to the side of the road next to the bridge. He looked out across the bay at the collection of black dots he knew to be fishermen's ice shanties. Someone had fired up an auger in preparation for fishing. Looking east, he noted a deer making its way from the lake into the trees. The escarpment glowed gold in the morning sunlight, as if floodlit against the intense blue of the winter sky.

The night alone with Jess had been wonderful, the best in his dark and troubled life since the days of his carefree youth. He thought of her now, and a warm sense of happiness spread through him. But this moment of contentment was brief. Who was he kidding? A cold stone settled in his gut, and joy turned to dread. Jess's face had betrayed her when they parted. Despite her declared enduring love for him, he knew they were both in denial. He knew that family would come first when a choice had to be made. During the night, they had blocked out the realities of life, facts that would have to be faced eventually.

His happiness felt fragile. Alan Fischer would walk through her door later that day, hold her in his arms as *he* had done, and love her in the same bed. The thought filled him with resentment. He pictured Fischer's face and his dull expression, wondering how Jess could have chosen such a man. He brooded for a few more minutes until he finally got a grip. *You're acting like a lovesick child.* Now he could add jealousy to his list of traits, along with bitterness and self-pity. He shifted the car into gear and drove downtown.

Detective Barnabas Lawrence finished his third cup of coffee. He lifted the carafe from the hotplate to pour another, swirled the dregs in the glass bowl, and noticed the dark brown sludge at the bottom. "How can anyone drink this crap?" he asked no one in particular. When he saw Ray at the door, he looked relieved. He grabbed a goose parka from the coat rack and made a "follow me" gesture toward the door. Ray tagged along without question.

"I have to get a decent cup of brew before I lose consciousness. That so-called coffee is a disgrace. I was in Mackinaw, a tiny village watch house. What have they got? A pod machine, that's what they've got. You can get a cappuccino, a macchiato, a latte for chrissakes. What do we get? Sludge is what we get. It's the reason I'm on medication."

Ray thought Barney did indeed resemble a man on medication. He winced every few minutes as if in pain or puffed out his cheeks like someone out of breath. He looked awkward and walked with the waddle of an overweight penguin.

A block from the precinct, they discovered Lawrence's home away from home; a small doughnut shop offering a variety of deep-fried treats to satisfy any cop's basic needs. Lawrence ordered two large Tim Horton coffees and two cream donuts.

"Whoa there, no donuts for me," Ray said.

"They're both mine, buddy. No offense, but if you come between me and my doughnuts, you're likely to lose a couple of fingers." Lawrence had finished the first mouthful even before he'd left the counter. The doughnuts were each covered in chocolate and chock-full of custard, the kind that oozes out the sides when you take a bite. Lawrence chuckled happily as he licked his fingers clean. "Cheryl would bust my balls if she caught me in here. She's got me on this alfalfa diet. That's grass on bird food slices she calls bread if you want to know." He sighed as he finished the second doughnut and wiped his hands on a napkin.

"Got anything on the Bird case?"

"I'm glad you came over, Ray. We haven't had much to discuss since we last talked. I'm still waiting for the DNA results on the hair samples. Forensics found plenty of evidence, but I won't have lab results for a day or two. We managed to expedite the DNA process, so hopefully, it will be soon. We have three separate security cameras that captured our female caller, but none were clear enough for identification. Not even close in that weather."

Chapter 19

Jess Fisher turned off the vacuum cleaner and wound the cord tightly around the cylinder before placing it in the storage cupboard. As she closed the door, she was startled to see Prescott Guziac standing in her kitchen, his boots dripping melting slush onto the wooden floorboards. He stood calmly and smiled when he noticed the surprise on her face. His left hand grasped his woolen beanie, while his right played with the drawstring of his coat.

"Scottie! What are you doing in my house?" Her tone was sharp.

Scottie's face turned sour, as if he found the question insulting. "Hi Jess, nice to see you too." His sarcasm dripped from his mouth like slime. He then tossed his hat onto the table and moved to the stove, where a simmering pan released steam into the air. He lifted the lid and gazed into the contents before inhaling the aroma deeply through his nose. "Looks like a nice pot of winter warmer you got going there, Jess. I could do with something to warm me through."

Jess wiped the palms of her hands on her apron and felt the sudden stickiness of nervous sweat, formed almost instantly by Scottie's presence. "It's for Alan and the kids; they'll be home soon. Any minute, actually."

Scottie smirked, a contemptuous curl of his lip creasing his face. He returned the lid to the pot. "I knocked, but you didn't hear me over the vacuum cleaner. Door was open."

Jess looked at his feet and saw the dirty water pool beneath them. He noticed her irritation and glanced down at his boots. "Sorry about that, I ain't got no manners, do I?" He stepped over to the table, seated himself at the head, and pulled his boots off. Jess watched as he took off his socks. Scottie snickered. "Wet," he said, hanging them over the back of the chair. Jess felt repulsed.

"What do you want, Scottie?" Her tone was impatient, aggressive, and tense.

"That's not the Jess I know and love. Do I sense some hostility there, sweetie? Because I do not get the impression you're over the moon to see me?"

She composed herself. Something about his mood troubled her, and her instincts urged her to be diplomatic, show some friendliness, and then get him to leave as soon as possible.

"I'm sorry, Scottie; it's just that I have Alan coming home, and I need to finish my chores before he gets here. How have you been? It must have been years since we chatted."

"Fifteen years, to be exact. We last chatted fifteen years ago, almost to the day. You told me to get a life, remember?"

Jess shifted uneasily. She recalled how his constant harassment had escalated in the lead-up to Christmas. He had repeatedly pestered her to start dating, but she had refused. What began as a friendly rebuff eventually turned into an emphatic no. One day, he cornered her in the washroom of the library where she worked as an assistant. She couldn't remember the exact exchange of words, only that they were unpleasant. At that time, she felt relieved that the confrontation seemed to end his infatuation.

She tried to smile and casually brushed aside the memory as if she hadn't given it another thought since. "Oh, that was years ago, must have had a bad day. Look, I'd love to chat, but I'm really pushed for time. Maybe we can get together for a coffee or something when Alan's back, the three of us."

Guziac looked her up and down; his cold expression made her skin crawl. He did not respond to her offer or try to leave.

"I see our best buddy has settled right back where he left off. Didn't take him long to start coming between us, Jess." He lifted his foot onto the table and began to pick a piece of white, crusted skin from his heel. This time, she did not attempt to hide her disgust, and he smiled when he saw her expression. "I'm sorry, sweetie, but I've had this blister gnawing at me for days. Must be from having cold, wet feet; do you get them in the winter, blisters?" His eyes wandered over her, forcing her to look away. "Where was I? Oh yeah, I was saying about you and Ray, Jess. You two carrying on behind my back like I wouldn't find out what you was up to. Jesus, Jess, you can't do that. A man's got to have some dignity! What does it say about our relationship?"

Over the years since their confrontation at the library, she'd managed to avoid Scottie. Most of the time, at least. She would cross the street or pretend she didn't see him when faced with the option. Occasionally, a meeting became unavoidable. She would bump into him in a store or while walking down Main Street. She limited these contacts to a nod of acknowledgment or a quick "Hello, how are you doing?" Since the incident at the library, he mostly stayed out of her way.

"We don't have a relationship, Scottie, you know that. As for Ray, I don't know what you're talking about. I haven't had anything to do with him since he left Fowler." Scottie shook his head in disbelief, so she added, "Yes, I did bump into him, and the other day we got together and caught up, that's all there was to it."

Guziac snorted loudly, throwing his head back to emphasize his amusement.

"You call all that fucking last night *catching up*! You two must have been at it from dusk 'til dawn. How many times did you suck on him, Jess? Don't tell me you only was catching up. I've been watching you."

Anger immediately replaced her initial nervousness. She hurried to the door and swung it open wide. "Get out!"

Scottie snorted again, a broad smile spread on his face. "Settle down, princess. Scottie ain't going nowhere 'til we finish our little chat. Wouldn't do for those kiddies of yours to come home and find themselves in the middle of our discussion now, would it? What about Al? I'm sure he would find it interesting. I think the sooner we finish this on a personal, one-to-one basis, the sooner you can carry on preparing that welcome home supper, that's what I think."

Jess felt her stomach knot. Scottie would reveal her secrets without a second thought; he was a snake. She seethed at the satisfaction in his eyes, closed the door, and crossed her arms in defiance. But beneath her defiant mask, she was panicked.

"You look so good when you're angry, Jess." He gazed at the stove and the steaming pot. "I sure would like some of that pot lunch you've been cooking up."

Jesse tossed her head back and laughed. "There's no way you'll eat in my house. What do you want? Is this an attempt to blackmail me?"

"Shit! You're so fucking pompous, always were, Jess. Why do you jump to those evil conclusions, girl? You have a bad mind, you do."

"Look, say what you came to say…"

"*Shut the fuck up!*" The outburst silenced her instantly. Moisture filled her eyes, and she began to tremble. "Now sit your skinny ass down so I can talk to you." She complied without speaking. "I'm very disappointed in you, Jess." He looked her up and down, his eyes resting on her breasts, then he squinted as though he imagined what lay beneath her clothes. "Can you still smell him on you, his body odor? Does it still cling to you?" She squirmed in the chair and said nothing. He sized her up and down again. "Maybe you need a long shower to wash all that sex from you." She didn't respond. "I mean, don't worry about me, I'll wait while you freshen up." His face cracked into a grin. "I must say I'm feeling kind of sticky myself, might even join you." She did not move or speak. She looked to the window, then the door.

"Relax, Jess." He paused for several seconds, then asked, "Why did you turn on me?"

"I didn't turn on you; life just took us in different directions. We all went our separate ways, didn't we? You, me, Ray? That's what happens to friends; they drift apart."

"We didn't drift apart; you two tore us apart. Then Ray left without so much as a by-your-leave. Now he rocks back in whenever he chooses, God knows how many years later, and messes with us again. That boy doesn't leave it alone, does he?"

She could see the anger in his face now and hear the rage in his words; he terrified her. She tried pleading. "Ray's dying, Scottie, he doesn't have much time left. How could I turn my back on him now?" Guziac kicked the chair back and rose to his feet, pushing the table into Jess's gut with a thud. She winced at the pain, and fear gripped her throat. She watched him pace the room.

"Ray's dying? *I'm dying*, we're all fucking dying; what about me, my feelings? I don't see you running to me to fuck me 'cos I'm going to die one day!" He was hyperventilating, trying to catch his breath. For several minutes, neither spoke as Scottie calmed.

A burst of snow slid off the roof with a thump, jolting Scottie out of his daze and causing Jess to jump.

"All my life, you two made me feel like I didn't belong."

"Scottie, that isn't true."

"Shut up and listen, for fuck's sake!" He placed his hand on his forehead and sighed. "You made me feel like I was the odd one out, a fucking intrusion. There were times you deliberately went out of your way to make me feel small, inadequate." She went to speak, then thought better of it. "You think I didn't hear the snide remarks, the jokes you shared with him? Whispers, I remember the whispers, all the time whispers so I could hear you but not what you were saying." She watched him pace anxiously back and forth, agitated, wound up like a tightly coiled spring. "One time you even screwed right there in front of me, remember, at the lake, in the boat shed? My God, you screwed right there for me to see, to tease me. You knew I was watching, and I could see your naked body moving against him. You even looked at me, looked at me as he thrust himself into you, and knowing I wanted you."

She blushed at the thought. She and Ray had made love many times at the lake, and, admittedly, they had been careless, but they were young and carefree, and... A rapid flush of blood rushed to her face, an electric tremor that ran the length of her spine. She felt it because, in that instant, she recalled that day too. The day she taunted Scottie. She remembered suddenly with such stunning clarity, and now she began to visualize the moment as the memories tumbled back into focus.

She was seventeen, and the summer had been long and hot. She and Ray were in the boat shed, flirting; she stood before him, love on her mind. But first, she planned to tease him with a playful strip show. Henry was out on the lake, which boosted her sense of bravado. The brilliant summer sun streamed through the cracks between the cedar planks of the siding, sending rays of light like shining swords cutting through the darkness of the old wooden building. She noticed movement against the bright lines of light on the far side of the wall. She knew it was Scottie; he spied on them all the time. She saw him crouched behind the wall, his shadow covering a dollar-sized knothole, and her heart quickened as a mischievous thought took shape in her mind.

On any other day, she would have called out, labeled him a pervert, and told him to get lost. But not that day; her lips remained sealed. She felt a thrill of excitement, an urge to be naughty, to tease. She said nothing to Ray, who didn't see Scottie or know of her plan. He stood before her with his back to the voyeur, unaware that she was about to perform for two.

She dropped her dress from her shoulders, allowing it to slide to the floor, revealing a sleek satin slip. She slowly peeled the clothes from her body, each movement a tantalizing tease to the onlookers. Her body glistened with sweat. Ray stood, staring with boyish pleasure as she moved in sensual twists and turns. She imagined the music, an exotic rhythm, and let herself drift into a seductive dance. Hers was a performance, a show for lovers and voyeurs, and she felt daring and outrageous, liberated, powerful, and sexy beyond imagination. She felt warm, moist, and electric.

She stood naked in the dappled light, golden bands painting her skin and accentuating the swell of her breasts, the dip of her waist, and the taut curve of her thighs. The air hummed with the musk of her arousal, thick and sweet, intoxicating even to her. She hadn't known she could desire like this.

Slowly and deliberately, she turned in place, allowing their eyes to drink her in. A temptress. A revelation. Ray's gaze burned as she stepped into his arms, her back arching against him, shielding the truth, Scottie watching, always watching. Her fingers deftly worked on his clothes, each button, each brush of fabric against skin a calculated tease. She held Ray's stare, willing him to be blind to anything but her.

Then they were on the floor, the rough wood biting into her knees as he took her with a hunger that matched hers. She moaned for Ray, writhing for Ray, but her stolen glances belonged to the shadow in the corner. Sin had never tasted so sweet.

Scottie's voice cut through the sterile chill of the kitchen, and the memory curdled. That day, the heat, the daring, the shamelessness, now felt like a curse. She crossed her arms over her chest, as if she could still feel the fingers of light licking her skin. Twenty-one years later, in the cold atmosphere of her encounter with Scottie, she felt only shame.

"I was young, stupid," she said at last, sitting. Tears rolled slowly down her face and dropped into her lap. She bowed her head and felt the misery of her disgrace. "It was so long ago," she said through the sobs.

"Hell, I knew it! I knew you'd seen me; knew I was there." Guziac banged his fist on the table; Jess stiffened. With his hand on his head, he quickly paced from one end of the room to the other. "All these years; all these years you stuck your nose up at me, made me feel like trash, and all the while it was you who was trash." He banged his fist again; this time on a cupboard door. He coughed out an ironic laugh and shook his head vigorously. "What a goddamn fool."

"I'm sorry," she said. That was all she could say.

A long pause followed, then he turned his head. "Sorry? You're sorry, you say? Well, sorry doesn't cut it, sugar. I..."

The noise of the front door slamming shut and the sound of a child's voice interrupted Scottie's speech, indicating the return of Al and the kids. Terror crossed Jess's face. She darted toward the door, but Scottie quickly moved to block her. Her mind raced. She didn't know what to do. Should she go in first and tell Al everything? Alan Fischer walked into the kitchen smiling. He carried Brighton in his arms while Abbie followed, phone in hand as ever, focused on the screen.

Brighton called out, "Mommy," excited by their reunion, but suddenly shied away when he saw Scottie. Al set Brighton down on the floor. He wrapped his arms around his father's legs and hid his face behind him. Alan Fischer noticed the distress on Jess's face. Her eyes were tearful, red, and puffy. His gaze flicked from her to Scottie and back again. He looked down at Guziac's bare feet, then at his boots on the floor and his socks on the chair.

"What's going on?" he asked. His voice was calm, but the tone was anything but. Al had a tall, robust build; lean and long, with large feet and hands. No one answered. Tension mounted, almost palpable. He knew who Prescott Guziac was, even though he had never exchanged words with him. His hands balled into fists. Jess noticed this, and her panic heightened. She searched Scottie's eyes for his intent. She should beat him to the punch and come clean before he could blurt out his accusations. She would rather Alan heard it from her than from Scottie. Then, Scottie spoke first.

"I don't think we've ever been introduced," he said. "Jess and me was just reminiscing about old times. Jess got a bit emotional. We're old friends; ain't that right, Jess?" He chuckled. "In fact, she was supposed to marry me." He glanced at Jess. His smug expression formed the briefest threat; she saw it in his eyes. But he broke into laughter once more. "When we was four years old," he added with a chuckle. He extended his hand, and Alan shook it cautiously, seemingly aware that the tension remained between the two. Scottie continued. "Pleased to meet the better man, the one that won her heart."

Alan Fischer didn't seem to know what to think of Scottie; something had happened to upset Jess, and Scottie appeared to be the cause. Fischer stood next to Jess and wrapped his arm around her. "Are you okay?" Jess nodded but didn't speak. She was trembling.

"Jess and I were catching up on old times," Scottie continued. "Unfortunately, the circumstances are not the best with the bad news, and we were just discussing what a dirty trick has been played." Jess's heart skipped a beat. "Come on, Jess, it's not the end of the world." Jess looked to Al; there was nothing she could do. Scottie continued. "I know she's hurting, Alan; I am too. But life isn't always fair. You see, our best friend is dying, and we were sharing the pain, trying to find comfort in each other. I live alone, Alan, and, like Jess, I'm a bit of an emotional wreck; I find it hard to cope in times like these, especially so soon after losing my daddy." Scottie placed his hand over his eyes and sighed deeply. Jess couldn't tell if he was actually weeping. His explanation prompted an immediate change in Alan Fischer's demeanor, the tension instantly relieved from his face. It was apparent now why his wife had been crying. And she knew he wasn't stupid; he was aware of how she felt about Ray. Jess felt sick at the deception.

Fischer watched as Scottie seemed to collect himself. "I'm sorry I interrupted, Scottie. And I'm glad you came to us for support." He squeezed Jess around the waist and gently kissed her on the forehead. "I'm sorry, honey, I should have called ahead." He glanced at the bubbling pot on the stove and then back at Scottie. "You'll stay for supper, Scottie?"

Jess jumped in before he could respond. "Unfortunately, Scottie has to run off. He has an appointment."

Scottie looked at Jess and sneered. "That's right," he said at length. "I've got a lot to take care of, Alan. Though it would be nice to share some company for a change."

Jess aimed a look that said, *Don't you dare! Don't you even think about it!*

"I don't want to impose on you, good folks. I can rustle something up from the corner store. I'm used to eating alone."

"Won't hear of it, Scottie, our home is your home, isn't that right, Jess?"

❄

Chapter 20

Ray wiped condensation from the windshield. He'd been sitting for so long that his breath was beginning to freeze on the glass. From his spot on the street, he could see the front stoop of the little house that Jody Callus called home. He'd watched three neighbors leave their homes for work, each going through the same winter ritual: sweeping two inches of snow from their vehicles, clouds of steaming exhaust billowing into the air.

He sat up suddenly when the door to Callus's home opened, and she stepped out. Taking a plastic snow shovel, she began clearing the night's snowfall from the step. She followed that by pushing the shovel along the path, stopping every few feet to tip the snow aside. When she reached the mailbox, she leaned the shovel against the picket fence and removed the contents of the box, scanning each item before slipping them into her coat pocket.

Finally, Ray got out of the car and walked toward her, his pulse racing. "Mrs. Callus."

She turned, tilted her head to one side, and squinted. "That's me, who's asking?" Before he could answer, her expression changed to one of surprise. "Raymond Waring." The words fell from her mouth rather than being spoken.

"Yes, Mrs. Callus, you remember me." It was a stupid thing to say. Of course, she would remember. How could she forget? She stood frozen; it felt like an eternity, her face unreadable.

"I surely do remember you, Raymond, I surely do," she managed at length.

Ray sat in the family room while Jody Callus made coffee in the kitchen. "Won't take more than a few minutes," she called out.

Ray had practiced the encounter many times, anticipated her reaction, and what he would say to counter it. But there was none of the anticipated hostility. Jody Callus acted as though he were expected. Her calm welcome had thrown him.

"Do you like carrot cake?" she said, setting down a tray with two mugs of coffee and two plates of cake.

"It looks very nice, but no thank you." He couldn't have eaten even if he wanted to. A framed photograph stared at him, burning his peripheral vision. He knew it was her and avoided looking. She tormented him, daring him to see her as she was. "I don't know why I came," he whispered. "I thought I did, but now I'm here, I'm not sure."

"I was sorry to hear of your illness, Raymond; how are you coping?"

"I'm fine. I mean, I'm coping well, Mrs. Callus. Got some big decisions to make."

She nodded in approval, and her lips curled into the faintest smile. "You're quite the hero around here."

Ray murmured. "Humph!"

"It doesn't sit well with you, the hero tag?"

"No, ma'am. I was doing what I was paid to do." He shifted uneasily in the chair and looked around the room as if distracted, continuously avoiding the photograph. This whole hero obsession was bizarre. He didn't feel heroic, far from it, yet everyone else seemed to get off on it. It was a wonder they hadn't thrown a parade for his homecoming. To make matters worse, it was distracting him from what he had to do, stopping him from shouldering the past. "Is Mr. Callus home?"

"My husband died four years ago last fall. John suffered a heart attack while helping a neighbor dig fence post holes."

"I'm sorry, I didn't know."

"How could you?" She sighed. "Raymond, I think I understand why you came here today. I hold no animosity toward you. What happened back then was a tragedy we all shared. I won't deny I was angry with you for a while. I was angry at Walter for leaving her. I was furious at God. But most of all, I was angry at myself for not being around when I should have been watching over her."

"But I ran away, left you all to..."

"You were in a bad way, I realized that. It wasn't the best of decisions, but believe me, there were times I would have run if I hadn't had John by my side." Jody stood and walked to the window. "Come here, I want to show you something." Ray went to the window, unsure what he was supposed to be looking at. "When Clair died, it was as though my heart had been ripped from my body; I was inconsolable. I wanted to know how and why this terrible thing had happened, but most of all, I wanted to know how I could go on living without her. I am not a religious person, Raymond. I never went to church except for the carols at Christmas.

"Nevertheless, I wanted Clair's funeral to be a Christian one. I asked the minister about my lack of faith and my need for answers. I was shocked by his advice. He told me to go and get thoroughly drunk. Can you imagine? There I was asking for divine help, and he told me to get drunk." She smiled and reflected for a long moment. "He went on to say that he had lost a brother in an accident. He was distraught and needed to find those same answers I searched for. He felt betrayed by life, by God, to whom he had dedicated his life. So, he turned to the bottle. I asked him if he found the answers he needed by getting drunk. He smiled and told me no; the same demons came to meet him the following day, and when he awoke, nothing had changed, plus he had a hangover.

"I began to think he had fewer answers than I did. He said he looked in the dressing table mirror one morning after waking from his drunken stupor; he looked at himself in the mirror, unshaven, with bloodshot eyes and smelling of dried vomit, which encrusted his hair and his shirt. As he regarded himself in this pathetic state, he saw in that same mirror, just above his right shoulder, a photograph of his brother. Encased in a gold picture frame, it sat on a shelf beside the sports awards his brother had won during his college years. He studied his brother's face, the light in his eyes, and the flash of his teeth as he proudly held aloft a basketball trophy. Then he looked back at his image, and he knew immediately what he must do."

"What did he do?"

"He got cleaned up, shaved, and went to the liquor store."

Ray frowned, his brow deeply puckered, prompting Jody Callus to laugh at his puzzled expression. "I know. I was thinking the same at this point," she said. She continued with the story. "He bought several bottles of expensive champagne and invited friends to his home, where they lovingly and proudly celebrated his brother's life." She added that the minister had indulged in only the occasional glass of sherry since, but that it had marked a turning point in his life. "I got the message as easily and suddenly as that. I did not take the minister's advice and get drunk, but I celebrated her life by planting a rose, a beautiful old-fashioned rose by the name of *Peace*. That's it, there."

Ray saw the thorny sticks poking through the snow in the yard.

"I thought I'd made a mistake that first winter when it died back to branches. But come spring, she blooms so brightly, it's like Clair is reborn each year, forever young."

Ray finally turned to the photograph of Clair. Tears rolled down his face. "Thank you," he croaked. There was no need to say more.

As he prepared to leave, he paused at a family photo. "I saw Walt."

Jody's face tightened. "His grief took a darker path. Drugs. Institutions. He rejects my help now." She

turned to him, her voice firm. "Promise me something, Raymond. Promise you'll spend the life you have left celebrating the ones you love. That includes your own. If you owe Clair anything, promise me you won't let her life be the cause of your despair."
She hugged him hard. Her wish for his peace, unmistakable.

Chapter 21

With Jody Callus's last words swirling in his head, Ray pulled into the ice rink parking lot. Scottie's Ram truck was parked right in front of the doors, occupying one and a half handicap spaces. Ray peered into the cab. A pile of fast-food wrappers and empty cups cluttered the floor. An empty rifle rack showed signs of wear and tear; one end was taped with plastic to keep it from falling apart. A large canvas tote bag sat on the passenger seat, but the zipper was closed. He tried the door, but the lock was engaged. A locked hardcover secured the tray. Ray hesitated, wondering if this was such a good idea, then went inside.

He'd already had enough of Scottie to want to skip the game. But some nagging questions needed answers. If the chance came, he planned to ask them. After putting on his boots, Ray grew irritated to find the right one pinched his little toe. He loosened the laces and adjusted his foot, but it didn't help. He muttered under his breath. After securing his helmet, he followed the rubber mats to the ice, where a group of men circled the rink, quickly sweeping several pucks back and forth. Scottie threw his stick in the air when he saw Ray and hurried over to him, splashing shaved ice into the air as he stopped.

"Hey, Ray! Thought you was a no-show, buddy."

"Why, you scared I'll kick your butt?"

Scottie wheeled in a circle as he talked. "Good luck with that, Ray. When was the last time you strapped on the blades?"

Ray didn't respond. Scottie was right; he hadn't worn a pair of skates in years. He continued to fiddle with his uncomfortable boot.

"Maybe you're right, Scottie. Don't know if this was such a good idea," he said eventually. "These boots must be twenty-five years old, and *I'm not*. Maybe it would be better if I sit this one out."

"The hell you will! I set this up specially for you, man. Hey guys! This here is Ray Waring, a super-hero and personal friend of President Carlton Crisp and yours truly. Two large defensemen skidded up to the boards, slamming their sticks against the hoarding with a clatter to create as much noise as possible. Ray nodded warily. He recognized the competitive look on their faces. Scottie opened the door, and Ray slipped out onto the ice for the first time in twenty-odd years.

"Like riding a bike, Ray!"

It was true in some ways; the familiar feeling returned almost instantly. However, he was way older now and felt utterly out of shape, as evidenced by the strain on his knees as he finished the first round of the rink, convincing himself how foolish the whole idea had been. This was supposed to be a friendly game of four-on-four, Scottie had told him, consisting of three ten-minute periods with a short break in between. Some of the guys were on their lunch hour, and they needed to keep the game moving.

"No time for a warm-up, Ray. Let's get ready to rumble."

The ice appeared freshly cut. Two teams of four, including the goalies, but Ray had no illusions; the real battle was between him and Scottie, two men who'd rather eat a skate blade than shake hands after a loss.

Scottie filled the center spot for the opposition while Ray slotted into a position on the opposite wing. Scottie quickly took control of the face-off, raced forward, and immediately attempted a shot on goal. One of his teammates made a critical comment about passing the puck, which Scottie ignored with a grin. Ray found himself with the puck and quickly passed it off, only to receive it back in short order. His lungs struggled to pull enough oxygen to support the sudden exertion. Scottie came close to checking him into the boards, but Ray dodged the hit and delivered a pass across the goal. Scottie skated closely beside him and heard him wheezing for air.

"A bit out of shape, aren't you, Superman?"

Ray pushed him aside and made a play for the puck, only to feel Scottie check him fiercely into the boards. Ray didn't complain; this felt like old times, and the day Scottie Guziac could get the better of him on ice would be a long time coming. Scottie barreled down the wing, eyes locked on Ray like a predator, but Ray's defenseman, a brick wall named Joe, stepped up. Boom! Scottie got plastered into the boards. The glass rattled, and Joe howled. Ray skated by, tapping his stick in mock applause. "Nice try, princess."

Scottie retaliated with a clapper from the blue line. Ray's goalie gloved it effortlessly. "That's all you got?" he barked, flipping the puck back with disdain.

The first period passed quickly and without a score. Ray was relieved when it ended, but he had little time to recover. He observed the others laughing and joking, but he lacked the energy for conversation; it was all he could do to breathe. He drank deeply from a water bottle before wheeling out onto the rink for the second period. Scottie circled him, laughing.

"Just a little friendly challenge, Ray. Hope you don't think I was too rough on you out there."

"Challenge? Man, I thought you were trying out for the girls' team. Give it your best shot, buddy, let's see what you can do."

Scottie laughed again; he was obviously relishing the rivalry. He called up the second period and made a play, combining with his winger to slap home the first goal. The goalie could do nothing to stop the blistering shot that found the top corner of the net. Ray switched positions with the center and faced off against Scottie, winning the puck in a flurry of sticks. He glided out, leaving the first defenseman struggling around the back of the net. A quick give-and-go saw the puck recycled before Ray delivered a perfectly timed pass to secure an assist, the score even at one-all.

His next contact left him sandwiched between players, and he felt Scottie's crunching check come in late from the side. Scottie's stick caught Ray in the nose, and blood poured into Ray's mouth.

"Want to quit?"

Ray paused briefly on the sidelines to stop the flow before returning to play. "Keep it coming, Scottie," Ray responded.

A breakaway from Scottie caused the puck to spill loose. Ray picked it up before being slammed into the boards behind the goal once more. As he skated back into play, he felt Scottie's stick wrap around his legs, causing him to tumble to the ice and crash heavily on his right arm.

Scottie grinned and circled him. "If this was a real game, I'd be out for tripping, eh, Ray?"

"Tripping is what lazy players do, Scottie, those who can't skate fast enough."

Scottie rounded the goal and picked up the puck, drawing two players to him before weaving to the side and charging up the ice. He slapped home the second goal and ignited a triumphant cheer from his team.

By now, Ray was exhausted, bruised, and bloodied. The last period saw him smashed against the boards multiple times, worsening an already fragile condition. Finally, a perfectly weighted pass reached him just outside the blue line. He stepped over the line and took a good old-fashioned slap shot from the point for the equalizer. A cry of offside went ignored as the two faced off for the final time. This time, Ray became the aggressor. He swept past Scottie, turned, and slammed him into the boards; an attempt at a trip that fell short. Ray left Scottie behind to finish the game with the sweetest snapshot, leaving the goalie stranded.

Ray circled Scottie in triumph. "Like I said, Scottie, tripping is for lazy players."

Outside the rink, clouds covered the once blue sky, and the temperature had dropped, signaling a change in the weather. Ray stood beside Scottie, feeling unashamedly exhilarated by his victory. "Don't take it so bad, Scottie. I had a bit of luck for once! I'm sore as hell, though. I've got blisters the size of speed bumps."

"Don't give me no bull, Ray. You was out to show me up in front of my buddies. Hell, you never fail to come through, Ray, you never fail me."

Ray didn't reply. Scottie had always been a sore loser. He figured now would not be a good time to ask his questions. He looked up at the sky and sensed that more squalls would come before the day ended. He turned toward his car to leave.

"Hey, Ray!" Ray turned to face Scottie. "Saw Jess yesterday. Invited me to supper, her and Al. She is one beautiful girl, old Jess. It was just like old times. Funny though, every time I mentioned your name, she seemed to change the subject. It was almost as though she was avoiding something, maybe even keeping something from Al." Scottie had that same smug look he always had when he was driving at something.

"What are you getting at, Scottie?"

Guziac opened the door and jumped into his truck. "Not a thing, Ray! Why don't you give Jess a call and ask her how our dinner party went? Al even asked me back. Maybe we'll start a regular little soirée."

Chapter 22

Ray glanced at his phone and saw a missed call from Jess. He dialed her number, but it went to voicemail. He didn't leave a message. He called Lawrence, and they arranged to meet at the Bird residence at three. When he arrived, he found Lawrence in the basement, poking at the floorboards with the tip of a knife.

"Something interesting, Barney?" He startled Lawrence and smiled when he saw him jump in surprise.

"Shit, Ray! You scared the bejesus out of me." He puffed out his cheeks and took a deep breath. "No, I was just checking out the timber; I have a nephew looking to buy a place in town, and I figured this place is a really nice piece of real estate; it may suit him and his new bride if the price is right."

Lawrence's opportunistic enterprise amused Ray. "I'm going to take a look around if that's okay?" Lawrence didn't respond, and Ray interpreted it as permission granted.

Celine Bird kept an orderly, well-maintained home. He would expect no less from the woman who preached what she practiced. The kitchen remained undisturbed, just as she'd left it. A mug of hot chocolate sat on the counter, untouched. In the lounge where she met her end, the scene appeared no less organized, aside from the missing tablecloth, taken by forensics along with the chair she had died on. The bloodstained furniture remained. She would be upset at the mess. Besides the jewelry, investigators had discovered a large amount of cash in the house, and other valuables remained untouched. The mission to humiliate and kill this old woman seemed to be a single-minded affair.

A writing desk appeared perfectly organized and tidy. A journal lay in place next to a tray of pens and newly sharpened pencils, all aligned in regimented order. He flipped through the pages of neatly written notes and saw in them the mundane normality of a retired widow's life. He read a neatly written letter addressed to one Mary Jane Houston, in which she expressed her desire to visit the coast of Maine one more time before she became housebound. She ended the letter with a promise to write more often. An assortment of Post-it notes reminded her of upcoming dates and bills to pay.

Lawrence appeared in the doorway, looking flushed with dirty smudges of dust on his sweat-covered forehead. "I suppose you heard about the homicide up in Keweenaw Bay?"

"Nope."

"I got a call from there this morning, a Fed Agent, Dale Seymour. Know him?"

"There are a lot of special agents at the bureau, Barney. I imagine he'll be working out of Detroit."

"He's been working the Upper Peninsula with Tribal Police at Keweenaw Bay. They had a particularly gruesome case on the reservation in early Fall. A contract worker from an experimental power plant, Bradley Cover, was tortured and murdered after a night at the casino. The investigation hit a dead end after ruling out criminal connections, bad debts, and other motives for the brutal attack. Seymour says he's been twiddling his thumbs ever since, until he read about Ms. Bird's murder. It piqued his interest when he saw that she taught at Myerson. He noted in Bradley Cover's file that he was a Fowler resident and, after a bit of digging, found that Cover had attended Myerson and had been in her class."

Ray knew Cover. Everyone knew Cover. He was a year ahead of Ray. He came from a notorious family, known for trouble. He had also attended Bayside High alongside Ray before being expelled in tenth grade. That was the last Ray had heard of him. Cover's homicide was now the third incident that had connections to Ray personally.

"The fact that he went to her class is a weak link at best," Ray said. "I think Seymour is grasping at straws. Still, it is a coincidence."

"Yeah. I thought so too. He's coming down anyway. Compare notes, see if we have any other similarities. Speaking of notes, the killer left one behind up north. *'Don't remember? Here's a little reminder.'* Wonder what he didn't remember? Whatever it was, he must have pissed someone seriously off."

"Is Seymour certain the note was left by the killer?"

"Thirty-four nails from a construction gun, all over his body. Tortured. One to the temple pinned the note in place. It was the last nail in his coffin."

"Not funny, Barney."

"You got a theory, Ray?"

"Remember, you said someone might have had a grudge against Ms. Bird? I told you she was a tyrant, a bully." Lawrence listened attentively. "Well, I knew Brad Cover. He was what you'd call a classic class bully. He was a big kid, even in first grade, coming from a family of roughnecks. He was the same in high school. It's a stretch, but…"

"The same killer?"

Ray went back to Celine Bird's desk. He stood in silence, browsing the papers, coming to rest on a note about shopping.

"What are you thinking, Ray?"

Ray removed the little square of yellow paper and took it across the room to a side table. On the table was a well-used Bible, and on the Bible was another handwritten Post-it note. "*Here endeth the lesson.*" Ray read the words aloud, then compared the writing. The block-printed note, though neatly laid out across the little square, bore no resemblance to the precise hand of Celine Bird.

"What do you make of this note, Barney?"

Lawrence shrugged. "She was pretty religious. Isn't that what they say in church after they've been preaching, *here endeth the lesson?*"

"They do. But this wasn't written by Ms. Bird."

"Holy shit! You think her killer wrote it. Just like the one on the U.P."

"Maybe."

"Goddamn it, we got us a serial killer." Lawrence looked excited.

"Don't even mention that word. You'll have the place crawling. My advice is to keep that thought to yourself until you get the lab to process the notes. Besides, you need three or more to make it a serial case. Stick to the case at hand, Barney."

Ray took a small piece of paper from his pocket. He'd been carrying it around since Scottie discovered it pinned to his car. "Someone stuck this behind my wiper blade a few nights back. Have the lab look for any similarity in the handwriting."

Lawrence struggled to read the faded writing. The ink had bled into the paper. "Big mistake coming... here.' Does that say, here? 'You should have died in that, schume... Sch..ool. School. You should have died in that school.' Shit, Ray, someone doesn't like you."

Chapter 23

Aunt Eadie made it clear that Jess Fischer was a married woman with two small children. She held nothing back, telling Ray as much. Despite his attempts to reassure her that he had no intention of getting between Jess and her husband, he couldn't deceive Eadie. She had received at least half a dozen calls from Jess on the landline throughout the day. Jess wanted to speak to Ray urgently, but he wasn't answering his phone. Ray checked his cell and noticed four more missed calls. *Damn!*

"Jess is a wonderful woman, Ray, and I love her like she's my own, but her head is in the clouds right now, and I don't think she understands she's heading for tears with this nonsense. I love you, son, but I won't stand by and watch you wreck her life and the lives of those little ones." Ray listened without another word of protest. "Jess said you were to call her urgently. I could hear it in her voice; she's falling in love all over again, and it just isn't right."

Ray kissed Aunt Eadie on the forehead and assured her that he would sort it out. He found some privacy and dialed her number. Jess answered, her voice filled with anxiety.

"I have to see you. Where have you been?" She didn't wait for an answer. "It's late night at the store, and Al won't be home until close to midnight. But we can't risk meeting here. Where can we meet?"

Eadie's warning still rang in his ears. He tried to reason with himself, but he wanted to meet just as much as Jess did.

"Do you think it's a good idea, Jess? Maybe we should slow things down." A long silence followed.

"Ray, I need to see you, please. Scottie came to my house. He knows about us."

"Knows? Knows what?"

"Ray, I can't talk now. Where can we meet? My sitter, Sylvia, will look after the kids for a couple of hours... please, where?"

"Okay, Jess, but the town's too small; someone will see us. We'll meet at the lake, at Henry's place? The drive isn't plowed, but you can park on Falls Road and ski in from there. I'll meet you there in forty minutes."

❄   ❄   ❄

Jess hurriedly pushed her cross-country skis into the car without strapping them onto the roof rack, leaving the tips to protrude through the front passenger window. After dropping the children off at Sylvia's house, she drove quickly to Falls Road and parked the car at the edge of the unpaved road. By the time she snapped her toes into the bindings, the last light of day had vanished behind the escarpment, and an eerie purple haze illuminated the towering pines. There was no moon to brighten the sky, and only a faint orange glow from the cabin windows to guide her way.

On her arrival, the cabin door opened, and Ray stepped out to greet her. She untied her bindings and propped her skis against the cabin wall. They kissed briefly. Ray held her back from going inside. "What's all this about Scottie?"

Jess hesitated. "It's a long story. Is Henry here?"

"He is, and I'm glad we came. He's had another run-in with those guys who've been harassing him. They vandalized his shed and destroyed two of his hives."

"That's awful. Is he alright?"

"He's upset but not hurt."

Inside the cabin, Henry set aside his problems and greeted Jess like family. "Daughter, welcome home." Jess hugged Henry. "How does a blossom become even brighter with time? You defy Mother Earth's plan for autumn, my dear. Come sit by the fire and let an old man celebrate your return."

Ray left them to talk, saying he would head to the boat shed to clean up the damage. Jess made small talk, mainly about the past and their days at the lake. She glanced around the cabin, cluttered with books and collectibles, while Henry watched her, a glint in his eyes. She looked toward the door.

"Ray is busy, Daughter; you can speak your heart. But I am troubled. You carry a heavy burden today."

Jess turned to him, surprised by his comment. "You could always see our secrets, Henry. I remember I could hide nothing from you."

"I can see you're distressed."

Henry had always been easy to talk to. Jess felt an overwhelming urge to open up to the old man. "I don't know what to do."

Henry stoked the woodstove and waited quietly, his eyes reflecting the firelight. He stirred the embers as Jess found the courage to speak. Once she started, she couldn't stop, a spontaneous outpouring of her struggles. She spoke of her enduring love for Ray, but said that she still loved her husband. She said that Ray's return had torn her heart apart.

"My love for Raymond will never waver; he is my son, as you are my daughter. But he is weighed down by the past. He is a leaf now tossed in the wind. You too find yourself in the wind. You love your husband, yet your love for Ray stirs like a ghost. Ask yourself; does he return to bring you strength, or does he come to scatter the life you have built like ashes in the breeze?" The fire crackled as he continued. "Love is not just a feeling, it is a choice, a promise. Your husband walks beside you now. But Raymond? He lives in memories, and memories are sweet because they are untouched by time. But life is not lived in yesterday." He placed a gnarled hand on hers. "Ray brings with him many storms." Finally, he sat back. "The heart speaks, but the spirit knows. Listen to the deeper voice within you; the one that whispers of peace, not just passion."

Jess stood up and walked to the window. She noticed the shadows cast by Ray in the shed's light. "How did you come to be so smart?"

"Humph. Not so smart, according to the young of our tribe. They would rather find their wisdom in the phones they carry." Henry paused a while, then said, "Wisdom only comes from truth, Jess."

"He's a broken man, Henry. How can I desert him now when he needs me most?"

Henry's eyes carried the weight of years. After a long silence, he spoke. "Daughter, this wounded man who returns is not the same as the one who left. You love who he was, but do you see who he is now? Ray's broken heart still beats, but does it know how to love without breaking what it touches?" He stirred the fire again, watching the sparks rise and fade. "You have a husband who stands whole beside you. Does Ray seek you, or does he seek healing, and if so, are you his medicine or his shelter? Neither is the same as love." A log shifted in the fire, casting shadows.

"You're supposed to be the medicine man; can't you mend him?" Jess sighed and put her hands together as she would in prayer. "I'm so sorry. That was disrespectful. Please forgive me."

"There is nothing to forgive. You speak your heart. But I have no medicine, only advice born of years."

"You have to understand, this is not a new infatuation. My love for Ray has never been in doubt. The years apart have meant putting my feelings aside, but they have never wavered, Henry. Never."

His gaze softened, but his words grew firmer. "Perhaps you can choose to help him, but let it be from a distance; with open hands, not an entangled heart. Honor his pain. But do not mistake mercy for destiny. Some souls are meant to pass through our lives, not stay. Let him heal on his journey while you walk yours."

"What if my love for Ray is stronger than my fear of losing Alan?"

Henry exhaled slowly; the firelight flickered across his weathered face. His voice was quiet but heavy. "Then you have already chosen, daughter. But you fear the cost." He held up a hand before she could speak. "Love that feels stronger than fear is still just love; it does not mean it is wise, or kind, or true." His eyes darkened with sadness. "A broken man can be mended, but not by breaking another's heart. If you leave your husband for Ray, you will break what is whole to mend what is shattered. And then, who will mend you?"

Henry leaned forward; his voice dropped to a whisper. "You ask what to do with this storm inside you. I say, sit with it. Let it rage until the quiet comes. If this love is real, it will wait. If your marriage is true, it will endure the questioning. But if you act now, in the fever of this longing, you will lose not just a husband, but the woman he believed you to be. And that, daughter, is a loss even time cannot heal."

*　　*　　*

The door opened, and Ray walked in, abruptly ending the conversation. He held a rusting chain and mechanism in his right hand. "What is this?"

Henry looked indignant. "I think it is quite clear. It is a bear trap."

"A bear trap?"

Henry turned to Jess. "Perhaps it is I who does not speak clearly. Or is Raymond having difficulty understanding?"

Ray walked into the room and set the trap on the floor. "With great respect, Henry, the nature-loving man I know would never use a trap like this on an animal."

"But a man? Maybe."

"Henry! They'd lock you up if you did. You can't be serious."

"Calm down. I am old, not deaf. Is not a broken leg better than a bullet from a rifle?" Before Ray could answer, Henry laughed. "Don't worry, my son. I have had time enough to reflect on that course of action. The bear trap will remain an unused deterrent. Now, Jess and I have had time to reminisce. Let us drink some wine and allow the heat of the fire to calm our souls."

After a while, Jess and Ray went out to the boat shed to continue the clean-up, allowing them time to talk alone.

"Scottie came to my house," Jess started. Her face was full of concern. "I think he's been watching us, spying on us. Alan came home in the middle of a heated exchange. I thought Scottie would reveal everything about us, but he didn't. The more I see of him, the more I dislike him. I didn't want to say too much the other night, but Scottie and I fell out a long time ago. He didn't take it well. He can't be trusted."

Ray frowned. "I've got to admit, he's been driving me crazy. He's so eager to get together, but each time is worse than the last. He's manic at times. He thinks we'll pick up where we left off as kids. I plan to tell him to cool it for a while." Ray kept his more serious concerns about Scottie to himself.

Jess scoffed. "Where we left off as kids, really? He lives in cuckoo land. I can't remember when I started disliking him. I think we *were* still kids. I know you've been away a while, but the guy is a creep; it should be obvious even to you. He's got real problems with us, Ray; he's jealous in a big way and he frightens me."

Ray pulled her close. "He *should* be jealous. Who wouldn't be jealous when they see us together?"

As if she'd remembered Henry's words, she gently pushed Ray away before he could kiss her. "I'm serious, I thought he would lose it altogether before Al came home. Al invited him to supper for God's sake!"

"Why didn't you just tell him to leave?"

"I couldn't, he knows about us, he would have told Alan everything. Like I told you, he's watching us."

Ray's gut churned. He didn't know what Scottie was up to. His worries about Scottie were greater than Jess could ever imagine. "I'll have a word with him; tell him to back off," he reassured her. Then he sighed.

"You're not going to like what I am about to say, Jess." She wasn't the only one who had been pondering advice about their reunion.

"What?"

"Jess, I've been thinking about Saturday, you and me, and what we're getting ourselves into. We need to back off, too. I've been too obsessed with my own life to see what my being here is doing to yours. I came home to put things to rest, right the wrongs, and make amends. But I'm making things worse for you. I should never have drifted back in without considering what it would do to you." He paused when he saw new fear in her face. "Let's at least slow things down before anyone else gets hurt."

"I don't think I care about anyone else," she said abruptly.

The words didn't come easily to him. "You should care, Jess. First Henry, then Aunt Eadie. They may be old, but neither has lost their gift for good advice."

"You too," she said. "Henry just gave me what amounted to a lecture. The Buddha himself couldn't have done better. I'd forgotten what he's like. Talk about a guilt trip. So, what now?"

He saw she was angry. He took her hand and squeezed. "I was looking through old photographs. All the old faces, acting out and having fun. I was transported back in time, and it brought a sudden lump to my throat. I thought, God, how I miss those days. You, me, our friends; I miss them so badly it hurts. I sat feeling sorry for myself. *How could I have let it all go?* Then I realized why I hurt so bad, why I felt the empty longing inside. It wasn't just you, Walt, or the others I missed; the one I missed the most was me."

Jess remained silent for a long time. Eventually, she smiled sadly. "I can't pretend to understand what you've been through, what you're still going through. But whatever you face now, we can face it together."

Ray held her close. He ran his fingers over her cheek and smiled tenderly. "I'm going back to Washington just as soon as I settle things here. I decided I'm going to have the operation. There's a good chance of success, and I want to take it."

"Hold me," she said desperately.

Chapter 24

Ray awoke the following day to the chatter of excited voices. He wiped the sleep from his eyes and noted that the clock's red dial read 6:13 am. It should still have been dark, yet light filled the room from the street. He slipped out of bed and pushed open the drapes. Several high-powered floodlights temporarily blinded him. The drone of a large diesel generator made the window vibrate, and the street buzzed with activity. Satellite trucks were parked along the road, while men and women, dressed in winter coats and boots, unloaded equipment from the trucks and stacked it on the sidewalk. *What the hell?*

Aunt Eadie and Uncle Arthur were already dressed, watching the scene unfold through the downstairs window. Eadie jumped at the sound of fists thudding against the front door.

"What's going on?" Ray asked, still groggy from his medication-induced slumber.

Arthur turned and whispered, "News people."

"News people?"

"Where?" said Arthur.

"You said... Doesn't matter. What's going on, Aunt Eadie?"

"Television, everywhere up and down the street."

"We think we just saw Gary Cooper," said Arthur.

Aunt Eadie chipped in. "Anderson Cooper, and it wasn't him, Arthur, I told you, it was that Percy fellow from Channel Ten, the one you always said reminded you of Russell Crowe."

"Russell Crowe? Anderson Cooper looks like Russell Crowe?"

"Not Anderson Cooper, that Percy fellow."

Ray shook his head and chuckled at the back-and-forth. The heavy pounding continued on the front door.

"I already told them to leave you alone, Ray. They keep on asking for you."

He opened the door to a flurry of microphones and questions that reminded him of his time in Washington, a time he despised with a passion.

"Special Agent Waring! Do you have any suspects at this time?"

"Special Agent Waring! Do you anticipate a speedy arrest?"

"Raymond! Is it true the victims are known to you personally?"

The questions came fast and furious.

"Agent Waring, where do you think the serial killer will strike next, and will it be another of your acquaintances?"

Lawrence!

"Ray. You worked on a serial homicide case previously and successfully tracked the killer. You brought that man to justice. Did you ever imagine you would work a case that hits so close to home?" The voice was familiar. He glanced over the heads of the people to the woman without the microphone and saw the smiling face of Laura French. He smiled back and answered her directly.

"Ms. French, as you know, I'm retired from the Bureau. I'm not an active investigator in the recent homicides. I suggest you direct your questions to Detective Lawrence of the Fowler Sound Police Department."

A second familiar voice called out from behind Laura French, and as if on cue, Barney pushed his way to the front of the crowd.

"I think I can clarify that for you folks." He smiled excitedly at Ray, who returned the cheeky look with a condemning glare. "Special Agent Waring is acting only on a consultative basis and has been assisting the F.S.P.D. with his expertise. However, it is the F.S.P.D. that is conducting this investigation, and we would be more than happy to answer questions from the national press."

"Special Agent Waring, can you confirm that a serial killer known to you is on the loose here in Fowler Sound?"

Barney raised his hands high and called for silence. "Please, ladies and gentlemen, Agent Waring will not be answering any more questions. Now, if you folks want to pack up here, we will be holding a press conference at the town hall in exactly one hour. Thank you." He then took Ray's arm and led him back into the house without acknowledging any further questions.

"What in hell's name is going on, Barney? I thought we agreed to keep this under wraps until we had more information to go on. And another thing, I am not on this case as a consultant or in any other capacity. You asked me for an opinion. That's all I gave. For God's sake, Barney, I don't do this anymore. Now, take that crowd of parasites with you and leave me out of it from now on. I don't want anything more to do with it, understand?"

"Ray, listen. I may have let it slip that we have a serial killer on our hands, but I was only trying to protect the public. They need to know what we're dealing with here. You're the best there is, Ray; everyone says so. Give me a break here, will you?"

Ray opened the door. "Goodbye, Barney."

Lawrence left with one last plea before turning away. Ray watched him navigate the media circus as they packed their gear and headed for the town hall. Laura French waited until Lawrence turned the corner before approaching.

"Ray."

"Laura, long way from Buffalo... sorry, *L.A.*"

She laughed. "Yeah, maybe I was destined to learn to drive in this stuff after all. Then I can move to Buffalo and fulfill my life's dream of a place in the snow."

"Shouldn't you be hurrying on down to the city hall for the story?"

"You *are* my story, Ray, we only got through chapter one last time around. Seems to me there's a whole book to finish." She squinted as a shaft of sunlight cleared a rooftop and fell directly on her face. "How about breakfast?"

Chapter 25

Ray chose Verne's Diner, located on the north edge of town just before the highway. Frequented mainly by truck drivers, he figured this would be the least likely spot to be seen with Laura French. Four burly truck drivers quietly tucked into their breakfasts while a woman with an Adam's apple served coffee over the counter. Only Verne was in the tiny kitchen. He glanced up when Ray entered, closely followed by Laura, before returning his attention to the hot plate where he tossed pancakes, causing them to sizzle and release blue-gray smoke.

They took a seat at an empty table by the window. Ray ordered coffee, and Laura ordered a large cappuccino.

"We got coffee," the server told her.

"Fine," said Laura.

The server waited, pencil in hand, as the two looked over the menu. "Be lunch soon."

Ray shook his head and sighed. "I'll just stay with the coffee, thanks."

"Same." They both laughed as the server walked away in disgust.

"Nothing like small-town hospitality," Ray said. "I thought I was back in Washington for a minute."

There was a long pause before Laura spoke. "I thought about you a lot since Grand Rapids. Why is it that the nicest people seem to be married, gay, or...?"

"Dying?"

"I didn't mean that. I was going to say, out of reach." She scanned the diner before getting straight to the point. "So, this Jess Fischer, is she someone special to you?"

The server returned and placed two mugs of hot coffee on the table along with the tab. They both took a sip, and Laura spoke just ahead of Ray. "Surprise, coffee's delicious!"

"Not bad, is it?" He took another slurp. "So, you've been doing some digging since we last spoke."

Laura grinned. "That's my job, remember? Anyway, it didn't take much digging; I found out about her within five minutes of arriving in town. She's married." She waited for a reaction, but none came. She tried again. "With children."

"Jess is a friend from way back; we used to be close."

"How close is close?" He hesitated, trying to decide how much to reveal to Laura. She seemed to draw information from him effortlessly; it was alarming how freely he spoke.

"We were close."

"And then Squall Lake. The accident."

"You know about that?"

"Do you want to tell me what happened? Better from the horse's mouth than some rag making up the details."

Ray took time to decide how much to say. She was right; sooner or later, someone would print the story. "Clair was ten years old; I was nineteen. The day had started well, the sun was shining, and it was unseasonably warm. It was the first hint of spring, and we were all desperate to get some sunshine. At that time, Walter Callus, Clair's older brother, and I were best friends. Clair was nine years younger than Walt, and often tagged along because their mother worked shifts. We planned a lazy day at the lake with friends, hoping to enjoy music, drinks, and some hockey before the ice melted.

"Most of our friends were to arrive after midday, but me, Jess, Walt, and his girlfriend, Sue, set up camp in the morning among the trees along the shoreline. A last-minute shift change for Jody Callus forced Walt to bring Clair, but nobody minded. We adored his little sister. Jess and I volunteered to build a bonfire and start prepping food. Walt and Sue left for a beer run, leaving Clair with us. Ironically, Walt's last words, said in jest, were: 'Don't let her out of your sight, Ray. I'm trusting you with her life.' An hour later, that trust was shattered as Clair fell through the ice, drowning in the freezing lake."

Laura said nothing, and the silence hung between them. "I can't imagine how you must have felt," she said eventually. "You must've been devastated."

"How come you came after me? I thought you got what you wanted in Rapids."

"Are you kidding? I just finished writing my piece for the magazine when my editor calls me like he's just hit the jackpot. I asked him what he'd been drinking because I wanted some of the same. He told me he got a tip-off from one of the dailies saying you were back on the job and tracking a serial killer who had started taking out your old buddies. It was like, "HELLO, why aren't you on a plane to Michigan?" I didn't even have time to pack my pajamas; I just grabbed a toothbrush at the airport." She looked Ray up and down, and the corner of her mouth curled into a cheeky smirk. "Guess I'll have to sleep naked tonight."

Ray flushed at the innuendo and admitted to himself that her comment had piqued his interest. He thought of Jess, and the moment melted.

"First, let's get one thing clear: Fowler Sound is a small town where half the population knows the other half. Therefore, it should come as no great surprise that I knew both victims. They were not my buddies. Second, two murders don't make a serial killer. Someone got carried away with their imagination."

"But you *are* on the case? Who are you working with?" Ray shook his head in frustration. "Oh, come on, Ray. You know you can trust me. I want your story, and that includes your cases. Just tell me what you have on this guy." She placed a hand on his. "You and I have history, don't we?"

"That's not going to work this time, Laura."

"You're holding out on me, aren't you? There's more, isn't there?"

"I don't know what you mean."

"Peter Guziac."

Ray's heart skipped. She really had been digging. "I have to go, Laura. It was good to see you again."

"Come on, Ray? Please?"

"Bye, Laura."

Chapter 26

ay's Trans-Am purred its way down the First Avenue hill toward the river and rolled to a stop at the flashing red lights. A freight train was shunting across the road, sliding into the siding near the grain silos. The long procession of steel cars ground to a halt, blocking the road. Ray noticed the line stretching into the distance and switched off the engine, bracing for a wait.

A Silverado pulled up behind him, carrying five people, two in front and, from what he could make out, three crammed in the crew cab. The Chevy crept too close, stopping just inches from his bumper, so close he could no longer see their faces in his rearview mirror. Both crew cab doors swung open, and two men climbed out at the same time. Ray's hand went automatically to his holster, then he cursed under his breath. No weapon, no room to maneuver. He could only sit there, tense, as they approached.

One of the men rapped on the glass, a Staccato P4 steady in his grip, pointed at Ray's head. "Unlock the doors."

The gun didn't waver as the second man yanked the passenger door open and slid in beside him. His neck was a mess of tattoos, like some twisted roll-neck sweater. Hideous. He shoved a Glock into Ray's ribs. "Turn the car around," he growled. "Follow the Silverado." Ray obeyed. The Chevy peeled off down a gravel road, leading him toward the grain dock sidings.

* * *

Scottie watched from the hill. He saw the guy climb into Ray's car. "*Hello.*" He pulled over and waited as the two vehicles made a U-turn before heading along the railroad tracks. Scottie slowly drove out as the freight train rumbled into motion, passing the silos and leaving town to the east of the bay. Carefully keeping his distance, he observed the two vehicles come to a stop outside the old railroad maintenance shed. The two-story shed stood like a forgotten tomb in the middle of a freight yard, where all the other buildings had been torn down. Its rusted, corrugated walls supported a roof covered with snow. Scottie parked and unlocked the hardcover of the Ram.

He grabbed a ballistic vest, took off his coat, and quickly strapped the vest on. He reached into the truck again, pulling out an IWI Galil Ace. He slung the Israeli-made assault rifle and took two Sig handguns, one tucked into his belt. He released the manual safety on the other and carried it in his left hand. Scottie looked over the scene. The isolated shed made a covert approach tough. He decided to approach from the rail line, crossing open ground to a derelict boxcar parked on a siding. He crouched behind it, fifty yards away, with his Galil resting on the steel frame. He watched one of the guys patrol the shed, his rifle lazily slung over his shoulder. Scottie lined up his shot and hovered his finger over the trigger.

✳   ✳   ✳

Inside the shed, the guy with the tats tied Ray to a rickety steel chair using an old hemp rope, and Ray winced as the coarse fibers dug into his skin. The flimsy chair wobbled on the dirt-strewn floor, and Ray feared it might collapse at any moment. He planted his feet firmly on the ground. A strong smell of used motor oil filled the air, and a greasy layer of grime coated everything in sight. The only light came from dirty windows high on the shed walls. A steel staircase led to a catwalk that provided access to a mezzanine. A block and chain, like the kind used to hoist an engine, hung from the steel beams overhead.

"Special Agent Raymond Waring, still alive. Aren't we lucky?" The guy who spoke was the only one without a weapon. There were four men inside; one had stayed outside to keep guard. One guy inside had an AK-47, while two casually carried handguns by their sides. Ray didn't know what the guy outside carried, but he suspected an assault rifle would be his choice. "I'm glad your much-publicized impending demise has been delayed long enough for us to meet. I must say, you don't look much like a man on death's door."

"It's my winter glow." Ray assumed the guy talking was the one in charge.

"Funny man. We haven't had the pleasure. But you knew my brother intimately." Ray knew this must be Mateo Ramos, even though he didn't resemble his twin brother much. "Quite the hero you turned out to be. Tell me, what does it take to gun down an unarmed man?"

"You tell me. What does it take to shoot a five-year-old kid in the gut? Your brother was filth. An animal who deserved to be put down."

Ramos stepped into a beam of light from the window. He smiled and took out a packet of cigarettes.

He offered one to Ray, but Ray just sneered at the offer. Ramos was a stocky man with Latino features, but he had no accent. He spoke like a Harvard grad. Ramos lit a cigarette and inhaled deeply before continuing. "You think you can goad me into killing you quickly? No, I don't think so. I've got time on my hands. We're going to have some fun."

Ramos nodded an instruction to one of the guys, who stepped up and pistol-whipped Ray on the side of his jaw. Ray spat blood and laughed. "I thought you were going to take it slow. Another blow like that and this old tumor will be popping in my head. What will you do then, kill me again?"

"Thanks for pointing that out. You're right, it was stupid of me." Ramos took off his jacket. He had a Glock in a shoulder holster. "We're going to take it real gentle. I take it your condition isn't affected by fire?"

"Now you're talking; it's damn cold in here."

"Go on, laugh." Ramos smirked. "We can chat, crack a few jokes while Vince grabs gasoline from the truck."

The tattooed guy nodded and walked toward the door. Ray watched him go, just as Ramos lunged from the side and buried a blade in his thigh, like planting a flag. Ray screamed.

The raw sound made Vince pause at the threshold. He turned, just as his head exploded. The sudden violence erased Ray's pain, shoving it into the background. His mind sharpened, hunting for an opening. A second shot rang out. The lookout bolted inside, only for a round to punch through his skull mid-stride. His body slammed into Ray, dragging them both down. The rusted chair splintered, ropes snapping free.

Ray scrambled up and dove for cover as chaos erupted. Ramos locked onto the door. The AK guy moved to block Ray, but Ray dropped low, sweeping his legs. The man fell, trigger finger spasming. Bullets stitched the tin walls, glass shattering like confetti before hitting the floor in a second crash. Ray rolled behind an oil drum.

"Fuck!" Ramos yanked his Glock, firing blind through the doorway. Guy number three joined in, until his chest burst in a red mist. Ramos ducked behind crates.

The AK guy charged the stairs, taking them three at a time, and positioned himself on the catwalk above. Then, Scottie blew through the front door, spraying wild suppressing fire. Bullets shredded an oil drum. He spotted the shooter overhead and dove beneath the catwalk, barely in time. Ray spotted Vince's handgun. He rolled across the floor, snatching it up in one smooth action, and hid behind a tool rack. "What are you doing here, Scottie?"

"Good to see you too, Ray. How come I'm always saving your hide, buddy?" The guy with the AK fired a burst, rounds peppering the shed. "What have we got, Ray?"

"Guy up top and one hiding out somewhere near the far wall. He's carrying a Glock."

As if to confirm, a round from Ramos caught Ray, grazing his bicep. Ray winced.

Scottie slung the Galil and drew his Sig. "You okay, Ray?"

Ray felt the arm wound and winced again. "Been better."

Gunfire erupted from the catwalk. Scottie rolled, dropped to a knee, and fired upward, catching the high man in the thigh. The shooter screamed, tumbled over the railing, and hit the concrete with a sickening crack. Ramos emerged. He had Scottie in his sights, about to pull the trigger. Ray braced, took aim, and fired before Ramos could shoot. A single bullet to the temple brought silence to the building.

After a long, cautious wait, Scottie stood, brushing dust off his vest. "Is there anyone who likes you, Ray? Seems like they're lining up just to take a shot."

"Yeah, well, I am starting to feel unloved."

The pain in Ray's leg returned with a vengeance. He looked down at the damage. The wound oozed blood, soaking his slacks red. "Find me something to tie around this, Scottie." Scottie took a knife from his belt and came up close to Ray, holding it for a few seconds in front of Ray's face. He smiled, then cut Ray's sleeve from his shirt and wrapped it around his leg tightly. "How'd you know we were here?"

"Saw you roll down the hill on First, then watched these chumps take you. Figured you may be in trouble, buddy. Ain't that what friends is for?"

"And you just happened to be driving through the neighborhood carting your own personal arsenal with you, right?" Ray eyed the Galil slung on Scottie's shoulder.

Scottie chuckled. "Never know when you need to do some killing, Ray; you know that better than anyone."

Chapter 27

Fowler Sound hummed with the grim aftermath of gunfire. FBI agents moved like an occupying force, incorporating the attempt on Ray's life into their school siege investigation of Brothers for America. Familiar faces from the bureau questioned Ray between hospital exams while county sheriffs and town cops sulked in the background, their territory invaded. Scottie had given his account of the conflict and vanished—no goodbye when the ambulance doors closed on Ray.

The media siege was inevitable. Cameras staked out County General before the last shell casing cooled. Surgeons had excavated the knife's shattered tip from his femur. More repairs would come, but his wounds were superficial. By the time the night shift administrator declared to the waiting reporters that Ray was stable and in good spirits, even the most dogged reporters had begun to wilt under fluorescent lights.

Unbeknownst to the gathered journalists, as the spokesman addressed the crowd, Detective Lawrence pushed Ray in a hospital wheelchair toward a waiting vehicle parked at a side entrance. They slipped away unnoticed, heading west past the town mall and raceway, then followed the bay road south out of town. Lawrence had invited Ray to stay as a guest in his home, at least until the ruckus subsided.

Ray's phone buzzed with a number he didn't recognize. His first thought was to decline the call. He hesitated but then answered. It was Detective Carson from Traverse City. "This is a courtesy call, Ray."

"Shoot."

"Is Guziac a good friend of yours?"

The question had intonations. "I guess you've heard about the shootout." Carson hadn't; he'd been busy working. Ray gave him the short version.

"I guess that answers my question."

"Why do you ask?"

"Does he have a brother?"

"No. Scottie's an only child."

"You're sure about that? Only your buddy said he hadn't had contact with his father for years. The problem is, we have his DNA all over that apartment, and we even found it on Peter Guziac's clothes. Now, unless the old man hasn't done his laundry in a long time, I believe your buddy's telling some porky pies. We're going to bring him in, Ray. I just wanted to let you know."

"You're certain it's Scottie's DNA?"

"If he has no siblings, then yes, I'm certain. Father, son. The DNA doesn't lie."

Ray thanked Carson for the heads-up and asked to be kept informed.

"Bad news?"

"I think it is, Barney. I think it is." Ray shook his head. His mind was racing.

Barney Lawrence lived on the outskirts of the nearby township of Weaton with his wife, Cheryl, and an old hound named Rockford. The aluminum-clad, single-story home had a warm, lived-in feel. A large wood-burning stove heated the house to oven-like temperatures, and the interior had an immaculate touch, unlike Barney. Rockford sprawled across a rug in the center of the room. He managed only a cursory glance before rolling over and closing his eyes when Ray entered the house.

Cheryl Lawrence, a Maltese woman with a maternal streak wider than Barney's appetite, fussed over Ray like he was a stray pup in need of feeding. "Barney! Don't just gawk, get the man a beer." She snapped her fingers toward the fridge. "And take the trash out before you wash up. Honestly! That man needs a mother, not a wife." She turned to Ray, hands on hips. "You need to freshen up, sweetheart? Barney, run to town for more beer. What's your poison, Ray?"

Ray opened his mouth to answer, but Cheryl was already halfway to the kitchen, her kindness as relentless as her hospitality.

"Don't bother yourself, Cheryl," Ray said. "I'm not in the least bit hungry."

Barney snorted. "Famous last words." He clinked his beer bottle against Ray's, earning a wince as Ray's injured arm protested the motion.

"Hell of a homecoming," Barney said, wiping his mouth. "Town's crawling with feds like ants on a picnic sandwich. Where'd they all come from?"

Cheryl reappeared, plunking a steaming beef-and-bean casserole the size of a hubcap onto the table. Ray stared.

"Don't worry," Barney said, rubbing his hands together. "That's just the first course." A hopeful belch escaped him.

"Half portions, Barney!" Cheryl called from the kitchen. "Doctor's orders!"

Barney gazed at the casserole like a condemned man eyeing his last meal.

"You're a lucky man, Ray," Barney said, serving himself from the dish. "Lucky Guziac had your back."

He paused for a moment to fill Ray's plate with food and then continued. "He sure had some firepower, a truckload of military hardware to be exact. No less than five assault rifles. All licensed, it turns out, though what a man needs with all that stuff beats me." Ray noticed that Barney was studying his face, searching for some kind of reaction.

"Leave Ray be, babe, he hasn't even touched his food yet, what with your jawing at him." Cheryl gave Ray a wide grin, then pushed a basket of bread rolls closer to his reach.

They finished their supper with some casual conversation about Cheryl's friend Marcia, who suffered from terrible hemorrhoids and would, by all accounts, need surgery. She eventually cleared the table and left the two men to talk.

"God, I love that woman!" Barney said.

"I'm going to ask to be reinstated."

Barney raised his eyebrows and waited for Ray to continue.

"I'm going to ask for the case."

"Whose case? My case?"

Ray took a slug of beer. "It's going to be a federal case, too, now, Barney. Cover was killed on a reservation; that makes it federal. Link it to your case here, and it's a slam-dunk that the feds will take over. I'm surprised the Bureau isn't already all over you."

Barney frowned. "They are. That's what I've been waiting to tell you; there's a whole mess of your boys swarming all over the department. Half the guys who came up for the Ramos thing have stayed on. They're setting up shop. I've got orders to give them everything I have. There's this Captain Gruder, who thinks he's God's gift to law enforcement; he's running the show now. I think you're high on his list to interview, but I headed him off. Figured you could use a rest before you cross swords with that son of a gun."

"I know Gruder from my time at the academy in Virginia; he's a by-the-book man, a paper pusher." Ray wondered why Gruder had gotten involved.

Barney took a call on his cell. "You're sure?" He ended the call and turned to Ray. "Goddamn it, they match. Writing, prints, they match."

"DNA?"

"Too soon. But the report on the hairs found stuck to the bindings is back. Identical length, both dyed, same blonde hair color. Except that one has a different DNA profile. I mean, two blonde killers working together, what are the odds?"

Ray considered Barney's naivety. He couldn't help chuckling. "A wig."

"A wig?"

"A wig. Two blonde hairs, same length, same hair dye. Two different donors. It happens."

"You're shitting me. Oh, by the way, your note was written by a different hand. Whatever the motive, it wasn't our killer."

"You said Scottie went home after he left the scene. Do me a favor, run me over there in the morning before we head into the department."

"He's coming in to make a formal statement tomorrow."

"All the same, we'll go to his place first."

Cheryl Lawrence called out from the kitchen. "You boys ready for coffee and dessert?"

$$ * $$

Chapter 28

They made the short drive to Scottie's house, Cheryl's home-cooked breakfast swelling Ray's stomach. On the way, Ray updated Barney on the Peter Guziac murder and the overwhelming suspicion nagging at him. Ray's face had swollen, with a blue and yellow bruise on his cheek, growing more vivid by the hour. He'd taken painkillers, but both his arm and leg ached like hell. At least for now, he was thankful that his brain wasn't joining the orchestra.

Scottie's residence loomed against the backdrop of the escarpment like an old-world castle, a monument to Maria Steelton and her wealth. Signs of foot traffic were evident to and from the four-car garage, with tire tracks leading out of the property, though all were covered by a light dusting of the previous night's snow. Barney rattled the handle and banged on the door with his fist, but it was clear no one was home. They wandered to the rear of the property, where Ray slipped the catch on a rotting French window.

"Not exactly police procedure, Ray."

"Trust me, Barney, Scottie left me an open invitation."

Barney scoffed. "Yeah, right!"

They wandered through the ground floor, moving silently from room to room. Barney's eyes roamed the interior, taking stock of the once-opulent contents. "Holy crap! What in God's name happened?"

"Scottie canned his cleaner."

"No shit," he whispered. "His mom must have lived like a freaking queen once."

"Stepmom. She did. I can't imagine what she'd think if she saw it now."

Barney leaned in close to examine the signature on a painting and half expected the artist to be Picasso. "*Alberto Sanchez*." Barney lifted a mummified rat by the tail. "Even bigger question, how does someone let it go to ruin? Why didn't he sell it if he didn't want it?"

"It's complicated. Just like Scottie."

Upstairs, they entered what was once Maria's bedroom. Whispers of her life, evident in the perfume bottles, their contents long since evaporated. A vanity mirror, clouded with age, reflected only shadows. The canopy of the four-poster bed sagged, its fabric as brittle as cobwebs, while the mattress had sunk into itself, sprouting strange, dark growths. In the wardrobe, moth-riddled dresses hung like the skins of long-gone occupants, their sequins still catching the light in weak, desperate glimmers.

The musky air was thick with the silence of abandonment, broken only by the occasional creak of settling wood. The mansion was no longer a home, merely a carcass of elegance, slowly being reclaimed by rot and time. Each step felt like they were trespassing on a memory that didn't belong to them, a place where the past was both preserved and decaying, waiting for the final collapse.

"It's just creepy. This friend of yours is more than complicated. And this, this is just obscene."

They made their way through the bedrooms, one by one, each littered with dirty clothes, empty beer bottles, and discarded cigarette packs. A dried pool of vomit covered a pillow on a spare bed. Barney peeled back a bedcover and saw what looked like excrement on the mattress. He shook his head in disgust.

They climbed another flight of stairs to Scottie's apartment. Ray ignored the ballroom where he'd been Scottie's guest and entered a spacious bedroom overlooking the front of the property. The scene stunned Ray into silence. Draper's racks of suits, dresses, and costumes formed lines against the walls.

Other garments lay sprawled over another large bed, over chair backs, and tables. A theater make-up mirror, bordered by lightbulbs, sat above an antique dresser. Ray noted the theatrical makeup covering the surface: grease paint, lipsticks, powders, and eyeliners. A grubby plastic box lay open on a table, containing a surprising array of mustaches, eyebrows, and beards, along with trays of latex warts, pimples, and scars of every kind. A bottle of spirit gum rested on the side table beside a ginger-colored wig and beard.

"Well, I'll be a monkey's, will you look at that? He was the damned reporter at the airport!"

Barney didn't respond. He sifted through a box of wigs and pulled one out to place on his head. "What do you think?"

Ray managed a brief chuckle. "You look like Frank Zappa."

"Is Guziac some kind of actor?"

"He says he is, though some folks think he's full of it. I think the term used was 'failed actor'. He used to own the theater in town."

"Oh, him. Yeah, I read about that at the time. It's never reopened. You said you knew him well?"

"Knew being the operative word. To tell you the truth, Barney, I don't know who this guy is anymore. If you had told me Scottie Guziac dressed up in women's clothing, I would've said you were out of your mind."

He looked through the garments, trying to come to terms with the implications. A tartan kilt. *The Scotsman in the park. Unbelievable!*

Lawrence flipped open a laptop. "I think you should take a look at this, Ray."

The home screen displayed a recent photo of Ray and Jess taken on Jess's doorstep. Ray felt the hairs stand up on his neck. Barney tapped a key, and the password box appeared.

"You need to get someone over here, Barney. A patrol for when he returns. And get that laptop to someone who can open it."

"I'm on it. I'll call you when—" Barney froze. He heard what sounded like a paper cup bouncing down the stairs. Someone was outside the room. He raised a finger to his lips, took out his weapon, and moved forward cautiously. After a deep breath, he awkwardly pounced into the hallway, bent his knees, and aimed his handgun in the Weaver stance. Ray cringed at Barney's cumbersome technique as he struggled to get a bead on the target.

"Ma'am, what are you doing here?"

Ray heard Laura French introduce herself to Lawrence. She followed up with a barrage of questions he struggled to answer. She told him she was there at Scottie's invitation. Then she asked if he was a suspect in the recent string of killings. Ray listened for a moment before stepping out of the room.

Laura looked past Barney and smiled. "Hi, Ray."

"You two know each other?" Barney asked, lowering his weapon.

"We've got some history. Hi, Laura."

She smiled. "Oh, I wouldn't call it history, not yet anyway. I was just asking your friend here if you believe Guziac is your serial killer?" She looked past him into the room. "My, my, he does dress well, doesn't he? I bet that woman you've been searching for evolved right out of that bedroom, am I right? Like Eve from Adam's rib. Tell me, Detective," she said, turning to Barney. "Do you have a warrant to search his home? And, I understood it was an FBI investigation now."

Her question about a warrant seemed to rattle Barney. "It's a joint investigation, and you shouldn't be here."

"You're off the radar, aren't you?" Laura said, smiling like a cat who'd just swallowed the canary. "That could cause a lot of problems for you, if it became public, I mean."

Ray watched Barney flush, then turned to Laura, a hint of a smile on his lips. "This is Barney, Laura. He's leading the local investigation, liaising with the Bureau. He's one of the good guys." She acknowledged Barney, and he her. "Give us a minute, Barney. There are a couple of rooms up top that you might want to check out. Then we'll head back to the precinct."

Barney made his way to the attic, allowing Ray some space with Laura. He stopped on the stairs to observe a large photograph, a woman with her face scraped away.

*　　*　　*

Damn annoying! "Hell, that Galil rifle could have been a family heirloom. It would have been if I'd shot my pa with it. Ha!" Scottie gave himself a pat on the back for that clever witticism. He wished he'd shared it with someone who could hear. The assault rifle had the weight and balance he had sought for so long, and the action was so smooth that he felt as if it were an extension of his body. Now, it was locked away in an evidence room along with his Sig, no small thanks to Ray Waring.

Still, it was kind of neat that he used it to save his best friend from certain and painful death. *Fucking ironic!* The news shows were broadcasting his own story of heroism right at that moment, while Ray lay bedridden in the hospital, like a big, soft girl; now that was really ironic. Little did those reporters know that they would write a different story of his exploits before the end of day. His smartphone pinged. An alarm triggered. Scottie flicked on the app and watched Barney Lawrence searching through his stash of survival gear.

"Son of a bitch. Good thing I saw this coming." Scottie switched to multi-room view. "Hello there! So, they let you out. And who's the bitch, Ray? Looks like you've been holding out on me and Jess." He zoomed in on Ray and Laura French. "Cute! Okay, Ray. Have a field day. There's a bed you can use, but don't go dirtying the sheets now." Scottie laughed heartily and turned his attention to a workbench.

He kept one eye on his phone while dismantling a Smith & Wesson handgun. He stared down the barrel and sighed. The house in Saginaw was a masterpiece of forethought, even if he did say so himself. An investment property purchased by his mother, he had allowed the home to remain vacant since inheriting it as part of the estate. Although it was ostensibly owned by one of her trusts, he had kept all the paperwork at arm's length ever since. He enjoyed the anonymity that the hideaway provided. He came and went in obscurity while the quiet neighborhood went about its business.

He visited the house every month, posing as Emanuel Hardcastle. The nerdy character was developed almost supernaturally based on a real person named Luis Crump. A real estate salesman, he called one day, canvassing potential sellers. Luis left a lasting impression on Scottie. He loathed the little geek from their very first encounter. His whining voice, sheepish face, thick bushy mustache, and greased black hair were more than any real man could stand.

Scottie remembered the night he followed Luis home, how easily the man had welcomed him inside, like a rabbit ushering a fox into its burrow. All it took was the promise of an imminent sale and a few convincing words, and Luis had swung the door wide open. That was the first and only time he'd strangled someone to death. Old tweetie didn't count because she never died until he stuffed her with toilet paper. Even now, the memory warmed him. The bulging eyes, the disbelief twisting Luis's face as Scottie's fingers tightened around his throat; what a rush. But the real magic came after, when the high faded and he was left staring at the corpse's glassy, wide-eyed gaze. That was when inspiration struck.

"Thank you, Scottie. You've done me a big favor." Luis's voice slithered into his mind, unbidden. No movement of the lips, no breath behind the words, just silence, and then that eerie gratitude. "Thank you for freeing me of this worthless existence." Freaky? Hell yes. But also... spiritual. The dead man was in his head now, whispering, pushing, as if trying to crawl inside his skin. Maybe it was the meth talking. Either way, Scottie wasn't about to let some weakling like

Luis become him. Prescott Guziac didn't share his soul with anyone. So he did the old switcheroo; he took Luis instead. Not his name, that would've been stupid. The cops would've caught on fast. But his essence? That, Scottie could use. Like a vampire feeding on blood, he absorbed the man's identity, reforged it into something stronger. Something his. And just like that, Emanuel Hardcastle was born. A man after Luis's own heart, or what was left of it. Who would ever suspect that a tricky bastard like Scottie Guziac and soft-spoken Emanuel Hardcastle were one and the same person?

Scottie watched Ray leave his house with the woman and the cop. Soon, the place would be crawling with pigs. He peeled the fake mustache from his lip and stuck it to the coffee table glass, right beside his freshly cleaned arsenal. Enough firepower to outfit a small militia. He had everything he needed here: supplies, weapons, a fortress. He could vanish for months. *Years*, even. But where was the fun in that? He had chores to finish. Games to play. And he was only getting started.

*　　*　　*

Ray led Laura down the stairs to the door. "I get the feeling you're tailing me, Laura."

Laura made a sound almost like a hiccup. "I wouldn't tail you, Ray. You make me sound like a stalker. I was following up a lead, actually." She brushed past him into a side room, browsing as though she were at a department store sale. "My God," she said, running a finger through the dust on a table. "I overheard you and the detective talking; you really think your friend is the killer, don't you?"

Ray's mind raced off on a tangent; he was already trying to anticipate Scottie's next move.

Laura continued. "I don't get it. This lunatic friend of yours just saved your life."

"What's to get? He's unwell."

"Are you going after him?"

"Of course."

"His saving your life must make it hard for you to bring him in."

"If he murdered anyone, he'll be brought to justice like anyone else, and I'll help if I can."

"*If he killed them?* You're not so sure?"

Ray appreciated her inquisitive nature. It indicated she was a good investigator. "I can't tell you any more than I already have, Laura. When there's news, I'm certain that you'll be the first to know."

"Oh, come on, Ray, you know me well enough to give me more than that."

She followed him out of the house, and they joined Barney on the street. Her nose was red from the cold, and her breath rose in clouds from her brilliant red lips. He noticed the thin black line she used to outline them and how they curved into perfect Cupid's bows. She had a face of many moods, he thought; she could appear voluptuous or vulnerable, determined or indifferent. Now she looked as attractive as he had ever seen her.

"Let's go get a drink!"

"Later, Laura."

Chapter 29

Sardines. That was Ray's first thought when they arrived at the C. P. D. The briefing room was thick with the mingled scents of coffee, stale sweat, and the faint metallic tang of gun oil. Every inch of space was occupied; uniformed officers in pressed blues stood shoulder to shoulder with detectives and agents in rumpled suits, their badges glinting under the harsh fluorescent lights. The low hum of murmured conversations, the rustle of notepads, and the occasional crackle of a communications radio created a restless undercurrent.

At the front of the room, a large case board dominated the wall, plastered with crime scene photos, maps, and timelines. Gruder stood beside it, his voice cutting through the noise. "Listen up!" The room snapped to attention. Chairs creaked as those seated in front leaned forward; those standing shifted weight, straining to hear. A homicide detective chewed on an unlit cigarette, eyes locked on the action up front. In the back, a few latecomers pressed against the doorframe, craning their necks over Ray's shoulder to see. Not that they'd have difficulty seeing the man about to take center stage. He must have been six-eleven, a stick insect with glasses. Ray shuffled in along the back wall. He saw Barney hovering outside with a cup of coffee and what looked like a box of Krispy Kremes.

The stick insect introduced himself. "Jorge Dyer, good morning. Let's cut straight to it." His pointer tapped the whiteboard. Ray craned his neck but only caught fragments of text. "We're dealing with a killer who's hunting people tied to Myerson Public School. This isn't random. It's personal. Victim One; Bradley Cover. Ex-student, seasonal laborer. Petty criminal, known bully. Thirty-four nails from a construction-grade gun before the kill shot to the temple. A taunting cryptic note left by the killer: *'Don't remember? Here's a little reminder.'* Remember what? Remember what you did to me? Remember what you owe me? Bradley Cover terrorized people for years, including kids he went to school with. The nails weren't just torture; they were counting something. Possibly symbolic; a count of grievances, time passed, or, like his second victim, biblical references, e.g., thirty-four lashes. These elements are ritualistic and symbolic. He was asking his victim to understand the why, to take responsibility."

Dyer scanned the room as though he were waiting for questions. "Victim Two," he continued. "Celine Bird. Retired teacher. Bound to a chair. Tortured with a switch, like the one she carried in class. Strangled and then suffocated. Staged crime scene with underwear on her head and a note: *'Here endeth the lesson.'* Bird was strict; some say cruel. Students called her "The dragon bird." This crime was brutal in its need for retribution." Dyer jabbed the crime scene photo. "Control, theatrical humiliation, she was made to surrender her dignity. The biblical note? A mockery of her profession. She wasn't just killed, I believe she was sentenced."

A hand shot up. "Did the victims know each other?"

Gruder cut in. "Save it."

Dyer pressed on. "The killer's profile: Organized. Ritualistic. They're not just murdering, they're executing. Bird for authority, Cover for brutality. Both being bound to a chair is significant. Total control. The wig fibers at Bird's scene? They're disguising themselves, maybe to avoid cameras or recognition. The killer is known to the victims and probably locals. This is planned. Precise." He leaned in. "Our killer is a former student; someone who blames the school for something, such as failure, punishment, or trauma. The religious phrasing '*Here endeth the lesson*' suggests a warped moral code. They see this as justice." Murmurs ran through the room. "They're not done. If we're right about the pattern? More are on the list. Teachers. Bullies. Anyone they think '*deserves*' it." Dyer scanned the room again. "This is a serial case. And they will kill again."

"They already have."

Heads pivoted, searching for the speaker. Those closer to Ray looked in his direction. Gruder moved alongside Dyer and scanned the crowded room. "Who said that?"

Ray stepped forward as people moved aside. "We believe there's a third victim, the killer's own father." A spontaneous outbreak of chatter followed as Ray pushed his way to the front. "We're looking for Prescott Guziac," Ray said, approaching Gruder as everyone looked on, eyes wide, mouths agape.

Gruder looked stunned. "What in God's name are you doing in here, and who's we?"

"Detective Lawrence and I have good reason to think that Scottie Guziac is our killer. And Dyer's right, he's not done yet, not by a long shot."

Gruder sneered. "Last I heard about you, you were hospitalized, and this fella Guziac was your savior. What in hell's going on, Waring?"

Gruder's reaction was predictable, or at least it would have been if Barney had known him better. As it was, he walked naively into a hornet's nest when he triumphantly entered the chief's office. Ray was already there alongside Gruder, Chief Sullivan, and Agent Moises Rocha, the lead Special Agent assigned to the case. Barney had thought congratulations were in order; he had just cracked the case wide open. The reception he received was colder than the ice on his backyard fish pond.

"You had no warrant," Sullivan said, steaming.

"I went to his home to take a statement over the railyard shooting, sir. I wanted to tidy up the county's involvement with a report. When I arrived, I discovered the French window had been forced open, and I became concerned for Guziac's safety. So, I entered the premises."

"How well do you know Raymond Waring, Detective?" Gruder looked him in the eye as he spoke. Barney's eyes flitted to Ray and back.

"I can't say I know him well, Captain."

"Well enough to share confidential police business with him, though, important clues in a federal case. You do know he's no longer a law enforcement officer?"

Barney knew where the questions were headed. "Sir, I think Ray's involvement here can only benefit the..."

"So, you admit he's involved. What kind of goddamned outfit are you running here, Sullivan? I made myself perfectly clear when I said we were taking over the investigation and I would be managing the operation. I told you Waring had no place in all this."

Ray interjected. "I encouraged Barney to enter Guziac's home. And, like I told him at the time, Scottie left me an open invitation to visit."

Gruder scowled. "Get out of here, Waring. You may think you're some hero with special privileges, but to me, you're just another civilian. You're up to your eyes in this, and I'm going to find out why. Rocha, escort Mr. Waring out and place him in the interrogation room. I'll be with you shortly—"

"Hold up, Captain," Sullivan interrupted. "Until now, this has been our operation, and everything we've achieved is thanks to the hard work of our team, with or without Waring's assistance, who, I might add, is not *'just a civilian'*, but a department consultant to my team. Now, unless I'm mistaken, the FBI has no authority over local law enforcement. You are welcome here as our guest to collaborate with my department on what is a concurrent jurisdictional investigation."

Chief Sullivan took a moment before speaking again. "We have a good team here, Captain. Harmonious. Don't bring whatever beef you have with Waring into it. And another thing. I don't like your tone, Captain. I'm a religious man, and I don't take kindly to offensive blasphemy and people taking the Lord's name in vain, especially when spoken in my place of business and directed at my staff. You may be in charge of the FBI investigation, but you sure as hell aren't in charge of me or my men. Now get the hell out of my office; I want to talk to Detective Lawrence and Mr. Waring in private."

Gruder appeared surprised by the Chief's outburst and obeyed with a sneer. He paused at the doorway, turned around, and spoke. "I am going to make a phone call to the capital, then we'll see who takes the lead on this." Sullivan closed the door on him.

"I didn't know you were a religious man, Chief?"

"Before you say another word, Lawrence, don't even think about pleading your defense, because sorry will never be good enough to excuse you. You had no authority to involve Waring in this case, and what in God's name were you thinking going into a suspect's home alone and without a warrant?"

"I wasn't really alone. It's like I said, Chief, I went to…"

Sullivan held up his hand to silence him. "I said no excuses. Now, tell me everything, and I mean everything from the start before that goddamned irritating son of a bitch comes back."

Before Lawrence could speak, they were interrupted by a uniform. "Sorry, Chief. They just got confirmation on the prints from the note at Bird's house. We have a match to Guziac; his prints were all over it. No doubt about it, he's our man."

"He's got a record?"

"They were on record after he was charged with a misdemeanor two years ago. Using a telecommunications device to harass and intimidate. It involved emails sent to the governor over a property dispute. They managed to get a partial print on the other note, too, the one left on Agent Waring's car. Walter Callus. He has a record of minor offenses, mostly related to DUIs. Oh, and Gruder is gathering a unit to take down Guziac."

Sullivan turned to Ray. "Welcome to the team, Waring. You are now officially consulting the department. Now, please tell me what we're dealing with. I want to know what's behind all this. This is our town, for chrissakes; not a freaking federal circus."

Ray had Barney drop him off at home. He needed his meds and a clean set of clothes. Aunt Eadie opened the front door and recoiled in horror. "Oh! What have they done to your face?" She extended her arms to guide him inside, as if he needed help getting through the door. "You just missed Scottie," she told him. "He filled me in on those terrible men. It must have been horrifying. It was fortunate he was there to help you. Scottie said he would catch up with you later when the dust settles. We had reporters around too, three or four groups throughout the day. Scottie had to sneak in through the back door to avoid them."

"Scottie was here?" Ray rushed to the window and scanned the street. "How long ago, Aunt Eadie?"

"Oh, five minutes, it's a wonder you didn't see him driving off. That boy gets stranger as he gets older, I do declare. He was gibbering and jabbering, making no sense at all. Said he was going to leave everything he owned to his son. I said, Scottie, you don't have a son, do you? He said, 'I will have, Eadie, just as soon as I settle down and get married.' I told him he would have to get moving and find a young woman, or he would run out of time. You know what he said? 'There's always time to start a new life, Aunt Eadie, especially when you're playing God.' He's mad as a hatter." Eadie shook her head.

Ray sat down with Aunt Eadie and shared everything with her. Her face went pale as he spoke.

"Scottie, a murderer?"

Ray's phone rang. Number unknown. "Waring."

"Hey, buddy, I would have stayed for lunch, but you know how it is. We both got our list of things to do. Did you have any luck searching my place? I noticed you found my kilt."

"Where are you, Scottie? You know they're going to bring you in. And, knowing Gruder, it'll be in a body bag."

"Come on, Ray, you don't think these chumps are going to come between us, do you? You and I still got some dancing to do."

"What's going on, Scottie? What's all this about?"

"You're a smart man, Ray. You know what it's about. Cover got what was coming. I've thought about this a lot, and seeing you're the man with all the answers, we're going to have a game of who's next? I give you a hint, and you try to stop me. It'll be like we're playing Cluedo or some shit like that. I set the clues, and you have to solve them before I tick another off my list."

"That's just dumb, Scottie. I don't know what's driving this, but I'm not playing your game. Tell me where you are and I'll come and bring you in without anyone else getting hurt."

"Now you're starting to annoy me, Ray. So, I'm going to give you your clue, like it or not. Don't play the game, and the killing just goes on without you. Now, keep your stupid mouth shut while I talk." Ray let the silence hang. "Good. This one should be easy: *What turned beauty into a beast?* Don't answer that; I haven't finished; there's a part two: *There are some beasts, only an Angel could love.* What d'ya think?"

Aunt Eadie stood beside him, looking terrified. Tears rolled down her cheeks, emphasizing the wrinkled skin of her aging face.

Ray sighed. "I think you're crazy; that's what I think."

"See, that's you all over, Ray. Never gave me credit for anything. Well, the clocks are ticking. *Better get to it.*"

Chapter 30

Laura French stood on Jess's doorstep, her practiced smile faltering slightly as she took in the woman's guarded expression.

"I'm not talking to the press," Jess said, already moving to shut the door.

Laura wedged her foot just enough to stall her. "I'm not here as press. Not entirely." She softened her voice, letting a hint of sincerity slip through. "I'm a friend of Ray's."

Jess hesitated, her fingers tightening on the doorframe. "Ray doesn't have many friends."

Interesting. Laura filed that away. "No, he doesn't. Which is why I'm here." She held up her hands in surrender. "Five minutes. If you want me gone after that, I'll go."

Jess exhaled sharply but stepped aside.

Inside, the house was warm, lived-in, a stark contrast to the polished edges of Laura's own apartment. A child's laughter echoed from another room, followed by the tinny jingle of a cartoon.

"You're writing about him," Jess said, arms crossed.

Laura nodded. "A profile. Not the usual hero-worship piece. Something real." She studied Jess's face, the way her jaw tightened at the mention of Ray. "He's hard to pin down. I thought you might help me understand him."

Jess's laugh was brittle. "And why would I do that?"

"Because you know him better than anyone." Laura let the words settle. "Because you *care*."

For a moment, Jess looked like she might argue. Then... A sharp cry cut through the house. "Brighton!" Jess was moving before Laura could react, bolting toward the sound. Laura followed, her reporter's instincts kicking in.

In the living room, a little boy, Brighton, she guessed, was howling, his face red, tiny hands clawing at his nose.

Jess dropped to her knees, panic lacing her voice. "What's wrong, baby? What happened?"

Laura watched Jess lose all rational thought; her hysteria, a mother's rush to protect her child, took over completely. She'd never seen anyone transition so quickly from calm to terror over what appeared to be an unknown cause.

"My God, what's wrong?" Jess screeched.

Laura spotted it first, the glint of red wax wedged deep in his nostril. *Crayon.* Without thinking, she reached into her bag, pulling out a pair of tweezers. "Jess, hold his hands."

Jess shot her a wild look through welling eyes, but obeyed, gripping her son's wrists as Laura leaned in. One steady motion, and the crayon was out. Brighton's wails hiccupped into sniffles.

Jess sagged, pressing a kiss to her son's forehead before looking up at Laura. "Thank you."

The gratitude was real, unguarded. Laura smiled. "Kids are terrifying."

Jess laughed, shaky but genuine. "You have no idea."

They settled in the kitchen, tea steaming between them. The near-crisis had thawed Jess's defenses, just enough.

"You asked about Ray," Jess said at last, tracing the rim of her cup. "He was different before the accident. Kinder. Less... closed off."

Laura stayed quiet, letting her talk.

"He loved kids," Jess continued, almost to herself. "Used to coach the neighborhood team. Then..." Her voice hitched. "Then Clair died, and he just... shut down."

Laura nodded. "Guilt's a hell of a thing."

Jess's gaze flicked up, sharp. "You sound like you know."

Careful. Laura sipped her tea. "I've interviewed enough veterans, survivors. The ones who blame themselves never move on."

A beat of silence. Then, softly, "Do you think he ever will? Move on, I mean?"

The question hung between them, raw and unflinching.

Laura hesitated. This wasn't just about the story anymore. "I don't know," she admitted. "But I think he wants to."

Jess studied her, really *looked* at her, for the first time. "You like him."

It wasn't an accusation. Just fact.

Laura didn't deny it. "I barely know him."

Jess smiled, sad and knowing. "That's never stopped anyone."

The moment stretched, two women bound by the same complicated man, neither willing to say more.

Finally, Jess stood. "You should go. My husband will be home soon."

Jess was still shaking. Laura decided not to push. "Perhaps we can do this again?"

"Perhaps. Thank you for your help with Brighton. I don't know what I would've done without you."

Laura rose, but paused at the door. "For what it's worth... I think he still cares about you, too."

Jess's expression flickered: pain, longing, resignation. "Cares? The time for caring has long passed I'm afraid."

Laura recognized the lie in her expression. She was still in love with Ray, though she tried to conceal it. She observed Jess's uncomfortable body language, and the truth hit her. She realized how slow she had been to understand it.

"Jess, you and Ray aren't... You haven't been seeing each other since he returned home?"

Jess stood up as guilt washed over her face before smoothing into something polite. "Good luck with your article, Laura."

The door closed between them.

Laura exhaled. *Well. That wasn't in my list of questions.*

Chapter 31

A snow blower growled in a nearby street. Ray hadn't slept. He'd tossed and turned, praying that the dull ache would remain just that, long enough for him to find Scottie and put an end to the senseless killing. The ache had appeared soon after Scottie's call. He couldn't face the extreme agony and the seizure that usually followed, at least not today.

He'd spent the previous evening with Barney and Sullivan, brainstorming Scottie's threats and childish clues. Clues that could either save a life or end one. They had no choice but to play the game. Someone out there was at risk, and they didn't even know it. Sullivan decided on two courses of action.

"I'm going to run an appeal on the local television station, warn the community of Guziac's intentions."

"Gruder won't like it," Ray said. "He still thinks he's got the lead on this."

"Son, I know you're still a fed at heart, but this is our town, and I'm not about to let this psycho kill someone else without warning them that he's out there. Hell, I'll even publish the clues he provided."

"There's no love lost between Gruder and me, but keeping him and his team onside gives you resources you don't have, Chief."

"I take your point, Ray. But he won't stand in my way on this."

Before they could debate any further, Ray had a dizzy spell. This was often the prelude to a seizure, and Ray didn't want his presence to distract the team. He left Sullivan and Barney to decide on the press conference, hoping a night's sleep would reinvigorate him for the challenge ahead.

It was still dark outside. A second snow blower started up. Ray figured there had been a heavy snowfall during the night. He thought of Jess. Somewhere out there, she lay beside Alan Fischer. The thought irritated him. Why, when he had made his choice years ago? If he was honest with himself, there were long periods when he didn't think of her at all. Now, after waltzing back in, he was threatening her marriage just by being here. How could he have imagined she would still hold such feelings for him, still love him? *Liar, you knew!* Hoped for it at least; another example of his selfishness and arrogance.

His thoughts drifted again to Scottie. How had he ended up at this terrible point in his life, and why drag Ray into his nightmare? Sure, he'd had a tough childhood, like a thousand others, but that didn't turn them into killers. And his life got better, didn't it? He got the things he wanted, wealth... he was going to say happiness, but that was ridiculous. Wealth, what good was it alone, and look what he did with it? No, looking back, Scottie got nothing he genuinely wanted. What he really wanted was to be loved. Perhaps Scottie's life was always destined to turn out poorly.

There were signs and warnings, if anyone had cared to see. Even as a young child, Scottie had demonstrated dark tendencies. He recalled the day he led Jess and him to a spot in the woods where he showed them a gun. Scottie had just turned eleven years old the day before. He'd stolen the shiny handgun from a cupboard in his father's bedroom. Ray recalled the pistol wrapped in a dirty rag, along with a handful of bullets. Scottie took a bullet and appeared to load the weapon. He pointed the gun at Ray's head and squeezed the trigger. He then fell to the floor, laughing hysterically.

"What the hell? You could have killed me!"

Scottie got a bloody nose for the prank. The following day, Scottie told them he'd used it for real this time. When Ray called him a liar, he said he would lead them to the body if they wanted proof. He led them to a spot in the woods. He could still hear Jess's piercing scream. The victim in question turned out to be Scottie's white rabbit. It lay bloodied and lifeless at the base of a tree. Ray remembered the flies buzzing around the corpse in a whirling mass, the rabbit's eyes, glazed and dull. He knew now that it augured the future, the classic behavior in the profile of a psychopathic killer: Animal cruelty and torture.

✳   ✳   ✳

It was six o'clock in the evening when Myra Burke tuned into local TV while getting ready for work at the Harbor Inn. She called the number on the screen, but a recorded voice told her the line was busy and that someone would get back to her shortly. She'd called three more times in the last two hours with the same result. Just seeing Prescott Guziac's face on the TV made her shiver. "Jesus Christ! That sicko killed that old lady, and now he's coming after me. Can you believe that?" she said to nobody.

She wasn't going to hang around any longer. She grabbed a pair of blue denim jeans from a pile of clothes and started pulling them on. The snug stretch denim hugged her legs, and she struggled to lift them over her hips. She lay back on the bed, pulling, squeezing, and kicking to get into them, anxiety growing with every attempt.

She dug through a pile of dirty laundry and pulled out a black lace bra from among the crumpled bed sheets. A loud bang startled her as she got dressed. She froze. A second bang came from the front door. She glanced out of the bedroom, down the hall to the glass-paneled door, then quickly stepped back. A man's face pressed firmly against the frosted glass.

"Ms. Burke, please open the door!" *Shit, it's him!* "Ms. Burke, open up, please!" he repeated.

Myra began to tremble. Her lip quivered, and tears welled up in her eyes. A tightness in her chest turned into numbness in her legs. She resisted the urge to scream.

"What do you want?" she croaked eventually, unable to hide the fear in her voice.

"Ms. Burke, I'm Lieutenant Getty with the F.S.P.D. Ma'am, could you please open the door? It's about your phone call." Myra was skeptical; she hadn't seen Guziac in years, and the TV had warned of his many disguises. The person behind the door could be anyone, and she wasn't willing to take that risk. She grabbed her keys and purse from the table and retrieved her phone from inside her purse. Her fingers trembled as she pressed the small buttons to dial 911. She waited.

"Ma'am, is something wrong inside?" His fist pounded harder against the glass, causing it to rattle. He tried the doorknob. "Ms. Burke, I'm coming in!" Myra gasped and dropped the phone. The door handle rattled violently again.

"Fuck you, Scottie! I know it's you; I called 911, they're on their way!" Terrorized, she ran to the back door. She wailed, her mouth curling into the expression of a frightened child. Tears streamed down her face, and snot dripped from her nose. She slid the latch on the door and dashed across the yard to the broken fence. She heard glass shattering and the front door crashing open. She screamed hysterically. A sudden warmth filled her pants as she lost control of her bladder. The jagged edge of the broken fence caught her belt loop. She screamed again, twisted to break free. A strong hand pulled her back into the yard.

❉　❉　❉

Ray lay on his bed, eyes closed, trying to blank out the pain. His thoughts returned to Scottie's deadly game. The clues he'd given were typically Scottie; overdramatic. However, they pointed to his next victim, which made them critical. This was all about people he thought had wronged him. Beauty and the beast; he couldn't, for the life of him, see what it meant.

Jeeze, this is ridiculous! Think. Could the beauty be Jess? No doubting she was beautiful. Perhaps Ray was the beast. Ray jumped to his feet, suddenly panicked. Why hadn't he thought of that already? He called Barney. If Scottie was going after Jess, they needed to be there to protect her. Barney answered on the fourth ring.

"Barney, we have to get over to Jess's place. I think Scottie's referring to her when he talks about beauty. And..."

"You haven't heard? We believe we have her; the next target, that is. We're going to interview her now. Her name is Myra Burke."

Lieutenant Getty briefed Ray as they headed to the interview room. Gruder was noticeably absent. The case was theirs alone for now.

"Has anyone informed the bureau?"

"Sullivan's orders. Keep it in-house."

"He's playing with fire."

Barney waited inside. Myra Burke sat clutching a polystyrene cup. Mascara streaked, hair matted. Beautiful underneath the distress. She glared at Ray as he entered; his offered smile withered under her contempt.

Barney began. "You dated Prescott Guziac. When was that, Myra?" She squinted in disgust.

"You might call it dating, I call it a mistake. Not that he was up for it!" She yelled at Getty. "Jerk!" He flinched. "Made me piss my fucking pants, he did. Why didn't you show your badge, you moron?"

Getty's shrug was confession enough. A faint smell of urine confirmed her story.

"Do you need clean clothes, Myra?" Barney asked. "We can send someone to your house?"

"Yeah, I need clothes, but I ain't having him go through my panties drawer." She jerked a thumb at Getty. "And get someone to fix my goddamn door while you're at it, before someone moves in with me. The Incredible Hulk here thinks doors are for doormats; he's a walking disaster!"

"Tell me about your relationship with Guziac. How long have you known him?" asked Barney.

"Is there a reward?"

"A reward? For what, Myra?"

"For me telling you what I know about the guy."

"Myra, he's trying to kill you, and you want us to pay you to stop him?" Barney shook his head.

"Well, you guys need me, right? To find him?"

"Jess doesn't have time for this." Ray made a move for the door, turned, and said to Barney, "Send Myra home."

"Wait!" Myra's bravado cracked. "You can't do that. He's out there looking for me. I want protection!"

Ray stopped at the threshold. "Then talk. Fast. Can't help you if you won't help yourself, Myra."

"You goddamn son of a bitch. You cops are all the same." She lit a cigarette with a trembling hand. "He was a regular at the Harbor Inn. Lonely. Weird. Started buying me drinks. After a few weeks, we went to my place." She barked a bitter laugh. "His idea of sex was a solo performance. He just... played with himself. Couldn't get it up. I offered to help, and he lost his mind. Didn't see him for weeks."

"Then?"

"Then he shows up with a grand in cash. A gift," she snapped, preempting Getty's look. "I ain't no prostitute. So, he says he wants to go again, but this time we went to his place.

God almighty, have you seen it? I thought he was joking when he said it was his. A fucking museum of crazy. We drank. He flashed money. I thought, 'This could work.'" Her face darkened. "He takes me upstairs. There's this goddamn four-poster bed. Tells me to get comfortable. So I do. I'm waiting. And waiting."

She took a drag, her eyes distant. "I found him in another room. Standing in front of a mirror. Dressed like Marilyn Monroe. I kid you not. Wig, white dress, the works. I figured, whatever gets you going, buddy. So, I start teasing him. And it... works. He's got a smile as wide as your butt," She smirked at Barney, who

looked hurt. "That's when I lost it. This guy is standing there in sequins and gold, wearing a dress I would die for. There's a bulge in the front that Superman would be proud of, and I start to laugh. I couldn't help it; I lost it completely. Of course, Superman turns into Superwoman real quick and he…"
The memory stole her voice. The room was silent.
"What happened, Myra?" Ray asked eventually, his voice low and soft.

"The smile died. He went cold. Tried to kick me, his heel snapped, and he fell off his pumps. Just lay there. I tried to apologize, touched his shoulder… Then…" She took off her blouse with stiff fingers, revealing a complex web of silvery scars, front and back. "He used an extension cord." She paused again. "I begged. He didn't stop until I passed out."
Barney looked sick. Getty turned away. Ray forced himself to look at the scars, then into her eyes; the deeper wounds were there.

"You didn't press charges?" Barney whispered.

"He locked me up in that house of horrors. He nursed me back. Bathed me, fed me. Was so gentle. I was confused… grateful, even. Eventually, he stopped locking the door. When I could walk, he paid me off. Bought me the house." A tear finally fell. "I should've known better than to laugh at a man's pecker."

Chapter 32

Gruder faced the barrage of camera flashes and TV floodlights, adjusting his tie as he prepared to speak. Sweat beads covered his forehead.

"Special Agent Gruder, how close are you to bringing Prescott Guziac into custody?"

Gruder shaded his eyes to better see the questioner's face. "It's too soon to say, but I can reveal that we have his intended target in protective custody. The quick actions of the FBI and others allowed my team to move swiftly to secure her safety."

"Can you identify this woman, Special Agent Gruder?"

Gruder smiled at the reporter and took his time answering. "That's Captain Gruder; spelled g.r.u.d.e.r." The reporter snickered. "At this time, her identity will remain confidential. Until Guziac is brought in, she will stay under our protection."

"Are there other victims and more importantly, any more targets at risk of this serial killer?"

"We know nothing of additional targets at this time. Guziac is now on the run, and so we don't expect him to risk capture by targeting anyone here in this city. We are close on his heels, and it's my opinion he will be apprehended soon. Anyone seeing Prescott Guziac should not approach. He is considered armed and dangerous. If you have any information that may lead to his capture, contact the bureau at the number provided or call 911. That's all I have to say at this time. Thank you."

✳　✳　✳

Barney turned to Ray as Gruder strutted across the screen. They were in the FBI field office, waiting for Gruder to finish with the press. "So now we're 'others.' The bastard! Did you hear him, taking credit for our work? Where did the FBI find a man like that, and how in hell did he become a captain?"

Ray shrugged. "He is truly something else, isn't he?" Ray's phone buzzed.

"This Gruder guy a friend of yours?"

"Scottie!"

"Don't bother with the trace, Ray; it's a burner, and I won't be on long."

"This is insane, Scottie. What the hell is it all about? I don't get it. I'm pleading with you. Whatever the problem is, I promise you we can sort it out. I know this isn't you. Whatever's going on, there are people, professionals who can help you. Let me help, Scottie."

"Help? You saying I'm schizoid or something, Ray?"

"I'm saying you're sick. You saw Gruder's presser, so you know we've got Myra. Why don't you come in and talk? You owe me that much." Ray heard Scottie's familiar snort.

"Excuse me? I owe you Jack shit! You seem to be forgetting all those times I saved your butt. What the hell do I owe you, Ray?"

"Alright, I owe you, I know that. But you owe it to us, Scottie, us as friends. You owe it to yourself to come in and put an end to this madness. I can get you help."

"Madness? Madness, maybe, but it falls on your shoulders, Ray. This madness, as you call it, is the result of *your* madness." There was a long pause. "This is your game, Ray, you started it, and now you leave me no choice but to finish it."

"Started what? Help me out here; what have I started?"

"You know what I'm talking about. But now it's no longer about starting; it's about who finishes on top."

"Finish what? Finish your life on a table with a needle in your arm? Finish what, Scottie? Is it about you getting bullied? Do you think killing those people will change the way they treated you? It won't, it won't change a thing."

"I wasn't bullied, Ray. I could have turned on them any time I wanted."

"Okay, you weren't bullied. So, tell me what you think they did to deserve it?"

"You don't get it, do you, Ray?"

Ray looked to Barney, who stood in the doorway, shaking his head. "*Keep him talking,*" he mouthed.

"This is not about them," Scottie continued, "this is about you; it's about you and me. It always *has* been. When these people die, it will be because you let them down. Just like you let Clair down."

Blood rushed to Ray's face. His mind began to spin. A trickle of sweat ran down his nose, and his hands turned clammy. *Not now!* He fought the feeling.

"I may have let her down, and I may have let you down, Scottie. But I will do everything I can to stop you from taking more lives. Myra's safe, so what's next? Give me a clue. I'll play your game."

Scottie laughed. "I gave you the clue, the trouble is you're not getting it, Ray. Myra was never in danger.

Myra's okay; I like her. At least she did the right thing by me. No, I think you have the wrong girl, buddy."

Jess. "You leave Jess alone, Scottie; like you said, this is about me and you."

"Very noble, buddy, but I wouldn't hurt Jess either. I think she's been hurt enough by you already. The one thing I can guarantee you is that Jess will not die. What I will tell you is..." He paused a moment. "Okay, here it is. You listening? One perfect little lady will be dead before her next birthday. That's it, last clue, last chance. Oh, say hi to Myra for me."

Scottie was gone before Ray could respond. He turned to Barney, who looked miserable in the doorway.

"The boys couldn't pin him down, sorry."

Ray's phone pinged. He received a message, a photo. It was a selfie of Scottie wearing a long black wig and a thick mustache. He had his arm around Cheryl Lawrence.

Chapter 33

In a small Baptist church on the edge of a rural town just south of Fowler Sound, a church minister was being amused by a visitor to the chapel. A curious fellow, a stranger, who seemed intent on preparing the minister for a surprise.

"Sit down. I have something for you," said the man.

Pastor Singleton sat down and smiled. She wondered if someone had put him up to it. He appeared extremely happy, she noticed, as he lifted the bucket of water into the air.

"Be careful," she said as the water slopped from the rim. She had visions of him slipping on the wet floor and ending up on his back. "You might hurt yourself."

The shock of the cold water cascading over her body struck her like a freezing bolt from the blue. It immediately took her breath away. She stood rigid, raised her hands to her face, and wiped the icy water from her eyes as it flowed down to the floor. At first, she felt an urge to scream, but she resisted and focused on calming her breath before speaking.

"I told you to be careful!" she said, her mouth still wide with shock. She had to see the funny side, and her lips curled into a smile. This was definitely somebody's idea of a prank. She started to laugh. Her moment of jest was brief. She felt the blow from the mop handle and crumpled to her knees, stunned by the unexpected assault.

"Hallelujah!" said the man.

"What are you doing? Please, I don't understand." A second blow struck her squarely on the chin, and she swayed before collapsing back to the ground.

The man lifted her from the floor and seated her in an empty pew. His face was an expressionless mask of calm.

"Shit, that's better, I've been waiting to do that for years," he said.

What had brought such violence to her house of God? Another protester, a religious fanatic who believed women had no place in the ministry? She had encountered her fair share of those over the last two years, but never to this extent. Things had settled since the near riots her ordination had caused. She tried to stay calm, though she could already feel her face swelling. She noted her attacker's grin. He appeared elated by his actions.

"You obviously have issues with me," she managed breathlessly. "And I have no idea what they are. Can I ask at least, what has brought you to this action?" She placed her hand on the swollen lump above her temple and felt the pain beneath her palm. She thought her jaw must be fractured; it hurt so much.

"I can't believe you packed all that fat on, Polly. Why, you must weigh a hundred and eighty pounds, am I right?"

She smirked, but it brought a severe stab of pain. She had passed that little benchmark long ago under the influence of comfort food, as she called it. The stress from her battles put a strain on her that only God and food could ease. She knew all too well that the pounds had accumulated because of her excessive eating binges.

"No one has called me Polly for years. Do I know you?"

The man sat close to her and pressed his face against hers. "You still have those beautiful eyes, Pol. And that cute little nose, the one you looked down when you looked at me, remember? As though a bad smell had crept up from the gutter and stuck in your nostrils." He was touching her cheek with his as he spoke. "I think you might be glad for old Scottie's attention now, eh, Pol, now that you're all fat and everything? Not many good-looking boys like me would take an interest in you now, not looking like that."

The pastor's head began to clear. She had to think more clearly, although the throbbing in her head made it difficult. She was composed under the circumstances. Although she'd never faced a situation like this, she'd always managed to stay calm amidst everyone else's panic.

"I'm sure you're not here to help me manage my weight, so can I assume we've had some kind of disagreement? Is this about women in the ministry? I'm afraid I'm at a disadvantage. You seem to know me; do I get to know who you are, Scottie, I think you said your name was? What's this about, Scottie?"

Scottie stepped back and placed the mop against the wall, much to her relief. "Let's play a little guessing game, Pol. You were ten years old, the proper little madam. Not my description, you understand; no, mine would be, stuck-up little bitch. But let's just call you a little madam for now, shall we? It's your tenth birthday, and you invite all the kids who are anybody to your little soiree. All in their finery: pretty cotton dresses, lots of ribbons and bows, a real tea party. Are you getting it, Pol?"

She tried to remember. She always had birthday parties, and her tenth would have been no different. Her guests were mostly church folks. A birthday party was the one indulgence her father allowed when growing up. He didn't believe in luxuries.

"I'm sorry, I don't remember that particular party. Should I?"

"Well, you probably don't, Pol. You probably never gave it a second thought." He began to pace up and down. "I must say it does surprise me to see you've let yourself go so much."

"You already made that sensitive point, thank you very much. Though I must say, I have been hearing a lot of that lately from people who call themselves Christians. Do you know, my own father, God bless him, he's no beanpole himself, told me I looked like a beached whale. Thank you very much, Daddy! There are too many skinny people in the world, if you ask me. Feed them burgers, I say. No, I shouldn't jest when there are so many starving people in the world. Look at you, you look in good shape; how do you manage to stay so slim?"

"Pol, I think you're missing the point here. You and me are going to dance with the devil before this day's out. You may think this is all a joke; some prank or other, but I don't think you've grasped the gravity of your predicament." He paused for several seconds, then frowned. "Did your daddy really call you a beached whale?"

She nodded sadly. "'A beluga whale', I think, were his exact words. 'You look like a beached Beluga Whale'. Bless him; he hasn't coped easily with my ambitions. He thinks that women belong in the kitchen and the marital bed. No sex unless it's for making babies, mind you, procreation, certainly not ordination." Scottie gazed at her, a bemused expression on his face.

"That ain't no right thing to say to a daughter, no matter how fat. It's one thing for a stranger to say it, but another for your pa to hang on you."

She started to shiver as the winter air filled the empty church, and her wet clothes sapped all warmth from her body. She ran the boiler only on Sundays, and the little oil she had left would not last her church through Christmas. He removed his coat and offered it to her.

"Here, put this over your shoulders, stop that shivering."

The gesture felt positive, she thought. There was hope if he began to feel compassion for her. She wrapped the coat around her, huddled forward on the wooden bench, and thanked him for his consideration.

"You said I treated you badly. Looked down my nose at you, I think you said. I'm sorry for that. Won't you tell me your name?"

"Guziac, Prescott Guziac. Scottie to my friends. You invited me to your tenth birthday party." He sneered. "I must have been some fool to think you actually liked me enough to invite me. If I'd knowed it was all for the amusement of your friends, your little charade, I..." He stopped, hung his head, and sighed dramatically. "Never figured anyone could be so cruel."

"I'm sorry, I still don't recall the day. I invited you to a birthday party?"

Scottie sprang forward and spoke abruptly. "Jeez! Does it mean so little to you? I even bought you a gift. Pa was drunk, so I took a few bucks from his wallet." He glanced at the cross on the wall. "It was my allowance anyway. She left it for me," he said, as if he were talking to God. "I went down to the corner store," he continued. "Bought the biggest box of chocolates I could find. I bought wrapping paper too; I took care wrapping it. Then I put on my best clean clothes, even shone my shoes, and brushed my hair. I knew Ray wasn't invited..." She stopped him mid-sentence.

"I'm sorry, Ray?"

"Ray Waring!" She drew a blank; the name meant nothing to her. "I knew Ray wasn't invited, so I figured you thought I was special."

His face changed, and she noted a flush of anger. She tried to calm him. "You were special; I didn't invite just anyone to my parties." She beamed a smile. "Now, what was so bad about my party that gave you such a bad time? Probably my father's awful party games?" she said, unable to conceal the patronizing tone in her voice.

Motionless, he stared at her for a long time, looking confused. "Do you really think it's all so funny?"

"I'm sorry, go on, please? I shouldn't have interrupted."

She was still smiling when he smashed his fist into her face. She slid to the floor. He dragged her, barely conscious, to the baptismal pool. She had no strength to resist. *Heavenly Father, give me the strength to put my own pain aside. To help this man find peace.* Scottie pushed her head beneath the water, his hands firmly on her neck, and held her there. After several long seconds, he allowed her to slump, choking, to the floor. Blood poured from her twisted nose and spread across the white tiled floor. He was calm and relaxed now. He said nothing while she struggled to recover.

The light streaming through the long windows had lost its warm glow, and the unheated building began to chill rapidly. The adrenaline that had briefly warmed her body now dissipated, causing her to tremble uncontrollably from the cold. Eventually, she spoke again.

"I did something terrible to you, didn't I?" Scottie looked down on her, sprawled pathetically across the floor.

"When I arrived at your house, you were all waiting. You up front, all your friends looking on from behind, grinning. I stood at the door, proudly held out my gift to you, imagining all the fancy food inside, all the games we'd play. I'll never forget the look on your face. You just stared at me and asked what I wanted. When I told you I was there for the party, your friends all laughed. You didn't. You just kept staring at me like I was a piece of dirt. You said, 'Why would I invite a filthy heathen like you to my birthday celebrations?' and slammed the door in my face. I could hear you all laughing as I stood there humiliated."

"My dear Lord, I don't remember. I really did that to you?"

"Worse still, I had to hear you snickering about it at school. Everyone knew; everyone laughed at me for being a fool."

She was shocked by the story of her callous prank, ashamed of her cruelty. "*What a horror I was!* I'm ashamed to say I'd genuinely forgotten, blocked it out of my mind, I suppose. I was such a brat back then. It left you terribly hurt; I can see that." *But thirty years later? This is still haunting him?* "You've every right to feel the way you do."

"Oh, now you know how I feel? And how do I feel, Pol?"

She thought about her answer carefully. She wanted to keep him calm and prevent him from harming her further. Not for her sake, she told herself, but for his, for his future. The more violent he became, the greater the consequences of her cruel actions, even all these years later. If he continued to hurt her, his punishment would increase for *her* crime.

"There can never be an excuse for what happened to you back then; there can be no excuse for me. I'm left stunned by your story, who I was and what I was. I won't try to come up with reasons or excuses for what I did to you. The truth is, I don't know the reasons. I don't know how I could have been so evil. I have changed, Prescott, believe me, I've changed. I hope you can forgive me."

They sat in silence. Her mind now fixed firmly on her childhood. How could she go from that person to who she was now? How could she preach compassion when she herself had been so compassionless? Recent events had brought her to her knees, forcing her to question who she was and where she was going. In her youth, she had been a reluctant Christian. How was it that she now lived the life she had loathed in her past?

And why had she chosen the path of her father when she had tried so hard to fight it, to be everything he despised? There were so many questions testing her faith. She studied Prescott Guziac as he sat with his head in his hands. Perhaps he was the answer to all her prayers. God's way of saying, you don't belong here, not in My house.

"My father was right," she said absently.

Scottie lifted his head. She was bleeding heavily from the nose; it was surely broken. "About being fat?" he asked seriously.

She began to laugh, but her swollen mouth stopped her in time. She didn't want him to think she was laughing at him. "Oh, he was right about that alright. Blubber belly!" she quipped, painfully. "No, I was thinking about his determined opposition to my becoming a minister of the church. He bitterly resisted my efforts. The trouble is, I'm as stubborn as he is. The more he tried to throw obstacles in my path, the more fight I discovered within myself. He campaigned against me at the highest levels. I think it was all about me, more than about women in general. I believe it was me he thought he must stop, no matter what it took." She reflected on the long battle.

"Why would he want to stop you? You're his flesh and blood; you would think he'd be proud to have you follow."

"You're the living proof I don't belong here, Prescott. My father knew how black my heart was. He knew there could be no place in God's house for one like me!"

Chapter 34

Barney couldn't hide the fear he felt when Cheryl failed to answer her phone. He tried every thirty seconds as they raced across town toward home. "The photo was taken outside the house," Barney said. "I recognize the tree in the yard."

"All cars are on route, Barney. They'll get to her first."

"I don't know what I'll do if anything happens to her, Ray. That woman is everything to me."

Ray didn't answer. His eyes stayed fixed on the blur of countryside racing past the window, his anger simmering over Scottie's reign of terror. It felt like a lifetime since that damn message.

Barney's squad car fishtailed on the icy road, slamming into a snowbank with a jolt. Ray lurched forward, his seatbelt snapping tight just before his face could meet the windshield. Without a word, Barney reversed back onto the road and kept driving. No apology. Not that Ray expected one. Desperation made men reckless.

When they turned onto the side road leading to the house, a dizzying array of flashing lights filled the night: county cruisers, sheriff's department vehicles, at least half a dozen in all. Ray's gut twisted as their car skidded to a stop.

Barney was already out before Ray could unbuckle.

Cheryl stood on the stoop, worry etched on her face as Barney rushed up to embrace her. Tears welled in his eyes. "I thought he would kill you."

"Barney Lawrence, you had everyone panicked about me. I told them I was fine. I met him this morning. I didn't know it was him, the one who'd done all those terrible things. I came out of the mall, and my car wouldn't start. He was standing nearby and offered to help."

"He probably messed with the motor."

Cheryl continued. "He had a fiddle under the hood and said he couldn't fix it. I wanted to call you, but then I couldn't find my phone. I looked everywhere."

"He must have taken that too."

"So, he called a tow truck on his phone and offered to drive me home. He was so nice, I accepted.

We got home, and we stood right over there, because he said he wanted a selfie. If I'd known... Anyway, no harm done. I thanked him, and he said it was his pleasure. He was really nice and even drove off singing. It made me laugh. Then, when all the boys showed up, well..."

Scottie's assurances hadn't convinced Ray that Jess was safe, not in the least. He wanted to see her, to reassure himself, and he figured she might be the key to solving Scottie's riddle. And if trouble came, he'd be close enough to act. He called ahead, telling her to think about Scottie's past enemies. He needed her help.

Inside Jess's home, Ray fought to keep his composure. Every instinct screamed at him to go to her, pull her close, like a dog straining at its leash. The urge to shove Al Fischer aside burned in his chest. Being this near and not touching her was agony.

Al stood behind her, arms locked around her waist. Fear made him look younger, softer than Ray remembered. He waited, tense, for Ray to speak.

"I need to ask Jess some questions," Ray said. "Scottie's targeting someone from our past. He means to hurt them."

Jess locked eyes with Ray, her face tightened, not with fear of Scottie, though that was there too. No, this was something deeper, private. A fear only the two of them shared. The dread of losing each other all over again.

"Is Jess in great danger?" The tremor in Al's voice revealed his apprehension.

"I don't think so."

"You don't think so? What kind of..."

"Please, Al, let Ray speak," Jess interrupted.

"Scottie's disturbed."

"To put it mildly," Al chipped in.

"Al!"

"He has this idea that everyone who has ever slighted him, bullied him, or wronged him in any way must pay for it now. He's taking his revenge for the past by playing a twisted blood sport: ticking off a list of victims, people he feels have hurt or betrayed him. In his sick mind, it's a game. He's giving clues for me to solve, like in a kids' board game. He's challenging me to stop him."

"But why?"

"I think he blames me more than anyone for the hurt in his life. He wants me to suffer along with his victims."

Jess sat on the couch and offered Ray a seat. Al quickly moved to sit next to her.

"I don't understand," said Jess. "You grew up together. He was always welcome in your house when he dared not go home; Aunt Eadie practically raised him. If it weren't for you, he wouldn't have had any friends."

"There's no time to figure him out, Jess. But we do have to figure out his intentions. I need your help finding his next victim before he strikes again. He's already killed Brad Cover. We believe he was the first victim. I know you remember him; he was a nightmare in both our schools. Everyone breathed a sigh of relief when he left to work for his dad, including teachers."

"You got on with him, though," said Jess. "Ray was on his hockey team, their star player." Al couldn't help a slight sneer. Jess continued: "Cover reveled in the reflected glory. You made him look good." Ray felt himself blush. "No wonder Scottie felt bad. While you were his new best buddy, Scottie was getting beaten up."

Ray moved on quickly. "Next, came his dad. Peter Guziac."

Jess jumped in. "My God, it's so obvious why he chose him. And you're in the picture there too, Ray." She directed her explanation to Al. "Scottie's dad used to ridicule him relentlessly. When he was sober, he would say Ray would make a better son, ask him to trade places, mocking Scottie. 'Why can't you be more like Ray? He's a good kid.' He used to tell Scottie he was useless. 'Better I have Ray for a kid.' He'd say things like that all the time."

"I don't think it was quite like that, Jess. Once or twice, maybe."

"Oh, come on, Ray. Poor Scottie got it from all angles while you were the bees' knees. Scottie's dad once said he'd never amount to half the man Ray would. Scottie always laughed it off, but I wonder now just how deeply it cut him."

"Then came Ms. Bird," Ray said, moving on with an irritated frown. "Scottie wasn't the only one singled out by her in class. We all felt her wrath; we all disliked her."

Jess raised her eyebrows. "You must be joking. She had a soft spot for you. She had more than a soft spot; I think she adored you."

What the hell, Jess? Ray was beginning to feel like she was deliberately trying to make him look like a toady. "She had it in for everyone, including me."

Jess turned again to Al to give the background review. "Ray was the teacher's pet, everyone said so, and it drove everyone wild, including me."

"I don't remember it at all like that," Ray said, indignant. *Can we just move on?*

"Do you remember when she caught Scottie stealing? He was about six or seven years old when he stole a chocolate bar that she'd confiscated from someone in class. He took it from her desk drawer and hid it down his pants. Bird noticed it was missing and made everyone empty their bags, pockets, and belongings while she searched the classroom. She got to Scottie and instantly knew it was him."

"Hell yes, how could anyone forget that day?"

Jess turned to Al. "She made him stand on his chair and demanded he turn it over. He pulled the chocolate bar from inside his pants while the class looked on in stunned silence. Poor Scottie was totally humiliated. Someone started to snicker, then someone else, until the entire class erupted. I'm ashamed to say that I did too. Bird allowed it to go on for ages before she called for silence. Then came the worst bit..." Jess stopped mid-sentence.

Ray let the silence linger for several long seconds before he solemnly concluded the story. "Scottie's still standing on the chair, and he starts to cry. Bird didn't relent; she just stood there, looking at him, the slightest smirk on her face." Ray hesitated. "A wet patch appeared on the front of his pants." Ray sighed. Jess stared at the floor. "It bloomed like a fucking flower, and still she let him stand there, several long seconds until she told him to get down and go to the restroom."

"It was horrible," Jess finished. "How could she have done that to a kid? He was just a little boy."

Disturbed by the recalled memory, everyone needed time to reflect. Jess made coffee while Ray and Al engaged in small talk. Eventually, they returned to the main issue.

"Gruder thinks Myra Burke was Scottie's intended victim. Scottie says she was never on his list, and I think he's telling the truth. So, if it's not Myra, who is it? This is what he gave me as a hint. What turned beauty into a beast?' And then he added, 'Some beasts, only an Angel could love'."

"The guy's crazy," said Al. "You should be out there finding him, instead of playing his stupid game. What if he comes after Jess?"

"I don't believe it's you either, Jess. Scottie swears he doesn't intend to harm you, and I believe him." Jess glanced at Al, the ghost of a smile on her lips.

"Oh, so everything's okay because Ray thinks Guziac can be believed. Please spare me the cavalier assumptions. My wife's life is at risk, and you're sitting here talking about board games!"

"Al, please. Where do we start, Ray?"

"Let's start with school. That seems to be where Scottie focused first."

A sharp rapping on the door silenced the conversation. Ray removed his handgun from its holster, a move that startled both Jess and Al. Ray pressed against the wall and slipped into the hallway. "Who is it?"

"It's Laura. Is that you, Ray?"

Ray opened the door, checked the street, and pulled Laura French inside. "What are you doing here, Laura?"

"Laura! Come in." Ray turned to see Jess, arms out in welcome, smiling like she was an old friend. "It's okay, Ray. Laura might be able to help too. The more heads, the better, right?"

"You two know each other?" Ray reluctantly stepped aside as Laura removed her coat, hugging Jess as she entered the room. Ray exchanged curious glances with the women, then picked up where he had left off. "So, if there are no more interruptions, who would you describe as beauty turned beast?"

"It seems to me you're looking for an ugly person." Everyone turned to Al, who shrugged as if to say he might as well participate since they were playing the game anyway. "Well, the first part says beauty turned beast, and your second clue says beauty only an angel could love. I mean, it's like, when you see an ugly kid, you say it's a face only a mother could love."

"Mother disappeared right after he was born. Stepmom is dead," said Jess.

"He could have tracked her down. The mother, not the stepmom," said Al.

Ray pointed a finger at Al. "It's a possibility, Al. But you said something about ugly kids. Who do you remember that was, well, ugly?"

Jess frowned. "I would never call someone ugly."

"Oh, come on, Jess, you said Mary White's baby looked like it had been hit with a bat," said Al.

"I did not! It was you who said that."

"Can we, please?" Ray interrupted. Al and Jess exchanged dirty looks. "It's a thought, but no one springs to mind. Maybe we're looking at it the wrong way, too literally. Perhaps by ugly he means their personality. After all, he's been going after people he believes are cruel. Could that be the ugliness he sees?"

"But why refer to beauty at all?"

Jess brought Laura up to speed on the clues. Laura added her thoughts. "How did Scottie get on with girls in general? Did he have girlfriends?"

Ray answered. "Scottie never dated, at least, not in the years I knew him. I remember Jane Rand saying he was good-looking once."

"Once. Most girls ran a mile when he came near," Jess added. "Scottie was an outcast in high school, a loner. Everyone thought he was weird by the time he reached his teens, especially the girls."

"Come on, Jess, you're not giving him much credit. He wasn't always that way."

"And you *are* giving him credit?" Jess looked irritated by Ray's defense. "He was weird, and you know it. You were the only one who'd give him the time of day. He was irritating and obnoxious. I always thought he liked it that way; he thrived on deliberately turning people off."

"Forget who he may have dated, did anyone reject him? Who did he like that gave him the cold shoulder?" Ray looked at Jess. "Apart from you." Jess poked out her tongue. Ray grinned.

Al fumed at the exchange. "Can we just focus?"

Ray felt duly censured. Al was right, this was no time for joking around. "Who would you consider beautiful out of all the girls we knew? Glamour girls, cheerleaders, that sort of thing; come on, Jess, think! Maybe he had an experience with one of them and it ended badly."

"I'm going back a bit now, before high school even. Remember the pretty kid? The one who always wore frilly dresses and ribbons? She was only at our school for a short while and left even before grade seven. Her family moved away, and I think they were very religious, Mormons maybe. I have a vague recollection that Scottie liked her."

"Well, the angel bit would tie in," said Laura.

Ray had a hazy image of the girl in question. He remembered the ribbons. "Do you have a name?"

"Pauline? Pauline perfect? No! Poly Perfect. That's what I remember calling her. And it's coming back to me now. I think her father was a Baptist Minister. She had a small group of friends who always stuck together, and they all tried to copy her. I always thought they looked like a box of Barbie Dolls."

Ray filled Barney in on Pauline Singleton. It didn't take him long to track down the surname, tracing Pauline (Perfect) Singleton to Colby, a town barely more than a crossroads, anchored by the First Baptist Church.

Barney called the Colby office just before six. Normally, the sleepy place was staffed from nine to five by a single state trooper and a clerk. But today, Trooper Burt Power had ducked out early for his wife's birthday, leaving the clerk to close up and forward calls to his cell.

In her hurry to escape, she forgot to switch the phones. The line rang and rang, unanswered.

"There's no answer, Ray. Colby's an hour and forty ride from here. That road is usually the last to be plowed, and it can become impassable at times in winter. We'll take my Sierra."

Barney didn't exaggerate. Even in the four-wheel-drive truck, he had to concentrate fully to stay on the road.

"Do you think she's the one?" Barney asked.

"Pauline Singleton? I don't know, Barney. She was ten or eleven years old when she moved away with her family. It's hard to imagine anyone could hold a grudge for so long, let alone one against a little kid he barely knew. It's a long shot. Hard to believe she's a minister. Once I realized who Jess was talking about, I'd have had her down for a modelling career. She was pretty and let everyone know it." He thought about Jess, with only Al to protect her. "We're probably chasing shadows here while he's back there making his move on Jess, another diversion. It makes me nervous."

"We've got a patrol posted outside Jess's place. If he makes a move for her, we'll get him."

Ray looked at his watch. "How far now?"

* * *

Scottie sat next to her. The austere little church made him feel small somehow. The cold wooden bench lacked any kind of comfort. He wondered why anyone would want to be part of its congregation. Pauline Singleton cradled her face in her hands. She was not what he'd expected, and it bothered him. It bothered him that she seemed nice. He felt a connection, and didn't know the reason. Her recounting the story of her father brought back his own memories.

"One time when I was a little kid, maybe five or six," he said, breaking the silence, "I climbed onto my pa's lap when he was sleeping. He was drunk; he was always fucking drunk. Anyway, he was making this sound through his nose. Like most kids that age, I found this sound real amusing. I watched his cheeks puff in and out and vibrate, like when you blow up a balloon halfway and let the air out again. He didn't often make me laugh; in fact, he never did it on purpose."

Pauline raised her head. "Dads are supposed to make you laugh."

Scottie continued. "There he was, this colossus of a man, making all these noises and funny faces. I thought he was pretending to sleep. I figured he was doing all those funny things just for me. Of course, he wasn't."

"Still, it's a nice memory."

"I squeezed his nose and giggled, like kids do when playing with their pa, and he woke up real suddenly, shocked. He backhanded me so hard I flew to Dallas and back before I hit the floor. That was the only time I ever sat on my pa's lap. He was a mean sonofabitch. Maybe our fathers are the same in a weird sort of way."

"I'm sorry. Sorry that you had to go through that." They sat again for a while without speaking. She put her hand on his, and he let her. "I'm sorry," she whispered again. "Your experience at the hands of your father was not an isolated incident, I'm guessing. Did you suffer a lot of abuse?"

Scottie knew what she was doing. She was trying to get inside his head, attempting to make him lower his guard. He shrugged off her hand. "Make no mistake, Pol, I give you no excuses just because you had a piece of shit pa like me. What you did to me, you must pay for. You have no one to blame but yourself."

He stood and took up the mop handle in both hands. He grasped it firmly like a baseball bat. She closed her eyes and began to pray aloud. "Do you want me to kill him after you're gone, Pol? Take him to the grave where you can meet him, cast scorn upon him, like you preachers say. Do you want me to teach him the error of his ways, Pol? Teach him respect for who you are? Say the word, Pol, say the word, and it's done. But don't take too long thinking about it. Your time is just about done."

Chapter 35

"Breakfast is served, gentlemen!"

Marlene Beachy's high-pitched voice didn't wake Ray; he'd hardly slept. He glanced at Barney and figured he had a similar story.

"I do hope you weren't too uncomfortable last night," Mrs. Beachy prattled on. "We had a spare room in the basement before Tom turned it into a garbage dump. And might I add, he never empties it! Thinks life's one big scavenger hunt, that man. He'll drag anything in from the street and haul it downstairs. 'Saving it for a rainy day,' he says. 'What rainy day?' I ask. 'You never know when you'll need this stuff,' he tells me. 'Never know when the Ruskies will come knocking. All this junk'll keep us alive.'

"I tell him, 'The Russians are our friends now. The Wall came down ages ago. Where've you been hiding?' And he says, 'Don't you know there's a war on?

Haven't you heard of Ukraine?' 'Keep a big gun under the bed, ' he says. 'And an eye on the horizon.' Well, I don't know about any war, do I?"

She barely paused for breath, rattling on for another five minutes about Tom and his Russian obsession. Barney shot Ray a look, and Ray knew exactly what he was thinking.

Stiff from his night on the sofa, Ray still looked better than Barney, who'd drawn the short straw and been stuck in a lumpy armchair. Dark circles hung under his eyes like bruises.

"Could've been worse," Ray said, trying to cheer him up. "We could've slept in the car."

As head of the church welfare committee, Mrs. Beachy was eager to help when Ray and Barney arrived late the night before, stranded with nowhere to stay. She gladly offered her family room and relished the chance to act in an official capacity.

She was waiting at the Baptist church door around eight last night, her face drawn with distress as they approached. Inside, their worst fears were confirmed: Scottie had beaten them there.

Ray's heart sank. The main sanctuary was a slaughterhouse. Bloody handprints streaked the stark white walls, and a thick, congealing pool darkened one of the pews. White tile floors were pooled with water and blood, smeared with drag marks. When Barney yanked back the baptismal curtain, the water glowed crimson.

No sign of the minister's body. That meant hope. Until they found her, nothing was certain.

Barney called Fowler and briefed the Chief. The roads were blocked until morning, but the chief promised to have the team there as soon as possible. There were no motels in town, and that was when Mrs. Beachy had come to the rescue.

After a large cooked breakfast, they thanked Mrs. Beachy and headed back to the clapboard church. She could hardly contain her disappointment when she realized they were going over without her. Crisp and clear, Ray thought it was one of those mornings when it felt good to be alive. It seemed ironic that he should feel this way while on his way to investigate a brutal homicide.

They had barely entered the church when a shout from behind signaled the arrival of State Trooper Burt Power. He sprinted from his cruiser and slipped on the ice-covered step, crashing to the ground at Barney's feet.

"Nice of you to join us, son," Barney said with an amused grin. He helped the embarrassed officer off the floor, and Ray noted the youthfulness in the man's face.

"Pastor Pauline has been murdered?" he asked breathlessly. "Mrs. Beachy said it was the serial killer; the Recess Reaper."

Ray exchanged bemused looks with Barney. "The Recess Reaper? Really?"

"Fox and Friends has it all over their bulletins. 'Schools out for winter', that was their opening line. Sir, shouldn't we cordon off the area, bring in the coroner?"

Ray smiled. He knew what it was like to be a rookie cop. This blush-cheeked kid was going to remember this day forever. "That's a good idea, Trooper. Why don't you start on that while we go have a look inside?"

Barney added, "A hot mug of coffee would be good, son. Mine's white with four sugars; Special Agent Waring takes it black with none." The trooper nodded enthusiastically and hurried off to find coffee.

"Stop with the Special Agent shit, Barney. You'll have me arrested for impersonating a federal officer."

"Sorry, slips out."

Mrs. Beachy managed the cross-town pursuit in less time than it took her to pack the breakfast dishes into the dishwasher. She entered the church with one hand on each of the double doors and appeared silhouetted against the morning light. The two men turned to see the steam rising from her head in the sunlight. The woolen poncho she wore made her look like a giant bat just raised from hell. She could hardly catch her breath.

"Mrs. Beachy, this is a crime scene, ma'am. I'm sorry, but you'll have to remain outside." She lowered her hands, let the doors swing closed behind her, and staggered forward to the nearest pew.

"Oh, I think we're almost family now, Barney," she said, breathlessly. "Just let me rest here a minute while I get some air back in my lungs. Don't mind me."

"Barney." Ray knelt beside the baptizing pool. Barney came to join him.

"What've we got?" Barney knelt alongside. "This is the first time I ever knelt in church, Ray. I'm a full-blooded heathen like my father and his father before him. What is that, buddy?"

Ray took a pen from his pocket and probed the narrow gap between the pool and the wall. He fished out a small white object. Barney put on a plastic glove and lifted the object so both men could see. "A front tooth," said Ray.

Barney placed it in a zip lock. "Oh boy," he said sadly. "I think our lady pastor may be missing something."

"I think her tooth may be the least of her worries, Barney."

"There's a lot of blood. It doesn't look good, Ray."

They both stood up and found Mrs. Beachy standing directly behind them.

"Oh, poor woman. You're right, it doesn't look good, Barney." Mrs. Beachy shook her head. "But your CSI boys might find something. They can work miracles, you know! Why, I saw this episode where they had nothing but a scrap of paper, smaller than a pinhead, and they traced it to a passport, then matched it to the killer. DNA, confessions... marvelous what science can do." Her voice trailed off as if replaying the scene in her mind.

Barney sighed. "Mrs. Beachy, you need to wait outside until forensics arrives." He moved to guide her out just as Trooper Power entered, balancing two coffees on a plastic tray.

"Mrs. Beachy!" Power grinned. "Didn't realize you were here; I'd have grabbed you a cup."

"Oh, I'll survive, Burt," she said, beaming. She plucked invisible lint from his jacket and straightened his collar. "We were just discussing the evidence. Those CSI fellows can do anything, though you already know that, don't you, Ray?"

She barely paused for breath. "I found all this blood last night, lights on, water everywhere. At first, I thought Bill had hurt himself fixing something, but when I called, he was fine. Then these two showed up."

She eyed Ray. "Though you're shorter than on TV. And older."

Barney exchanged a glance with Ray. Interrupting was impossible; her words tumbled out like a burst dam.

"Pauline always courted trouble," she continued. "Even with her father, old-school fire and brimstone. I heard him once: *The Lord will smite thee down!*" She shuddered.

Ray seized his chance. "Trooper, take Mrs. Beachy to your cruiser and get her statement."

She latched onto Power's arm, chattering as they left.

Barney watched them go, then muttered, "Guess Daddy's prayers got answered. Handy having God on speed dial when you want someone smote."

❄

Chapter 36

The Fowler Sound Brass Band played beneath the town's towering Christmas spruce, cycling through crowd favorites to the delight of gathered families. Al Fischer had closed his pharmacy for a few hours to join Jess and their children at the annual carol sing. It seemed somehow important to be with them. Cradling Brighton in his arms, he watched his son trying to sing along, his face a beaming smile. Even Abbie had taken her eyes off her phone to join in the singing.

Jess stood beside them, her gaze distant. She didn't notice Al studying her face—not when the music played, not when she gave him an automatic goodbye kiss. "Don't work too late," she murmured, already turning away with the children. Al watched their retreating figures disappear into the festive crowd.

"Hey!" he called out after her, and ran to catch up. "Let's take the kids to the park for some chocolate. Mary's got the store."

The park kiosk was busy as always. A cozy glow lit the interior. A Christmas tree twinkled, and an overhead speaker played more holiday favorites. Jess settled the kids with hot chocolate and muffins. She and Al had coffee.

"I'm losing you, aren't I?"

The question hit her like a slap. Jess opened her mouth, then closed it. A forced laugh escaped her lips, but her eyes flickered with something akin to panic. "No! God, Al... where is this coming from?"

"Please, Jess, don't take me for a fool."

He sounded calm, reconciled, but she went on the defensive. "Al, please, this is not the time..."

"You want to leave me and go to him, don't you? You want to be with him right now, right this minute." Jess didn't answer; she couldn't. He spoke the truth. "I guess I always knew you were never really mine. I was a poor second choice from the start."

"Don't say that."

"It's true. I convinced myself that he was gone from your life, gone for good. I knew you didn't love me, but I believed you could learn to love me eventually."

She avoided eye contact, speaking in a low whisper, her voice trembling with emotion. "You don't understand; of course I love you. You've given me so much, so much I thought impossible after..." She paused, and he finished her sentence for her.

"After Ray left you, you thought it was impossible after Ray left you." Al let the words hang between them. "Now he's back, and I can't compete. I'm just Al Fischer from the pharmacy, no hero. I don't know how to fix this, Jess. I'm watching our family fall apart, and I can't..." His voice cracked.

Tears streaked Jess's cheeks as she seized his hand. "You listen to me." Her thumb brushed his knuckles. "You gave me hope when I had none. A family when I was alone. You..." A wet laugh escaped her as Brighton emerged from his hot chocolate with a chocolate mustache. She wiped it away with her napkin.

"But it's not enough." Al's jaw tightened. "I knew when you invited him to supper. I'm not blind, Jess. I know what I am, the guy people pity. When I asked you out, I never dreamed... But then I saw how broken you were, and I just wanted to..." He swallowed hard. "This family, you three, you're my whole life."

His raw vulnerability made her chest ache. She pressed her fingers to his lips before he could beg.

"Someone told me that when they looked back on the time of their youth, they saw they were a very different person, and they now missed that person terribly. They said they disliked the person they'd become and craved who they once were. Yes, I do love him." She inhaled shakily. "But Al Fischer, look at me. Look at them." She guided his gaze to their children: Abbie absorbed in her phone, Brighton demolishing his muffin. "I don't miss the woman I was before you, and I don't crave the past. I'd miss the woman you helped me become." She brought his hand to her lips. "I don't want you to compete for me, Al; I'm already yours." Al crumpled against her, sobbing into her sweater. A few diners glanced over.

She'd said what she must, and she meant every word, even as they carved hollows in her chest, ripping her heart apart.

"Why's Daddy crying, Mommy?" Brighton asked, chocolate smeared across his chin.

Jess smoothed Al's hair. "Happy tears, baby. Just happy tears."

❋

Chapter 37

Six days. No Pauline. No Scottie. Ray slumped into the watchhouse; the investigation's stagnation preyed on his mind. Scottie was out there, planning, waiting. The media circus had packed up. "*Recess Reaper*" never caught on (too clever by half). Even the Post's "*Guziac's Gambit*" chess analogy had been buried, literally, by California's earthquake. Now? Just silence.

A team of twenty-five Bureau staff, including sixteen field agents, had filled the ranks and made Fowler Sound Police Headquarters their home. Arriving in the aftermath of the Ramos shootout, they remained to collaborate with county officers on a task force, code-named Northern Frontier. But all that was about to change.

"They're pulling out, Ray." Chief Sullivan was the one to break the news. "Gruder said they were all wrapped up with their Brothers for America investigation, and he said his help with Guziac was always going to be temporary. He's passing it on to the field office in Rapids."

"Can't wait until after the holidays?"

"Seems not. He said that now we've identified Guziac as the lone killer, it's more of a manhunt than an investigation. He says we should bring in State Police, they have the resources, and we no longer need such a large contingent of men. His resources are stretched, he says, what with the holidays coming up and ongoing investigations elsewhere."

Ray sighed. "Wants to get home for Christmas more like."

"We get to keep two field agents and a techie to support the task force until Grand Rapids gets involved, but it's all up to us for now to find Guziac and put a stop to these murders; that's it. We're about to have a briefing; you'll sit in?"

Ray closed his eyes. His head throbbed, and he could sense another seizure approaching. "Maybe I'm more of a hindrance than a help, Chief. It's not my place to be part of this investigation."

"I know you're not with the feds anymore, Ray. But make no mistake, you are part of this investigation whether you like it or not. In fact, you're smack dab in the middle of it. Let's not forget, it's you he's baiting every time he kills." Sullivan paused. He looked bereft of answers. "Look, to be honest, we need you, Ray. We need your help. I know you're…"

"Dying?"

"I know you're unwell. But help us out here."

Ray felt weary. But Sullivan was right; he was in the middle of all this. And it was becoming increasingly clear that he was the root cause. He nodded, and Sullivan took that as a yes. He was still part of the team. When they walked into the briefing, Gruder pulled Ray aside.

"I guess you've heard. I'll be heading out right after the meeting. The boys will pack up and be gone by this afternoon. I just wanted to say that I'm sorry for your, you know, condition."

Ray couldn't help but sneer. "I know there's no love lost between us, but don't pull the guys out because of me."

Gruder studied Ray's face before speaking. "You think that's why I'm pulling the plug? You conceited son of a bitch! I've never liked you, Waring. You're a show-boater. You don't follow the rules. You could've gotten agents killed at that school. Worse still, you could have gotten all those kids killed. Now this. You're in the middle again, grandstanding. Well fuck you, Waring. Fuck you. And good luck with your friend

Guziac. We'll be here mopping up long after you're gone."

Ray stood back while Sullivan and Barney summarized the current progress of the task force. Gruder kept to himself, casting Ray irritated glances now and then, until he'd finally had enough and stormed out of the room. Barney was becoming more confident, summarizing the case so far and embracing his lead role. The priority now was to find Pauline Singleton, dead or alive. The fact they hadn't heard from Scottie was both disconcerting and a relief. Ray had the naive hope that he'd finished his rampage.

The investigating team had swept the church and the surrounding area, discovering a blood trail that led to tire tracks in the snow. DNA tests were being conducted on the samples, along with the tooth, but there was little doubt that both belonged to Pauline Singleton. The tracks suggested Guziac had loaded her body into the bed of his Ram truck before driving away. His reason for removing the body remained unclear, but its absence raised another possibility: that she might have survived the attack.

Carson listened in on a Zoom call from his office for the briefing. He reported on the findings in Traverse City, and there was no doubt that Peter Guziac was murdered by his son. The evidence against Scottie was overwhelming. Dale Seymore noted that there were no new updates on the Brad Cover killing; he was one of the special agents now assigned to the task force.

Barney provided an update on the search at Scottie's home. "Oh, and the bank has foreclosed," he added. "They now own his house, cars, everything. We ran Andre Fishburn down: he's the bank manager who declined Guziac's loan extensions. We figured he was an obvious target. He quit the bank and moved to Florida when news first broke of Guziac's motives. Said he wasn't sticking around to be picked off like the others."

"What about his theatre?" asked Carson.

"That went to the receivers eighteen months ago. A bank loan default," said Barney. "He has no access to it now."

The briefing had not long ended when Ray's cell buzzed. The call from Scottie was somewhat inevitable. An automatic trace started the moment Ray received the incoming call.

"Did you think I'd gone away for the holidays?"

Ray inhaled sharply. "Where are you, Scottie?" A chill shot through him as a thought flashed in his mind. Scottie was in Florida, chasing Fishburn.

"Got you wondering, eh, buddy?"

"Where's Pauline Singleton?"

"Good question, Ray. Now, where would Scottie hide a big bundle of lard like that?" Ray heard that irritating snort of a laugh and almost ended the call. "You were quicker than I thought, Ray; almost had me if you'd been an hour earlier. Weren't far behind me. But let's not dwell on that; it's time to move on. So here it is, one last clue before we dance the last dance."

"Where is she, Scottie? Where's the pastor?"

"Oh, you'll find her right enough. And just you wait 'til you see her. You won't believe it, Ray. But stop interrupting me; I'm losing my train of thought. Oh, and I know you're stalling for time; got a trace on. So, listen carefully because I won't say it again. You're going to love it, Ray. I spent hours on this. It's going to be a red-letter day for justice. You ready?"

"This is bullshit, Scottie."

"I'll take that as a yes." Snort. "Here we go. Find him where the eagle cries, but I see clear through all his lies, better be quick, Ray, 'cause next, he dies. Like it? It rhymes."

"You're sick, Scottie. You need help."

"Yeah, you said that, Ray. But here's the thing, you're sicker than me. Get moving, buddy. I'm already on my way."

Scottie ended the call as Barney approached. "Zach's working on it."

"I think we're losing the battle, Barney. Scottie won't stop until we stop him, and we're no nearer catching him."

Bureau technician Zach Chase shook his head. "Ten more seconds, and I'd have had him pinpointed exactly. I can narrow it down to St. Ignace; that's all I got. The phone went dead after the call. Most probably took the battery out."

It was no more than Ray expected. "What's he doing in St Ignace?"

The team gathered, and Ray repeated Scottie's cryptic clues. Barney wrote them on the whiteboard.

Find him where the eagle cries, but I see clear through all his lies; better be quick, Ray, 'cause next, he dies.

"Who does he think he is, the Zodiac Killer?"

"Who's the Zodiac Killer?" asked Zach.

"Serial killer from the sixties. Before you were born, Zach. He left notes, clues for the FBI investigators. Never caught. It was a big embarrassment for the bureau," said Barney.

"He mailed letters to the newspapers and demanded they print them," Ray added. "Let's concentrate on Scottie. The first thing he said was that it's going to be a red-letter day for justice."

Bill Getty interrupted. "Hey Barney. My sister's car broke down and the kids are being sent home from school; there's a major storm on the way. I hate to do this to you, but if I don't pick them up, no one will. I'll be gone an hour, tops." Barney nodded absently.

*   *   *

CBM BREAKING NOW—A MAJOR WINTER STORM IS BEARING DOWN ON THE UPPER GREAT LAKES AND MICHIGAN, PROMPTING OFFICIALS TO ISSUE A WINTER STORM WARNING.

The National Weather Service warns that this system could bring blizzard-like conditions to Northern Wisconsin, Upper Michigan, and Northern Lower Michigan, starting tonight and lasting through Tuesday.

Here's what you need to know: Heavy snow is expected, with totals ranging from 8 to 14 inches and localized amounts exceeding two feet in lake-effect zones. Dangerous winds are also forecast, with gusts reaching up to 50 mph, whipping snow into near-zero visibility and making travel extremely hazardous. Officials are urging residents to stay home if possible. Roads may become impassable, and emergency crews warn that response times could be delayed.

Stay with us throughout the night for live team coverage, featuring updates from Jim Clark in the Weather Center and reporters monitoring road conditions.

*   *   *

Ray stared at his trembling hands, slick with sweat. The room tilted, a dizzying carousel, his mind screaming as the walls spun. He grabbed for balance but could only brace for impact.

Minutes later, Barney loomed over him, that same worn look of pity on his face. It was becoming all too familiar for Ray. He hated it.

"Do you want to talk about it?" Barney said, passing Ray a glass of water. "It's none of my business, but maybe you need a second opinion. Just because one doctor thinks it's bad, doesn't mean…"

Ray interrupted. "Barney, you're a nice guy, but I prefer your wisecracks to your medical advice. Let me put you out of your misery; I'm going through with the surgery. The president's own surgeon is overseeing it, and he tells me they're confident of success." He lied about the confident bit. Wienberger pulled no punches when he spelled out the risks. But Ray was grateful to see the relief on Barney's face.

"That's great news, Ray. I'm happy for you." He slapped Ray on the back, a big, cheesy grin splitting his face. Then he adopted a more serious tone. "There're a lot of folks wondering if you're a danger to the team in your condition. If it comes to action, they say you could be a liability; you could get someone a bullet."

Ray had already considered that. He was fully aware of his condition, as Barney had stated. The last thing he wanted was to jeopardize the safety of those around him if he had a seizure at the wrong time.

"It's your call, Barney. You and Sullivan need to make that call. But I promise you, I'll step out of the way if it gets to be too much."

"Okay. Like the chief said, we need you. If you think you're…"

Ray's phone buzzed. It was Scottie again. "Hey, Ray, did you miss me?"

"Is St. Ignace nice at this time of year, Scottie?" Ray wanted Scottie to look over his shoulder.

"Oh, you're quick, Ray. I thought it was me that was too fast. I'll make a mental note; Ray is not as stupid as I thought." Scottie chuckled. "Listen, Ray, I just wanted to add some words of cheer to my buddy before I get out of range. Give some encouragement and all that shit. See, there ain't no cell coverage from now on."

"Heading for the North Pole? Must be nice to take a day off to meet Santa."

"No days off for me, Ray. I got too many things on my list. Checking it once, checking it twice. That reminds me, how's your list going?"

"Where's Pauline?"

"Move on, Ray, you ain't got time to dwell on the past, and I got business to attend to." There was a pause.

Then Scottie started to sing, his voice howling with a strong country and western twang.

> "Don't leave me, cos you'll make me cry
> You're my best friend, so tell me why?
> To let you go, I'd rather die
> Come home and let me love you.

"Remember, buddy, it ain't over 'til the fat lady squeals. Catch you later, Ray." The phone went dead.

"Tom Croon," said Barney.

"What?"

"Tom Croon and the Boxcar Band."

"The song?"

"Cheryl's a big fan. I've heard that song a thousand times. We went to see them in Detroit. Do you think it's another of his stupid clues?"

"I don't know, but we need to find out."

Ray watched the feds scramble, hauling gear, stacking boxes, loading vehicles, all racing the approaching storm. He stood in the doorway as Gruder's car rolled past. Their eyes locked just long enough for Gruder's contempt to cut through the snowfall already whipping in from the north. The storm front would hit soon. Ray turned to go inside, then froze. Someone sat watching him from a truck across the street.

Walt? Ray jogged over, curious, skipping ruts on the slushy road. "Jeez, Walt, please, you've got to stop following me."

"Free country, last I heard."

"You want to talk, let's talk; but you've got to stay away. Things could get rough around here."

"I already told you; the time for talk is over." Walt put the truck into gear and drove away, leaving Ray frustrated in his wake.

Back inside, Barney was prepping what was left of his team when a fed fumbled a whiteboard; it hit the floor with a crash.

"Jesus Christ!" Barney's roar cut through the chaos. "Hurry up and get the hell out of here. Let us work for God's sake!"

The room froze. Barney's patience was wearing thin. His glare locked onto a wide-eyed techie lingering in the doorway. "What?" Barney snarled. The kid vanished. "Happy freaking holidays," he muttered to the empty space.

The last fed closed the door behind him. "Alone at last," scoffed Zach.

"Good riddance, I say," mumbled Getty, who'd just arrived back after his school run.

Ray tapped Barney's shoulder. "Stress getting to you, Barney?"

Everyone took a break to calm their nerves, though an edge still lingered in the air when they returned. There wasn't a man in the team who wasn't committed to bringing Scottie down. Over the next hour, they dissected Scottie's cryptic clues. The eagle symbol screamed military or government, and Scottie's service record backed that up as a possible point of conflict. Ray remembered Scottie's old story about outmaneuvering a superior officer, inheriting his stepmother's fortune as the ultimate revenge. No real grudge remained there, just Scottie's trademark gamesmanship. Nevertheless, Karl Morris volunteered to hunt down the officer in question.

That left government. "Doesn't exactly narrow it down," Barney said. "What about courts, judges? He has a record."

"Let's get to the files," said Getty. "Oh, and that babe is still out there looking for you, Ray."

Laura French stood at the front desk. Ray thought she looked more attractive each time he saw her, and he struggled to reconcile this reaction with his feelings for Jess.

"Hi, Laura. How long have you been waiting?"

"Not long. It's good to see you, Ray. I'm sorry about Pauline Singleton, sorry you were too late." Her sympathy only served to feed his frustration, the feeling of helplessness, and anger at his impotence. Rage that Scottie could take an innocent life and think it's a joke. "Are you any closer to catching him?"

Ray shook his head. "We're still hopeful Pauline is alive. But Scottie's already moved on to his next target. I can't give you more than that."

"I wasn't asking as a journalist, and I'm not still here in Fowler Sound for the story, Ray. Can we talk?"

They found a quiet spot, and Laura bared her heart. She'd fallen in love with him. Her candor shocked Ray.

"I don't know what to say."

"At least tell me I'm not crazy, that you feel something too." Her flushed cheeks and forlorn eyes pleaded louder than her words. This... this he hadn't anticipated.

"Laura, this is not a great time..."

"Right," she said, resignation in her voice.

"No. I mean, this is *really* not a good time. What with Scottie and..."

"People like me don't usually find anything worth fighting for," she interrupted. She paused and looked away, a tear in her eye.

Ray reached out and took her hand. "I do have feelings for you; I'm just kind of confused about what they are. I had no idea you felt anything for me."

"You were not in my plans, Ray, not at all in my plans. But here I am, putting you on the spot like a schoolgirl with a crush, an irrational, dim-witted schoolgirl."

"You do know my life's a little complicated?"

Laura laughed through her tears. "Really? I thought you were just bored."

The truth was, Jess or no Jess, Ray found himself drawn to Laura; each encounter pulling him deeper. That spark between them, the one he'd tried so hard to ignore, had first appeared in Grand Rapids, before his return home. How could he have known then that Jess would still figure in his future? Part of him wondered if this interest in Laura was just armor against the coming storm, against watching Jess fall back into a life with Al.

"Let's see how this plays out," he said, as much to himself as to Laura.

Barney poked his head through the door. "Update, Ray. Guziac's CO when he left the Army was Captain Harmon. He's currently deployed overseas in Germany. Looks like a dead end. But we got a break on Guziac's movements; we have him on camera, crossing the Big Mack two days ago. Ram truck with cloned plates."

"Big Mack?" Laura interrupted.

"The Mackinac Bridge. Wherever he's heading, he's got a hell of a head start on us, Ray."

Ray turned to Laura, looking apologetic. "Sorry. We're going to have to take this up later. Are you staying here tonight?"

"Do you want me to?"

Barney made himself scarce.

"I want you to. But I have to..."

"I know. Go be the hero. I'll be around when you're ready. Is there somewhere I can sit to write some emails?"

❄   ❄   ❄

CBM BREAKING NEWS UPDATE: HISTORIC BLIZZARD TO HIT MICHIGAN

An urgent winter storm warning is issued for Michigan and the upper Great Lakes as a once-in-a-century blizzard threatens the state. A major arctic front is set to collide with intense lake-effect snow bands. Fueled by seventy-mile-an-hour wind gusts, we can expect whiteout conditions, near-zero visibility, and life-threatening travel. Power outages are likely.

Stay prepared, stay alive.

Chapter 38

An hour later, Ray hung up with Detective Carson in Traverse City. "Scottie was booked on a misdemeanor; that's why his prints were in the system when they found them all over Guziac's apartment." He briefed Barney on the conversation. Scottie had been charged with using a wire service to harass a government employee.

Barney called the Michigan State Police in Lansing while Ray and Zach scoured online records for the case.

"Threatening letters to the governor's office," Barney announced, buzzing from his call. Ray looked up from a monitor. "Guziac tried getting a state grant for his crumbling theater. He won approval, but the new administration axed it after the election."

Ray tapped the keys on his computer. "Got it. Says he sent three hundred letters to officials before fixating on the governor, another hundred twenty emails and tweets, some just one or two words. But the frequency escalated, and they saw it as a threat. That's when they arrested him."

"That's got to be the connection," Zach said.

Getty frowned. "You all know the governor's a potential presidential candidate? Guziac wouldn't be that deranged, would he?"

"Makes sense, eagle and all," said Barney.

The team split tasks, zeroing in on Scottie's possible targets. The governor, the arresting officers, the prosecutor, Judge. If it was the governor, they'd need capital coordination and caution.

"Still doesn't explain why Scottie's up north," Ray muttered.

"Sir?" a tech interrupted. "Lansing's on the line; Governor Shepherd's security detail. They're... not cooperative."

Barney took the call in Sullivan's office. Through the glass partition, Ray watched him slam a fist on the desk, toppling a paper cup. Sullivan listened to the call, then waved Ray inside.

"This looks bad, Ray. According to his detail, the governor's out of town on a personal trip. He's hunting deer, would you believe?" said Barney.

"Isn't deer season over?"

"Not if you use a bow and arrow. Apparently, the governor's a fine archer," Barney added.

"This is at the summer residence on Mackinac?"

"No, Ray, that's all closed up for the winter. He's got a lodge north of the Big Mack. It's a secluded spot on an isolated lake."

"Shit."

"Shit is right, buddy," Sullivan said. "This is confirmation. He's after the governor."

Dale Seymore burst into the room. "Just got off the sat phone with Bruce Quail after his office in Lansing relayed our concerns. Quail is the security chief at the lodge. No cell coverage apparently. Says they're locked down tight: five people total. Quail, another private security guy, the governor, and two armed guests. Claims they're prepped if Guziac shows. I tried to emphasize the threat, but he seemed unfazed. But here's the kicker: he says the roads are already impassable. No one's getting through."

Sullivan said, "Well, that's something, I suppose."

Seymore continued. "Quail's a smug son of a bitch, informed me that the governor receives at least one death threat a month from every type of lunatic known to man. The fact that this particular lunatic has already killed at least three people didn't seem to worry him. He asked if Guziac had made a direct threat against the governor's life, and I had to tell him, no, not in so many words."

"No secret service detail?" Barney asked.

"He's a candidate, not a president," Ray said. "The governor relies on private security and state police."

"Quail says he won't have more than two PSD's when he's hunting."

Barney shrugged his shoulders. "So, what now?"

"I-seventy-five is closed," Zach called out. "The bridge is closed because of falling ice, and there's a multi-vehicle blocking all lanes further north. Even emergency vehicles can't get through."

"He could already be at the lake," Ray said. "He had a head start. We have to let Quail know; Scottie is ex-Special Forces, a winter sportsman, a shooter, and a skier. He can't be taken lightly."

"Quail's adamant. He has the threat in hand."

*   *   *

Quail hung up the phone and chuckled. He was approaching his fourth year in the governor's service, and he had yet to encounter a credible threat over the phone. The world was full of nutcases, and ninety-nine percent were a waste of his time. Still, he would remain vigilant. The lodge was so isolated that he felt the threat was slim due to the weather. This Guziac guy was more likely to freeze to death trying to reach them.

❄   ❄   ❄

Ray stood outside with Barney, pulling on his gloves. They had decided there was little they could do while the storm threatened. Sullivan had told them to seize the opportunity, go home, and rest. "I think we could have made it in the Sierra if the bridge had been open," said Barney.

"God, I wish, Barney. I feel helpless."

"What if there was another way of getting there?" Laura French came up behind them.

"You're still here," said Ray.

"What if I could get you there?"

Barney smirked. "What are you going to do, fly us there?"

Laura smiled. "Exactly."

Ray tilted his face to the heavens as the first fat snowflakes spiraled down, silent as falling feathers, relentless as time itself. This was how the heavy snowfall usually began, slow and steady. The wind had calmed momentarily, but it would return. The blizzard was approaching and was nearly upon them.

"Look at the sky, Laura. Scottie's probably holed up somewhere trying to stay alive."

"You don't believe that."

"The storm will keep him locked in, and by the time it's blown over, the governor will be pulled out of there faster than a jackrabbit. State cops will pour in a small army just as soon as the weather clears, believe me. I'm going home, Laura; I'm tired and unwell. I need a rest."

"We can still get to him," she said confidently.

"Go home, Laura. I'll call you." He stepped off into the snow and pulled the hood around his head.

"I meant what I said; we can get up there. I have a helicopter waiting in Pellston." She waited for him to stop, but he didn't. "I'm going anyway, Ray."

Ray waved his hand without turning. "Hope you get a good story," he said insincerely.

Barney watched her run after him, undeterred.

"That's just it, it's your story, Ray; it's up to you how you finish it." He stopped and turned.

"It's a hundred and fifty miles, maybe two to the lake, and helicopters don't fly in snowstorms, Laura." She glimpsed a glimmer of hope, a possibility in his voice.

"This one will!"

Chapter 39

Norm Medway was a self-proclaimed hotshot. A chopper pilot for indie press, stunt flier for films, and at forty-five, a legend. The best and worst in the sky, depending on who you asked. He flew like a god, gambled like a fool, and drank like he was racing death. With his wild Christopher Lloyd, *Back to the Future,* looks and a barstool always waiting, he didn't just chase thrills, he outran them.

"I can't!"

"What do you mean you can't? You're the *man,* the *king,*" Laura pleaded.

Ray sneered; they were just wasting their time.

Laura noticed Ray's skepticism. It made her angry. She turned back to Norm, who was about to head to the restaurant. "Are you getting chicken in your old age? I thought this was your bag."

She was baiting him.

"It's got nothing to do with chicken or chumps; I can't fly in the storm because the machine can't fly in snow like that. Besides, they wouldn't let me take off if I wanted to. Wait 'til the storm passes, and I'll take you wherever you want. Now I'm going to get myself a steak and some beer and watch some hockey."

Laura's frustration was evident, yet she remained unyielding.

"The forecast says the main storm won't hit for at least another hour. Look at the snow, Norm; surely a few flakes can't stop a man like you."

He said nothing but glanced at Ray for support. Ray shrugged.

"The lodge is a hundred miles, not even that," she said. She was determined to break him. "You flew rescue up in Denali in worse storms. We can be there before the weather closes in. Think of it, Norm, what a story this will make, front page stuff, and you'll be right there in all your glory: Flying Ace Foils Governor's Assassination Against All Odds!"

Ray shook his head. Still, she was a trier; he had to give her that.

"Come on, Norm, we can turn back if it gets too bad," she persisted.

Norm shook his head doubtfully, but she knew exactly which buttons to push.

*　　*　　*

The Detroit Free Press | Updated 3:30 PM EST

BREAKING NEWS – WINTER STORM "ATLAS" SET TO HAMMER MICHIGAN, UPPER GREAT LAKES IN HISTORIC BLIZZARD

Dubbed "Atlas" by meteorologists, a once-in-100-years winter storm, has already totally paralyzed Manitoba and large parts of Ontario as it heads for Michigan and the Upper Great Lakes with near-zero visibility, 60 mph winds, and snowfall rates of 3 inches per hour. The National Weather Service warns this could surpass the Great Blizzard of 1978 in severity, with some areas projected to hit 40-plus inches by storm's end.

Travel has been banned in 12 counties; I-75, I-94, and US-23 have been shut down statewide.

Conditions over the border are unprecedented, with thunder snow reported in Winnipeg.

QUOTE OF THE HOUR:

"This isn't just a snowstorm, it's a blitzkrieg." - NWS Meteorologist Sarah Kowalski

*　　*　　*

In twenty minutes, the rotor blades were turning on the R44 Raven. Barney pleaded for sanity, shouting above the swirling blades that whipped the snow into a driving vortex. Ray ran out after Laura to the waiting chopper. Laura took a back seat; Ray sat beside the pilot. Norm conducted preflight checks as Barney came up alongside, his hand on his head as though the wind would blow his hair off.

"Hell, move over," he yelled above the chopper noise. "I'm coming too." He squeezed in beside Laura, and the bird lurched into the air.

"Just tie that rope around the door handle, Barney. I don't want it flying open."

Barney looked aghast. "You're shitting me?"

"I've been meaning to fix it for some time."

Barney wrapped the thin hemp rope around the handle and secured it to a seat strut. He looked nauseous as the chopper swung left, shaking like a jackhammer. "This is insane!"

Norm set the GPS and quickly ascended to a higher altitude. A power line would be hidden in the driving snow, and they would encounter it before realizing anything was amiss.

"At least there won't be any other air traffic to worry about," Ray Hollered.

"Zebra 692, this is Air Traffic Control. Do you copy? Over." The voice came through the radio just as expected.

"Air Traffic Control, this is Zebra 692, over."

"Zebra 692, please return to Pellston. You haven't registered a flight plan, and we have a weather warning in effect, over." Norm sighed.

"Negative, Air Control, we have a medical emergency, and there was no time to file a flight plan, over." There was silence for a long moment before Air Traffic Control responded.

"State nature of emergency and your intended destination, Zebra 692, over." Norm looked to the group for help. Ray took the microphone.

"Air Traffic Control, this is Federal Agent Raymond Waring. We have a medical emergency at the governor's winter lodge. Estimated flight time..." He paused, looking to Norm for an estimate. "Maybe two hours if the weather permits, over." There was another long silence.

"Zebra 692, this is Air Traffic Control. Agent Waring, your flight has been given emergency clearance. Please proceed with extreme caution; conditions are deteriorating rapidly; this looks like a big one. Godspeed to you all, over and out." Norm sighed with relief, but Ray knew they would be back. Someone was checking his story at that very moment.

*　　*　　*

Marcus Shepherd stretched his boots toward the hearth, watching the firelight lick the soot-stained chimney. His two buddies clinked whiskey glasses over a worn poker table, while a PPD officer, a rookie on his first assignment, pretended to read a hunting magazine. Every few seconds, the kid's eyes flicked up to study Shepherd. The governor noticed.

The Lodge, a sprawling A-frame fortress of glass and timber, perched like a crown above the frozen lake. Shepherd had bought it at the peak of his stock-market rush, though critics whispered *'wife's money'* and *'lucky bets.'* Didn't matter. The place was his sanctuary.

Here, he wasn't the man polling ahead for the White House. He was just a Michigan kid who'd learned to hunt these woods at twelve. Archery now, no rifles. More skill, more thrill. The proof hung outside: a 200-pound buck. Not *Andre the Giant*, though. That old bastard with the 30-inch rack still haunted these trees. And this storm had robbed him of the chase.

Shepherd stood and sauntered to the panoramic window overlooking the lake. It was a wall of driving snow. A whiteout. A satellite call had crackled through earlier, relaying this guy, Guziac's threats: another lunatic, another Tuesday. Shepherd exhaled, watching his breath fog the window. *Democracy needs leaders who don't flinch.*

The door slammed open. Snow howled in as Bruce Quail staggered inside, shaking off a coat crusted white. "Ain't nothin' out there but snowmen and yeti," he barked. "If that nutjob's stalkin' us, he's froze to a tree. I couldn't see my own damn gloves out there."

Shepherd didn't turn.

At the table, Joe Barton tossed down his cards. "Storm's a blockade. No one's crazy enough to…"

"No one steps outside without me," Quail snapped. "That goes for you too," he said, glowering at the PPD kid. "Period."

Barton raised his palms. "Ain't got no argument here."

The rookie's grip tightened on his magazine. Outside, the wind screamed as though it were something alive.

Chapter 40

Norm Metway glanced at his instruments, then out to the turbulent sky. Snow peppered the expanse as though a million moths had been caught in the headlights.

The Raven shuddered violently as it sliced through the howling arctic wind, its rotor blades fighting against the thickening snow. Inside the cramped cabin, Norm gripped the cyclic stick with white-knuckled focus, his breath fogging the windshield faster than the defroster could clear it. Beside him, Ray clutched the edges of his seat, his eyes darting between the swirling void outside and the grim set of Norm's jaw.

"I've never flown in a helicopter before," Barney said from the rear, fear in his voice.

"Me neither," Norm said, deadpan.

"Funny."

Barney, sitting directly behind the pilot, was now soaked in cold sweat. His fingers clawed into the seatback as if he could dig his way to safety. Every jolt, every stomach-dropping lurch, sent new waves of nausea through him. He had protested this flight; begged to wait it out, but the urgency of reaching the remote lake had overridden his terror. Now, his worst nightmare was unfolding.

Laura, the quietest of the group, stared out the window, but there was nothing to see, just an endless, suffocating white. No horizon. No ground. No sky. The world had disappeared.

"Norm..." Ray's voice was tight. "Can you see anything?"

Norm didn't answer. His eyes darted between the instruments, the altimeter, the GPS, searching for anything to prevent them from crashing into the unseen dangers lurking in the storm. The helicopter bucked once more, dropping suddenly before lurching upward. Barney let out a strangled cry.

"We're fine," Norm lied. "Just some turbulence."

But the instruments revealed a different story. The GPS flickered, signal lost. The altimeter wavered. The storm was swallowing them whole.

The chopper bucked again, but Norm never flinched. He glanced over at the cowling and noticed the ice build-up. He pushed on the stick and found the bird sluggish and unresponsive. They had managed to cover a good one hundred forty miles since take-off, which surprised Ray, who had thought they would have turned back long ago. He looked at Barney, whose face was deathly white, terror in his eyes. Then, without warning, the world tilted. The helicopter banked sharply, throwing them sideways. Laura gasped, and Barney screamed. The windshield was a solid wall of white.

"Norm?" Ray shouted.

"I've got it!" Norm growled, fighting the controls. But the wind had other plans. The R44 shuddered, its tail swinging wildly. The engine whined in protest.

Barney's breath came in ragged, panicked bursts. "We're going to die!"

"Shut up! "Ray snapped. The storm was relentless, pressing in from all sides, a raging animal, tearing at the chopper.

"We can't go on much longer, Laura, she's getting iced up. If the ice builds up on the rotors or the intakes, we're going to go down." For the first time, Norm sounded concerned.

Barney searched for an airbag in the seat pocket.

"Just a little longer," Laura said as she peered hopefully out into the dull maelstrom through which they continued to fly blindly onward.

Norm tapped the GPS readout. "I think we're about ten miles from the lodge, closer than I first thought. Maybe we'll make it after all." Norm managed a triumphant smile.

Just when Ray thought their prayers had been answered, a mighty gust sent the chopper spinning rapidly in a long drop toward the ground.

Norm struggled to hold the aircraft steady. "We're going down, guys. Hold on!"

Barney braced himself and prayed aloud to the God he didn't believe in. He called out for Cheryl and told her he loved her. His white knuckles gripped the seat tightly. Laura, ever the strong, independent woman, simply closed her eyes and waited for the impact.

"I see a light! To your right, Norm, to your right!"

Norm saw it too and pulled hard on the stick. The rotors were heavily iced, and it was all he could do to regain some control of the falling chopper. The light provided a vital reference point in the bottomless free fall. He fought fiercely on the stick. Then, impact. A deafening crunch as the skids struck something solid. The cabin jerked violently, and the passengers lurched forward, harnesses biting into their shoulders. The helicopter spun, skidding and tilting. Then, silence. The engine had cut out. The only sound was the wind screaming outside and Barney's hyperventilating breaths.

"Everyone alive?" Norm's voice was steady, but his hands were shaking.

"Holy crap!" was all Ray could muster, and he repeated it several times; the others just laughed.

A chorus of shaky affirmations. They had landed, somehow. But where?

Laura gazed out the window, wiping the condensation from the glass. Outside, the snow swirled just enough to reveal the light.

✳   ✳   ✳

Bruce Quail turned the radio up and leaned in to listen to the station's weather report.

"The National Weather Bureau has upgraded its warning for the upper and lower Great Lakes region to catastrophic conditions. A spokesman for the Met says that the major storm hitting all parts of Michigan could turn out to be the worst in living memory. Fronts from the Arctic have now combined with a low from the Midwest. Lake effect bands off Superior are compounding the severity of the storm. The National Guard has been mobilized. Residents are advised to remain indoors until further notice."

It was probably a good thing, Quail conceded. If Guziac *was* a threat, he was unlikely to get near them while the storm raged. Come morning, it would all be over, and he could get the governor back to the capital, where he had better control.

Joe Barton called for a game of five-card stud. It bothered Quail that everyone seemed so relaxed. He was about to remind them that a killer was out there when Shepherd joined them at the card table.

"Why don't you sit down, Bruce?" he said as the others shuffled to make room for the governor.

"Sir, I prefer to stand."

"You should relax more, Bruce. This is one night when nature is on the job for you. Come and play cards." Quail sat beside Shepherd but declined the invitation to join the game. "You believe this lunatic is really out there stalking me, Bruce?"

"I don't know, Sir. All I know is we are isolated from all assistance at this time, and it makes us vulnerable." It was a sore point with Quail that Shepherd liked to hunt in the bush, putting himself at needless risk where it was difficult to secure a given perimeter. He had only Ziegler out of his regulation team at the lodge, a result of the governor's obsession with the wilderness and his need to hunt in isolation. The fact of the matter was, the governor seemed to thrive on the threat from maniacs like Guziac, viewing it as a challenge. News that some new cuckoo had him as a target came as a sort of test to his manhood, to his credentials for the presidency. He told Quail that he would be happy to meet this serial killer and deliver his own form of justice. Bravado at its worst.

*   *   *

The beacon of light had appeared out of nowhere, an answered prayer, just as they'd resigned themselves to death.

When they staggered from the chopper, they found its source: a lone homestead standing defiant in a snow-rimmed pasture. A diesel generator growled somewhere in the darkness, its pole-mounted spotlight carving a halo of light around the farmhouse. The occupants hadn't heard the rotors over the storm's roar. When Ray's fist pounded the door, the crash of knuckles against wood sent them reeling back in shock.

Inside, the world changed. Heat rushed over them, thick with the scent of roasting meat and fresh-baked bread, laced with herbs and the faint, comforting tang of woodsmoke. The windows trembled against the wind's fury, but here, for now, the storm couldn't reach them.

"God, I'm hungry," said Barney, smelling the hot food.

The large room combined a kitchen, dining, and living space into one open area. A large cast-iron stove dominated the cooking area; its surface cluttered with simmering pots and a kettle whistling softly. Open shelves showcased jars of preserves, sacks of flour, and bunches of dried herbs that hung from hooks.

The occupants, a family of five, sat around the room, watching the visitors recover from their ordeal. Barney cheerfully accepted a mug of coffee from the young mother's warm hands and asked her what she was cooking. Ray explained their brush with death and the urgent mission that had brought them to the remote lake.

"I figure we're exactly six and a half miles from the lodge, twenty-three by road," Norm said as he recalculated their last position based on the output from the GPS unit.

"It might as well be one hundred," Ray replied, smiling at the curious boy who was watching him from the corner of the room.

Laura picked up a mug of coffee and took a sip. "Do you have a truck?" she asked the man, who had hardly spoken until now.

"Forget it, Laura. The roads are impassable and you can't see a damn thing out there. We're going nowhere in no truck, no way!" Barney's words carried an angry tone. He pointed out that they had just barely survived. It was time for more rational thinking.

"I have a Ski-Doo out back. Fact I got two of them," the man said. He looked blankly at Barney, then at Ray, and back at Barney.

"Twenty-three miles in this weather; we couldn't find it if we wanted to," Barney said. But he wasn't getting through to Ray. He watched Ray and noted his eyes on Laura and hers on him. Neither had to say a word; he knew what they were thinking. The man jumped in again without invitation.

"Twenty-three by road maybe, but the governor's lodge is directly across the lake, due east. You could see smoke rising from the chimney if it weren't for the blizzard."

Barney shook his head. "No, Ray, you can't be serious; six miles across a lake? It's a whiteout for God's sake! Go out on that lake, and there's no way you can find your way to the lodge."

Norm stepped forward, sensing the new challenge, adrenaline still pumping. "GPS will work on my phone. No need for any cell connection. It uses a direct satellite link, and I've got maps already loaded."

Fifteen minutes later, the snowmobiles were out of the barn and ready to go. Ray flicked the ignition, and the engine roared into a high-pitched squeal. The machine's owner watched on, bemused, then casually added to his earlier statement.

"Course, the lake's not fully frozen yet."

Everyone stood silent, and Ray cut the engine.

"Come again?"

"The lake doesn't usually freeze proper 'til January, less it's a particular hard snap. My reckoning says it's still weeks away from a proper freeze. Oh, she'll be frozen alright, just not froze thick." The group exchanged worried looks before Ray kicked the engine over one more time. Norm Medway straddled the other ski.

"You can't be serious, Ray, you're not still going out there?" Barney's voice was incredulous. The whole idea was becoming more nonsensical by the minute. "You heard the man, the ice won't hold up under the weight. Give it up, buddy, while our luck holds out."

Ray felt the wind bite as it whipped around the barn. It wasn't just blowing; it was gnawing. It came in great, starving gusts, teeth of ice bared against his body. It was a foolish idea, and Ray knew it, but they were close, and he sensed Scottie was even closer.

Laura spoke; the tone in her voice had changed. "I don't want you to go, Ray. You were right earlier; we should wait 'til the weather clears." But it was too late now; Ray had already made up his mind, and he twisted the throttle to drown out further pleas for sanity.

"Stay here, Norm," Ray bellowed. "We may need that chopper of yours in a hurry if the storm passes." Norm couldn't hide his disappointment but nodded his agreement. He would be ready when called upon to do what he did best. Barney jumped onto the second sled and flipped it over. Ray raised a gloved hand and shook his head vigorously.

"I'm going alone, Barney. Stay here and try to contact Sullivan on the radio. Tell him where we are and that I'm going over to the governor."

"Like hell! I'm here now anyway, so I might as well get some of the glory. Besides, who's going to watch your back when the bullets start flying?" They moved out to the edge of the lake and edged slowly onto the ice.

"The faster you go, the less likely you are to break through," said the man. "And don't stop," he added.

"Comforting words," said Barney with a sigh.

Ray pulled the visor down over his eyes, took a deep breath, nodded at Barney, and then lurched away at high speed. Barney followed, determined to stay right on Ray's tail. If he lost sight of Ray, he was done for.

Chapter 41

How long have you known me, Bruce?"

The governor's tone carried that familiar needle, the one that meant he wasn't asking, he was prodding. Quail knew the answer: Seven years. Two terms. Countless threats neutralized before Shepherd even noticed. But the man only cared about his own point.

Quail kept his voice flat. "Can't say exactly, sir. Is there a point to your question?"

Shepherd's smile didn't reach his eyes. "My point is you've known me long enough to realize I don't scare. Modern leaders? Hiding behind bodyguards like cowards. If I were president..."

Here we go.

"I'd lead from the front. Like the old days. First into battle. And you?" Shepherd clapped Quail's shoulder. "You'd be right behind me. In *my* protective shadow."

Quail said nothing. Bravado won elections. Stupidity got people killed.

Shepherd wasn't done. "First act in office? March this nation into a new era. No more Senate rats gnawing at every bill. A president should be able to make decisions without being second-guessed."

Trade legislation. *'Crisp's a lame duck president,'* jab coming. Quail had heard it all before.

He stood, cutting off the tirade. Let the card players absorb the governor's fire. The kitchen's solitude beckoned, somewhere the man's *shadow* wouldn't reach.

✳ ✳ ✳

Prescott Guziac lay prone on a snow-covered bank, his body pressed low against the ground. The Remington MSR rested atop a compact bipod, its suppressor jutting forward like a silent promise. He pressed his cheek against the cold, textured stock, his eye aligned with the high-magnification scope. The crosshairs hovered over the distant target, a figure barely more than a smudge at eight hundred meters. He moved in closer, finding a stump to reset himself, his eye back on the scope. Two hundred meters. Four men at the table. One was standing, leaving for a back room.

His breathing slowed, deliberate. He inhaled. Exhaled. He paused. The world narrowed to the scope's field of vision, disappearing in and out of view as the wind-driven snow hurtled across his sight, swirling waves distorting the air. His gloved finger rested lightly on the trigger, taking up slack. The rifle settled into him, an extension of his will. "Like fish in a fishbowl." He wasn't sure which one was Shepherd. He'd seen pictures, but that was a while ago now. "Can you believe these bozos, sitting there in plain sight?" he said aloud. *Could be bulletproof glass. Why else would they leave themselves open like that?* Though he doubted it, the cost of so much glass.

"Don't leave me, cos you'll make me cry," he whispered low to the tune. "You're my best friend, so tell me why?" he added, the sound barely audible. That damn song was stuck in his head. *Concentrate.* A gust kicked up powdered snow, spinning it violently. Hard to judge the wind speed. He adjusted the weapon, dialing in the last fraction of a mil. Heartbeat steady. His finger squeezed, not a pull, but a smooth press.

The shot broke with a muffled thump, passing through the glass and leaving a neat round hole in the pane as the bullet found its mark. The guy's head seemed to fold and distort, like that painting, the scream, or some shit like that. The guy held onto his cards, but Scottie knew without doubt, he was *deader than disco.*

He cycled the bolt; eyes still locked on the targets inside.

*   *   *

The snow wasn't just falling; it was being hurled, a furious white delirium spinning in the dark, erasing the farm behind them, the trees, the very horizon, until all that remained was the storm's blind, howling throat. Ray pushed up the fogged visor and peered desperately at Norm's phone. It was nearly useless in the blizzard conditions. The guy at the house had set them on a diagonal course across the lake, but it hadn't taken long for them to become disoriented. The small blue blip that signaled their position was barely visible, but by his own reckoning, they should have been near the shore by now. He searched the distance for any sign, but there was none. The air thickened into a writhing mist, each flake a needle, each gust a scythe against his face. The world was no longer land or sky but a churning, formless thing, a beast that thrashed and roared and swallowed all light.

Below them, the surface groaned under the weight of the two snowmobiles racing across it. Ray took the lead, his motor screaming, and his breath coming in sharp white puffs. Right behind him, Barney leaned low over his handlebars, teeth clenched in a bare smile. He had ditched the helmet altogether.

*　*　*

Scottie lay silent in the snow as the wind howled around him. The log cabin sat on a prominent outcrop, a gold tooth in the jaws of the wilderness, smoke curling from its chimney, all lit up as though it were a Christmas tree. *Call themselves security?* They might as well have staked the governor out like a goat. Four more now hiding inside, waiting. They think they're safe. They're wrong. "Oh, hello." A door opened on the back wall. Bruce Quail emerged in a crouch. Scottie tracked him in the scope. He dashed for the light switches, M15 in hand. Scottie squeezed the trigger. Again, the bullet punched through the plate glass neatly. Quail's hand was almost on the switch when his body twisted and tumbled lifeless to the floor.

*　*　*

Ray searched the expanse for a landmark, anything, trees, a shoreline. But there was still nothing to go by. He glanced back again and saw Barney slowing. *Don't stop, big man.* Ray had no time to shout a warning before the world dropped out from under Barney's sled. The ice shattered, swallowing his snowmobile whole. Ray circled back; he didn't want to stop in case he broke through the ice. Barney flailed, clawing for the surface while his heavy snow gear dragged him down.

Without an option, Ray skidded to a stop, his heart hammering. The hole in the ice was a jagged maw, the water already smoothing over, sealing Barney beneath. *No. No, no, no.* He leapt off his machine, scrambling to the edge. The ice groaned ominously under his weight. One wrong move, and he'd join Barney in the depths. "Barney!" he bellowed, peering into the dark water. Bubbles surged.

Suddenly, from the depths of his subconscious, there she was: a vision of Clair Callus struggling amid the broken ice. Ray felt as though the world had come to a standstill. He was paralyzed. Her eyes staring lifelessly, her long hair waving in the water. Perhaps it was only a second, a moment frozen in time, but for Ray, it was a lifetime. He stretched out a hand to save her, but her face melted away. Only the bubbles remained.

A gloved hand broke the surface, grasping blindly. "Ray!"

In that instant, Ray regained his senses. He dropped flat, spreading his weight, and lunged, grabbing Barney's wrist just as he began to sink again. The ice shrieked in protest, spiderweb cracks racing outward.

"Hold on!" Ray growled, hauling with everything he had. Barney's body was dead weight, his clothes waterlogged, his limbs already stiffening from the cold. Inch by agonizing inch, Ray dragged him onto the ice. Then, snap! The edge gave way.

Ray plunged waist-deep into the frigid water. It swallowed his legs, the chill so intense it burned. The cold tightened around his chest, stealing his breath. Barney lay half on the ice and half off, his face blue, his lips trembling.

"Move!" Ray roared, shoving him forward. They crawled, gasping, as the ice fractured beneath them with each desperate lunge. Briefly, the squall cleared, Ray spotted the shore, only twenty feet away. It might as well have been a mile.

Barney collapsed onto his belly, his strength gone. Ray grabbed his jacket and pulled, his muscles burning and his vision blurring. The cold was winning. They tumbled onto the snowy bank, heaving and shuddering. The lake exhaled behind them, the broken ice shifting, a stalking beast, hungry and unsatisfied.

Ray rolled onto his back, his breath ragged and his body numb. Barney coughed violently beside him, but he was still breathing. They both were. For now. The real fight wasn't over. The cold would pursue them, creeping into their bones, waiting for a sign of weakness. Ray looked back at the ice where his snowmobile sat, waiting. It was too risky to go back. What to do? He could feel his own body shutting down. They had to keep going. A shot rang out. Then another, and another. An automatic rifle firing a burst. Two more bursts. *Scottie.*

Ray forced himself up. "We gotta move," he gasped. "Or we die here." Barney didn't answer. He'd slipped into unconsciousness. "Shit, Barney." Ray looked back at the snowmobile out on the ice.

❄   ❄   ❄

Scottie moved unpanicked, his boots sinking into the deep snow. He hesitated at the hanging buck. "Nice catch!" Inside, he heard shouts and boots scrambling, someone firing randomly. He moved quickly, kicking in the door, rifle leveled. He saw a man spin out from behind a wall, rifle coming up, but Scottie fired first. The blast tore through his chest, slamming him back into the wall. Blood sprayed the logs. Scottie scanned the room and guessed there was one behind the sofa and another hiding behind an upturned table. Did they really think furniture would protect them from a three-three-eight round? "Come out, come out wherever you are!" Scottie chuckled. "I promise, I won't hurt you." A shot cracked past Scottie's ear, splintering wood. He dove, rolled, and came up behind the stove. The guy fired again, wild. Scottie heard him fumbling behind the table. Was it the governor or his PPD? He didn't want to kill the governor by mistake. Not yet, anyway. He slung the rifle and took a handgun from his belt. "Hey, governor, you come on out and nobody else gets killed on account of you. You hear me?"

"You'll kill us anyway," came a voice from behind the sofa.

"Thanks for the tell." Scottie sprayed the table with his Sig. Mitch Ziegler stood up from behind it, his shocked face covered in blood. Scottie put a round in his forehead, and he dropped. "That leaves just you and me, Governor. Why don't you throw out your weapon, and we can have a nice chat? Are we cool?"

"I don't have a weapon," Shepherd said solemnly, emerging with his hands above his head. The cabin reeked of gunpowder and copper. Scottie stepped over a body. Outside, the wind howled through the trees.

"You kill that big buck?"

The governor nodded. "With a bow and arrow."

Scottie grinned. "A bow and fucking arrow? Just like them Indians, huh?"

Shepherd didn't answer. "You know why I'm here?" Scottie kicked away a nine-millimeter on the floor. "Don't answer that, 'cos I'm here to kill you. Don't need no reason. Just like you didn't need a reason for ignoring my emails, my letters. That right?"

"I don't know what you're talking about."

"No, you wouldn't." Scottie looked to the window and noticed lights out on the lake. Headlights perhaps, swallowed by the night as quickly as they'd appeared. He turned his attention back to the governor. "Where's your bow?"

✻　✻　✻

Time was the new enemy. Ray twisted the throttle slowly. The ice creaked. He edged toward the shore without falling through. He checked Barney for vital signs and felt the faintest trace of a pulse beneath his icy skin. He needed to get the wet clothes off him, but they were already too stiff to remove. He looked up the shoreline. A lull in the gale gave him a glimpse of the governor's cabin, all lit up in golden light. It was their only chance, even if it meant facing Scottie head-on. Barney opened his eyes, gazed lethargically at Ray, then closed them again.

"That's a good sign. Stay with me, buddy, we only just bought ourselves some time," Ray said. Barney was a dead weight, but Ray managed to lift him over the seat. There was no time to hesitate; he set the Ski-Doo skidding across the bumpy shoreline and headed for the lodge.

The lodge glowed warmly and brightly, welcoming, an illusion that masked the violent scene within. The vast expanse of glass rose to a towering apex. There couldn't have been a more exposed position to defend. A diesel generator rumbled from a shed at the back. Other than that, no sounds of life. The circumstances called for caution, but Ray knew speed was essential for their survival. The snowmobile hit a stump, causing Barney's lifeless form to slump forward, pinning him against the handlebars. What had been waterlogged clothing was now frozen solid. Ray's legs were lead. Heat was their only chance of survival. Ray revved the motor and sped to the lodge. The sight of a body brought him to an abrupt stop.

The governor lay half-curled in the snow, as if paused in the act of rising. One elbow was propped beneath him, his bare hand clutched over his heart, not in ceremony, but in a final, futile attempt to stem the pain. His face was turned toward the iron-gray sky, teeth bared in a silent grimace of protest, a deathly grin stretching his skin, skin already fading to wax. Snow gathered in the folds of his shirt, dusted his eyelashes like fine ash, and began to fill the hollow of his open collar.

"I didn't do it, Ray." Scottie's voice came from behind. Ray went for his handgun; the cold steel burned his skin as he drew it. "Would you believe it, he done killed his self. After all my effort, dumb son of a bitch has a heart attack. Got to watch him die though, Ray."

Ray quivered, unable to stop shaking. "It's got to end, Scottie. Right... Right here and now."

"Aw, come on, Ray, what are you going to do with that gun? You don't want to spoil all the fun by shooting me, do you? We got lots to do yet. We ain't half ended." Scottie looked down at the governor's body. "We was playing *Archer Clash*, know that game, Ray? It's cool; you should try it. Governor here was playing the *Hog Rider*. I made him run like he was a wild hog. Told him to squeal, but he wouldn't.

"He stumbled and fumbled like a real pig, though, trying to get away. I can tell you, Ray, it's not easy that bow and arrow shit. I missed him twice. Then he goes down clutching his heart, begging me to get help. Well, I wasn't going to put an arrow in him there, like that. What would be the fun in that? So, I watched that son of a bitch, laughed in his face 'til he turned blue and died. Funny how life goes, huh, Ray?"

Scottie kicked the governor's body and turned to Ray, grinning. He made no attempt to unsling his rifle or go for his Sig. "Now, we've got a pickle, Ray. My truck's up to its axles, going nowhere fast, as they say. So, here's the deal. I need that there sled of yours, and you need to get your buddy inside. Now, you got a choice: worry about taking me in, or your fat boyfriend there, dying of cold. He don't look too good, though, Ray; may not even make it inside. That old clock's ticking again. What's it going to be, Ray?"

Scottie's words sounded muffled and distant. He flickered in and out of Ray's vision. Ray tried to keep a steady aim. He couldn't stop shaking. His body was breaking down with every passing second. Finally, the gun slipped through his fingers and fell to the ground.

Chapter 42

107.1 FM The morning drive.

"Hey, Andy, how was your Christmas? And what about that storm! My goodness, was that a doozy or what?"

"It certainly was, Dianne. Five days later, and we're still cleaning up the mess. Roads finally open upstate. And, to answer your question, I had a great Christmas; how about you?"

"Didn't get the big house I wanted. Santa didn't come through. It must have been the weather; that's my only explanation. So, what are you going to be covering on the ten o'clock bulletin?"

"We've got lots to get through, Dianne. The manhunt continues for Prescott Guziac. The National Guard joined the FBI and the State police in the search, sweeping large parts of Upper Michigan. No sign so far of the fugitive, last seen when he attempted to hijack a truck in the Crystal Falls State Forest. It's feared he's crossed into Wisconsin or doubled back and into Canada, but many experts think he most likely perished in the wilderness somewhere this side of the border. Meanwhile, the hearing into the governor's death and the killing of those in his entourage is set for January sixth. Heads will roll at the FBI."

*   *   *

Ray walked out of the hospital with Cheryl by his side. The day was a glorious blend of crystal blue sky and crisp, fresh air. It seemed so far from the depths of the storm that Ray sometimes wondered if it had all been a terrible nightmare. "Your hands are looking better," said Cheryl.

"Yeah, they're still sore, and the right one is numb most of the time. But the doc says they're doing well, considering." Ray left out the extreme pain he felt in both his hands and the difficulty he had making a grip. He'd spent two nights under observation in the trauma unit alongside Barney, who'd been in an induced coma until yesterday. Ray felt he'd gotten off lucky. "Barney looked a lot better," he added.

"He's alive thanks to you. The opioids seem to be helping with the pain. He's worried about nerve damage. The doctor says severe frostbite and hypothermia can have long-term effects, both physical and mental. He's already starting to peel like an orange. Don't tell him I told you, but he broke down and cried like a baby this morning. I think the mental trauma may take longer to heal. But we'll get through it, one day at a time." She turned and hugged him, holding him for a long time, as though she was scared to let him go. "Thank you," she said.

Ray's mind snapped back to the lodge, to dragging Barney's half-frozen body inside. He'd barely been able to stand himself, yet he'd done it. They collapsed onto the floorboards, their bodies wracked with tremors.

Ray tore away Barney's frozen clothes, each layer peeling free with a sick, sticky *rip*. The stove fought him, flames licking grudgingly at the fresh logs. Wrapped in blankets, he pulled Barney against him, skin to skin, breath to breath, two men stripped bare in every way that mattered. Outside, the wind prowled the eaves, a sound like death crying to get inside to take them.

Ray turned his face to the sun. He could still feel the firelight gilding their faces, stitching them back into the world of the living. Beyond the walls, under that same warm glow, snow buried the governor's body. And every time Ray thought of Scottie, the cold slithered in again.

Ray was waving off Cheryl when Sullivan arrived. "Just going to see my boy," he said. "How are you doing, Ray?"

"Getting there, Chief. Barney will be glad to see you."

"I don't know about that, but I want him to know he's in my thoughts. Are you done with the feds?"

"I've had a few interviews, and I'm sure there'll be more to come. It looks like Gruder's going to be the sacrificial lamb for pulling his team during an active threat to the governor. I doubt he'll go down easily. Watch your back; he'll want to take you down with him."

Sullivan shrugged. "Well, if he does, I'll get to enjoy my retirement all the sooner. I have my own boss to worry about, and she wanted me to quit years ago. A little ice fishing sounds good right now. Take care, Ray."

"You too, Chief."

Sullivan walked away, then stopped and turned. "Hey, Ray! You think Guziac's dead out there?"

"I guess we'll find out, Chief."

❋　❋　❋

"What do you think, Pol?" Scottie held a white silk dress against his body and spun around. "I think it's perfect. It was made special for a musical: *The King and I.* You heard of it? I was set to be the leading man, Pol, until that stupid bitch, Chelsea Frye, walked out with the rest of the cast. Frye my ass. I should have fried *her* ass there and then. You know, I'd forgotten about her. Why didn't I put her on my list, Pol? Anyway, what was that guy's name, Pol, the one in the movie? The baldy bastard; what was his name? Yuletide or some shit like that. Hey, I could do that, Pol. Shave my head like him. Shit, that's a great idea. I'm going to do it, Pol."

Scottie turned. "You ain't still pissed now, are you? I already told you why I couldn't get back sooner. I didn't aim to be away for so long. You're sulking, aren't you? Now that really pisses me off, Pol, it truly does. Do you know what I went through trying to get back here for you? I had to take the long way around; that's what I had to do. All over the damn country just to get here. Weren't nothing but a miracle I got to Madison and out on a flight home. I had a nice flight back from there to Saginaw, though. Them cops didn't have a clue. Out the back door, back in through the front. They're still looking up there in the forest, Pol.

"Good thing I went prepared; no one was looking for Emanuel Hardcastle." He laid the dress on a table and smoothed out the creases. "Let's not dwell on it any longer. I'm here now. And! We got the big finale to come. Are you excited, Pol? Cat got your tongue? Oh, I forgot, you can't talk, can you? Yul Brynner! That was the name: Yul fucking Brynner. Think I look like him, Pol? Wait 'til I shave my dome."

❄   ❄   ❄

Ray woke, gasping, his sheets soaked with cold sweat. Barney's face still haunted him, those panicked eyes staring up through shards of ice as he thrashed, each movement driving another razor-edged fragment into his flesh. Blood bloomed in the water like ink, the air bubbles glinting like bullets as they rose. Just as Barney began sinking, Clair appeared beside him, their hands reaching for Ray in silent accusation.

He staggered to the bathroom, splashing water on his face, but the vision remained. Cheryl's words echoed: 'The mind heals slower than the body.' Poor Barney, so desperate to do his duty, to prove himself. Ray should never have let him come. That chopper ride where Barney's knuckles had gone white on the seatbelt. The snowmobile skittered across thin ice. Every decision now felt like a failure.

His mind flipped back to his hospital bed.

"He's alive, thanks to you." Those were Laura's words when he'd asked about Barney. "He's in intensive care, but they expect him to survive." She took Ray's hand, held it in hers, lifted it to her lips, and kissed it. "Jess was here. She stayed with me most of the night until we heard you were okay. We had the chance to talk a lot while you were in dreamland." Ray had been given a sedative. "We didn't stop talking all through the night, mostly about you, of course. She's a sweetheart; I can see why you love her."

Ray got dressed, went down to the kitchen, and made himself a cup of coffee. He heard snoring from the bedroom on the next floor and did his best to avoid waking Aunt Eadie. She'd fussed over him nonstop since he came home, even though she struggled to walk at times. He took his coffee into the family room without turning on the light.

"I'm going to write a book," Laura had said. She lowered her eyes and released his hand, her fingers lingering for half a second too long before retreating to her lap. "I got an offer... one I couldn't refuse."

She looked up then, searching his face, not frightened exactly, but braced. He could see the calculations behind her eyes: *Would he understand? Would he hate her?* Of course he'd known. She'd been a journalist first, always would be.

"You knew," she said, sharper now. Not a question, but armor. "You knew this was always going to happen."

"I knew. I knew that's what you'd do, Laura. I don't have a problem with it. Just don't hurt Jess, is all I ask." Ray thought she would write what she wanted, regardless.

"Of course, I would never do that." A long silence followed. "So, what about you and Jess? She's having a hard time finding her way forward."

Ray felt that familiar pang of guilt. He didn't know his own way ahead, let alone Jess's. "I honestly don't know." He reached out and pulled her toward him. "How does it end, this book of yours?" he asked.

Tears rolled one after another as she dropped to her knees by his bedside and sobbed. "It ends when the hero breaks everybody's heart and rides off into the sunset, that's how it ends." He ran his fingers through her hair and kissed her head.

"It's okay," he said, and kissed her again. "You do realize I don't ride horses?"

Later that morning, Ray attended Doc Galaway's surgery. "The hands are coming along nicely. How about the feet, Raymond?"

"They're fine, doc. I need my new meds, keep me going until Thursday."

"I've upped the dosage. It should reduce the likelihood of more seizures and lessen the swelling that's causing pressure within the skull. I know the last thing you want is more sleep, but it has a strong sedative effect, so I'm afraid you're going to want to sleep some more. You've been through a traumatic time, Raymond, and you have a big week ahead. A little more rest won't harm at all."

It was probably what he needed, although the thought of more night terrors didn't exactly make the prospect enticing. He decided to go home, eat some lunch, and maybe watch some news on CNN. Aunt Eadie made a fuss; she cooked him a grilled cheese sandwich, which he ate after feeling surprisingly hungry. He followed lunch with two Clobazam capsules washed down with grape juice. After that, he settled on his bed and browsed the internet for news.

Two hours later, exhaustion came in waves. The pull of sleep dragged him into a twilight zone of consciousness, where dreams were not quite dreams but torture to his brain. He tossed and turned in restless sleep.

His cell buzzed. Ray rolled over, letting it die against the sheets. Silence. Then,
Buzz. Buzz. Buzz. Minutes later, the damn thing still insisted. He grabbed blindly, fingers numb with sleep, the phone clattering to the floor. His fingers searched the rug until he retrieved it. *Jess.* Her name glowed on the screen. Hers was the only voice he'd crawl through glass to hear. Every hour without her these past weeks

had been a slow suffocation. Now, with his thoughts syrupy from meds, he couldn't come up with a single coherent word.

"Jess, I..." His tongue felt swollen. "Can we... hold on." He hauled himself upright against the headboard, knuckling sleep from his eyes. The room swam. "Jess?"

"Hey, bud! How's it hanging?" The voice, real or imagined, faded in and out like a distant radio signal. He tried to grasp the words, to understand. "Thought old Scottie was a popsicle somewhere out in the cold, eh, Ray? Well, there ain't no snow deep enough to bury this snowman." Ray was confused, his thoughts smudged at the edges, dissolving before they could fully form. The harder he fought to focus, the deeper the fog rolled in. But slowly, the realization struck home, and a chill ran down his spine.

"Scottie?"

"Hi, Ray!" The voice was cheerful, filled with mischief. "You sound a little confused there, buddy. I'm having a bit of a get-together. You know, the old gang. Oh, and a special guest, but that's a surprise."

"Scottie, where's Jess?" Ray's head swam as he began to focus. He jumped out of bed, nearly toppling over, his balance wavering.

"Jeez, Ray, don't get so excited. Jess doesn't want to talk to you right now; she's kind of tied up."

"You hurt her; I'll kill you."

"You already had your chance, Ray, remember? Now, shut up while I give you your invitation. Listen carefully, Ray, because you need to know what I'm going to tell you, assuming you don't die of that brain turnip in the meantime, of course." He snorted like a pig in heat. "Brain turnip, I like that one."

"I'm done playing your game." Ray's voice was steel. "I don't believe you have Jess. Go haunt someone else, Scottie." He ended the call before his shaking thumb could betray him. Silence. Then, the buzz. He let it die, needed time to get his head together. *What was he doing hanging up?* The panic came hot and fast now, clawing up his throat.

The phone vibrated again, insistent against his palm. He hit the green button.

"Had me going for a minute, Ray. But no more fooling around, no more chances. Either you get yourself to the party or Jess... Well, I'm not going to spoil it by saying more."

"Tell me what I have to do?"

"That's better, Ray. Jess and me have decided we're going to shack up together by the lake. We're going to celebrate with that crazy old coot up there. Now that's a clue in case you didn't realize, but it's a real easy one, seeing as how you seem a little light in the head. This is the final chapter before happily ever after, Ray, so don't mess up."

Scottie's voice echoed in his addled mind, thoughts swimming like eels, slipping in and out of focus. *Concentrate!* "Scottie, listen, I... I..."

"I, I, I nothing. You listen, Ray! I haven't finished yet; this is important. Bring any cops, feds, or the Lone fucking Ranger within a mile of me, and her life will be on you. Try anything that looks like a heroic rescue, and all bets are off; you don't want to know what will happen. Do you get it? Do I make myself clear?"

"I got it."

The threatening tone shifted instantly, giving way to Scottie's sickly cheerful repartee. "Hey, Ray, this is going to be so cool, the three of us together again with old friends, just like old times, eh? Now don't be too long, buddy, I don't want you to miss a thing."

Chapter 43

Scottie's stolen Chevy fishtailed wildly down the snow-choked trail, tires spitting rooster tails of slush. The wheel fought him like it was possessed as he wrestled it between drifts. One wrong twitch would send them nose-first into the hidden ditch. Beside him, Jess jerked against her bonds with each violent swerve, the grocery sack taped over her head rasping against her frantic breaths. Scottie had punched a single air hole near where her mouth should be.

"Yeehaw, motherf...!" Scottie's laugh cut off as the Chevy slammed into a snowbank, frame groaning against a rock as it came to a standstill, balanced high on its axle. Thirty yards short of the boat shack. "Shit."

Silence. Scottie cranked down the window and listened. Dead silent. Quiet only the deep woods could weave.

Jess stayed statue-still.

Winter's bite flooded into the car, the Chevy's stale heat fleeing like a coward from Scottie's close quarters. He glimpsed his youth in the familiar surroundings, and for a moment, felt warmth at the memory. "Nostalgia's for pussies," he mumbled, and pushed the thought away before it could slither under his skin.

"Henry's got a fire going, hon," Scottie mused, nodding toward the thin gray ribbon unwinding from the rusted stovepipe. "Think he's expecting company, darlin'?"

The smoke curled lazily and low, hovering just above the pines before the wind tore it apart. For a breath, he smelled the air like another memory, sweet and sticky, maple sap bubbling in Henry's old evaporator pan. Spring mornings. Simpler times. Then the present snapped back. *Fuck! Got to stop that shit poisoning my mind.* He turned to Jess and laughed. "Shit, you look dumb in that hat, Jess!"

Scottie stepped out of the car and strolled to the trunk. He popped open the lid to reveal Pauline Singleton tied and gagged with duct tape. Her eyes clenched tight as the bright daylight poured in. He watched her casually for a few moments, then took out a pocketknife and slipped it between her legs, severing the bindings that pulled them tight up her back to her wrists.

"Get out, Pol." The command was abrupt. She clambered out clumsily, banged her head on the lid, and stumbled into the snow. Bare feet hit the frozen ground, and she hopped as the cold stung her skin. His hand clamped onto her arm, marching her to the passenger door, where she saw, for the first time, that she wasn't his only captive.

"Pol, meet Jess. Jess, Pol." His voice dripped with mock ceremony. "But, you two go way back, don't you? Little sorority sisters all growed up."

A jagged smile split his face. "Oh Jess... wait 'til you see her, see Pol now." His fingers picked at the tape sealing the bag over Jess's head, nails scrabbling for purchase. "Remember how pretty she was? That fucking Barbie smile?"

Pauline stood rigid, shivering through cold and fear.

When the tape refused to yield, Scottie's breath turned ragged. With a sudden animal snarl, he wrenched the fabric violently back and forth until she could see Scottie through the torn breathing hole, his face contorting, veins bulging like roots across his forehead.

Then, as suddenly as it came, the storm passed.

"You ready for the big reveal, Jess?" he snickered, his voice sweet as poisoned honey. His hand fisted in Pauline's hair, yanking her forward until Jess could see her beaten face inches from her own. Pauline's whimper strangled into a gasp as he twisted harder.

Scottie threw his head back and roared with laughter, a sound like a Halloween soundtrack. Jess sobbed uncontrollably, while Scottie laughed, hysterical, like he'd just pulled off his favorite party trick. "Can you believe it? All that fat and ugliness? And her being so stuck up about how she looked, remember? Never would've thought Pauline fucking Singleton could end up like this, eh, Jess?" A snort. Then, he let go. "Beauty becomes the freaking beast.

"Ok, introductions over. Let's go see if that old bastard has a brew for me." Scottie dragged a large canvas tote from the back seat, slung it over his shoulder, and pointed the way forward. He took Jess by the arm, and they trudged to the shack. Jess's hands stayed bound, and the bag remained tattered around her head.

Pauline Singleton walked slightly ahead, clearly relieved to be free from the dark confines of the trunk. "That was the most terrifying ordeal of my life," she said, almost casually. "I could face anything the good Lord puts in my way, except another stint in that claustrophobic space. I'm very grateful you allowed me out, Prescott."

"Shut up, Pol."

Henry emerged from the shack as the threesome approached. "What do you want? I have nothing for you here, now go!"

Scottie noted the rifle hanging loosely at Henry's side. "Hey, Chief, you old son of a bitch, that ain't no way to greet the wedding party." He stepped closer and drew a nine-millimeter from his belt. He aimed it at the old man's head. "I know you've seen what one of these can do, old man, so let's go inside where it's warm and cozy because Jess and I got some good news to tell you."

Henry groaned as though he were in pain when he saw the women tied. He stepped aside as they entered the cabin, wary of the gun in Scottie's hand.

❋　❋　❋

As soon as the call with Scottie ended, Ray dialed the department number, hoping Sullivan would be in his office.

"FSPD, how can I help you?" Ray hesitated. "Hello, FSPD, how may I assist?"

Ray's mind raced. "Hey, this is Ray Waring."

"Ray, how are you? This is Kay." Ray remained silent. Scottie's threats echoed in his head. "Ray?"

He closed his eyes and sighed. *Damn it!* "Hey, Kay," he said, taking a breath. "Sorry, pocket dial. I didn't mean to call."

"No problem," she said, then: "Ray, I just wanted to say..."

Ray ended the call, speed now imperative. He loaded his handgun and strapped the holster over his shoulder. He slipped two more clips into his pocket and dashed for the door, his mind already clearing.

Chapter 44

Scottie pawed through Henry's shack like a starving raccoon in a dumpster while the old man worked the duct tape from Jess's neck. The bag came away with a sickening peel, revealing Jess's tear-streaked face. Her sobs hitched in ragged gulps.

Pauline's face told its own horror story; swollen nose split like overripe fruit, lips purpled with bruises, the angry red welts from days of taped-up gags still branding her skin. She pulled Jess close, her good arm cradling Jess's head against her shoulder. Fingers trembling, she stroked Jess's matted hair, ignoring her own pain, a gentleness that belied her ruined face.

Henry tossed the bindings on the floor like they were too hot to handle. He stood motionless by the stove, his eyes on the poker as he tracked Scottie's every move.

"Look at this; do you remember this, Jess?" Scottie held a framed photograph of a Chippewa chief in full headdress. "Your daddy," he said to Henry. "I remember." He tossed the photo carelessly and took a fishing pole from a rack on the wall. He flicked it back and forth as if he were casting.

Eventually, he returned to where the women sat huddled. He pulled up a chair opposite them, straddled it, and rested his arms on the high back, then placed his chin on his arms. He said nothing; he just stared at them with a straight face. They clutched each other for comfort. Jess stopped crying and turned her head into Pauline's shoulder, unable to meet his gaze.

"Why do you bring such distress to this house?" Henry asked, visibly agitated.

"Distress? Do I look distressed?"

"I was referring to your captives."

"Shit, Henry, you saying I'm keeping them against their will?" Scottie stood up and walked over to a bookshelf. He picked up a volume, flipped through the pages, and then tossed it thoughtlessly to the floor. "Well, here's the thing. We're here for a reckoning, Henry. This little get-together is going to sort the men from the girls. And the girls will learn what it means to be Scottie's squaws. So, sit down, old man, before I knock you down."

"A reckoning? You think forcing a woman to fear you makes you a man? That's not power; that's the whimper of a dog who's never known respect. You want the respect of a woman? You've got a choice. You can be the man who takes or the man who rises above and earns his place by a woman's side."

"You hear this crap, Pol? He talks like he's better than everyone else, always has. Full of shit. Thinks he's a big chief, Pol. Henry talks in riddles, Pol. Like he's some ancient spirit."

"All spirits are ancient, Scottie, even yours."

"See what I mean?" The shack grew silent. Scottie moved to the window, gazing out at the track.

"Do you think we could have a drink?" Pauline asked eventually. "I'm parched and need water badly. Jess could use some, too."

"Get Pol and Jess a drink, old man, and don't think about guns. I know you've gotta have more than a rifle around here."

"A willow bends, but can snap when it gets old," Henry mumbled under his breath as he walked to the faucet.

Scottie chuckled. "*I heard that*. Stupid old coyote." He turned to Pauline. "I never did introduce you to old Henry, did I, Pol? Henry here is a genuine Indian relic. He should have been dead long ago, 'cept he's too stubborn to die like most old folks, ain't that right, Henry?"

"Why are you doing this?" Jess asked in a whisper that barely traveled across the room.

"Why am I doing what, Jess? Putting our lives in order, putting the past wrongs to right? Oh, I think you know why, Jess, and I think you secretly approve. Why, even Pol understands what needs to be done when it comes to comeuppance. When I'm finished here, Pol, I promise, I'm going straight to your pa's to fix his sorry ass for you. I'm going to put one right in his ear for you, Pol, I swear!"

Pauline stiffened at the promise. "Oh, you don't have to do that, Prescott. It could hurt your chances of getting the help you need. I can get you that help, Prescott. We should talk about it."

Scottie's silence stretched like old rope. "Where are you, Ray?" he finally muttered. His gaze drifted out the grimy window to the bridge beyond, then swung back to Jess with unsettling focus. That faraway look settled in his eyes again. "Remember when we used to dive off that bridge? You always..." he began, voice gone soft and dangerous. "You always acted like you was Queen of the fucking lake."

The shack's silence thickened. Jess might as well have been carved from ice.

His gaze returned out the window. "That boy's pushing his luck." A muscle jumped in his jaw. *Clock's ticking, Ray.*

Five endless minutes oozed by before Pauline dared try again. Henry's expression never changed. He just watched, steady as a gunsight.

"You had a traumatic childhood, all those stories you told me about your father, your stepmother. People will realize all this is a consequence. It isn't your fault; the things that happened to you as a child leave psychological scars that only professionals can help heal. Everyone knows that. Let me get you the help you need, Prescott. You have problems, and I can help you. And, if you look to God, you can find forgiveness."

Scottie sat motionless. He studied Pauline with blank eyes, revealing a distant mind. "*I* need help?" he said eventually, snapping out of his reverie. "You have to be kidding, Pol. Look at you for pity's sake, the only reason I didn't gut you like the pig you are is because I need you." He stopped and thought for a moment, then once again his demeanor changed in an instant, and he quipped, "Not in a sexual way, you understand, Pol, more a matter of I need you for professional shit." He retrieved his tote bag from where he'd dumped it by the door, delved inside, and pulled out a bottle of bourbon. He unscrewed the top, took a long slug, then offered it to Pauline. She shook her head. "What, don't like my hospitality all of a sudden?" She took the bottle and tipped it to her mouth, but didn't drink. Scottie knew she'd faked it.

Chapter 45

Ray's legs nearly buckled with each step toward the boat shack. Exhaustion dragged at him, his body a lead weight. His Firebird, first mistake since coming home, lay abandoned in a ditch after skidding off the icy track. Now he fought through knee-deep snow, the half-mile trudge stretching into eternity. Three times he went down hard, the cold biting through his clothes each time he struggled up.

He came upon the stolen Chevy. Tilted at a drunken angle over a boulder, trunk yawning open. He moved in with caution, saw the driver's door gaping. Keys still dangling in the ignition. A glance inside; cartridges scattered on the floor. Scottie's calling card couldn't have been clearer.

Thirty feet ahead, the shack crouched under fresh snow. To the left, Henry's woodpile leaned dangerously on crumbling posts. Beyond it, the boat shed's roof peeked through a drift, someone's fresh graffiti staining the tin. Ray's breath came in ragged clouds as he turned and saw the apiary. Not a single hive standing. Just splintered wreckage poking through the snow.

Those guys again! "Goddamn animals." His voice sounded alien in the frozen silence.

Ray knew Scottie would be watching from the windows. No point in stealth, even if he were capable. He trudged straight to the front porch. The door swung open before he could knock. Jess stood there, ghost-pale, her eyes red-rimmed and hollow. She stepped back wordlessly, her silence louder than any scream.

Inside, Scottie lounged at the table, head shaved, Wild Turkey in one hand, 9mm Smith & Wesson in the other. The gun's barrel gleamed dully under the cabin lights. Then Ray saw Pauline. Her face was an injured wreck: split lip, swollen nose, one eye purpled shut. Dried blood crusted her temple, matting her hair in stiff clumps. But she was alive.

Henry noticed Ray falter and moved across the room to offer him support. "What's going on, Raymond?" he asked quietly. Ray took a deep breath and patted Henry's hand to reassure him.

Scottie smiled when he saw Ray's face and the pain reflected in its grimace. "Come on in, Ray, make yourself at home." Henry guided him into the heart of the room, and Jess shut the door before going to his aid.

"Hold on now." Scottie pointed the gun at Ray. "Open that jacket, let me see you're not carrying."

"I'm carrying, Scottie." Ray unzipped his jacket, being careful to avoid sudden movements. He used two fingers to remove the gun from the holster and placed it on the table beside Scottie.

"Shit, you look pooped, Ray. I would've given you a ride, but I had a car full. Sit down, buddy, take a little while. We've got all the time in the world."

❄   ❄   ❄

Scottie felt good. He was in control. Everything was unfolding exactly as he'd envisioned. He watched Pauline guide Ray into the chair like some nursemaid, Jess clinging to his arm as though he might dissolve before her eyes. Scottie didn't need to check the windows; he knew Ray too well. He couldn't, wouldn't jeopardize Jess's safety by bringing backup. Besides, the self-righteous bastard always had to play the hero, show everyone he could handle it alone. But not this time. This time, the script was Scottie's to write.

His mood shifted suddenly, like a record scratch mid-tune. A second ago, he'd been chuckling at their little caretaker routine, Pauline's doting hands, Jess's desperate grip, but then Jess whispered something in Ray's ear; he was sure of it. His vision swam red. Before anyone could react, he was on them, jamming the 9mm hard under Ray's jaw, forcing his head back. "I could end this right now, Ray," he hissed.

Jess's scream pierced the cabin as she launched herself at him, her fists beating uselessly against his chest. "What are you doing, you sick fuck? Leave him..." Tears streamed down her twisted face. He backhanded her without looking, sending her sprawling.

Ray tried to rise, but Scottie lashed out, catching him in the mouth. His boot crushed into Ray's sternum, sending him gasping back into the chair. "Down, boy," Scottie mocked, wagging a finger. He turned to Jess, sobbing on the floor. "You'll need to learn some manners, darlin'. Future wives don't talk to their men like that." He turned back to Ray, lips curling. "See what you've done? Turned her into a spoiled little brat."

The smirk returned, wider now. "Good thing I like my women with some fight in 'em."

❄ ❄ ❄

The pressure behind Ray's eyes threatened to crack his skull. He forced air through his nose, *in, out*. He tried to compartmentalize: his condition, the fear coiling in his gut, concern for Jess, the need to think and act like a pro. *Bureau training. Hostage situation. Just another assessment.* But his hands betrayed him with the faintest tremor; this wasn't just any hostage. This was Jess. *Concentrate!* Ordinarily, he would have already done it. It was an automatic response after years with the bureau: check out the location, his surroundings, and the physical terrain. Look for makeshift weapons, exits, and the time needed to reach them. Evaluate the hostage's condition and the perpetrator's state of mind. Finally, assess the options for a course of action.

His eyes roved the cabin. Henry's lifetime of clutter stacked haphazardly against log walls. The iron belly of the woodstove glowed cherry-red. Three doors to the back, a bedroom, a kitchen, and an unknown exit. Weapons? The axe by the maple pile. The cast-iron skillet on the stove. A poker. *Too far.* Henry's rifle was lying on the table alongside Ray's 9mm within Scottie's reach. An assault rifle poked out from a tote on the floor. The only other weapon was the gun in Scottie's hand.

His gaze flicked to Pauline. Bruised but steady, her eyes locked onto his with tactical clarity. That was unusual. She was watching for him to make a move. *Composed. An ally.* Jess shuddered against her, all raw nerves and adrenaline terror. *Volatile. Protect first.*

Henry stood quietly, mumbling to himself. Hard to read. The old man's stare never left Scottie, lips moving in silent calculation. Ray worried that he was planning a move against Scottie. Henry was a peaceful man, but he had the heart of a lion. Ray knew he would not stand by if the situation worsened.

And Scottie? The S & W wavered lazily in his grip, his free hand drumming, a psychopath's rhythm on the whiskey bottle. Every twitch screamed *unstable*.

Ray's muscles coiled. *One move. One chance.* The woodstove's crackle timed with his pulse.

"When we was just kids..." Scottie's voice slithered through the cabin's heat. The gun spun on his finger, *click, click, click* against the trigger guard. Ray tracked the safety's red dot. *On. For now.* "You always had to be the big damn hero, the big shot." Scottie's grin showed too many teeth. "Your games. Your rules. Where we went, what we did, and who with. You started dragging those college pricks around even though you knew they hated my guts." The gun stopped mid-twirl, barrel suddenly pointing at Ray's left knee. "But..." Scottie sneered. "Today we play my game."

"Is that what this is about, Scottie? You're pissed because we didn't play dress-up when you wanted? What's the deal with this dressing-up anyway, Scottie? I didn't know you were into panties and bras."

Scottie paused. But he wasn't going to bite.

"You liked my little charade then?" He chuckled and shook his head. "I can't believe you fell for it so easily. If you'd seen your face, Ray, at the airport that night, you looked like a frightened girl, I swear. I was inches away from you, and you never knew it was me."

"You went to a lot of trouble just to be left standing with your dick in your hand."

"Wasn't my dick, Ray. It was a microphone, and you fell for it. Listen to this, Jess. Shit, I thought for sure you would see through it, Ray, being the big FBI man and all. I even put my own name on the press pass that was hanging from my jacket, but you never spotted it."

Ray felt embarrassed by his own gullibility. He should have known from the very beginning and seen through the crude disguises. "Maybe they'll give you that Oscar you've been lying about."

Scottie ignored the jibe. He jumped to his feet, raised his hands above his head, and yelped in delight. "Oh, oh, but the best! The best was in the park." He roared with fake laughter. "Pol, Pol, you got to hear this. These two were sitting in the park. I don't know what they was doing sneaking around behind Al's back, if you know what I mean." He gave an exaggerated wink. "They was sitting like two lovebirds on a bench by the ice, and guess what? I skated right past them, looking like Bonnie Prince Charlie, kilt and all. Talk about in-your-face, I practically waved my balls in them. It was magic!"

"You should have been on the stage, Scottie; you have a natural talent for trying to be the man you're not." He paused briefly, then added, "Or woman."

"Woo, that was hard, Ray. Don't you think that was below the belt, Pol? That was below the belt, Ray; I'm hurt." He snickered to emphasize his sarcasm. "Talk about being the man you're not, what about getting away from the man you are, Ray, let's talk about that." He moved inches from Ray's face. "You couldn't face who you are so you ran away, ain't that right, Ray? You couldn't face being the coward of the county, as the song goes. Remember that song, Pol, Coward of the County? Who sang that song? Don't matter. Ray here's a coward, ain't you, buddy? Tell Pol about Clair Callus, about the way she got drowned while you two was making out, tell her, Ray."

Ray felt a crawling sensation on his skin and tightness in his chest. The vivid image of Clair was impossible to remove from his mind's eye, a permanent scar. To have Scottie raise it now was a knife in his gut.

Scottie didn't wait for Ray to respond. "See, Pol, Clair was only ten years old. She had all her life ahead of her. Isn't that right, Ray? They said it was an accident, but I know better. Ray here sees her in his sleep. He says he can't get her out of his mind. It's slowly destroying him from the inside out. Why, I bet that's what caused that big old tumor in his head. Guilt, Pol. Guilt."

Ray's head felt like it might explode. "She should be alive," he whispered.

"What's that, Ray?"

"She should be alive," he repeated. Tears welled in his eyes.

"Damn straight she should." Scottie showed no mercy, no pity for Ray, only fresh contempt. "But you had to make it all about you, didn't you, Ray. Well, let me tell you something, Ray. We all had to face it. That guilt gnawed at us all, gnawed at me, Jess, Walt, all of us. Why was it you thought it was only you who felt the pain, only you had the right to claim you suffered because of what happened? We all had to go through it, but you, you had to run away. You're a coward, Ray. You left us behind."

"For God's sake!" If looks could have killed, Jess would have killed Scottie right there and then.

He's baiting you. Ray drew himself up, the movement sending a spike of pain through his ribs. His words came razor-edged and deliberate. "You did all this because you thought I *left you?*" A hollow laugh escaped him. "You weren't even an afterthought, Scottie. Not a single second of my life was wasted worrying about you."

He leaned forward, blood trickling from his split lip. "Yeah, I ran from things that actually *mattered*. I lost everything that counted. But you?" Ray's smile was colder than the wind outside. "You were never in the equation."

Scottie's face darkened, veins bulging at his temples. His grip tightened on the gun. Ray saw the knuckles bleach white. Then, like a switch flipping, the rage dissolved into that familiar, mocking grin. "Oh, Ray, Ray," he crooned, tilting his head. "You're going to love what I tell you next." Scottie paused, scanned the gathering, and sighed. "You thought it was an accident that killed her, Ray?" His mouth twisted, a smile like a cocked trigger. He leaned in close, breathing into Ray's face. "Well, I got news for you, bud, she got what was coming. A teaser, that one."

The words hit Ray like a gut-punch, each syllable dripping with venom. Scottie rose slowly, letting the silence stretch taut between them, a snare of unsaid things, waiting for Ray to step into it.

Ray's thoughts scrambled through the shock. Was Scottie saying what he thought he was saying? "What the fuck are you telling us?" His voice came out strangled, jaw clenched so tight his molars groaned. The cabin walls seemed to pulse inward, the woodstove's heat suddenly suffocating. Scottie just watched him, that same evil smirk, as realization crawled up Ray's spine like an insect.

Scottie paced the floor, gun in hand. "Okay. Why not? It won't matter soon anyway." He stopped pacing and took a deep breath. "That day, I got to the jetty. No one else was there when I arrived, so I hung out with the kid. We was sitting there talking about stuff, school, boyfriends, all that shit. She said she didn't have one; she was saving herself for you, Ray. Imagine that, even the kiddies all gooey-eyed over you.

"Anyway, we got to fooling around, laughing and such. I said she was pretty and she laughed, pretending to be shy. I kissed her." He suddenly stopped and raised his hand in protest. "Don't look at me like that, Ray, not like that. I was just having fun. She was a tease, you know that. It wasn't nothing but a bit of fun."

"She was a child!"

"That may be, but she knew stuff. I know she did. Then, she starts making out like she was wronged in some way, like I was some pervert." Scottie's face screwed up, a bad taste in his mouth. "She started saying she would tell her brother how I touched her. Which was a lie. She was going to tell you. She kept saying, 'I'm going to tell Ray. He'll kick your butt.' I wanted to talk some sense into her. Told her to shut up. But she wouldn't stop, wouldn't listen to sense. Then she ran out onto the ice. She was gone before I could grab her. She stood out there taunting me. Kept saying over and over, 'I'm telling Ray, I'm telling Ray.' I told her to come back in, but she wouldn't."

Scottie went silent, his eyes suddenly distant, the hint of a tear, but Ray wasn't sure. Eventually, he went on. "There was this God-awful noise, a gunshot, but different; this metallic crack, like when a fence wire snaps under tension. Then there was another. Clair was suddenly struck dumb. Stupid grin gone from her lips. Fear on her face 'cos she knew. That noise was the sound of breaking ice."

The air left the room, leaving a hollow silence, but for the fire crackling, absurdly cheerful.

"She went through like a stone," he continued. "I went in straight away to rescue her; I did, Ray. The water was up to my armpits, cold. I had to break the ice as I went out. Wading toward her as fast as I could, I only had one thought; to save her." There was no longer any humor or malice in his voice. He was reliving the moment, immersed in the memory, immersed in the dark water of his past. "When I reached her, she wouldn't let me help. She thrashed and clawed at me. 'Get off me! I'm telling. Ray! Ray!' I told her to be quiet and let me help, but she kept on calling for you. I pushed her under just to shut her up, thought it might get some sense into her. But she kept fighting, fighting." Scottie took a deep breath. "Fighting until she didn't. She went limp. Her eyes just stared at me from under the surface, pieces of ice floating everywhere, covering her face. I pushed them away.

"You know how quiet it could be up there. I was sure you'd come running. But no one heard. I looked around. No one came. I held her there beneath the surface, just holding her. After a long while, I got cold. I heard cars. That's when I started shouting for help. That's when Walt and the others arrived. And last came you, Ray. Too late to the party. She would've been okay, Ray, she would have if you hadn't been her damn hero. She would ..." His voice tailed off.

Chapter 46

The words lingered, grotesque and undeniable. Jess tightened her grip on Pauline's arm. Her breath faltered, turning into an audible wheeze; a strange, sorrowful recognition of the gravity of what they had all just heard. Her lips trembled and parted, but no words emerged. Only the faintest moan betrayed her despair.

Ray went rigid. His jaw clenched, the muscle twitching like a live wire. He recognized the shape of evil, but hearing it spoken so casually, as though he'd been admitting he'd scratched your car, made his stomach turn. His fingers curled into fists, the instinct to act surging inside him, but the gun in Scottie's hand kept him frozen. The weight of his uselessness pressed down on him, heavier than he'd ever known.

The room felt colder. Pauline wept, unable to stop the tears. A scripture rose in her throat. "Suffer the little children..." she started, but choked it back. There was only a hollow, aching silence where her faith should have been.

Henry sat with his back straight as a cedar, his expression unreadable. But his eyes, sharp as flint, remained fixed on Scottie's face.

Pauline's voice cut through the silence. "You've taken the first step to God, Prescott." Her swollen lips trembled around the words. "You finally said it. After all these years carrying Clair's death alone."

Ray's stomach heaved. *Absolution? Now?* The words didn't strike him so much as seep into his veins, slow as freezing water. His hands went numb against his knees. Behind his eyelids, he imagined Clair's mittens clawing at the ice. The wet choke as Scottie held her under. The dreams that still left him screaming into his pillow twenty years later.

A log shifted in the stove. Embers flared and died.

"Shut up." Ray's whisper barely moved the air.

Pauline pressed on, raw courage in every word. "It was an accident. Kids horse around; terrible things happen..."

"*Shut the Fuck up!*" Ray's roar shook dust from the rafters.

Scottie's head snapped up from where he'd been focused on the floorboards. "You think I'm some fucking charity case, Pol?" His laugh was spilling sewage, loathsome in its spite. "Save your church-lady pity for someone who..."

"Is this all for Clair?" Pauline's interruption hung in the air. Ray was about to protest when he suddenly understood; she was working him like a hostage negotiator, trying to get inside Scottie's head. "Are you making innocent people pay because no one helped *you* grieve?"

Scottie's face purpled. The slap, the sound of a whiplash, sent Pauline sprawling against the log wall. Ray was halfway up when the pistol's barrel froze him mid-motion.

"*Innocent?*" Spittle flew from Scottie's lips. "That drunk bastard I called Daddy, was *he* innocent? The world's better off!" He paced like a caged animal, the gun weaving dangerously. "But Ray? Oh, Ray could do no wrong in my pa's eyes. He had him fooled, same as everyone else. Even Tweetie Bird acted like he shit sunshine! Ray..."

"Ah. Now we reach the rotten core of it," Henry interrupted, catching everyone off guard.

"What did you say, old man?"

"This was never about anyone else but Raymond. And just like your father and Clair, Jess is collateral damage, a consequence of your hatred for Raymond. This is about Raymond, your *friend*. The one who had the love you starved for. The one life smiled on while it spat in your face. You saw him as the competition. You don't want Jess. You want him to hurt. And she's just the knife you'll twist in his gut to do it."

Henry let the words hang, watching the rage flicker in Scottie's eyes before pressing deeper. "But here's the joke, brother; he didn't even know you were playing the game. You've been keeping score your whole life, every slight, every laugh you swore was at your expense. You've been consumed by hatred while you could have been living. And now? You'll make Jess your prisoner, wasting your hate on a woman who'll never see you as anything but a curse... and for what, so he cries at this phony wedding? You think that'll fill the hole inside you?"

Henry's voice dropped to a whisper, lethal as a blade slipping between ribs. "You're not his villain. You're his footnote. And when this is over, his spirit will still be whole... and you? You'll still be empty with blood on your hands." He paused, letting the weight of his words crush down. "So do it," he said at last. "Take your pound of flesh. But know this: the only heart that will stop tonight is yours. And no one will mourn it."

Ray braced for the explosion, for Scottie to put a bullet in Henry's skull right there. But the moment stretched, thin and brittle. Scottie just stood there, his face unreadable as a storm cloud, eyes drilling into Henry's. Long seconds passed, then Scottie broke away. "Enough of this shit." His voice was eerily calm. "We got a wedding to enjoy."

He whirled, yanking Jess up violently by her hair and slamming her to the floorboards. Her gasp of pain seemed to delight him. "Open the bag, Jess." A singsong command. When she didn't move fast enough, he stood on her fingers. "I said open it." Her trembling hands unzipped the tote.

"There's my girl." He crouched beside her, suddenly tender, as she pulled out the white silk dress. It pooled in her lap, a ghost of a thing, empty and cold.

Scottie tilted his head, studying her face for a reaction. "What do you think?"

"Think about what?"

"Don't give me no lip now, girl. Think about the dress is what. Think about your wedding dress."

She grinned, all teeth, a chuckle that held no humor. "I already have a wedding dress, Scottie, the one I married in. I have a husband, too, in case you hadn't noticed. You never were very smart, were you, Scottie?"

"Yes, you always did think that about me, didn't you, Jess? But okay, I ain't mad at you on our wedding day. Get into it." Contempt painted her face. "I said, get into it." She didn't move. Scottie strode to where Ray sat and put the blue metal muzzle to his temple. "Well?" Jess took the dress and headed for the bedroom.

"Hold on there, Jess. You ain't going nowhere out of my sight. Get into it here. There's no one here ain't seen what you got before." He grinned at Pauline. "You girls in the school shower, I heard all them stories." He turned back to Jess. "Come on now, let's show Ray what he'll be missing out on while you and old Scottie here are jumping each other's bones."

Ray lunged, but Scottie was prepared. He kicked out, driving his heel into Ray's knee. Ray crumpled, unable to suppress a scream of pain.

"*Get out of them clothes, Jess!*" Scottie screamed. Jess flinched. She removed her clothes and quickly slipped into the gown. "You ready, Pol? Ready to do some marrying?"

"You can do what you want, Scottie. I'm married to Al, and that's the way it will stay. What you do here will mean nothing; it will be a sham."

Scottie howled in delight. "A sham! I don't think so, Jess." He stepped forward and marked an imaginary line, dragging the heel of his boot across the floor. "Okay, all those who are widows step up to the line." He waited a beat. "Come on, Jess, why aren't you moving, woman?" He howled again; it was his sick idea of a joke. He looked her in the eye as the laughter drained from his face. A cold, hard expression replaced it. "Oh, I forgot to tell you, Al won't be coming to our wedding. In fact, Al won't be doing much of anything anymore since he's dead, which is pretty convenient seeing as how that makes you an official widow."

Jess wavered, then toppled; she crumpled to the floor, wailing. The news, too much to bear.

Ray felt an overwhelming urge to reach out to Jess, to hold her and comfort her. The intensity of that urge was matched only by his desire to take Scottie's gun and beat him to death with it. Pauline moved to Jess's side, cradling her sobbing body in her arms and rocking her gently like a baby.

"Oh, don't start crying now, Jess." Scottie sighed, rolling his eyes. "Nothing worse than a sniveling woman." He turned to Ray, grinning. "Guess we're on hold while Princess here composes herself."

He circled Ray, taking in his battered state. "Christ, you look like roadkill. All that chasing must've really worn you out." A chuckle. "Gotta admit, I was good, wasn't I? Had you running around in circles, a dog chasing its tail. Never faced anyone like me in your vast FBI experience, huh?"

Ray let the silence stretch just long enough to needle him. "Actually?" Ray's voice was ice. "You were textbook. FBI profiler nailed you first go." He leaned forward, blood dripping from his split lip. "Whiteboard had your whole life story in red marker: *Bed-wetting loner. Compensates for his inadequacies with violence. Below average intelligence, unable to cope in society.*"

Scottie's grin faltered. Ray pressed harder. "We even had a betting pool. Odds you were impotent? Even money. That you still cried for Mommy? Three-to-one."

"You lying sack of..."

"Retarded, was the final conclusion," Ray goaded.

Scottie's breathing turned ragged. The gun trembled in his hand. Ray saw the anger building. He was ready to make his move when Scottie snapped.

"I never wet no bed in my life, and you know it. There ain't nobody done what I done and got away with it. I could keep on killing and still not get caught. If I hadn't left all those clues, you'd be scratching your heads, wondering what to do next."

"What I'd have added to that profile, if I'd known before your little confession, was that you're a pedophile."

The dam broke. "I ain't no goddamn pedo!" Scottie's roar shook the cabin walls. "We were just..."

A gunshot split the world in half. For one suspended second, no one moved. Then Ray staggered back, hand grasping his shoulder where the bullet had punched through, warm blood already seeping between his fingers. Behind him, a brass pot screamed as it spun across the floor, the ricochet's whine fading into ringing silence.

Scottie's eyes beaded. "Happy now?" He waved the smoking barrel between them. "This what you wanted? Make me the monster so you can play hero one last time?"

Ray knew it was a clean through. No bones shattered. Pauline rushed to his side, pressing against the wound.

"He's okay, Pol. Let's get this party going. And Pol, toss another log in the stove, girl. We don't want Jess getting cold feet." Snort.

"Wait." Henry's voice cut through the chaos. "He's bleeding out. I'll get a towel."

Pauline caught Ray's eye as she stood, one searing look that said everything. *Enough.* "I'll get it," she said, moving quickly toward the kitchen.

"Argh!" Ray's fake groan snapped Scottie's attention away just as Pauline passed the woodstove, her fingers closing around a thick maple log.

"Argh!" Ray groaned again.

Scottie sneered. "Aw! Hurts, Ray?"

Behind him, Pauline pivoted on her heel, swinging the log in a vicious arc. Crack. The impact sent Scottie reeling. Ray was already moving, a linebacker's charge straight for his ribs. They hit the floor hard, the gun skittering into shadows.

Fists rained down on Ray's skull. He took the blows, using his weight to pin Scottie. Fingers stabbed into his bullet wound, twisting. Ray's scream filled the cabin as Scottie bucked him off. A rib snapped under Scottie's boot. A knee crunched under his heel.

"Son of a..."

Click. Pauline stood statuesque, an avenging angel, the 9mm shaking in her grip. "Move again," she breathed, "and I'll paint the walls with your brains."

Scottie froze, chest heaving. Blood dripped from the gash on his scalp, mixing with the sweat and hatred on his face. "Well, well, well, now that's the Poly of old. 'Paint the walls with your brains?' Really?" Pauline shrugged. "You going to shoot me, Pol? After everything we've been through?"

Ray struggled to his feet. Pain wracked his body, head, legs, and hands. He steadied himself and took the gun from Pauline's trembling hands.

"Now what?" said Scottie.

"Now you're going down, is what." Ray's chest heaved. "Anyone got cell coverage?"

The door exploded inward just as the last word left Ray's mouth. Walt Callus filled the doorway; shotgun braced hard to his shoulder. "Gun down. Now." The command left no room for debate.

"Walt? Jesus..."

"Drop it now, Ray, and kick it over here."

"Walt..."

"You've got three seconds." The shotgun roared, peppering the ceiling with buckshot. Plaster rained down. "One..."

The pistol clattered to the floor before he reached two.

"Kick it." Walt's finger never left the trigger. The gun skidded across the boards, coming to rest behind Walt's boots. He didn't even glance at it.

"Thank Christ!" Scottie's voice oozed relief. "He's lost it, Walt! Was gonna execute us all!"

Pauline lunged forward. "He's lying..."

Ray's knee buckled. "Walt, Scottie killed..."

"Done talking." The barrel of the shotgun didn't waver. "Scottie, get out of here. I've got no quarrel with you. At least you tried."

Scottie moved quickly past Walt to the door. Pauline called out in panic. "You've got this all wrong! He's..." But she wasn't quick enough.

Scottie turned, scooped up the pistol, and fired in one fluid motion. Walt's knees hit the floor first. The shotgun tumbled from dead fingers. For three terrible heartbeats, he remained upright, the gaping exit wound in his chest pulsing crimson onto the planks. Then he folded and fell.

Ray moved on pure instinct, rolling, grabbing the shotgun, coming up in a crouch, just as Scottie's barrel found his forehead. "Walt never was too bright." Click. Click.

"Fucking Smith and W garbage." Scottie hurled the pistol against the wall.

Blood spread around Walt's body in a dark halo. Scottie stood in it as he backed toward the door, hands raised in mock surrender. "But you're not going to shoot me, Ray. Not in cold blood."

"The hell I'm not." Scottie stepped back. "Don't do it, Scottie."

The shotgun's pump-action racked. Scottie kept moving, executing a slow shuffle backward, hands in the air. "Live to fight another day, Ray. That's my motto. You and I still got games to play."

"I'm not playing, Scottie. We're done with your games." Still, Scottie backed off.

"Gonna borrow your Ski-Doo, Henry. Hope that's alright?"

Scottie plucked the keys from their hook, stepping backward through the door, never breaking eye contact with Ray's shotgun sights. The barrel followed his every movement, steady, deliberate.

"Let him go, Raymond." Henry's voice was gravel.

"Like hell." Ray matched Scottie step for step across the frozen yard, boots crunching in the snow. "This ends today."

Scottie grinned, arms wide. "You won't shoot me. We're brothers, Ray. Ain't that what you always said?"

Henry came up alongside Ray. They shadowed Scottie, ten paces behind. The women watched from the deck, breath fogging in the air.

"Let him go," Henry repeated. Ray shot him an irritated glance. Henry met his eyes. "The bear must walk the dangerous path alone."

Ray froze. His gaze darted to the shattered beehives, then back to Henry's weathered face. "You didn't..."

"That's me, Ray; I'm the goddamn bear."

Henry's eyes were flint, but his words were hushed, almost serene. "Some paths are best left to fate, Raymond. Let the spirits guide him home."

"Listen to the old man, Ray. Back off and let them spirits guide this old grizzly the hell out of here."

"Scottie, stop..."

The world snapped into a single, silent frame. The wind's howl, the creak of the pines, all sound bled away into a deep, resonant hum. Ray watched, suspended in that impossible stillness, as Scottie's heel caught on a tree root. He tipped backward, arms windmilling, hands flailing at the air, not in panic, but in a slow, almost graceful surrender. Surprise flickered across his face, a child's brief, uncomprehending blink, and then it was gone, smoothed into something terrifyingly serene.

In those fractured seconds, a lifetime scrolled. They were boys again, knees scraped raw from tumbling off a shared bike, laughter echoing through humid summer air. Slapping a puck on a frozen street, jumping off the escarpment into the bay, the future stretching out like uncharted seas.

Every triumph, every failure, every silent exchange, it all flashed in a furious, beautiful montage. Four seconds in which the world remained frozen: a single snowflake hung in the air, a vein throbbed in Scottie's temple, Ray's breath a ghost between them.

Then, Scottie thumped to the ground, his head snapping back against the pressure plate. The trap's iron jaws snapped shut with a squeal of rusted hinges, followed by the dull wet thud of jaws crushing bone, flesh, ligaments, and arteries. A fountain of blood arced across the snow, impossibly red against the monochrome world.

They stood transfixed, a wave of disbelief washing over them. Jess's hands pressed to her mouth,

Pauline's breath caught mid-gasp, and Ray's shotgun slowly lowered. Scottie's legs gave one last shudder, then he was still.

Only Henry stood unmoved, his face as weathered and unreadable as the ancient rocks. He gazed at Scottie's crumpled form, the snow drinking his blood in greedy gulps. "Some men," he said, his voice the quiet of snowfall, "are born with poisonous thorns in their souls. They tear at everything they touch. The ancestors say such souls are trapped in their own darkness." Henry turned to Ray and placed a hand on his shoulder. "You pity him, but sometimes the world can only grow lighter when that poison is removed." Henry looked once more to where Scottie lay. "The universe settles its own debts, Raymond, and justice is not always kind."

Epilogue

The nurse adjusted Ray's pillows with practiced hands, sliding his tray table closer before placing his buzzing phone within reach. As the door clicked shut, Jess's voice spilled through the speaker, sunshine in her voice.

"You sound happy." Ray closed his eyes, picturing her smile.

"Brighton made you a nice get-well card." Her laughter was medicine. "You've got a pumpkin head, four fingers total, and clown feet that would make Bozo jealous."

Their shared laughter faded into comfortable silence.

"How's Al?"

"He's down at the boat show in Tampa." She told him about Al's newfound passion for boating. "He's settled on a twenty-footer and lessons instead of a solo round the world cruise." Ray could almost see the man's spring-loaded step. As it turned out, Al had been safe all along, oblivious to Jess's predicament. The memory of Al's hospital reunion with Jess surfaced unbidden: her rush into his arms, the way they'd clung like survivors of a shipwreck. It was a moment of acceptance for Ray. He still loved her, but the truth settled over him gently and without regret: he had to let her go. And so, with a quiet resolve, he loosened his grip, knowing that sometimes love meant stepping back.

"You'll make a great first mate."

"We've been spending a lot of time with Pauline. We've formed an unbreakable bond."

"Shared trauma will do that to people."

"She's decided to stick with her church and work at her congregation. She says her father is a tougher prospect, but they are at least talking, and she tells me they're making progress. She's a funny woman once you get to know her. She keeps us laughing with her quick wit and humorous remarks. She says she's got you to thank for bringing her out of her self-pity and saving her from a life in the French Foreign Legion."

Ray chuckled; he liked Pauline, too. She had called him twice since his operation, and both times, she left him in danger of popping his stitches from laughing.

"And Henry?" Ray asked.

"He's good. I visited twice in the last week. It seemed as though the whole tribe was there last time I went. They're watching out for him. The kids from the high school are building new hives. He asked about you."

"I'm looking forward to putting a pole in the water with him. Maybe soak up a bit of his wisdom."

"He'd like that." A beat of silence. Then, softly, "How are you *really*?"

"Alive." He paused, traced the scar on his head. "Weinberger says it's a complete success; no speech loss, no blindness. Just months of pretending I like kale smoothies."

"Laura's visiting?" she asked with a teasing lilt.

"Book research."

"Mhmm. What chapter's titled 'Handsome Patient'?"

"It's the title of the whole book," he said, laughing.

There followed another long pause, and he was about to wrap it up when Jess spoke. "We all share a little blame, don't we? For what happened to Scottie, I mean. We're all responsible in some way."

Ray knew what she meant, and he felt the same way. But he could never forgive him for what he did to Clair.

"Our lives, the three of us, were always intertwined. Maybe we could've done more to help him, but there can never be excuses for what he did. And we've all spent too long blaming each other, blaming ourselves. Enough regrets; we have to live with it and move on."

"What happened, Ray? What happened to the three of us, those three little kids, that it could all go so wrong?"

"We thought we were invincible, didn't we?" Ray let the words hang. He thought he heard Jess sob. Outside, a lawnmower droned. Ray watched its shadow pass the window.

"Is this the end of our story?"

"Scottie's gone, Jess, but it's not the end of our story; it's the beginning of a new one."

THE END

Acknowledgments

I would like to thank all those who supported me while writing this novel. Thanks to Daniel Lee for his brilliant photography, and to Cheyena Lee for lending her gorgeous face in such dramatic fashion for the cover of this book.

Thank you, Des Lewis and Anthony Lee for their always honest feedback as beta readers. Special thanks to my editor, Steven Moore for his speedy work and constructive feedback. Thanks to all my family for their love and support.

Lastly, to my darling wife, Christine, thank you for keeping me sane and for everything you do to support me. I could write a book on all you do to make me love you.

About the author

Lee was born and grew up in Liverpool England where he married and fathered three sons. The family emigrated to Canada where Lee spent ten years working throughout the Great Lakes region, servicing American and Canadian industrial clients.

The family moved to Australia in pursuit of Lee's business career. After years in international management, Lee swapped spreadsheets for manuscripts and is now writing full-time from his home in the Southern Highlands of New South Wales.

He is also the author of the Australian epic drama, Black Bones, Red Earth, and the Young Adult novel, Alexander Bottom & the Dreamweaver's Daughter.

leerichie.com

www.ingramcontent.com/pod-product-compliance
Lightning Source LLC
Chambersburg PA
CBHW050104120726
47904CB00004B/1213